Conqueror

The Branded Trilogy
Book 3

J.A. Guynn

Acknowledgements

Thank you to my wife for supporting me throughout the entire crazy process of creating the Branded Trilogy. Your encouragement and understanding made this all possible. Let's see what comes next.

Thank you to Emily Armstrong! You stuck with me through thick and thin. Your feedback improved not only this story but my writing skills. Because of you, I am a better author. Also, I can't wait to see your story continue. I'll always be your biggest cheerleader on this side of the pond.

ISBN: 979-8-9856947-4-1

Library of Congress Control Number: 2023922983

Cover Design by 100Covers.com

Editor: Charlie Knight at cknightwrites.com

Proofreader: Mark Schultz, the Hyper-Speller at www.wordrefiner.com

Publisher: 3220 Group, LLC. Alvin, TX

Publisher Note:

Chapter 1

The steel left a cold line as it slid across the back of my neck. Hairs on my arms stood tall. Light from several candles burning on the table beside me cast dancing shadows on the wall. Bracing my back against the chair to hold myself steady produced a quiet creak from the wood. My ears filled with the raspy sound of metal scraping metal as Tindra trimmed my hair with a small pair of shears.

"The timing of this meeting is still suspect if you ask me," she said, resting the cool metal below my left ear. "Since my parents will be here no more than a day after you leave."

Reaching back, I patted her leg as she continued trimming my hair. "I'm not leaving to avoid your parents. Riding out with this caravan is the perfect opportunity for me to meet with Crum after he officially promotes Lieutenant Aerison to Commander. Along the way, I can survey my old skati. I won't let people resettle there without seeing how bad it is myself."

She tapped her foot while trimming around my ears. As she worked, the shears grew warmer.

"I will dump you in a watering trough if you burn me." I rubbed the upside-down T burned into my left cheek. "I don't need another brand. What's bothering you?" *Firesyths. I swear.*

"Sorry." The metal cooled. "I worry."

I sighed, pushed my talent into the stone floor, and spun my chair around to face her. "You have nothing to fear. There are no threats left in my old territory. Once I lead our army into Satra, I promise to stay out of the fighting."

"Maybe our victories have come too easy. What if it's all a trap to get you into Satra? After all, we don't know what lies Porsey fed them." She snipped the front of my hair short. "I think success clouds your memory. Don't ignore the week they held our forces at bay before running back into Satra.

"I haven't forgotten."

"Good. Lather your face; I'm shaving your beard."

I laughed. "Given the mood you're in? There's no way I'm letting you put a blade near my neck."

"Fitzeirick, dear husband." She touched her forehead to mine and kissed me on the nose. Sparks flared in her eyes. "My love, I know where you sleep. If I wanted to slit your throat, I could do it any time. Lather your face, or I'll shave you dry."

I pulled her into my lap and kissed her until she pushed away.

"Keep this up, and your warriors will leave without you," she said, smiling.

I laughed and let her go. "I'm the king. They won't leave until I give the order."

She smiled and shook her head before pointing. "Soap. Face. Now."

"I thought you liked me with a beard," I said, reaching for the soap.

"I don't mind you having a beard, but your helmet will be more comfortable without one. Plus, they can be a liability on the battlefield."

I nodded and dipped the soap into the small bucket of water sitting on the table. It wasn't long before the hair on my neck was loaded with frothy bubbles.

Tindra drew a short knife from her belt and rested the edge lightly against the base of my throat before pressing the stump of her right wrist against my forehead. "Don't move. My left hand still isn't as steady as my right was. I'd hate to cut you by accident."

"Let me shave myself," I protested.

"If I don't practice, I'll never get any better," she argued, and quickly scraped the hair off my face, only slowing when she had to work around the brand. "Much better," she said. "Rinse. I'll gather your things."

"I'm packed. The only thing left is to put on my armor," I said, reaching for her. "Why are you trying to busy yourself? What's bothering you?"

She sighed and took my hand. "Everything. My parents are coming—"

"Aren't you happy to see them?"

"Of course, but you're leaving, and I know something bad is going to happen to you. Also, you expect me and Roi to work together with the builders working on our castle. We're getting along better, but...honestly, if I wasn't friends with Grima, I wouldn't be allowed in their house."

I shook my head. "Roi's not as bad as you think. Give him something to focus on, and you two will be fine. And stop worrying about me. I killed my half-brother and took leadership of Croy while leading only five people. Imagine what I can do to Satra with an army."

She smiled, hugged my face to her chest, and ran her fingers through my hair. "So confident. It's one of your better qualities."

I hugged her back. "I know losing your hand cost you more than you want to admit, but"—I rubbed my smooth chin—"you're adapting well."

"Thank you for understanding," she said, "and for your support. I'm glad you don't treat me like I can't do anything for myself."

"A queen who couldn't take care of herself wouldn't be any good for me or our country," I said and stood. "I need to put my armor on and get going."

Tindra nodded. "Let's get you dressed. After I walk you to the caravan, I'll talk to Einns and get a list of how he wants the castle kitchen."

"Assuming all goes well, I should be back in time to move into our new home," I commented.

Although the steel sandwiched between the inner and outer layers of my dark-green-and-brown leather armor added a lot of weight, I had worked the thick skins enough to make the protective garment easy to put on. Having Tindra's help wasn't necessary, but I could tell it made her happy.

With a quiet click, my metal-and-stone battle hammer stuck to the magnets on my back. I hefted the saddlebags filled with spare clothes and supplies to clean my armor. If I learned nothing else while training with the Varian army, the importance of well-maintained armor stuck with me.

"Don't forget your helmet," Tindra said, picking it up from the table.

I took it from her, and she planted a long, hard kiss on my lips before letting me slide the leather-covered, steel helmet in place.

"To remind you why you need to come back home."

I raised my eyebrows. "What makes you think I could ever forget you?"

She smiled and took my hand. "Shall we go?"

"You're going out unarmed?" I asked.

"How would it look for the queen of Croy to walk to her friend's house with a sword on her hip?"

I shrugged. "Whatever you think is best."

"Remember to keep using those words when you get back." She laughed and pulled me toward the door.

Chapter 2

As we passed through the courtyard, she squeezed my hand. "How long will you be gone?"

I pursed my lips. *The last time I guessed how long I'd be away from home, I ended up in a lightless dungeon for nine months. Now, I'm leaving a new home and heading into known hostile territory. At least, I'm prepared for threats this time.* "No way to know. I'll return as soon as possible."

She nodded but didn't say anything.

Though I'm not an overly large man, I must make an imposing figure when dressed in my dark armor. We had no problem getting through crowds as I made my way to the warrior caravan.

Quartermaster Rafberg noticed us and pushed through the crowd of warriors and porters loading wagons. "My queen, it's a pleasure to see you this morning." He bowed.

"I trust preparations are going well," she said, nodding.

"Not as quickly as I'd like, my lady," he said, frowning, "but the caravan will be ready to leave soon."

"Do you happen to know if Andale is ready?" I asked.

Rafberg nodded and looked back toward the stables. "I saw Bior leading him out earlier, m'lord."

"Is he riding among your guard?" Tindra asked, eyebrows raised.

"I asked Agrim to send someone as a companion. Bior practically begged to go," I said. "I suspect he wants to make up for his failure last time he rode with me."

Tindra's hand grew warm. "Why only one guard and no archers?"

"I'm riding with *two* warrior companies. I am in *no* danger. Bior's serving as my steward more than anything else," I said. "Calm yourself, and don't make a scene."

"Fine. Make sure he knows I still expect him to keep you safe," she replied.

"I will. Don't worry."

She cocked her head for a moment, then smirked. "Give me a kiss, and I'll be on my way."

"Of course, my love," I said, and kissed her deeply. "Tell Mikael and Margit I regret not being here to see them."

She reached inside the helmet and caressed my cheek. "You come back. Come home to me."

I kissed her again, gently, and smiled. "Whatever you think is best."

She replied with a weak smile before turning on her heel and walking away.

I looked around and found all eyes were on me, except for a few men watching Tindra. Raising my eyebrows and grinning, I turned back to Rafberg. "Do you know if Varian Lieutenant Aerison has arrived yet?"

"Yes, Sire. He's riding on the lead wagon."

"That will make him easy to find," I said. "Is Vestmar with him?"

"The Varian soldier? Yes, m'lord."

"Thank you for the information. I know you're busy, but may I ask a favor?"

He nodded. "Of course, Sire."

I took a sealed message from one of my saddlebags. "When you get the chance, have a messenger deliver this to Commander Galtis where he's training men on the barges."

"Consider it done, m'lord," he said, dipping his head before taking the parchment. "Anything else?"

"No, that should do."

"Then I hope you have a swift, safe journey, my king."

I thanked him, turned toward the front of the caravan, and dodged men rushing to get the last of the supplies loaded before reaching the lead wagon. "Well met, Lieutenant Aerison. Vestmar, I trust you are doing well."

My good friend's escort nodded to me. "Aye, King Fitzeirick, I am. A little sad to leave your fine city but happy to be headed back to Varia."

I smiled and nodded. "Always nice to return home after a long time away."

The Varian lieutenant stood, shaky until he steadied himself against the wagon. "Good morning, King Fitzeirick." He glanced toward the eastern horizon before continuing, "Good day for travel, assuming those clouds don't mean rain."

I followed his gaze. "Never been a good judge of weather myself. The last time I was in the central forest, my friends and I were caught in a bad storm. I'd like to avoid repeating the experience."

"The sooner we get going, the sooner we find out what awaits," he replied.

"You speak the truth," I said. "I'd best get in the saddle and see what's holding us up."

Aerison nodded and returned to his seat.

I left them to find Bior and Andale. A stablehand told me the horses were readied on the other side of a warehouse not far away. Following his directions, I found two rows of armored men mounted on horses, looking bored. The warriors brought their right arms to their chests, saluting as I passed.

I spotted Bior grooming Andale. Though the arrow wound he sustained when we were ambushed shortly before I started the war had healed, it still bothered him. It was easy to notice how Bior favored his right leg if you knew what to look for.

I clamped my hand on his shoulder. "Brush him much more, and there won't be any hair left on his flank."

He jumped and turned to me, light-blue eyes open wide. "Oh, Sire." He bowed, and his silver-streaked, curly, black hair fell forward, covering his cheeks. After brushing his hair back, he continued. "It's... Sorry. I didn't see you coming. Was trying to pass the time and wanted Andale to shine for the trip. Would only be right for the king's horse to look its best."

"Thank you. I trust he's ready to go," I said, securing my saddlebags.

"Aye, Sire. Put the tack on him myself," Bior said, tugging on the stirrup.

"At least I'll know who to blame if the saddle falls off along the way."

"Won't happen," he replied, smiling. "Checked it twice."

"Having a little fun before the ride," I said, mounting Andale. "Get in the saddle so we can get going,"

He bowed once more and mounted his horse so fast, his sword slapped its flank, causing it to rear.

"Careful," I said. "Wouldn't want you to get hurt before the trip begins."

Several of the warriors near us laughed.

"Aye, Sire ... would be terrible. Injuries should wait for the return trip." Bior patted his leg. "We're ready to go."

I nodded to him and turned Andale toward the front of the line. "Warriors. Follow me."

Men cheered and fell in line. As we passed the warehouse, all but four turned toward the back of the caravan. The four who stayed followed Bior and me to the front.

Turning to Bior, I said, "I only asked for one guard."

"Scouts," he explained, "or heralds, if you'd prefer, m'lord. Roi insisted."

I bit my lip for a moment. "Do they know where to go?"

Bior looked at me with a slightly confused expression. "Last I was told, we were leaving through the southern gate, following the trade path east through the Carved Scar, and continuing to the first supply camp. I was there when Agrim gave the instructions. Has the route changed, Sire?"

"No, and if we don't get going..." I shook my head. "I don't want to keep King Crum waiting."

Bior nodded. "I believe everyone's waiting for your command, my king."

When I reached Aerison's wagon, I called for the caravan to get underway.

Chapter 3

The scouts trotted ahead of the caravan, heading for the southern gate.

Vestmar popped his reins, and the wagon lurched forward. Shouts rose behind us as drivers urged their teams to move. I heeled Andale and trotted to lead the group. Bior took his position on my right flank.

Citizens waved and shouted their support as we made our way through the city. *A welcome change from the treatment I received when I first took power a few months ago. Victory should bring even more happiness, provided it isn't too costly.*

My half-brother let the enemy take my homeland and convinced everyone Satra had no desire to take more territory from Croy. Their incursions past the central forest after I overthrew Eirickson proved they were an ongoing threat to our country. The second attack exposed traitors in my army.

Though the executions that followed cost me several veteran leaders, their deaths secured support for my rule. *I didn't want to spill more Croian blood, but it had to be done.*

At the southern gate, the guards stood with their swords and axes across their chests, saluting their fellow fighters as we passed.

I looked at the sky as we turned east. Clouds floated on the horizon but didn't look to be gathering for a storm. *We're starting later than I wanted. Nothing I can do about it now.*

• • • • ● • ● • • •

As we approached the mountain range dividing Croy nearly in half, Bior spoke up. "Ready for a bite, Sire?"

Before answering, I glanced toward the sky, forgetting the peaks would block my view of any worrying weather ahead of us. "Yes, thank you for reminding me."

He nodded and trotted toward the end of the line of wagons.

I looked over my shoulder and found Aerison and Vestmar eating lunch. Aerison lifted a waterskin and smiled before taking a drink.

My steward soon returned with my meal. He handed me a waterskin to sling across my chest and a small bag. "Hard biscuits and dried rabbit," Bior said.

"With lukewarm water to wash it down," I replied. "Can't complain about eating the same food we're winning a war on."

Bior coughed, spraying crumbs from his mouth. "At least we'll be stopped for dinner. Warm food goes down easier."

I shook my head. "Spoken by someone who's forgotten what it's like to eat on the move."

He patted his stomach and laughed. "Aye, m'lord."

I joined him in laughter before putting a piece of meat in my mouth and taking a drink of water. Even taking my time to eat, I finished my meager lunch shortly before the Carved Scar came into view. As the caravan turned toward the pass, someone came riding toward us—fast. "Bior!" I called out and pointed toward the rider.

He nodded and galloped ahead to meet them.

I slowed until Aerison's wagon caught up with me. "What do you think?" I asked the lieutenant.

"Messenger?" As he finished the word, Bior turned to lead the rider toward us.

"I'd guess you're right," I said. "But I'm not expecting any messengers."

"Kings aren't the only people who get messages," Aerison commented.

I chuckled. "True enough, but you have to admit, lots of parchment passes between the capital and the battlefield."

"Yes, but not all of it goes to you."

I nodded and rode ahead to meet Bior and the messenger. As I got closer, I noticed it was one of the scouts and slowed Andale's pace.

"Umm ... well met, Sire," he said, keeping his gaze down. "I bring word ... from the Scar."

Please don't say it's blocked. We haven't had heavy storms recently to wash down mud and stones. At least this time, I'd have plenty of help to clear the debris if it is. I raised my eyebrows and nodded.

"Speak," Bior prodded.

He looked a little pale when he turned to Bior. "Sorry ... I, uh ... I've never spoken with the king before."

"What's your name?" I asked.

Shifting in his saddle, he shivered before turning toward me. "Th — Throst ... Sire." He avoided looking me in the eyes.

"Throst, relax. Tell me what's going on at the Scar before the caravan passes us."

He bowed. "The pass is crowded, Sire. Between people and wagons, there isn't much movement at all. Um ... Hallkel and Brondulf rode ahead ... to the far end. They're ordering people to ... to clear the way for us — I mean you, Sire — and Thorvid stayed on this side to make sure no one blocks the entrance."

I pressed my lips together to keep from laughing at the nervous young man. *I suppose I'd be much the same had I not grown up in a royal court.* "Thank you for the report. Ride back and help Thorvid."

"Yes, Sire. With all haste," he replied, bowing as he turned his horse and left at full gallop.

Concern furrowed my brow. "Bior, do you know how much experience these scouts have?"

"From what Captain Agrim said, he and Roi hand-picked the top four warriors from the men traveling with us."

I crossed my arms. "In other words, they have no experience in the field."

Bior nodded. "Green as new grass, m'lord."

Great. I looked back to see how close the caravan was to catching up with us. "Another question. What had him so scared?"

"These fresh warriors haven't had a chance to get to know you. Veterans still talk about Eirickson's cruelty. Maybe he expects you're much like your half-brother, m'lord ... being Eirick's blood and all."

I hung my head and sighed. "Why do people continue to believe I'm anything like my father or half-brother? Haven't I proven myself to be better?"

"To those of us who are close to you, aye. But you did nearly split Eirickson in half with one blow from your hammer, Sire ... on his wedding day, in front of half the country, no less. Soon after, you had your guard killing people resisting your rule, Satran and Croian alike ... right out in the open. Those actions make lasting impressions."

The creaking sounds of wagons on the move drew closer. *This is not the time or place to discuss this.* I nodded and put my heels to Andale. "Bior, I appreciate your honesty. You've given me much to consider. Thank you."

"Agrim's always said you want the truth," he replied, shrugging.

The first travelers we met before reaching the Carved Scar gave us plenty of room to pass but otherwise did not acknowledge us. As we got closer, the way grew crowded, slowing our pace. Masses of people, horses, and wagons stretched into the pass beyond the first curve. *I'd be surprised if the other two scouts made it to the other end.* I noticed angry looks cast my way as we jostled our way inside.

Throst and Thorvid were doing their best to move people out of our path, but two men against the masses was a losing proposition. Raising my fist above my head, I signaled for the caravan to halt.

Vestmar yelled my order as I dismounted. Pulling stamina from the ground as I shouldered my way to Throst. "Get Thorvid over here and be ready to catch me if I pass out."

He swallowed and looked from me to his fellow scout on the other side of the crowd. "If you pass — Yes, Sire. Um ... What are you going to do?"

"Something I've never done on this scale before," I said, closing my eyes. "Hope it works."

My hand quivered with the energy I'd gathered. Pressing my fingers into the Carved Scar's stone wall, I took a deep breath. The shaking in my hand worked its way up my arm and into my chest before I released the energy, and my frustration, into the wall. "Make way for King Fitzeirick and a warrior caravan!"

The cliff face shook as my voice roared from the stone, echoing through the pass.

My ears rang. Bright spots winked on and off behind my eyelids before my legs went limp. Hands grabbed me, holding me by my arms.

"We have you, Sire," someone said. "My king will not fall in front of all these people."

"Th — Thank you," I whispered.

"I'm here for you, m'lord," Bior said. "Lean on me if you need."

I nodded as another hand steadied me. It was tempting to relax, to sink into a deep sleep, but I knew we needed to get moving again. My breath came in shaky gulps while I sythed a little strength from the ground to steady my legs. Once my breathing slowed, I opened my eyes and took my weight off the warriors propping me up.

Throst, pale and wide-eyed, stepped back as I stood.

Thorvid hesitated before releasing my arm. "Are you well, m'lord?"

I nodded. "Thank you for your concern and support."

He bowed. "As you need, Sire."

I turned to face Bior.

His brow was deeply furrowed. He wiped the sweat from his face and looked me over. "That was awesome and scary and dangerous. We can pass now, but you've spooked many horses and upset no small amount of the traders and travelers. Perhaps you should've warned us first if I'm not out of line for saying so, m'lord."

I looked past him to the crowd pressed tight against the walls, clearing the majority of the pass. More than a few people looked angry. "I didn't mean to upset anyone. Your suggestion is noted. Stay by my side until I get on Andale. I'm not sure I trust my legs yet."

Bior snapped his fingers. "You heard the king. Escort him to his horse."

"No," I said. "Throst and Thorvid, ride along the line of people and give them my thanks and apologize for our passing delaying their travel. I'm nothing if not polite."

"But, Sire. They weren't cooperating with us," Thorvid protested.

"They moved when *I* asked. Thank them."

"Yes, my king," Thorvid replied. "As you say ... with all haste."

"Bior, let's get moving. I want to make the central forest by dusk."

He moved to my side as I walked. "Lean on me if you need, Sire."

I patted him on the shoulder and strode to Andale, doing my best to hold my head high. Had I been anything other than a stonesyth, though, I might not have been able to get back in the saddle. As it was, I had to pull more strength from the ground and hop three times before I mounted my horse. Once I was mounted, Bior yelled the order to move again.

I made sure to nod and wave to the crowd waiting for us to move through. Along the way, my thoughts drifted to how impressive the man-made pass was. Long ago, several stonesyths, each much stronger than any I've met, had poured tremendous amounts of energy into a natural flaw in the mountain range, opening it into a winding path wide enough for at least four horses to ride side-by-side. *My display pales in comparison.*

The scouts were waiting as I exited the pass. "You men did your best. I wanted to thank you for the effort."

"Much appreciated, m'lord," Throst replied, sounding more confident.

"I have another request. Keep us well south of The Traders Cup. Geri is a good man, but..." I paused, unsure what to say about how I was received when I last visited the inn.

"Geri? A good man?" Bior sputtered. "He housed us in the stable and fed us cold gruel. He's a horse's ass if you ask me. If I hadn't been carrying an arrow in my leg, I'd have set him straight."

"My order stands; stay away from the inn," I said, before turning to Bior. "As far as you setting him straight ... you might find his blade is as dangerous as his temper."

"Understood, Sire," Thorvid said. "Scouts, move out."

"How can you defend Geri after the way he treated you?" Bior grumbled. "You are the King of Croy. He treated you and the men with you worse than servants."

"If not for him, his aid and understanding, I may not have lived to have a chance at being king. He took me in, fed and clothed me when I needed help most. Ultimately, he helped me find Crum at his own expense and asked for nothing in return. Had I not reunited with my best friend, good chance I'd be dead ... likely by Eirickson's hand, certainly at his order. I owe Geri a debt I have not yet repaid."

Bior stayed silent until I turned to look at him. "Thinking about what you said. Him helping you and all ... well ... I take back calling Geri a horse's ass. It's possible pain clouded my judgment that day."

I fought back a grin but couldn't stop the chuckle. "I didn't say you're wrong in your assessment. He *can* be a horse's ass, but in his heart, he *is* a good man."

Bior nodded but didn't reply.

I looked at him before turning my attention to the path ahead of us. A few homesteads had popped up along the trade path before we reached the bridge crossing a river running near the halfway point between the mountains and the central forest. What was once open grassland was slowly turning into farms and grazing pastures. *How many people will be comfortable moving back east, farther from the capital, once the war is over? How long will it take for us to settle in the former nation of Satra once those brutes are no more?*

The sound of Andale's hoof beats changed when we stepped from the packed-dirt road onto the bridge. I pushed my concerns to the back of my mind, more things to figure out later, and forced myself to pay attention to my surroundings. More homes and livestock greeted us on the other side of the river. The path north, toward the Trader's Cup Inn, ran between two homesteads. *The last time I was this way, there was nothing but grass and trees lining the route.*

"My lord," Bior said, riding to my side. "Not trying to be a bother, but in case you hadn't noticed, the sun's getting low in the sky. If we don't pick up the pace, the last wagons won't reach the camp until after dark."

He was right; I hadn't noticed. *Too worried about people and land.* I looked at him and nodded. "Ride back and pass the word. I want the drivers to push their teams so we can arrive while it's still light."

"Aye, Sire." Turning his horse, he shouted orders as I put my heels to Andale.

My big horse protested with a loud snort, speeding up after a second poke.

Chapter 4

Bior galloped to my side. "One of the horses pulling the last wagon is moving slow. Might pull up lame. I'm going to ride ahead and get a couple of horses ... just in case."

The light breeze became a steady headwind as the central forest's treetops came into view. It carried the distinct smell of roasting meat. I licked my lips.

I eyed my companion sniffing the air, trying to decide if he was telling the truth or making an excuse to get to camp ahead of everyone else. "And maybe get the first cut?"

His face contorted, making it obvious he was fighting to hide a smile. "Sire, you wound me. I'm motivated by nothing but keeping this caravan moving. Surely there's enough meat for everyone to have a hot meal ... but I could secure a serving or two. Wouldn't be right if your steward let you miss a meal that smells so good."

I made sure to keep my expression neutral. "And your king, whom you are so deeply concerned about, is to trust your judgment on if there's enough for everyone?"

"I'll only turn my attention to food after securing the needed horses. You have my word, m'lord."

I nodded. "No doubt your concern for the warriors came first."

"Of course, Sire."

"Go ... and use your best judgment."

He smiled, gave a quick bow, and took off.

"Bior!" I yelled.

His horse slid to a stop before my steward turned toward me.

"Bring me back a bite if I don't reach camp before you leave!"

His jaw dropped before he laughed and sped off.

• • • • • • • • • •

As the camp came into sight, Bior returned, leading two horses. He glanced over his shoulder. "There are several deer cooking ... plenty to go around, Sire."

"Thank you for the report," I replied, smiling. "See to the last wagon. I'll make sure you don't go hungry."

He nodded and headed toward the end of the caravan.

Slowing, I waited for Aerison's wagon. "Lead the caravan to the right of camp; we'll circle the wagons there, corralling the horse teams inside for the night."

"Varian army training stuck with you, did it?" he asked, smiling.

Vestmar chuckled.

"More than I'll ever admit," I replied, returning his smile. "Can you handle things, or do I need to stay and give orders?"

"I may not be a Croian commander, but a well-trained man recognizes authority when he hears it."

I gave him a quick nod and turned back to camp. Once inside the wooden fence, I asked the first warrior I saw where his commander was.

He bowed. "Sire, Commander Kalf's in the third cabin on the left."

"Take my horse to the circle of wagons and see he's cared for."

The warrior reached for the reins. "Of course. Gladly, Sire."

I strode down the path with my shadow stretching ahead of me. My legs protested as tight muscles worked loose with each step. *Should've been riding more often.* I stopped at the door of a simple, wood-walled cabin, about a third larger than the surrounding structures, and knocked.

"Come in and make it quick," someone called from inside. "I'm expecting the king soon."

Stepping inside, I said, "King Fitzeirick is here."

Torches mounted to the left and right walls gave the room a warm glow in the fading daylight. Two candles, sitting on a large, wooden table sitting in the center of the room, lit the space. Three men, two with their backs to me, sat, looking over a large parchment.

Commander Kalf's eyes opened wide. His chair fell over backward as he quickly stood. "Sire, I wasn't expecting you to arrive alone."

The other two men jumped from their seats, turned, and bowed.

"Everyone else is busy with wagons or horses. I saw no reason to wait for an escort," I replied.

"Of course, Sire. I trust your travel was easy. Would you care to sit? I'll send for some ale. We can talk. Have you met Sergeants Boe and Ingjald?"

The men nodded when he said their names.

"I have not. Well met."

"Well met, Sire," they echoed.

"The Carved Scar was crowded, a good sign in general, but it slowed our pace. A drink sounds good. It's been a long ride. My legs need to stretch. I'll stand, at least until dinner's served."

Kalf nodded. "Sergeant Boe, a cask of ale and cups."

"Aye, Commander. With all haste."

"A favor, while you're out," I said.

They froze mid-step.

"Find Varian Lieutenant Aerison, the Varian soldier Vestmar, and Bior. I'd like for them to join us."

"Of course, m'lord," Ingjald said.

"Thank you," I replied, making my way to the table. "What do you have here?"

"Reports and supply requests from Southold, Sire."

"Anything I need to know?"

"Nothing surprising in the requests. Between our stores here and what the caravan holds, we'll send everything they asked for with you, m'lord. As far as the report." He shrugged. "Looks much the same as the last several reports. Little fighting. General Gudmann suspects it's a trap."

I nodded. *I've heard the same during my recent meetings with General Heming.* "Given the way Satra ran back to their lands, I can't fault anyone for thinking they're planning something big when we cross the border."

"Better to advance with caution than be caught by surprise, m'lord. I'm sure plenty of barbarians will be there, regardless of when we arrive."

I chuckled. "True, but the longer we give them to prepare, the worse it may be. Changing the subject, have you been past the central forest?"

"Far enough to investigate the nearest Satran stronghold."

My chest tightened. "How bad is it? What sight awaits when I return to my homeland?"

He shook his head. "It's not pretty, m'lord. We've made a safe path through the murder ground, but the surrounding area is untouched. Haven't had enough spare strong stonesyths to work the land flat again, much less make sure it's safe. I strongly suspect traps are waiting for anyone fool enough to venture too far into those pits and barricades alone."

"But it's safe to pass on the path and through the fortress?"

"Aye, it is."

"And beyond?

"No reports of any problems since the enemy fled south."

I nodded. "Good. It hurts my heart knowing Satra tore up my homeland, but I'm looking forward to good Croian citizens settling there again. Soon, I hope."

The door opened. Boe entered, hefting a small cask on his shoulder.

Kalf gathered the parchments and moved them to one corner of the table before Boe placed the ale on the side nearest to him.

As the sergeant filled a stone tankard, Ingjald came into the room. "I have the Varians with me, Sire. Bior isn't far behind. He insisted on bringing the food."

I tried not to smile at my travel companion's antics. "Thank you, Sergeant."

Aerison followed, red-faced and leaning on Vestmar.

I pulled a chair out and motioned to Aerison.

He nodded and hobbled over to the seat.

Bior entered, streaks of meat juice in his beard shining with the torchlight. He carried a platter of food with several forks jabbed into it. "Told you I wouldn't let you go hungry, Sire."

Ingjald closed the door behind him and joined us at the table. "Anyone goes to bed hungry or thirsty, it's their own fault."

Boe placed our drinks on the table as we took our seats.

"Sire," Kalf said, "You first."

I looked at Aerison. "You're a valued guest in our country, a great leader, and a good friend. Would you start the meal with a toast?"

Lifting his tankard, Aerison cleared his throat. "To strong warriors, battles well fought, and long live the victors. To a long and prosperous alliance between Varia and Croy and to ridding our world of the Satran plague."

I reached to him and patted his shoulder as the echo of 'aye' drowned out the sound of mugs clacking together. We set into the meat like a pack of wolves.

Typical of my home country's cooking style, the meat was unseasoned but not as bland as it could've been. Whoever cooked it chose the firewood to add a nice touch of smoky flavor. Between bites, Bior explained one of the horses pulling the last wagon had something wrong with a hoof. The driver thought it might be a cut, but it was getting too dark to tell. The head groom agreed to look at it in the morning.

"If it can't pull, we've got plenty here you can use, Sire," Kalf offered. "But if anyone can get a horse right, it's Borgar. Don't know if there's such a thing as a herbalist for horses, but if there is ... he's the best."

Boe and Ingjald nodded their agreement, not speaking with their mouths full.

"I'll trust your man's judgment. Thank you for offering more horses, if needed."

"Anything to support the war effort, m'lord," Kalf replied.

I lifted my tankard to him before taking another drink. "Aerison, I trust everything else is in order with the wagons and horses."

He swallowed. "No doubt you've got some tired stonesyths among your men this evening. Your group isn't as well trained as I thought. Took three tries and way too much yelling on my part before the wagons were pushed together well enough to contain the horses. I'd advise you to run all your future recruits through the exercise until they can do it correctly the first time with their eyes closed. I promise this group won't have a problem doing it when we stop tomorrow."

"That explains why you were so winded when you got here. I'll pass your suggestion on to Agrim next time I see him," I said.

"What were they doing?" Kalf asked.

Vestmar and Aerison described the Varian practice of circling their wagons to act as a makeshift corral when a caravan stops for the night. I had experienced it first hand, traveling from Varia into Croy as part of the coup resulting in me taking control of the country from my half-brother.

Bior's fork was the last one dropped on the platter. Despite our best efforts, there was still meat after we'd eaten our fill. However, the cask had run dry.

"While I *am* enjoying the company, we have an early start tomorrow. Where are we sleeping?" I asked.

"The cabin to the right of this one, Sire," Kalf said, pointing. "Boe will take the lieutenant and his man to their quarters. Bior, follow Ingjald to the barracks. Ingjald, take this platter for the night watch to finish off."

"Bior's my right hand on this trip. I'd prefer he stays close to me."

Everyone turned to look at me.

"Sire," Kalf said, "you're in no danger here."

"I'm concerned with any danger. He should be close enough that I don't have to search for him if I have a task for him."

Bior nodded. "I'll sleep outside your door if that's what you need, m'lord."

"Won't be necessary," Kalf said. "Boe, see the Varians to their rooms. Ingjald, help Bior get a bed from the barracks and put it in the front room of King Fitzeirick's cabin."

"Aerison, Vestmar, sleep well," I said, as they headed for the door.

"With a belly full of deer and ale, I'll sleep like a babe," Aerison said.

Bior chuckled and nodded as he followed Ingjald out of the building.

"Would you like me to escort you to your cabin?" Kalf asked.

"No. I'm sure you've had a long day and need to sleep soon yourself."

Kalf bowed. "As you say, m'lord. Sleep well."

"And a good night to you, commander."

Entering the cabin, I fumbled in the dark to find the tinder box and light a candle. *If only I was a firesyth.*

Dust hung in the air as I removed my armor. *Probably should clean it before going to sleep.* Tired, and more than a little drunk, I wiped the leather clean and flopped onto the bed.

I don't know when Bior entered.

Chapter 5

To his credit, Bior woke early enough to have a large cup of tea and a small loaf of bread coated with honey waiting on the table for me. After breakfast, I did my best to ignore a slight headache and changed into a fresh set of clothes. *Where do they bathe around here?* Bior wasn't around to find out for me, so I set out on my own.

Commander Kalf walked past my quarters as I opened the door. "Morning, commander," I greeted him.

He bowed before looking at me, eyes a little bloodshot. "Good morn, Sire. Did you sleep well?"

"Better than I expected. I'm sure the ale helped."

He nodded. "But it hurts a little this morning."

I chuckled. "Yes. It does."

"Anything I can do for you?" he asked. "Breakfast?"

"Bior took care of my meal, but where do I clean up? I'd like to bathe before we hit the path."

"Come with me," he replied. "I was headed to the pond myself."

"Pond?" I asked, as we walked. "I don't recall any stream nearby."

"A couple of stonesyths found an underground spring, opened a well, and fed it into a small depression. I will warn you, it's chilly enough to wake an exhausted warrior."

I nodded. "Thanks for the warning, but I figure warm baths are a luxury I'll do without for some time."

"Aye, Sire. They are few and far between out here."

Kalf led me past several rows of small cabins to the northeastern corner of the camp, nearly inside the central forest. Five or six warriors dried themselves near the bathing pond, about a dozen more were washing.

"How's the water this morning?" Kalf asked the men getting dressed.

"Cold as usual, commander."

He chuckled and pointed toward a set of stone shelves a couple of paces away. "Sire, you can store your clothes there. Drying cloths are on the left. Wet cloths go in the small cart. Soap cakes are in the buckets at the edge of the pond."

I undressed and took a deep breath of warm air before stepping into the pond. Cold water stung my feet as I bent down to get soap.

"Best to get in quick, m'lord," Kalf said, passing me. "Get the shock over so you can wash and get out."

A shiver ran up my legs. I nodded before willing myself into the water. As the chilly water lapped at my stomach, my legs went numb from the cold. I stopped when the pond was mid-chest deep and made sure to keep my hands out of the water, afraid my fingers would lose feeling and drop the soap. Ripples of cold tickled my back as men waded past, getting out to dry.

After a deep breath, I dunked my head under quickly and soaped from head to toe as fast as I dared. Kalf chuckled before I dunked myself again to rinse.

The commander got out of the pond a few steps ahead of me and tossed me a drying cloth. I dried quickly and shook my legs, trying to get some feeling back in them, before dressing. Returning to camp, I pondered where to look for Bior first and asked Kalf if he knew where my steward might be.

"No, Sire. I went straight from eating in my quarters to bathe. Perhaps he's with Borgar checking on the injured horse."

I thanked him for the suggestion and turned to leave camp.

"If I don't see you before you leave," Kalf said, "may you travel swift and safe, my lord."

I waved and kept walking. *For someone who's supposed to be at my beck and call, Bior made himself scarce this morning.* Dodging warriors, doing my best to not interrupt their business, I reached the western edge of camp and stopped at the exit to talk with the guard. "Have you seen Borgar this morning?"

"Yes, Sire." He pointed toward the caravan. "The head groom went that way shortly after first light."

"Was Bior with him?"

"Don't know who that is, but Borgar was alone when he passed through."

Dead end. I tapped my foot and scratched my chin for a moment. *Where else could he be?* The answer came to me. "Where do the warriors eat?"

The guard pointed back into camp. "Follow the fence south to the training grounds, and keep going to the mess hall."

I smiled and offered him my hand. "Thank you."

He bowed before shaking my hand. "My pleasure, Sire. Best of luck with your search."

Hurrying along the edge of the camp, I reached the training grounds and was tempted to stop and watch the men sparring. As much as I wanted to know my warriors were at their best, I needed to find Bior and get the caravan going again. *We are on a schedule.* I kept walking, trying to keep my mood from getting any worse.

The chaotic sounds of mingled conversations hit my ears when I opened the door to the long, rectangular, stone building used as the mess hall for the entire camp. No one looked my way while I swept my eyes across the room. On the third pass, I spotted Bior and called his name.

He stood, still chewing whatever was in his mouth, and waved me over. He returned to his seat as I stomped my way to the table. "We don't have time —"

"Sire, I'd like you to meet my cousins," Bior interrupted. "King Fitzeirick, allow me to introduce Skap and Kotkel. They're family from my mother's side. We haven't seen each other in months. Cousins, this is King Fitzerirck."

At first glance, the two men looked a little younger than Bior. They stood and bowed low. "Honored to meet you, my king," one said.

"Please, join us," the other added.

I understand, all too well, how important family is, but we don't have time. "I'd like nothing more, but as I was saying, we need to get the caravan on the move." I moved beside Bior and clapped my hand on his shoulder.

He stiffened under my grip.

"I need *your* assistance," I said, frustration evident in my voice.

"I ... yes, m'lord. My assistance, of course ... anything you need." He stammered. "I — we were catching up and ... and I must have lost track of the time."

"Skap, Kotkel, thank you for everything you do for Croy," I said. "I don't want to seem rude, but we must be going. Duty calls."

They bowed again. "We understand, Sire. Travel safe and swift."

"It was good seeing you two," Bior said, before I squeezed his shoulder and turned him toward the door.

We wound our way through the camp, dodging warriors. Bior tried several times to explain himself, and I kept telling him to keep quiet. Once we reached the cabin, I opened the door and motioned for him to go in.

"If you would let me explain—"

I pointed to a chair at the table. "Sit. I'll talk. You'll listen."

He squinted for a moment before hurrying to the chair.

Crossing my arms, I glared at him for a moment. "While my rule is more secure now than it was, I'm not confident there aren't people still conspiring against me."

"But we're among —"

"Don't talk...listen, and listen carefully. I didn't balk at you traveling as my steward because I know you are a good man, reliable and loyal. However, I need you to set the example, at least in public, showing my authority over my guard and our army is absolute. I did not berate you as we walked across the camp because I didn't want anyone to see me as a harsh tyrant. I'm not asking you to be a bootlick; I'm asking you to do what you know how to do. Be a loyal, observant, and capable servant."

"I brought you breakfast."

"You did, and I appreciate it, but *I* had to ask where to bathe because you were nowhere to be found. I don't doubt Kalf's loyalty, but how does it look when I have to ask him a question my steward should have already addressed? Does it give him a reason to consider I don't command respect? Does he slip up, mention it in front of the wrong person, and start a rumor that undermines my effort to keep Croy whole and safe?"

Bior wrung his hands together. "I ... I'm sorry, Sire. I didn't think you'd mind me visiting family."

"I don't. Believe me, I know family is important. Had you asked or even let me know where you would be, I'd have gladly given my permission. The problem is I had to go looking for you."

He cast his eyes to the floor. "Understood. Do I resign to you, or should I ride back to the capital and resign to my captain?"

I sighed. "I don't want you to resign. I want you to act as my right hand."

He nodded but didn't look up. "Professional. All business. I understand. It won't happen again."

After rubbing my forehead for a moment, I said, "Look at me. I don't want this trip to be a burden. I like having fun as much as anyone. I like to laugh. I enjoy playful banter ... when it's appropriate. When we're alone or riding out of earshot of anyone else, you have my permission — my encouragement even — to speak freely. Around everyone else, I want you nearby and alert. I need you ready to act as necessary. When I don't have an immediate need, do as you like, so long as I know where to find you."

"Understood." He stood and put his arm across his chest. "I'll take my assignment more seriously and be mindful of your request."

I smiled. "Perfect. Now, for the first order of the day. I'll pack my clothes. Take the saddlebags and get Andale ready to travel. Let everyone know I'm getting ready and expect the caravan to be ready to move soon after I arrive."

He nodded. "Gladly, m'lord."

Once Bior left, I pulled my armor on and headed to the wagons.

Aerison was seated on his wagon, shouting orders as warriors went about getting the horse teams harnessed.

"How's it feel to be in charge again?" I asked, as I got close.

"Same as I remembered," he replied, smiling. "I was born to do this. Shame I can't go into battle with my soldiers."

"But you are getting command of an important post. If you remember, I was the one who said you can't keep a good man down while you were on the mend at Abi's."

"True, but we would have never had that conversation if you didn't have traitors in your midst."

"They're all a bad memory now," I said, as Bior approached with Andale in tow.

"He's ready to go, Sire," Bior said, patting my horse's neck.

I thanked him and got into the saddle with no problem. "How's the horse with the hoof problem?"

"Borgar insisted on keeping him here. Said the wound needed time to heal, or the horse would go lame. He made sure we had a good replacement. I sent the scouts ahead when I arrived. Everything's ready to go ... on your order, m'lord."

"I'll trust the groomsman's judgment. Ride back and remind the drivers to keep their reins tight. If they get off into those obstacles between here and the stronghold, it could hurt a horse or damage a wheel ... or worse."

He nodded. "With all haste, Sire."

I turned to Vestmar and pointed toward the forest.

He snapped his reins. "Move out!"

Chapter 6

I led the caravan along the fence surrounding the camp to the path leading into the central forest. After passing through the shattered remains of the wall Satra built to slow down any attacks we might launch, we entered what was left of the once-majestic stand of trees known as the central forest. Satra had decimated it while they occupied the territory.

My last memory of this place was traveling to the capital with Roi and Crum. I smiled, for a moment, before a frown forced its way onto my face. *Had I known then what I know now, I would have killed Eirickson on sight. Yes, I may have died as well, but it might have saved many lives.*

Lost in my thoughts, I barely noticed the hoof beats as Bior returned. "I've spoken with every driver about the dangerous path ahead, Sire," he said.

I turned to look at him, frown still twisting my lips, and blinked a couple of times.

Bior raised his eyebrows. "What troubles you, m'lord?"

"Memories. Good and bad," I said, shaking my head. "Recent events which feel like a lifetime ago."

"It'd be a lie if I said I understood but ... I'm here if you need to talk."

"Thank you, but your responsibilities are enough of a burden," I said.

"I have broad shoulders, m'lord, and a shared load is easier to bear. I'm supposed to help you as you need. Am I not?"

Whether he intended it or not, his statement brought a smile to my face. "Yes, you are. If I want to share, I'll ask for your ear. Until then, your support is welcome."

"As I can," he said, bowing.

We exited the forest much sooner than I expected—*It used to be much deeper. To the fire with the Satran for wasting the trees*—to a breathtakingly horrible sight. None of the descriptions of this maze, the killing zone Satra made here, prepared me for it. Hills, valleys, pits, large sharp-edged stones jutting from the ground at random, and smaller stones strewn about to trip men and horses, slowing any advance for archers to pick them off from the fortress wall.

This is what Fastulf led the guides through in the pitch black of night, preparing our surprise attack. Pride swelled in my chest. "Can you imagine what the first attack was like?"

He laughed. "I'd never cross this broken ground without hurting myself somewhere along the way."

"Yet the company Fastulf and the guides led across made it through without being detected," I said. "Amazing to it for myself."

"Aye, Sire. It is a sight."

The Satran fortress loomed ahead, looking foreboding with a wide section of the western wall torn open. Tension drew my shoulders higher. My hands gripped Andale's reins.

"Have you seen anything moving about since we exited the trees?"

He looked left and right before glancing back at the caravan. "Can't say I have. Why?"

"I haven't seen anything either, but since we exited the woods —" I shrugged.

"I know what you mean," Bior said, nodding. "There was some death here, and the fortress ahead isn't inviting. Perhaps it's all weighing on your mind, Sire. If there was something, the scouts would have noticed and sounded an alarm, or we'd have heard fighting."

I rubbed my forehead before looking toward what remained of the Satran fortress. "Perhaps. But stick close anyway."

"I'm here until you tell me otherwise, m'lord."

Ravens squawked and cawed as we entered the abandoned fortress. The noise twisted my nerves tighter. A faint smell of death hung in the air though I didn't see any bodies nearby. Heart pounding, my eyes flitted from one shadow to another, looking for places someone might hide as we rode through the stone structure. Splintered, wooden doors lay inside ragged, stone openings to barracks, storehouses, and other structures. Piles of rubble sat on either side of the path through the site of our first attack.

As much as the victory made me glad, I couldn't keep from thinking about the people, my people, who once lived beyond where this horrid, stone structure now stood. The innocent farmers, ranchers, and tradesmen who worked with the land. People who wanted nothing more than to provide for their families, help their neighbors, and live in peace.

The memory of a family I stayed with came to mind. A farmer, his wife, son, and twin daughters ... decent people making a life for themselves. *No doubt the Satran invaders killed or enslaved them. Protecting the good folks who can't protect themselves is why we fight to remove Satra from our world.*

The exit on the far side of the stronghold was larger than the entrance we came in. I remembered a report mentioning something about needing more room to get warriors out faster when the Satran soldiers turned tail. Leaving the ruined structure, I should have known better than to expect the land to be in usable condition. The ground was gouged by routed soldiers trying to slow down their attackers or make crude hides and holes to fight from. Where once there were homesteads with farms and livestock, vast areas of devastation dominated the landscape. Sorrow gripped my heart before anger settled in my gut like a cold stone. *It's going to take the sweat of many men and women before my old skati is livable again.*

"All this damage," Bior said. "It's like they had no intention of settling here. Why plunder the land instead of settling here?"

"Eirickson convinced them they would split Varia with him. Perhaps they planned to use the resources here to build weapons, enough to arm the whole nation of Satra, to continue the invasion."

Bior shook his head. "But you twisted their agreement off, right at the root. So, they turned their forces toward us."

"Maybe my actions forced them to give up settling here." I shrugged. "Who knows how a Satran's mind works. Regardless, the war isn't over until the last Satran draws their final breath."

"I'm not sure General Gudmann agrees," Bior commented.

I swept my arm ahead of us. "How can anyone see this and not want to wipe them out? When Eirick attacked Varia and captured this land, he didn't leave it unlivable. And he didn't kill or enslave the Varians who didn't escape. My father left them the option to leave or stay and live under Croian rule. Can you say the same about Satra? No. They slaughtered our people or took them as slaves. I'll strike the last one down myself without a second thought."

Bior raised his hands. "Sire, I'm not saying I agree with the general. Even if I did before, seeing this would change my mind. You mentioned the possibility of disloyalty earlier. If there is any, perhaps General Gudmann is a source."

"He and I have disagreed before," I said, shaking my head, "but I've never had a reason to question his loyalty. I trust him to do what needs to be done when ordered without delay. We may have a heated disagreement afterward, but he will obey."

"As you say, m'lord. You know him better than I."

I hope so. "I need a subject to take my mind off all the destruction. Tell me about your cousins."

Bior chuckled. "I figure their story's about the same as many other warriors. As young boys, they did more to get into trouble than anything else. Nothing serious, mind you—typical kid stuff. Skap's older by about a year, but Kotkel's the thinker of the two. I helped them both prepare once they decided to become warriors. Their pa expected them to work in the family business. He's a cobbler." My escort pulled his boot from the stirrup and kicked his leg to the side. "Makes the finest boots you'll ever wear."

"I'll keep it in mind next time I'm looking for new boots," I said, smiling.

"Let me know, and I'll get you the family price," Bior said. "Not that you couldn't afford them anyway, m'lord."

"I don't mind paying for good work."

He nodded. "As I was saying, working leather and hammering soles didn't appeal to either boy. Like many, they wanted to go on an adventure."

"So, your cousins haven't learned adventures are funny things," I said. "People love to talk about their adventures, making them sound exciting. The truth is, adventures are only fun to talk about after the fact; they are miserable to have."

He scratched his head. "Not sure I get your meaning, Sire."

"We've been on an adventure before, you and I ... the ambush at the Carved Scar. I'm sure you've shared the story of how you got your limp, maybe even embellished the tale for laughs or to impress a lady or two ... right?"

"Well ... m'lord, I'm not sure I'd confess to bragging to you. I mean, you've had much worse."

I shook my head. "Regardless, you've talked about it since and made it sound exciting. But, and tell the truth, was it any fun at all while it happened?"

"No. I was hurt. You were hurt. Everyone was miserable."

I chuckled. "Thus my point. Adventures are fun to talk about but no fun to have."

Bior pursed his lips and stroked his beard several times before nodding. "I see the wisdom in your statement. I'll share it with the boys next time I see them."

"You can," I said, "or wait until they are telling a tale of some adventure to point it out."

His eyes lit up. "Oh, that should be good for a laugh. Thank you, Sire."

"I'm nothing if not helpful."

"And I'm getting thirsty," Bior said, grinning, "and this waterskin's empty. Want me to bring you a full one?"

The uncomfortable suspicion someone or something was watching us still nipped at the base of my neck. I looked back at the Varian wagon. Aerison's eyes were closed, but Vestmar was alert, sweeping his gaze right and left.

Does he have the same feeling?

Galloping hoof beats ahead of us caught my attention.
I spun my head around.
"Wait. Let's see who's headed our way."

Chapter 7

Topping a rise, we almost ran into Thorvid.

Yanking the reins, his horse skidded to a stop. "Sire," Thorvid said, "we noticed something moving through an overgrown field ahead."

I glanced at Bior.

He returned my look, eyebrows raised.

"What have you found?"

Thorvid shrugged. "I don't know, m'lord. Maybe nothing. Throst called out when he spotted some tall grasses twitching. I sent him and Hallkel into the field to look for tracks while Brondulf kept watch while I rode back to alert you, Sire."

"I've felt like someone—or something—has been watching us for a while now," I said, "but I haven't seen anything."

"Same," Bior added.

"How far away is the field?" I asked.

Thorvid twisted in his saddle and pointed. "You can see it from here, Sire."

Leaning so I could look past him, I saw two men ride out of a patch of knee-high grasses about twenty paces off the southern edge of the road. The clearing could hold our caravan with room to spare. The third scout, hand shading his eyes, stared at a stand of trees stretching away from the field's far southern edge.

"Bior, ride back and let Aerison and Vestmar know we might have something to watch for ahead of us. I'm going ahead, with Thorvid, to look things over for myself."

"Is that wise, Sire?" Bior asked. "This could be a trap."

"I am aware and won't be alone." I pointed toward the field. "They haven't raised an alarm, and two companies of warriors will be along shortly. For all we know, it could be a bear or a wild pig."

My steward pressed his lips together for a moment before nodding. "As you said, my king. Keep yourself safe."

I nodded toward the lone scout. "Thorvid won't let me take any risk, right?"

"Yes, m'lord. Your safety is my highest concern."

Smiling, I glanced back at the caravan. "Go, Bior. We'll wait at the field unless there is danger."

"Aye, Sire."

"Take the lead, Thorvid, and stay to my right. I'll keep to the northern edge of the path...in case someone emerges from hiding."

"Of course, m'lord," Thorvid said, bowing before he turned to lead me to the field.

Riding at a comfortable trot, I watched for any suspicious movement. Nothing caught my eye by the time we reached the other scouts, talking among themselves.

"Anything to report?" I asked, bringing Andale to a halt.

Hallkel cleared his throat. "A few broken branches, not far from the field's edge, Sire. We rode a short distance into the trees to see what we could find and." He shrugged. "No tracks in the ground ... nothing to follow."

"So, it's not an animal. If anything, it's a stonesyth wiping their tracks as they pass. Keep a sharp eye," I said. "A lone stonesyth isn't much of a threat, but we all know how deadly a surprise attack from a small force could be."

"Aye, m'lord." Thorvid said, before sputtering as I got off Andale. "What are you doing, Sire?"

"I want to check the field myself, and it will be easier to do without the caravan shaking the ground on its way by."

"Sire," Throst said, "is it wise for you to be on foot? Someone could be watching from the woods, waiting to spring an ambush."

I glanced toward the caravan. *They aren't far away.* "If they didn't attack you three, I doubt they plan to rush out when there's five of us here now. Keep your eyes open and yell if you see anything."

"As you say, m'lord," Throst said.

As soon as my feet hit the ground, I pushed my talent out ahead of me and approached the field slowly. Entering the overgrown vegetation was hard work. Interwoven grasses brushed against my calves. Low, rambling vines pulled at my feet, threatening to trip me. *It would take a woodsyth to move through here without leaving a trace. But if a stonesyth with woodsyth talent fled through the forest, why leave damaged branches?* The vegetation had deep roots, too, interrupting the smooth flow of energy, making it harder to hunt for anyone hiding.

By the time I forced my way near the center of the area, I had decided my efforts were pointless ... and I was growing tired from forcing my talent through constant resistance. Turning to the men behind me, I shook my head. "I'm finding nothing."

"Sorry, Sire," Thorvid said. "Probably best to come out of the field now. The caravan's almost here."

Glancing to the west, I saw Bior riding at the head of the line of wagons and mounted warriors. Two waterskins hung around his neck, bouncing off his chest. *Good, I could use a drink.* "Watch those trees while we wait, in case someone decides the supplies we're carrying are worth risking their life for."

"Aye," the scouts responded together.

Andale snorted a protest as I settled onto the saddle. After one last mouthful of grass, he did as I asked and walked onto the path where we waited for the caravan.

"All's well, m'lord?" Bior asked, lifting a bulging skin as he reached me.

"Scouts, ride ahead but keep us in sight."

"As you wish, Sire," Thorvid said.

I nudged my horse and fell into step beside him. I nodded, took the offered water skin, and quenched my thirst.

"Find anything?" Bior asked.

"No, and it bothers me. I want to talk to Aerison. Maybe he'll have some thoughts." Bior patted his saddlebag. "Once you're done, I have some dried meat for you."

I thanked him and turned Andale toward the approaching caravan.

"I know Bior told you the scouts saw something. Have either of you seen any movement?" I asked, slowing to match the wagon's pace.

"A suspicion but not much else," Vestmar said. "I've had an itch between my shoulder blades. Can't tell you why but it only happens when I should be paying extra attention to my surroundings. Has saved my life, once or twice."

"Once he mentioned it, I tried to listen for any unexpected sounds. Never noticed anything," Aerison added.

After describing what I'd found, I asked for Aerison's opinion.

"One thing is certain, animals don't cover their tracks," he said. "Perhaps it's a Croian who avoided capture, looking for safety."

"If so," Bior said, "why hide from us?"

The lieutenant looked at my companion and cocked his head. "You wonder why a frightened survivor would hide from four armed men on horseback? Anyone cunning enough to survive the Satran invasion wouldn't risk capture now unless they are desperate. It's likely they are trying to decide if it's safe to come out or not."

"I'd agree, assuming you're right," Bior said. "But what if they aren't peaceful? What if it's a trap?"

"Bior's point is solid," I said, glancing at him. "But it could be we're both a little fearful of an ambush." Pausing, I patted my chest where the scar from an arrow wound marked the time he and I got hurt during a surprise attack. "Regardless, unless the attacking force more than matches our numbers, I believe we'd prevail. After all, they showed themselves, so we know someone's out there."

"I agree," Aerison said.

"Aerison, given what little we know, what would you suggest?" I asked.

"Keep moving but have more of your mounted men ride along the southern side of the road."

I nodded. "Bior, give me my lunch, then go give the men the new orders."

"Aye, Sire," Bior replied.

"And make sure they know to raise an alarm if they see anything," I said, taking the pouch Bior offered me. "Unless they see a weapon, I don't want anyone to attack. I'd hate for one of our countrymen to die because a green warrior made a terrible mistake."

"Even if it's a Satran trying to surrender, m'lord?" Bior asked.

I scowled. "If our warriors see anyone with blotchy, gray skin...attack. Kill them where they stand."

"I'll make sure they understand, m'lord," he said, expression hard to read, before turning to spread my command.

After one more glance over my shoulder, in case I saw someone watching from the trees, I urged Andale to pick up his pace so I could keep the scouts in sight and tried to enjoy my meager lunch. *Dare I hope we reach the next obstacle in our journey without incident?*

Chapter 8

The sun sank behind us quicker than I wanted. A steady breeze rose as twilight crept closer. Grasses, wavering at the edges of the battle-disturbed ground, caught my attention, demanding I watch as I passed in case someone hid in the deepening shadows.

Daylight continued its steady retreat away from the approaching night, making it difficult to watch for movement. *Will we reach the wall before dark?* Nerves fought off the exhaustion nibbling at the edge of my concentration. Aching tension stiffened my neck. A firm knot formed between my shoulder blades.

I turned when something dark moved, at the edge of my vision, on my right flank.

Bior nodded to me and spoke.

I knew he wasn't a threat and turned my attention back to possible threats ahead without listening to him.

Near the top of a hill, yells got my attention.

All by itself, my hand reached back for my hammer as I put my heels to Andale.

Bior kept pace with me.

Topping the rise, I saw one of the scouts galloping toward us.

"Good news, Sire," Brondulf said, reaching us. He turned and pointed. "The wall's at the bottom of this hill."

"Good news indeed," I replied, taking my hand off the hammer's handle. "Bior, signal Vestmar to pick up the pace."

"Gladly," he said. Raising his hand above his head, he waved it back and forth.

Reins cracked behind me, and I nudged Andale to speed up.

Ahead sat a terrible, awe-inspiring sight. A rough stone wall, running north until disappearing into a small stand of trees and south as far as I cared to look.

Satra's soldiers used this as their last stand and held us off for several weeks before turning tail and running back to their country. The numerous battles left the ground looking like an angry, drunken stonesyth had attacked it.

A large gap had been sythed through the barrier, allowing passage for horses and wagons. I noticed a few smaller, man-sized openings. Their jagged openings made me think they were made by brute force.

"Brondulf, ride back and have the scouts check what's on the other side," I said. "There's no way we can make camp here."

"Aye, Sire. I'll return once we've found a campsite," he said.

"The drivers are tired; horses are about the same," Bior said. "We might have to make the best of it."

"Without unloading all the supplies, there's no way everyone could sleep in a wagon," I replied. "We push on and hope they find smoother ground."

Brondulf trotted toward us as we passed through the wall. "Sire, about thirty paces ahead, we found much smoother ground. I'd guess there was little fighting there."

Breathing a sigh of relief, I turned to Bior and smiled. "Pass the word."

He returned my smile and galloped back to the caravan.

"No sense in waiting for them," I said, to Brondulf, "I'm ready to get out of the saddle."

"Come with me, m'lord." He pointed ahead. "The ground levels at the top of that rise, and it's smooth and clear as far as I can see."

I nodded and looked around as we made our way. There was an odd, nearly uncomfortable, sense of familiarity. *This* was *your homeland. You grew up here ... governed this territory.* The farther we went, the deeper my unease became. Topping the rise, we rode to where the rest of the scouts waited.

"Hallkel, take Andale to the corral once the wagons are circled," I said, dismounting. "I'm going to look around a little, on foot."

"As you wish, Sire."

"Would you like one of us to go with you, m'lord?" Thorvid asked.

"No," I replied. "For what I want to do, I don't want any distractions." Reaching back, I tapped my hammer's handle. "I can take care of myself long enough to raise an alarm if I'm attacked."

He nodded but didn't hide his concern.

Several strides north of the path, I sat on the ground, closed my eyes, and pressed my hands onto the dirt in front of me. *Why is this place bothering me so much?* I tried to calm my thoughts and focus before pushing my talent out, searching for the source of my agitation.

Focusing on the emotion, I used it to fuel my efforts. Reaching farther down the path, I noticed something thirty or forty paces away. *Maybe a natural settling in the ground, maybe not.*

Getting to my feet, a horse snorted not far behind me.

"Sire, is everything all right?" Bior asked.

I nodded without turning to look at him. "Everything is fine. Well ..." I paused, searching for the right words. "Not everything. This place bothers me. I want to know why."

The saddle squeaked before his boots thumped the ground. "It'll be too dark to see soon. I'm not letting you wander around alone."

I shook my head and pointed toward the camp. "I'll be fine. Darkness doesn't hinder me on foot. Go. Eat and rest. Save some food for me. I'll find you when I'm done."

"Aye. Be careful."

I tracked Bior, making sure he didn't follow as I crept forward.

Dropping to one knee, I put a hand on the ground and carefully searched for what I found before. My energy tumbled past corners of compacted dirt too sharp to be natural. I squeezed my eyes shut, focused on a small area, and tried to fix the shape in my mind. After several breaths, it came to me. *A building stood here.* I pushed more of my talent out, widening the search. Similar shapes were nearby, some larger and a few smaller. *What is this place?*

My heart pounded as I stood. I kept the energy flowing and easily followed a path through the area, even though my eyes were closed. Ten paces in, I stood surrounded by the impressions of buildings. A rushing sound filled my ears as my heart thumped harder. *This was a market.* Little more than a year ago, I had to have passed through here on my way to the capital before the invasion. So much had changed. It seemed like a lifetime had passed.

My body shook as my feet carried me forward like they knew where I needed to go ... even if I didn't. I stopped near the largest plot yet, unsure why. It took a complete trip around the outside before I decided it had to be a hall.

Stopping at what had to be the front entrance, I pushed my talent ahead to search for the impressions left by the walls inside. Step after step, a disturbing sense of familiarity settled deeper into my mind. Echoes of footsteps on the—now missing—stone floors tickled my ears. Stopping at the entrance of a large room, my knees buckled. Tears flowed from my creased eyelids as a final thought forced its way to the front of my mind. *This was my home.*

Sorrow burned in my veins as memories flooded my mind. Power shook me. Short, ragged breaths rasped through my flared nostrils as I fought to keep control of myself. My will prevailed until I remembered Roi telling me how my mother had died. Killed by a hail of arrows while protecting our people from a Satran attack. I bellowed. Raw emotion ripped my resolve apart. My talent flowed out like a raging river, shaking the ground around me.

Curse the Satran people for what they did to my country, my people ... to me. Their debt demands blood. The life's blood of every man, woman, and child from that nation of blight. When I'm done, even the memory of Satra will go to the fire.

Forcing myself to stand, I screamed an incoherent challenge to the world around me before slamming my hammer into the hard-packed dirt.

The outburst brought clarity. *There's no better place than this.* I sat, pressed my hands onto the ground, and drained my emotions into it. Once my breathing slowed, I went to work.

Focusing my stonesything powers, I forced a slab of stone to the surface from deep underground. Channeling painful memories, my finger dug into the dark granite's smooth face. With practiced ease, I gouged out the words to create a memorial.

IN MEMORY OF LOVED ONES LOST TO THE SATRAN INVASION

Sar'sa

Aesa

Though the memorial began with my mother and fiancée, I intended this to be a growing tribute. We still didn't know for certain who had survived the invasion or the battles that followed. With that in mind, I left plenty of space for the names of those we lost. Near the bottom, I continued writing.

THE NATION OF CROY WILL NEVER ALLOW ITSELF TO BE INVADED AGAIN

As my finger dug the K in king, my hand paused. *They never knew me as king. Should I sign it as skald instead?* I closed my eyes and debated before deciding I was no longer the man they knew. I couldn't decide if I was better or worse, but I knew I wasn't the same. Making sure the K was still there, I finished the signature, *KING FITZEIRICK*.

Light flickered off the smooth stone. I reached for my hammer. Turning, I raised the weapon and prepared to face the threat.

At least a dozen men, carrying torches and armed with swords or axes, stood several paces away.

"S — Sire. Is everything all right? Are you hurt?" Bior called out. "We heard, well, something and came as fast as we could."

"I am unharmed, at least physically," I said, sything the dirt from my hammer before clicking it to the back of my armor.

Bior sheathed his sword before hurrying to me.

I pulled him into a tight hug.

He stepped back and looked over my shoulder. "Did the Satran leave a warning here?"

I shook my head and waved the rest of the men over. Swallowing, I tried to get rid of the lump in my throat so my words wouldn't catch on it. "I want everyone here to remember this place. Spread the word about it once we have peace. This land was once my skati. My hall, the place my mother, Sar'sa, and I called home, once stood right here. From what I know, she died here protecting my people, your fellow Croians, from the Satran invasion. This monument stands as a grave marker, raised for every citizen and warrior murdered by the uncivilized horde on our southern border. Once the war is over, I want the name of every Croian who died at their hand added. If need be, I will travel here personally to add names and syth more granite from below."

Men slowly dropped to one knee and bowed their heads.

Bior put his hand on my shoulder. "Sire, I can't say I understand your pain, but I grieve your loss with you. This is a good thing you've done ... for you and our country. Word will travel. Names will be added. Now, lean on me. Let me carry some of your weight back to camp. I'm sure you're tired. Come back. Eat and try to rest."

"Aye, my friend," I said, draping my arm across his shoulders. "It has been a long, exhausting day."

"Men!" Bior barked. "Escort your king to his tent."

As one, they rose and spread into a defensive line, leading the way back to camp.

A large, cloth tent served as my quarters. Someone had sythed a stone table and chairs near the entrance. Two, straw mattresses lay on the ground near the back.

Dinner was a bowl of watery stew, now cold, with a couple of mushy rolls soaking in it and a skin full of warm water. After quenching my thirst and trying to soothe my raw throat, I choked down the meager meal and flopped onto one of the beds. I heard Bior clearing the table before I surrendered to the darkness of sleep.

I've never believed in ghosts, not even as a child, but sometime in the night, my mother came to visit. I knew she was dead, gone over a year now. Still, Sar'sa stood near my bed, looking down at me and smiling. She looked the same as the last time I saw her. Dressed in a simple, tan gown with her brown hair cut short, the way she'd favored it. I stood and tried to touch her, hug her, but she kept out of reach.

"I'm proud of you, my son. Proud of the man you are," she said, her voice thin, airy. "Your journey has been hard. It will be harder. No matter, you must keep these words in your heart: Not everything you believe is true. Do not judge quickly. Always seek the truth first."

I reached for her one more time with tears clouding my vision. "What do you mean?" She cocked her head and stepped back, fading into darkness.

Chapter 9

A dull thunk woke me. Yawning, my body shook with a stretch. Instead of stiff straw, my body rested on grass. *Did I really chase Sar'sa?* After wiping chunks of grit from my eyes, I blinked and looked for the source of the sound.

Bior looked at me. "Breakfast's on the table, Sire. Boiled grains. Looks like you had a rough night, so I made tea for you too."

I stretched again before shuffling to the table. "Thank you. Join me?"

"I've already eaten. I'm going to see to our horses now."

"Any reports from last night's watch?"

He shook his head. "No one mentioned anything to me, m'lord."

I pursed my lips for a moment. "Good. Sounds good. Still, ask around after the horses are ready."

He eyed me. "Did something happen last night?"

Best I don't mention seeing my mother. "No, but if the scouts really did see someone yesterday." I shrugged. "Best to be cautious even though it was probably nothing."

"Aye, Sire. Be back soon."

"No need to hurry. I want to enjoy some calm before we hit the road again."

Bior nodded. "As you say, Sire. Andale will be ready to go when you are."

I wanted to take my time eating, to sort out my thoughts and feelings about the — *Was it a dream, or did she appear for real?* At the same time, warm, bland grains tasted better than cold, bland grains, and I couldn't take all day to eat.

With my stomach full of a warrior's breakfast, I drained the mug and got dressed. Sore muscles and aching bones disagreed with so much movement, but the sooner we left camp, the sooner we'd reach Varia. The caravan needed to get moving, and they wouldn't budge without me. As long as the weather stayed fair and the path was smooth, we should reach the eastern pass around midday.

I met Bior and a couple of warriors a short distance from my tent.

"We'll see to your things, Sire," he said. "Andale's ready and tied to the Varian's wagon."

I nodded. "Thank you. Don't hurry on my part. I'm moving slowly this morning."

"Considering what you did yesterday, I'm not surprised, m'lord," he replied. "Need help getting to your horse?"

"No," I said. "See to your task. I'll be fine."

He nodded and headed for the tent.

· · · · ● · ● · · ·

Vestmar gave me a shallow bow as I approached the lead wagon.

I had to pull some strength from the ground to get on Andale.

"Heard about what you did yesterday," Aerison said. "Of course, I guess the whole camp knows ... one way or another. That kind of loss is a hard thing to let go of. Remember, you're with friends. Can't say I've ever been through what you have, but I can listen if you need to talk."

"Same from me, King Fitzeirick," Vestmar added. "Haven't known you long, but I can tell you're a good man."

I nodded. "I appreciate the offer. I'll be fine. Seeing Crum again will surely bring a smile to my face."

"And being back in my home country will bring a smile to mine," Aerison replied.

I grinned and rode to find the scouts.

"Good morning," I called out, when I got close.

"Morning, Sire," Thorvid replied. "How are you?"

"Ready to get going. Plan on riding the same formation as yesterday. Stay vigilant, and keep within sight. We move as soon as Bior gets here."

"This path leads into Varia?" Thorvid asked.

"Yes. It curves to the north in about two hundred paces before turning east again, taking us to the pass. I suspect more than a few Varian soldiers will be in the area. Best if you look friendly."

Brondulf laughed. "Let Throst lead. Hard to find anyone who looks less threatening than him."

"Keep laughing, you big oaf," Throst replied. "You'll never see me coming until it's too late."

"I won't see you coming because you barely cast a shadow," the big scout countered.

"How about you two save it for when we enter Satra," I said, trying to not laugh but failing.

"Listen to your king," Thorvid ordered. "We have a job to do. Let's be at our best."

"Aye," Brondulf replied.

Throst nodded and turned to look away from us.

"Have your fun," I said, "but keep your eyes sharp."

"We will, m'lord," Thorvid said. "You have my word."

After a quick nod, I rode toward the path.

Bior arrived and let me know everything was in order.

"Give the signal," I said.

He whistled twice and raised his hand. Reins cracked, and wagons groaned.

The scouts galloped past us, and we were on the move.

It was obvious there was less fighting in this part of my homeland. Much of the land was undisturbed, but the Satran force had razed every structure and cleared swaths of trees. *So much senseless destruction. Why? Guess it doesn't matter now. Everything can be fixed with time and effort. Lots of time and effort.*

"Not trying to pry, Sire." Bior's voice shook me out of my thoughts. "But yesterday evening... That was—"

"A lot of frustration and anger. I'm sorry you had to see it."

"No need to apologize, m'lord. Had I known where we were, I'd have gone with you — helped as I could. Or kept you away. Whichever you needed more."

"At first, I didn't understand where I was, but part of me, somewhere deep inside, knew. Once I recognized the place, our army couldn't have kept me from my home. Eirickson and Satra kept me away far too long." I wiped a tear from my cheek. "Once, Roi and I made grave markers for a woman's husband and children after Satran raiders attacked their farm. I held the widow as she wailed while we buried her family. Some things, things like that, a person needs help with. Even the strongest among us can't do those tasks by themselves. What I did yesterday, I had to do alone."

He looked at me and brought his arm across his chest in salute. "I'm honored to be one of the first to see your memorial."

I took a deep breath and shook my head. "It's not mine. I may have started it, but it belongs to Croy."

He looked away. "Aye, Sire. Yes ... of course."

While we talked, my eyes kept moving from the path ahead to the scouts to any place a threat could hide. Once I realized Bior had nothing else to say, I let my thoughts wander to last night's encounter. *Since escaping the tunnels, I don't remember dreams often. Most that stick in my head are violent. Was it Sar'sa's ghost? No. It had to be a dream. But she seemed real, standing right outside my reach. And her words. I have false beliefs and should seek the truth. Good advice, in general, but ... If only Roi had come with me. I could use his council.*

"Sire."

Lost in my thoughts, trying to understand my mother's message, I jumped at Bior's voice. "What?"

"Want to eat before we reach the pass or wait?"

"Wait. Knowing Crum, there will be food and drink aplenty waiting when we arrive."

"And you *like* Varian cooking."

"I do," I said, grinning. "Eat now if you want, but don't blame me when you can't enjoy the tasty dishes at the celebration."

Bior chuckled. "I'll leave room for drinks."

I laughed and shook my head as he turned to ride back to the supply wagon. Lifting my gaze to search the cloudless sky for a hint of the cliffs at the border between Croy and Varia, the idea of seeing Crum again brought much-needed joy.

Chapter 10

The smooth, man-made cliff face creating an easily controlled eastern border between Croy and Varia came into view shortly before Bior returned. As impressive as the Carved Scar was, men had simply widened a natural fault in the mountains to make a pass. These cliffs were raised from deep below by the talent and will of many, exceptionally strong stonesyths.

Eirick's grand display of benevolence was a narrow pass left for any Varians wanting to leave after he captured this land. To me, it seemed like many chose to stay. It's possible my opinion was swayed because one of them was my mother, and she raised me around other Varians.

Thorvid yelled something I couldn't understand, snapping me out of a worsening mood.

Brondulf galloped back to me. "Sire, a small Varian force is not far ahead."

I nodded. "Tell the scouts to fall back. I'll take the lead."

"Aye, Sire." He put his heels to his horse and galloped ahead to pass on my order.

The dark cliffs made a foreboding background behind the first line of Varia's defense at the pass. Two armored soldiers stepped onto the path, crossing their spears.

"Bior, on my flank. Throst, signal the wagons to halt. Everyone else, wait here."

Continuing on, I stopped Andale where the spearmen couldn't attack without taking a couple of steps.

"Who are you? Why have you come this way?" one of them demanded.

"I am King Fitzeirick of Croy. On my flank is my steward, Bior. The lead wagon carries Varian Lieutenant Aerison and his escort, Vestmar. We are here at King Crum's invitation."

The one who spoke glanced at the other guard. "Give the signal."

The spearman thrust his weapon into the air. Flame engulfed the end before he waved it back and forth.

The spokesman bowed. "Welcome, King Fitzeirick of Croy. You and your caravan may pass in peace. King Crum eagerly awaits your arrival."

"Bior, signal the caravan," I said.

"Aye, Sire. With pleasure."

Reins snapped, and I nudged Andale to walk. Passing the guards, I bowed.

We passed two, maybe three, companies of men before reaching the guard post at the pass itself. *Seems Crum has taken the Satran threat seriously.*

Heavily armored men marched out of hidden passages and lined the walls, saluting as we passed. Their presence made the already narrow opening barely wide enough for a wagon.

The path led straight through the short, narrow pass and continued up to a rise not far away. A third group of soldiers met us as we exited the cliffs. One stepped forward and welcomed us before pointing to a clearing north of the path. "Set your camp there. A rider carries word of your arrival to my king. A carriage should arrive soon for you and the commander-to-be."

I nodded, turned, and trotted to the far side of the campground to wait until the wagons formed our corral.

"Sire, give me your reins, and I'll take Andale to the circle," Bior offered.

"Thank you, but I'll go myself. I want to talk to Lieutenant Aerison."

"Of course, m'lord. As you wish."

I looked around, trying to get the lay of the land while waiting for the drivers to unhitch their teams. Once the wagons were pushed together, I secured Andale and walked to Aerison's wagon.

"How's it feel to be home?" I asked, as the lieutenant clambered down from his wagon.

"Good. Even better with a belly full of lunch," he replied, grinning.

I nodded. "Any idea where your king might be? I don't see any place for him to stay around here."

He pointed up the rise. "If memory serves—mind you, it's been a while since I've been to this end of Varia—there's a keep atop this rise. It houses all the guards you see here. After my promotion, it will be my home for as long as I have this command."

"If it's close, why don't we ride on instead of waiting for a carriage?"

He shrugged. "King Crum was your best friend. You know him much better than I, but this is likely Anders' suggestion. My former king often demonstrated his absolute authority by making people wait for his bidding. Considering some see Crum's claim to the throne as weak, projecting power serves a purpose."

I sighed and looked around again. "What you're saying may be true, but this seems awfully formal. Crum's not big on formalities."

Aerison smiled. "The man you used to know, maybe, but he's a king now. Formalities are important, especially in matters of state. Surely you agree."

"Of course, but we're friends."

He nodded. "A meeting between kings is the definition of a matter of state, whether they are friends or not."

"You sound a lot like Roi," I said, and chuckled.

Before the lieutenant could respond, Bior and Vestmar approached.

"Vestmar," Aerison said. "See what you can find out about lunch arrangements."

"Glady."

"Any word from King Crum, Sire?" Bior asked.

As I opened my mouth to answer, I spotted several, large carts coming down the hill, leading a small carriage.

"Unless I miss my guess, that would be lunch and our ride," Aerison said.

"Am I going with you, Sire?" Bior asked.

"No. Spend time with your cousins. Enjoy the calm while you can."

"Yes, m'lord. I hope your visit goes well."

The carts pulled off the path, forming three rows, before reaching us. The carriage stopped beside us. The door opened, and a young boy exited. Bowing with a flourish, his long, brown hair tumbled over his shoulders. He looked to be barely in his teens, dressed in dark purple pants and a maroon jacket trimmed in gold. "Your Majesty, King Fitzeirick of Croy. I am Wilian, valet of Eastkeep. Your presence here honors us all. Welcome home, Commander-to-be Aerison. Both of you, please, accompany me to the keep."

The boy helped Aerison climb the steps into the carriage and held the door open for me.

I followed my friend inside and sat next to him.

Wilian closed the door and called for the driver to get underway before settling into the seat facing us.

Although the padded seat was comfortable, the back wasn't made to accommodate my hammer. I stood it between my feet.

Wilian cocked his head. "A fine weapon, Your Majesty, though I'm not sure you will be allowed to have it in the presence of my king."

"I've known Crum since we were younger than you," I said, smiling. "I'm no threat."

Aerison chuckled. "Formalities must be respected. Besides, you are in no danger here ... unless you are afraid your friendship is not as solid as you remember."

I looked sideways at him. "Crum once swore his life to me. I love him as family. His loyalty, our friendship, would stand any test without wavering."

The commander-to-be shrugged. "To be clear, King Fitzeirick, I'm not saying I know something you don't ... simply offering my opinion. You are both kings—leaders of two countries with past violence between them and their futures now tightly linked. Be mindful of my king's situation, my country's situation, when dealing with him."

Wilian gasped when I pulled off my helmet, hanging it on my hammer's handle.

"I believe the young squire is taken aback by your scar," Aerison said, a smile in his voice.

I brushed my finger across the upside-down T my brother branded on me.

The boy shivered. "I'd heard rumors ... stories meant to scare little kids, or so I thought at the time. I couldn't believe anyone would be branded, like livestock, especially on the face. But ... but your brother, he did this?"

Before I could answer, we stopped moving, and someone opened the door. Wilian stood, legs shaking. "King —" He swallowed, hard, and his body shook. "King Fitzeirick, crown guards wait at the keep's entrance to escort you. Commander-to-be Aerison, if you will, please follow me to your quarters."

I waited for Aerison to pass before standing. Tucking my helmet under my left arm, I grabbed my hammer and clicked it onto my back after stepping out of the carriage.

Two guards bowed. "If you will follow us, your Majesty. King Crum waits in his parlor."

I nodded. "Lead the way."

We approached an arched opening in a dark, stone wall. The courtyard was covered in bright, green grass. Grapevines clung to the keep's outer wall. We entered a hall; flickering torches lit the way to a staircase set into the wall.

I followed the men up the stairs to a small patio overlooking another, larger courtyard. A stone bridge arched across to another tall building. The grounds below contained a garden and a small orchard of fruit trees. We crossed the bridge, entered the second building, and climbed another set of stairs.

The stairs continued higher, but we stepped out onto a landing on the next floor and followed the hallway to the left. Two corners later, we turned left down another hall ending in a small entryway ahead of an iron-bound, wooden door. A pair of armored men stood on either side of the door and crossed their spears as we approached. "Halt and identify yourselves."

The escort to my right stepped forward. "Erwin and Karlo of the crown guard, escorting King Fitzeirick of Croy by order of King Crum."

The guard on the left side of the door nodded. "King Fitzeirick, I see a handle over your shoulder. Are you otherwise armed?"

I shook my head. "All I have is my hammer."

He pointed to a rack on the left wall. "I must ask you to leave it there. You have my word it will be safe."

With Aerison's statement about formalities fresh in my mind, I nodded and took the hammer from my back. Doing my best to look non-threatening — *This would be a bad place to get into a fight* — I moved slowly to the empty rack and leaned my weapon against it. Glancing at the helmet, I shrugged and hung it on the handle.

The other guard knocked twice on the door before opening it a crack. "My lord, honorable Majesty King Fizeirick of Croy is here at your request. Is he allowed to enter?"

"Did he bring three obsidian arrowheads?" Crum yelled.

The guard turned to me and cocked his head. "Do you happen to have—"

My hands balled into fists on their own. I groaned and took a step toward the door. "Crum!" I bellowed. "Let me in or you, and your treasured arrowheads, can go to the fire!"

The guards lowered their spears, bracing for my charge. The sound of steel sliding against leather came from behind as my escorts readied their swords.

The distinct sound of Crum's belly laugh burst from his parlor. "Let Fitzeirick in. He's always welcome to visit."

The guards looked at each other and shrugged before relaxing and moving back to their posts. Swords slid back into their scabbards behind me. As I pushed open the door, one of the guards muttered, "Royals."

Chapter 11

I felt the weight of the guards' gaze as I passed them.

A round, ornate, wooden table sat in the center of the room with my best friend seated on the far side. The walls were bare, dark stone, except for the one behind him. It was almost entirely glass, doing away with the need for torches or candles during the day. He stood when the door closed behind me. "Fitzeirick! It's good to see you again. Jesca and I missed you at our wedding. Your absence was most disappointing." He extended his arms, opening the red cape he wore, revealing a bright blue shirt and dark blue pants, and hurried toward me.

I met him and embraced the closest thing I ever had to a true brother in a tight hug.

He clapped me on the back a couple of times.

Releasing him, I stepped back.

He offered a folded piece of parchment. "Kurt asked me to get this to you."

Wasn't expecting anything from the war council. I furrowed my brow and took the message. "Let me see what this is about."

Your Majesty,

Negotiations with the Croian Trade Guild have gone well. Guildmaster Tore will trouble you no longer. Ultimately, his tight grip on old ways cost him everything. Many of his fellow leaders had the same problem. However, his sister was open to new ideas. She understood the wisdom in negotiating an agreement beneficial to all interested parties. I'd advise you to contact Tola should you need anything from the Trade Guild in the future.

No doubt our pact will strengthen the ties between our nations. My council extends their deepest thanks for involving us in this opportunity. We look forward to a lucrative future together.

Kurt

"Oh," I whispered, tucking the note into a pocket.

"All is well?" Crum asked, head cocked.

"I'd asked him to handle a problem for me. Seems he was able to sort it out." I pursed my lips for a moment. "Nothing to worry about. Where were we?"

Crum chuckled and lifted a pitcher. "Care for a drink while we catch up?"

I took the nearest seat. "Of course."

He poured a dark, amber-colored liquid into two cups. "Mapled ale. Grew fond of it at Stone Roof. Jahon's brewmaster gladly shared the recipe with the royal brewers after I was crowned."

I took a sip of the drink and found it tasted as good as the first time I'd had it at Swinter's famous inn. "Your brewers did themselves proud. Speaking of Jahon and his establishment—"

Crum smiled and shook his head. "It took a lot of explaining and no small amount of gild payment for the damages, but Jahon doesn't blame you for the fight. Still, I wouldn't be in a hurry to drop in unannounced."

"Seems I have a talent for upsetting innkeepers," I said. "Geri is still cross with me."

"Sorry," he said, after a long drink, "I can't come to the Trader's Cup and talk to him for you."

"Time heals all wounds," I said. "Speaking of healing, how's Jesca? I'd love to see her."

"I doubt you'd recognize her. She hasn't grown any taller, but her hair grew out, and she's healthy, happy, and full of life. That said, we decided it would be too risky for her to travel this far from the capital."

I cocked my head. "Surely no one in Varia would harm her?"

He raised his mug and smiled so wide I thought his cheeks would crack. "I'm going to be a father."

"You're going to be a —" Once my brain caught up to my ears, I jumped from my seat and pulled him out of his chair into a bear hug. "I'm so happy for you two. When? How?"

He wiggled free of my grasp. "If you don't know how by now, it's about time you learned ... but I'm not going to teach you."

I laughed and wiped a few tears from my eyes. "You know what I mean. She was so frail."

He nodded as we returned to our seats. "We talked, a lot, about what it would mean for us to have a family. Jesca wanted to raise a child of her own, if possible. She took treatments from several herbalists." He shrugged. "Seems my mother wasn't the only one with a talent for making over-effective vitality tea."

"The best news I've heard in a long time," I said, smiling. "When?"

He shrugged, still smiling. "Her herbalist says two full moons, three at most."

I clapped my hands together. "Wonderful and exciting. You will send a messenger. Even if I can't come, perhaps Tindra and Grima would make the trip. You're going to be great parents."

He pressed his lips together tightly. "Did you even look for Aesa?"

I glared at him. "Aesa's dead. Eirickson told me before I killed him."

His mouth hung open for a moment. "And you believed him. How would *he* know, anyway?"

"Stina wore the necklace I'd given Aesa when we promised ourselves to each other. I demanded to know where she got it, and Eirickson told me ... in explicit detail."

"Eirickson killed your fiancée?" he asked, face losing color.

I shook my head. "No. She killed herself to escape a worse fate in Satra. From what my worthless half-brother said, it was her best option."

Crum shivered. "I'm terribly sorry to hear this, especially from you, but was Tindra the best choice for a queen?"

I scoffed. "She's not the person you remember, partly thanks to you."

"Me?" he replied, brow furrowed. "What did I have to do with anything?"

"You made her see I was worth risking her life for. Tindra could have stood by and watched her king's youngest daughter slit my throat, but she didn't. She acted, saved me, and lost her hand. Might have been the first selfless thing she'd ever done in her life."

"Ander didn't blame her for Stina's death. When he heard what happened and who did it, he said, 'What a killer does in the heat of battle is no more their fault than a wolf taking a farmer's sheep. It's in their nature.' I'm not sure I could be so understanding." He shook his head and looked into his mug. "My cup's dry. You?"

I cleared my throat before finishing my ale. "Ready for another round."

He grinned and refilled our drinks. "Now, what's Roi up to?"

"Speaking of Roi, would you happen to know if Rorec's in Varia?"

Crum cocked his head and raised his eyebrows. "Figured Roi's father was dead. He seemed old when you and I were kids. Why?"

"Someone who escaped the Satran invasion swears he saw Rorec wearing Satran armor in my skati. Roi insists the man who recognized Rorec knew him well and was trustworthy."

Crum closed his eyes. "Why would Rorec, a loyal citizen of Croy and trusted agent of Eirick's, ride with the Satran army to attack his own people?"

"Doesn't make any sense to me either. But I'd like to find out to give Roi an explanation if nothing else."

"Understandable," Crum said, nodding. "From what I know, Satra moved to cut off access to the pass as quickly as possible. Few, if any, people escaped this way. But I didn't ask about Rorec. Tell me about Roi."

I shrugged. "Where to start? He married Grima, and they are the happiest couple I've ever known."

"Only because you haven't seen Jesca and me together," Crum countered.

"Maybe, but Grima has him wrapped around her finger, and he'd do anything for Einns." *I shouldn't tell him Einns is my nephew. He's not great at keeping secrets.* I grinned. "He's effective as my right-hand and most trusted adviser."

"So, nothing's changed," Crum commented.

I chuckled. "Since we're discussing advisers, how's Ander?"

Crum shook his finger at me. "Now, there's a difficult question to answer. Physically, he's in better shape than many men his age. He and I get along well. I seek his counsel often, and he's nearly as witty as me. His support for the wedding went a long way toward securing the throne for Jesca. Without it, I'm afraid Varia would still be fighting a civil war."

"I heard much the same from Kurt."

Crum nodded. "He told you the truth. With Ander's mind, things get more complicated. Jesca brings the biggest smile to his face every time he sees her. He seems deeply happy about the coming child but still mourns Inez and Stina. For a while, after he stepped down as king, he immersed himself in the war council's business. I think the thrill of working in the gray areas of the law took his mind off his loss. But...things like that take their toll on a man, you know?"

I took a long drink. "All too well."

Crum sighed heavily. "Look at us. We've managed to kill a good mood again. We must be getting old."

"Speak for yourself," I countered.

He gave me a weak grin and pointed over his shoulder. "Come see something that might make you smile."

"Outside?" I asked, raising my eyebrows.

He nodded, turned the windows, and waved me over.

I looked out to a field where a formation of Varian soldiers trained. "How many?"

"Two hundred men. Send word before you enter Satra, and General Rostik will lead them to secure your southern border."

"No reason to wait. They can ride out with us. I'm sure Satra's leaders know we're working together," I said.

"Because of Porsey," Crum muttered.

"May he burn in the fire."

"Slowly," Crum added, before clapping his hands together. "Ander made some deals to get the men here and agreed to use them only in Varia's defense. I can't knowingly send them directly into battle."

"But you're King of Varia," I countered.

"Only because I'm married to the queen. My rule is far from absolute," he explained, frowning.

"I see."

Crum put his arm across my shoulder. "Now, we've spent enough time making each other happy and sad. Let's get Lieutenant Aerison and make him a commander. Shall we?"

Chapter 12

I nodded. "Sounds great, but I'd like to get out of my armor first."

"You'll have time." He smiled. "We'll take the carriage back to the campground. The ceremony and celebration will happen there. I won't promote him until you're there with me."

"Why? I'm not part of the Varian army."

He patted my shoulder. "Aerison volunteered to go to Croy because he respects you and believes our countries should support each other. I heard about what you said to keep my soldiers from leaving after their lieutenant was ambushed by your detractors. You'll be there to honor our mutual friend because you've earned the respect of many powerful Varians."

"But I didn't do it to gain respect," I protested. "I did it for our country."

Crum grinned. "Correction. Croy's no longer my country. I may have been born there, and I want to see it prosper, but Varia is my home, my concern, now."

"Of course," I said, nodding. "A slip of the tongue on my part, nothing else."

He laughed and turned to the door. "I wasn't trying to be harsh, but choose your words carefully when we aren't alone. Some people are still looking for leverage to pry me from the throne."

"I know a little of how that feels. I'll try to be more mindful when I speak," I said, following him out of the room.

The guards stepped forward when the door opened. "Where to, Sire?" one of them asked.

"Commander-to-be Aerison's room."

"Can I get my hammer?" I asked.

"Finn, retrieve King Fitzeirick's hammer," Crum ordered.

"Yes, Sire," the guard replied, before bowing and hurrying to get my helmet and hammer.

"Surprised you gave it up without a fight," Crum whispered to me.

"On the way here, a friend reminded me formalities should be honored," I replied, clicking my hammer onto my back and tucking my helmet under my arm.

Crum chuckled. "Aerison's a stickler for following the rules. Another reason he's worthy of this command."

"If your majesties are ready, follow us," Finn said.

Crum nodded, and we were on the move. The guards led us on a long, winding route through the keep, stopping in front of a metal-bound, wooden door.

Finn knocked. "King Crum and King Fitzeirick request an audience!"

Aerison opened the door. "Please. Come in."

We entered a surprisingly big room and stepped onto a soft, dark carpet. A small desk and padded chair sat in the corner to our right. A larger table, with seating for six, sat near the center of the room, with more seating near an empty fireplace in the back wall. I noted a door near the middle of the right wall and decided it went to a bedroom.

Aerison had changed out of his traveling clothes into a light blue, long-sleeve shirt with darker, blue pants and tall, black boots that shined in the candlelight.

He closed the door behind us. "I wasn't expecting company."

Crum swept his hand toward the large table. "Sit. I'd like for us to talk before the ceremony."

"Of course, Sire. As you wish. After you."

Crum nodded and sat in the nearest chair. Aerison's shuffling walk set a slow pace as he moved to the table. I waited for him to sit before standing my hammer on the floor and taking the chair to Crum's left.

"So." Crum clapped his hands together, and Aerison jumped. "First things first. Aerison, breath. Relax and, maybe, smile. You earned this promotion. It should be a joyous occasion."

"Yes ... yes, my king," he said, sounding more nervous than he looked.

Crum nodded. "Second, Ander insisted I practice the ceremony until I could do it from memory without a single mistake. One difference, since we have a visiting king, Fitzeirick will stand with me when I announce your promotion. Before we proceed, I will ask for any who dissent to speak. Strictly a formality, of course."

And formalities must be honored. I bit my cheek to keep from laughing.

"Aerison, you'll stand before me."

The commander-to-be cleared his throat. "I believe I'm supposed to kneel, Sire."

Crum cocked his head. "Given your injuries, I thought standing would be more comfortable."

"It would, but if I can't kneel before my king, I have no business being a leader of men," Aerison said, closing his eyes.

Crum rubbed his chin and glanced at me. "I see your point. Kneel, as tradition demands. I'll place my sword on your shoulder and proclaim you a commander in the Varian army, charged with defending the eastern pass from all enemies. And tradition holds your first official action will be to order your soldiers to fall out of formation for the feast."

"Sounds like you have the ceremony well planned, Sire," Aerison replied. "But...may I speak freely?"

"You're among friends. Of course, you may," Crum stated.

Aerison pursed his lips for a moment. "I'm not sure I deserve this title."

Crum nodded. "Of course, you do. You've dedicated your life to Varia and trained our soldiers."

"I could name a dozen other soldiers who have done the same," Aerison argued, tapping his fingers on the table. "I haven't *earned* this."

"You led a volunteer force to aid our ally, survived an ambush, and continued leading from your recovery bed," Crum said. "If those actions aren't enough to earn a promotion, I hope I never have to meet your standards."

"Aerison," I said. "I agree with your king, and not simply because he's my best friend. You trained me. Your guidance readied me to overthrow a tyrant. I would not be Croy's King, might not be alive, if not for you. Then you came to my aid voluntarily and got hurt bad enough that we weren't sure you'd ever walk again. You earned this—more if it were up to me."

Aerison hung his head and sighed. "I *hear* what you're saying, but I don't *feel* it."

I leaned toward him. "Lieutenant, you spent weeks recovering. You've fought hard to regain the use of your legs. Now, it's time to rebuild your confidence. Trust me, you still have much to offer your country. You will serve Varia well here."

Crum nodded as I spoke, then added his advice, "Exactly. Bark orders at a few soldiers. Get men moving at your command. You'll be the man I remember in no time." He paused and raised his eyebrows. "More importantly, you'll be the man Varia needs here should the worst happen."

"If a couple of kings still believe in me," Aerison replied, squaring his shoulders, "I'll keep working on myself until I do too."

Crum slapped his hand on the table. "That's the spirit. Don't forget, I'll make sure you have all the support you need. If something, or someone, isn't working ... let me know, and we'll find a solution."

Aerison smiled. "I can't be much of a commander if I go running to my king with every little complaint."

"Nor do I expect you to," Crum replied. "Correct the problems you can; report the ones you can't address."

"Understood, Sire."

"Good. Sounds like everything's settled. Let's get to the carriage. The sooner the ceremony is over, the sooner we celebrate," Crum said, leaving his seat. "I expect the bonfires to burn well into the night."

"Far be it from me to hold up a celebration," Aerison said, pushing himself to his feet. "Especially one held on my account."

I chuckled and followed my friends out of the room.

Crum's guard led us out to a waiting carriage. Finn opened the door and closed it behind me. The vehicle rocked side to side, and I shot a questioning look at Crum as I stood my hammer on the floor.

"My guards have a small seat on the back to accompany me," he explained.

I nodded, and the carriage lurched forward. The ride down the hill seemed much quicker than going to the keep. We stopped, and the carriage rocked again before someone—Finn, I assumed—opened the door. The smell of spices and broiled meat filled the interior.

Bior hurried to my side when I got out. He had changed out of his armor into a tan shirt and matching pants. "My king. I have clothes ready in your tent."

I nodded. *Nice of Crum to take me to the middle of our camp.* Looking around, I understood why he chose to stop here. *It's not for me. He has an audience to entertain while I dress. Once a storyteller, always a storyteller.*

Crum began a tale as Bior closed the tent flap behind me.

"Sire, I selected a dark blue shirt and black leather pants for you. I'd suggest you wear the black cloak as well," Bior said.

I cocked my head. "I don't have a black cloak."

"Aye, Sire ... you do," he replied, grinning. "The queen had one made for you in case you decided to go sneaking about after dark."

My lips pressed together tightly, all on their own. I couldn't decide if I was suppressing a smile or a frown. "My wife seems to think of everything, doesn't she?"

Bior shrugged. "Not sure I can say, m'lord. You know her better than me."

I nodded and slid out of my armor before changing clothes.

"Let the fun begin," I said, opening the tent.

Someone had raised a stone stage outside of our camp. Crum stood in the center, with guards on his flanks. He seemed to have trouble organizing the growing crowd. Everyone seemed distracted by the food prepared for the celebration.

I hopped onto the stage, planted my feet, and announced, "Fan out and take a knee!"

The ground quivered as my voice traveled through the crowd. After the initial shock, every man in sight followed the order.

"Impressive," Crum muttered. "Thank you."

I nodded and relaxed, looking out over rows of Croian warriors and Varian soldiers mixed together. *United against a common enemy, as it should be.* I wasn't sure of the exact number, but there had to be well over three hundred men. My heart pounded. *We can't lose. Satra will disappear.*

Crum drew his sword and raised it over his head. "Lieutenant Aerison! Front and center!"

The commander-to-be shuffled forward, stopping in front of his king, and bowed.

"Your service to king and country, earning numerous accolades and praises. Years of leadership and guidance, even after surviving a vicious ambush and receiving injuries that threatened to end your career. For these reasons and more, I, King Crum of Varia, offer you the rank of Commander of the Eastern Guard."

Several men cheered.

"Aerison. If you accept this command, the responsibility and burden it entails, kneel."

He bowed again before slowly placing a knee on the ground.

Crum smiled and gently tapped his sword on our friend's shoulders. "You humbled yourself before me as a lieutenant. Rise a commander."

Aerison clambered to his feet and bowed again.

Crum nodded and sheathed his sword. "Commander Aerison, turn and issue your first order."

The new commander smiled before turning to face the crowd. "Fellow soldiers. Respected warriors. Let the festivities begin."

Chapter 13

Horns blared somewhere in the crowd. As the notes faded, unseen drums thumped. After the third boom, bonfires ignited around the field. The crowd roared loud enough to shake the ground as flames reached into the sky. Varian soldiers rushed to carts parked near the fires. My warriors didn't wait long before following their lead.

Crum turned to me, smiling wide. "Eat and drink your fill."

I swept my arm toward the nearest fire. "After you."

He nodded and glanced at the guards. "You are dismissed."

They bowed and jumped from the back of the rise, heading for a wagon.

Crum laughed and leaped from the front of the stage. He took off at a run as soon as his feet hit the ground. I couldn't keep from shaking my head at his antics before following his example, running with my cloak billowing behind me.

He turned as I caught up to him and shoved some kind of roasted leg at me. I took it and bit into the meat. Pork, well-spiced and cooked to perfection.

"Ale, wine, or mead?" he asked.

I'm not drinking any mead. "Mapled ale?" I asked, eyebrows raised.

He laughed, loud and long. "No. There aren't enough maple trees in all of Varia to serve this crowd. I will say this brew makes the typical tavern fare taste like pigswill."

"Sounds like I need to try the ale."

"I'm starting with wine but suit yourself," he said, shrugging before pointing toward a large mug.

I grabbed it and took a drink. It had a slight vanilla scent when it hit my nose but a wine-like feel on my tongue with a vague buttery flavor instead of the bitter taste I expected.

"Come on," Crum said, leaning close so I could hear him over the revelry around us. "Let's mingle and have some fun."

We made our way through groups of men, bragging and telling jokes. An impromptu wrestling match broke out near the next bonfire we approached. Seems my warriors were testing themselves against some of the Varian soldiers.

"Care to make a wager?" Crum asked, handing me a piece of sweetbread.

"I already owe you three arrowheads," I said, forcing myself to not laugh. "Why would I want to risk going further into your debt?"

He turned to me with a smirk. "If you promise not to use your talent, I'll face you. Best me and your obligation's erased, but if I win, it's doubled."

I shook my head. "You're not much faster than me, and I'm stronger than you. No reason the King of Varia should be embarrassed in front of his men."

He nodded, still looking mischievous. "Perhaps another ale would make us more even."

What is he doing? Crum's never challenged me before...why now? "All the ale in Varia isn't going to change my mind."

"Hold that thought." Approaching two men grappling in the middle of a crude circle, he tapped the soldier on the shoulder and leaned in, saying something I couldn't hear.

The Varian nodded and released his hold on my warrior before raising his hands and stepping back.

The warrior looked confused until he noticed Crum standing nearby. After a quick bow, he stepped away.

"Good fighting men of Varia and Croy! Everyone who can hear my voice! Listen close!" Crum yelled.

The crowd around us quieted to a dull roar.

Crum pointed to me. "Proud warriors of Croy. Fine men of my birth country. I don't mean to quell your celebration but hear me out. I, King Crum of Varia, challenged your king to a friendly contest of skill and strength."

Several of my warriors cheered.

Oh, no.

"Varian soldiers. He begged out of the challenge. Claimed my quickness is no match for his brute strength."

A couple of soldiers near him sneered. Some laughed.

What have I gotten myself into?

"I say he relies on his stonesything too heavily and declare myself more than his equal. He still refuses." He paused and shook his head.

I'll never live this down if I refuse.

"Fine warriors of Croy, surely you can convince your king that he can best a thin, weak, woodsyth like me."

"Aye!" one of the warriors yelled.

"Skillful soldiers. Do you believe your king to be weak? Easily bested by the King of Croy?"

"No!" they shouted together.

"As allies, maybe the two groups can convince King Fitzeirick to accept my challenge," Crum finished, bowing with a flourish.

It's not like you gave me much of a choice.

I waited for the jeers and name-calling to die down and stepped into the circle.

My warriors cheered again as I removed my cloak, dropping it to the ground. "Before I go through with this, what are the conditions for victory?"

Crum cocked his head. "Both shoulders flat on the dirt." Raising his eyebrows, he tapped his foot. "Three times to make it interesting?"

I nodded. "Agreed."

"Oh." He offered his hand. "Being kings—and gentlemen—we should set an example to our men. We try not to intentionally injure each other."

"Of course," I replied, gripping his hand tightly. *I won't have to hurt him to put him on his back three times.*

"And," he added, squeezing my hand back. "No sything by either of us."

"Goes without saying, I would think," I replied, shrugging.

"It's settled." He released his hold. "As the challenged, you make the first move ... my good friend."

I'm sure he expected me to charge. He didn't know I'd sparred with Tindra and learned a few lessons the hard, painful way. Though I didn't have my wife's grace, I moved smoother than the typical stonesyth.

Concern spread across Crum's face. He shifted his feet, trying to anticipate my attack.

Several men shouted, goading me into attacking quickly, but it wasn't their fight. Crum motioned for me to get on with it, to charge him.

I know that look. He's trying to cover his worry with fake bravado. Faking a quick move to my right got the response I wanted.

Crum's legs crossed as he turned.

Got you. I rushed forward, dropping my shoulder to hit him about waist-high. As soon as my body touched his, I wrapped my arms around his legs and knocked him to the ground. His back hit the dirt with a hollow thump. Several of the soldiers watching groaned.

Warriors behind me cheered as I got to my feet.

Crum shook his head when I offered to help him stand. I shrugged and backed away to prepare for his assault.

I didn't have to wait long. As soon as his feet were under him, he sprang.

Keeping my feet planted, I twisted my hips and shoulders to make it harder for him to grab me.

He latched onto my arm and pulled with my movement, taking me off balance.

Before I could free myself, he let go and threw himself into the back of my legs. My feet flew out from under me, and I fell to the ground, landing on my back. Hard.

"One," Crum gasped, standing over me, "to one.

"I may be stone-headed for letting you manipulate me," I said, before rolling away from him and getting to my feet. "But I can count."

Taking a moment to catch my breath, I weighed my options. *Doubt he'll fall for finesse twice.* I stalked him for four steps and found I was right. He didn't move when I faked this time.

Still, closing even a short distance kept him from having as much time to react to my charge. His shoulders stiffened when I grabbed them.

Instead of reaching for my arms to grapple, he pulled the cords keeping his cape in place and dropped to his knees.

I was left holding nothing but fabric and leaning too far forward.

Crum grabbed my shirt and pulled while slamming his shoulders into my thighs. My feet slid back, slamming my chest to the ground. The breath left my body with a loud 'whuff'.

Soldiers cheered when he easily rolled me onto my back while I fought to breathe.

He held two fingers over my face. I nodded, slapped his hand away, and tried to convince myself I'd be able to live if I could catch my breath again. *Dirty my shoulders one more time, and I owe him six stinking arrowheads.*

Forcing myself to yawn filled my lungs with air. After another deep breath, I groaned before pushing myself to my feet.

Crum charged.

I grabbed his cape from the ground and tossed it at him as he ran. It fell over his head. While he struggled to untangle himself from the garment, I lifted him under his shoulders, raising his feet off the ground. Somewhat gently depositing him on his back, I pressed a shoulder down with my boot ... to be sure the fall counted.

"Cheater!" a soldier roared.

I turned toward the call. "He used it for defense; I used it for offense. Seems like a fair balance to me."

Some warriors laughed.

A couple of the Varians scowled.

Shrugging, I turned back to Crum. "We're even," I said, nodding. "Call it a draw now?"

Crum got to his feet, red-faced, and flung his cape into the crowd. "A draw? Is King Fitzeirick scared he'll lose?"

"Not one bit," I replied, smiling. "Figured I'd make the offer to save you what little pride you have left."

The crowd chanted, "One more fall."

I glanced over my shoulder. "Seems our men demand a victor."

Crum nodded and returned my smile before squaring his shoulders and charging.

Determined to not wait and see what he had planned, I took a few quick steps back before charging too.

I raised my arms, acting like I was going to push him back.

He brought his hands up to fight off any attempt to grab him.

I snarled, slapped his arms up, and slammed chest-to-chest into him. Quickly wrapping my best friend in a tight bear hug, I lifted him from the ground and twisted so he hit the ground before me.

He yelped as we fell.

I landed on him with all my weight, and something in his chest cracked. *Stones and sticks, I've broken his ribs. So much for not hurting each other.*

Hands grabbed me, lifting me from my best friend before I could get off him.

He groaned, coughed, and groaned louder as I got my feet under me.

I reached down to help him, but soldiers pushed me away.

Chapter 14

"Crum, are you all right?" I yelled.

He coughed again before wheezing, "I'll live."

A big soldier stood eye-to-eye with me. He poked a finger into my chest. "You agreed to not hurt him."

I backed away into a wall of warriors. "Peace. I didn't mean to injure your king," I protested. "He *is* the closest thing I've ever had to a brother."

"That means nothing to you," the man replied, raising a fist. "Seeing as you killed your brother by blood."

I sythed some strength from the ground. *The match with Crum was for fun. This won't be.* "Don't talk about things you don't understand. Back off before we do something we're both going to regret."

As two warriors brushed past me, someone yelled, "Stand down!" from the far side of the circle.

No one moved. If someone had told me the fire froze in place, I would have believed them. I flinched when something cracked across the soldier's back.

He yelped and spun around.

As he turned, I saw Aerison wielding a crude cane.

"Your commander gave an order!" Aerison yelled, before striking the big man's leg. "Stand down!"

The soldier's shoulders sagged before he reached to rub his thigh. "Aye, Commander. Didn't know it was you."

Aerison stamped his cane tip into the dirt. "Instead of threatening your king's guest, maybe you should see about finding a herbalist."

The soldier bowed. "Sire, shouldn't you lay still while I get someone to look at your injury?"

Aerison blinked several times before turning to see Crum on his feet, holding his right arm against his chest. "My lord. Are you well?"

No doubt, broken rib.

Crum shook his head and smiled weakly. "I've had worse. It's nothing a belly full of drink wouldn't cure for now. Fitzeirick, help me to the bonfire. Someone keep the cups coming."

"Are you sure, my king?" Aerison asked.

"Do I have to order you, Commander?" Crum asked.

Aerison closed his eyes. "No, Sire."

"I'll see no more harm comes to him," I said, trying to reassure Aerison and myself.

Crum put an arm across my shoulders. "Help me to the bonfire, my good friend. And pull a comfortable chair from the ground when we get there."

"As you wish, your Majesty," I replied, smirking and fighting back a laugh.

The crowd parted, giving us easy passage to the fire.

"Here. This is good," Crum said.

I nodded and raised a bench for us.

No sooner had we sat, a cup was pressed into Crum's hand, followed by one for me. Crum downed his drink and called for more before I'd half-finished mine.

As the celebration wore on, food and drink flowed freely. I lost track of how much I'd had of either. Something roared in my ear. I flinched and turned to find the source. Crum. His head rested on my shoulder, and he snored. Loud as ever.

I tried to stand, but the world tilted around me, so I kept my seat.

Bior appeared before me with a Varian at his side. "My lords, Vestmar and I will see you to your tent."

"But Crum," I mumbled.

"My king will sleep it off in your tent," Vestmar said. "We'll make sure you two are safe."

* * *

I don't remember laying down but woke, dressed in my clothes from the previous evening and wearing my boots, in my tent. *Can't remember the last time I was so drunk I slept with shoes on.*

Crum snored softly, for him, next to me. Stiff, sore muscles complained as I moved to get up without disturbing my friend. I slowly shuffled to the table, smacking my lips and trying to get the dry, cotton taste out of my mouth. *Guess it was fun at the time.* A chuckle fought its way up my sore throat when I noticed my cloak and Crum's cape sat, folded, on the table.

Bior stuck his head through the tent flap. "Sire, you're awake. Good. I'll send Vestmar to make teas for you and King Crum. Are you ready for some food? He's prepared boiled grains with some herbs to help with your aches."

"Aye," I croaked. "Whatever he thinks best. I'll wake Crum."

After a quick nod, Bior disappeared from view.

For a moment, I considered yelling at Crum from the table but decided my head wouldn't like the outcome. I pulled a little stamina from the ground to help me lumber back to the bed.

Kneeling, I nudged his shoulder. "Crum, get up. Breakfast is on its way."

He snorted and slapped at my hand before rolling over.

After a long sigh, I barked. "Crum! Food!"

He mumbled something and opened one eye. Seeing me, he sat up and rubbed his eyes before combing his fingers through his disheveled hair. A faint cloud of dust hung in the air near his shoulders. "Food?" he asked. "Where?"

"On the table ... soon."

He groaned, getting to his feet. "How much did we drink?"

"Don't know," I answered, shaking my head, "but more than we should've. Vestmar's working on a tea to help."

"Good," Crum muttered, and we hobbled to the table together.

"Sorry about the ribs," I said.

He cocked his head and then waved a hand toward me. "My ribs are fine."

Shortly after flopping into our chairs, Bior returned with big, steaming bowls. Fresh, herbal smells filled my nose when he placed my breakfast on the table.

Crum took a deep breath and sneezed. "Too much ginger."

Vestmar entered with a tray holding several cups. "My lords, these teas should help you feel better...if you can stomach them."

Crum swallowed a spoonful of mush. "We thank you."

I nodded, still trying to force the first bite of warm, soggy grains down my throat.

Vestmar nodded and placed the tray on the table. "I'll be outside. Call if you need anything."

"Same," Bior said, bowing before following the Varian herbalist out.

I grabbed a cup and took a sip to get the taste of everything out of my mouth. It didn't help. Whatever concoction Vestmar made tasted like a minty apple blended with some kind of slightly sweet onion. "Is there some contest between herbalists to make their cures taste worse than everyone else's?"

Crum laughed for a moment.

"How are you not doubled over in pain?" I asked, memories of broken ribs making my chest hurt. "I heard something pop when I landed on you."

He thumped his chest and shook his head. "No problem with my ribs. I took a hard hit protecting Queen Inez. It messed up my shoulder. Something in there didn't heal right. It catches and snaps sometimes. I'll be back to normal in a day or two."

"Good," I said. "I didn't want to leave you any worse for wear from a friendly wrestle."

"I'm fine as can be. How I feel after eating this big bowl of grains is still in question."

"Makes you regret your actions even more, doesn't it?" I asked, smirking.

He pointed his finger at me. "You fought dirty last night."

I put my hand over my heart. "Me? Fight dirty? You wound me."

"Trapping me in my cape so I couldn't see you attacking. Uncivilized and unsportsmanlike, if you ask me."

"You shouldn't have been wearing it to wrestle anyway," I countered.

"But it did let me escape once."

"Proving I wasn't the only sneaky one," I said.

"Point taken."

I smiled. "I've missed you."

He smiled back and swallowed more grains. "And I you. Too bad we can't do this regularly. So much changed in so little time."

My smile turned into a frown, both from drinking more tea and from his words. "I never expected a simple request for help, protecting my skati and my people, would put me on this path. I never wanted to start a war. But I will end it."

He grabbed my arm. "I wish I could do more to help."

"You could ride south with me."

"If only," he replied, shaking his head. "I'm not comfortable staying away from the capital much longer. Odds are there wouldn't be another major push to dethrone me, but someone could make a power play if I'm not there."

"I have some idea of how that feels."

"And I'm going to be a father before long. Ander himself might stir an uprising if I'm not there for the birth of the next heir to the throne."

"Your family's more important than more time together," I said, gripping his shoulder.

He looked away for a moment. "When are you leaving?"

"As soon as I feel I can walk straight, assuming Bior has done more this morning than check on us. But the sooner these men move south, the better."

He nodded. "Understood. If I give you Aerison's wagon, do you have a driver?"

"I'm sure I could find someone. Why?"

"It's always better to have more supplies than less. One big storm and you're slowed or stopped and in need of more supplies."

I nodded and smiled. "Like our first journey into Varia."

"Exactly."

"Glad you learned from your mistake," I said.

"Hey," he snapped. "We didn't starve, and it only put us about a day behind."

I scraped the last spoonful of my breakfast from the bowl. "No harm done. You gained some wisdom, and everything turned out for the best. What more could you ask for?"

"Better breakfast," he said, after gulping down another cup of tea.

I nodded before draining my cup. "Time to change clothes and get these wagons moving. Too bad you can't ride beside me."

He nodded and wiped his eyes. "One day, likely sooner than we think, we'll ride together into some kind of mischief. For now, let me get some soldiers loading the spare wagon."

I stood and hurried around the table to pull him into a hug. "At least stick around to see us off."

He patted my back. "Of course."

"And you take good care of your wife and new child."

Squeezing me tightly, he nodded against my shoulder.

"One last thing," I said, letting him go.

He looked at me with tearful eyes. "What?"

"If it's a boy and you have trouble deciding on a name ... I won't be upset if you *don't* name the baby after me."

Cocking his head, he snickered. "Why would I?"

"We're like brothers," I said. "Maybe closer."

"Fair enough, but then, wouldn't you be honored if we named our child after you?"

I shook my head. "Fitz doesn't apply. You two are married, and I've already decided Eirick's name dies with me."

A weak smile crossed his face. "Sure. Makes sense. But I'm not naming my child after *my* father, either. He never wanted me anyway."

I clapped my hand on his shoulder. "You two will pick the right name, no doubt."

He nodded. "We will. Now, if you keep talking, you're never going to leave."

Chapter 15

I let him go and turned to pick through the clothes Bior left near my bed. After dressing, I pulled on my armor and snapped my hammer in place.

Stepping out of the tent, Bior was nowhere in sight.

Crum's voice carried as he shouted orders.

I stopped the nearest warrior and asked where my steward was.

"Headed toward the wagons, last I saw him, Sire."

I thanked him, headed toward the circle, and found my travel companion tacking Andale.

"I need you to find a wagon driver."

He looked at me, brow furrowed. "Why?"

"King Crum is letting us take extra supplies on Aerison's wagon."

"How nice of him," he said. "I'll find a couple of volunteers and have your tent packed so we can get moving."

"The sooner, the better." I mounted my horse with more ease than I should have. It only took two hops and a little extra strength from the ground. *As horrible as the grains and tea tasted, can't complain about the results. I'm feeling better than I deserve.*

The sound of a wagon approaching got my attention. I turned to find Crum, still wearing his slept-in clothes, driving toward me.

"You decided to join me after all?" I asked, smiling when he got close.

He pulled the reins to stop and shook his head. "Figured this might help get your caravan moving, and I could see you off at the same time. And it kept me from walking here."

I looked over my shoulder and frowned at the men taking longer than I wanted to get their tasks done so we could get moving. "I'll take all the help I can get."

Crum chuckled. "Maybe the celebration got a little out of hand last night."

After scratching my chin, I shook my finger at him. "If only we could figure out whose fault that might be."

He nodded. "I suppose I could shoulder some of the blame."

"A good ruler would," I said, suppressing a smile, "but I'd hate for anyone to get the wrong impression about you."

A sly grin wrinkled his cheeks. "No doubt I've cleaned up my act, even before I took the burden of ruling Varia, but I'm far from perfect."

I chuckled. "You and me both, my friend. It's been good spending time with you, even if I don't remember all of it."

"It's always good to see you, my brother —"

The sound of hoof beats coming closer cut him off.

"King Fitzeirick, King Crum," Bior said, bowing in his saddle, "I found two drivers. They're heading this way now."

"Good news," I said, nodding. "Send the scouts to me and get the rest of the warriors motivated. We need to get moving."

"Aye, Sire," Bior replied, bowing again before riding away.

Turning my attention to Crum, I frowned. "Not sure when I'll see you again. I hope it's sooner rather than later."

"Send word when you're returning home for a victory celebration. I'll make sure to meet you along the way."

I nodded. "Oh, how I miss your persistent overconfidence."

He laughed and hopped from the wagon as two warriors approached. "Fitzeirick, travel safe and swift. Strike hard, and try to not get into more trouble than you can get yourself out of."

"Thank you, Crum," I replied. "I'd give you the same advice, but with a baby on the way, you may already be in more trouble than you can get out of."

"*Me*?" he asked, pitching his voice high. "I can talk my way out of most any problem."

"Except for an angry father-in-law," I countered. "Go home, take care of your wife, and do your best to lead Varia to a prosperous future."

"Fight smart. Many people are expecting you to bring peace to the world."

"A burden I gladly carry," I said, bowing to him.

Smiling, he bowed and waved before turning to walk away.

Hope that's not the last time I see him. All it would take is one fight not going in our favor. A surprise attack could leave me dead.

The scouts arrived before any darker thoughts crept into my mind. "You sent for us, Sire?" Throst asked.

"I did." Making a show of looking at the sky, I continued, "Assuming we get underway before nightfall —"

Thorvid snickered.

I nodded. "I'll lead us out of Varia. Once we return to Croy, fan out ahead and stay in sight until we reach the wall. From there, ride three men near the wall and one on the eastern side of the path. Pay extra attention to any place there's a hole in the wall. Would make a great place for an ambush."

"I agree," Thorvid said, nodding, "Brondulf, the east is yours."

He nodded.

Bior trotted to us, red-faced. "You'd think the lot of these boys had never done any work after a night of drinking. They expected half a day's rest to recover. Can't remember how many times I had to point at you and insist some knot-on-a-log get moving. Sire, if not for the example you set sitting on your horse, I might still be yelling."

I nodded as my steward ranted. *Better not mention I'd have stayed another night if we had time.* "Glad I could do my part to motivate the warriors. Are we ready to go?"

"Aye, Sire. We are."

"Scouts, take your positions. Bior, give the signal."

Reins cracked behind me, horses neighed, and I nudged Andale to a comfortable pace. Varian soldiers lined the way as we got close to the pass, saluting as we rode by. Commander Aerison stood at the entrance of the split between the artificial cliffs. He tapped his cane on his chest, saluting before wishing us swift and safe travel. Once the scouts cleared the pass, they trotted ahead.

Continuing west, the wall came into sight sooner than I expected. I waved Bior to my side when the scouts turned south.

"Yes, Sire?"

"Stay close and keep your eyes open. Not sure we have anything to worry about but better safe than sorry."

"Aye, m'lord. I agree."

From memory, I expected to ride through mostly clear land until we passed a small forest before we stopped for the night. *If there's going to be an attack, it would likely come from there.*

The sun reached the height of its daily climb, and I tired. *Paying constant attention takes a lot out of you.*

Bior cleared his throat. "Umm...Sire? Hallkel is riding toward us. Looks like he's in a bit of a hurry."

I raised my head and blinked several times.

"Are you well, m'lord?" Bior asked, eyebrows raised.

"Resting my eyes," I said, as the scout got close.

"Sire. Thorvid spotted—" Hallkel paused for a moment, some color leaving his face. "—something not far ahead. Perhaps the caravan should stop while we investigate."

Chapter 16

Bior shrugged when I looked at him. "Hallkel, ride back, and tell everyone we're stopping for lunch."

"With all haste, m'lord," Hallkel said.

"Bior, let's see what they discovered."

Our horses' hoof beats echoed off the wall as we trotted ahead.

Thorvid and Throst sat on their horses near a large patch of torn-up ground. Brondulf had ridden a little farther south, taking a watch position.

Throst rode to meet me us. "Sire, a warning. It's a ... unsettling sight."

"I'm sure I've seen worse," I said. "What have you found?"

"When I first saw it, I thought it was more ground disturbed by a battle. As I got closer, I saw..." He shivered. "...bodies. Was there a graveyard here?"

"Not when I was Skald. Let me see."

He nodded and led me to the edge of a crude burial ground. I'd never seen anything like it. Jumbles of bones jutted out of the dirt among partially covered bodies. Judging by the lack of stench and the drawn, weathered look of the blackened flesh, the burials weren't recent. Neither was their exposure. The sun hadn't bleached dirt stains from the bare bones. Sweeping my eyes across the open grave again, I noticed most of the dead were missing heads, arms, or legs. In some cases, there was nothing but a naked torso with jagged wounds where extremities should have been.

A shiver shot down my back. My blood ran cold. "I don't recall any reports of our warriors burying anyone on this side of the wall," I said.

"No decent Croian would have cut someone up before burying them," Throst insisted.

"So, Satran soldiers did this?" Thorvid asked. "Are these our people?"

"I don't see any clothing," Bior said, "and the skin's too rotten to tell."

"It doesn't matter," I said, disgust at the treatment of these people gave an edge to my words. "Even weak stonesyths could do a better job than this. Buried this shallow, it's no wonder animals scavenged on the bodies."

Even ignoring the missing pieces, I'm not sure animals did this," Bior said.

Throst grunted.

"Why?" I asked.

My steward pointed. "No tracks in the dirt. No gnaw marks or bones split to get to the marrow."

I scratched my chin and looked for the missing details he'd pointed out. *He's right.* "Why would someone disturb a shallow grave?"

Thorvid rubbed the bridge of his nose. "Makes no sense to me either, Sire."

"Wouldn't be right to leave them like this," Throst added.

"Keep an eye out, and give me a minute."

"Aye, Sire," Bior said. "Scouts, keep a sharp watch."

Brondulf arrived as I slid out of the saddle. Bior ordered him to join his fellow scouts watching for threats.

I went to my knees and pressed my palms against the dirt. Holding a deep breath to a count of five, I focused my outrage and sent my talent toward the shallow grave. When the energy met on the far side, I forced the field down about half my height.

Andale whinnied and pawed as the ground quivered around us.

Once I was satisfied the remains were deep enough, I changed my focus and shifted dirt to fill in the hole.

With the work completed, I raised my hand. "Bior, I could use some help getting to my feet and some water."

Bior's feet hit the ground with a soft thud. He grabbed my hand and leaned back for some leverage to help me to my feet. "Don't have any water with me, Sire. Sorry."

"Take my waterskin, m'lord," Thorvid said, motioning he would toss it to me. "I'll get another before the caravan gets underway."

I nodded, caught the half-empty container, and drained it in a long gulp. "Good enough to get me moving again. Thank you."

As I turned to find Andale, Brondulf yelled, "Movement!"

"Go!" I barked, reaching for my hammer.

Bior drew his sword and ran to stand in front of me.

"On my left," I said, backing toward Andale. "Standing in front of me is a good way to get hit."

He shook his head. "Putting myself between you and a threat is the best way to keep you safe, m'lord."

Not seeing an immediate threat, I put my hammer back in place and mounted Andale as quickly as I could. "Keep an eye on the scouts. Raise an alarm if anything gets past them. I'm going to let the warriors know so they can ready themselves for combat."

Bior nodded, squared his shoulders, and shifted into a defensive stance.

Is it possible Satran soldiers have made it past the army? Are they scouting for an attack? Afraid to waste time, I set off at full gallop. "Archers!" I yelled, as soon as I saw a group of warriors. "Ready your bows! Take positions ahead of the wagons! Swordsmen! Axemen! Arm yourselves! Prepare to engage!"

While most of the men moved, a couple stood frozen, staring at me as I approached. I kicked at one as I passed. "Your king has given an order! *Move!*"

I didn't slow or stop bellowing orders until I passed the last wagon. Circling to the other side, I continued shouting commands in case someone didn't hear me until I reached the line of archers.

"What are we facing, Sire?" the nearest bowman asked.

"I'm not sure. The scouts noticed movement ahead. Bior stands watch ahead. Be mindful of him when we advance. I'd hate for him to get hurt by an arrow loosed mistakenly."

"Aye, Sire."

I nodded and looked over my shoulder. Two lines of warriors marched our way.

"Archers!" I yelled.

A couple of men flinched.

"Forward! Keep a sharp eye and do not, I repeat, *do not* let fly unless you are certain of your target."

Heads bobbed, and the line moved forward, more or less together.

The rest of the warriors made their way to me in a much less organized manner.

"What lays ahead, m'lord?" the first one to reach me asked.

I only want to have to say this once. "I'll explain when everyone has arrived."

He nodded and stepped back.

Before I gave in to the urge to ride around, kicking most of the warriors into action, the last stragglers meandered to the back of the crowd.

"Attention!" I barked.

Looking toward the line of archers, it seemed like nothing had made it to them, so I decided I had time to address the behavior of these green warriors. *Maybe Brondulf didn't really see anything.* "Form two lines, facing me, weapons at rest!"

After several moments of shuffling feet and muttered words, the warriors stood in two ragged lines.

"I gave an *order*! I didn't do it for fun. This is *not* a test or a joke. Does everyone understand me?"

A chorus of "Aye" came from the men.

"The scouts tasked with keeping this caravan from getting ambushed saw something and gave chase at my order. I returned here, leaving my right hand behind to alert us of any threat they missed, to ready you men for a fight ... should it be necessary. At least the archers took my direction seriously. If there was an ambush headed for us, you'd all be dead ... every one of you. Likely I'd fall with you. Is that what you want?"

"No, Sire," they yelled, almost in unison.

"Archers!" I bellowed.

The line turned enough to look at me.

"Fall back. Guard the wagons until I return."

"Aye," they replied together, turning to jog toward us.

"Warriors! Run to Bior's position and be ready to attack or defend as needed."

I followed the warriors to Bior. We found him on horseback, staring south.

"Warriors, make a defensive line twenty paces ahead," I ordered.

"Aye!"

"Anything to report?" I asked Bior.

"Nothing, Sire. Lost sight of the scouts after they went through the wall. No sounds of fighting. I'm guessing they are still looking."

I nodded. "Understood. If they don't return soon, we'll take the warriors to the hole and see what we find."

"How long do you want to wait, m'lord?"

"Not long. I'm still thirsty, and my appetite's coming back."

A horse and rider came through the hole in the wall, followed closely by three more.

"Warriors! At the ready!" I bellowed.

Thorvid led the group, stopping at the line of fighting men.

"Did you find anything?" I asked.

"No signs of an army, Sire," Thorvid said.

"You're certain there's no threat?" Bior asked.

Brondulf nodded. "As sure as I can be."

I pressed my lips together for a moment. "Warriors. Return to the wagons. Get ready to go," I said. "Make sure you pass the order to the archers."

"Aye, Sire!" they replied, before turning to leave.

"Give your report as we ride back," I said, turning Andale.

Chapter 17

Brondulf took a drink from his waterskin and cleared his throat. "I saw a man looking our way from behind the wall, Sire. I turned my horse to walk toward him, and he pulled back."

"You're sure it wasn't a bear, maybe?" I asked. "Burying those bodies disturbed the horses, could've stirred up other animals nearby."

"Yes, my king. I'm sure. He ran on two legs, with a dark cloak flapping behind him. Never seen a bear do either of those things."

"You saw him running?" I asked.

He nodded. "I gave chase after yelling the alarm. I heard you order the rest to go before I passed through the wall. He's a stonesyth. Messed up the ground behind him to slow my horse."

"It's true, Sire," Thorvid said, nodding. "We slowed but didn't lose sight of him until he hit a large stand of trees with lots of brush. It's got to be the same man as before, and he may have some woodsyth talent too. Passed through the undergrowth easily."

"I take it he escaped to the other side of the forest," I said.

"Not likely, Sire," Throst said. "Hallkel and I galloped around the sides of the trees and met on the far edge, no cloaked man in sight."

I nodded and scratched my chin for a moment before looking at Bior.

"Could have had a hide already set." He shrugged. "But who can say why."

"This cloaked man, did he say anything?" I asked. "Make a threat or show a weapon?"

"Nothing, Sire," Brondulf said. "He didn't even look back as we chased him. Like he knew where we were."

I nodded. *Not too hard for a decent stonesyth who knows how. Pretty sure I could track horses while running.* "If we start moving now, we can get the far end of the caravan past the opening in the wall. The trouble is, we don't know if there are more big holes in the barrier farther down this path. Did any of you happen to spot any?"

Thorvid looked at the other scouts. They shook their heads. "No, Sire."

"I'm open to suggestions," I said, as the caravan came into view.

"Perhaps it's best to make camp now with staggered watches when it gets dark," Bior said.

I looked at each scout, eyebrows raised. "Agree? Disagree? Any other ideas?"

"I was focused on the fleeing stranger and making sure I stayed in the saddle," Brondulf said. "Bior's suggestion makes sense."

"Making camp is our best option, Sire," Thorvid said.

"We don't know if this is the same person we saw before or if there is a group tracking us. Bior, do we have enough swords or axes to equip the archers with blades?" I asked.

He nodded.

"Thorvid, Throst, give the order to circle up and corral the horses. Organize watches *and* patrols. If a mouse moves near our camp, I want someone to know."

Thorvid nodded. "Sire, I know a few of the archers. They won't like carrying big blades."

"Shooting arrows at noises in the dark is a waste," I said. "Make it clear. I'm *ordering* them to carry a sword or an axe."

"Yes, m'lord," Throst said. "We'll make sure they understand."

"What do you want us to do, Sire?" Hallkel asked.

"Stay near me in case I need someone else to pass more orders."

"Glad to help, m'lord," Brondulf said, smiling.

"Those who abuse power don't hold it for long," I advised.

"Understood," Brondulf replied.

Bior snickered.

"Now we know someone's out there and can be ready. Best prepare for a long night," I said, after a long sigh.

Bior held Andale's reins while I helped circle the wagons to corral the horses. Thunder boomed in the distance as we secured our mounts inside. I saw no dark clouds and couldn't tell where it came from.

"Sounds like it could be a wet evening," Brondulf said.

"Bior, let's find my tent. Hallkel, Brondulf, find your fellow scouts. Help them finish their tasks and get some well-deserved rest. I suspect no one will sleep well tonight."

"Aye, Sire," Hallkel said, taking my reins.

Bior and I headed to a small field of tents, looking for the largest one.

Thunder rolled again. As the sound faded, a cool gust of wind rippled the walls of tents around us.

"Not good," Bior commented.

I searched the sky again but found no signs of a storm. "Maybe it's far enough away we won't get more than a breeze."

Bior grunted and turned down another row of tents.

"Remind me to ask about that burial site when we reach the battlefront. I'd like to know if it was there when they chased the Satran army south and, if so, why I wasn't told about it."

"Do my best," he replied, nodding.

We wove our way to near the center of camp before finding my tent. Another chilly gust pulled the flap out of Bior's hand as we stepped inside. It whipped back and forth, slapping against the front of the tent before he secured it in place.

My bed was in place near the back wall. To the left of the straw, my travel chest took up part of the wall. I put my helmet on the chest and leaned my armor against it before kneeling. Pushing my talent into the ground, I searched for any sizable stones near the tent's entrance to syth into a table or even workable seats. Finding nothing, I sighed and pushed my will into the dirt.

The taut cords holding my tent to the ground hummed as the wind rushed past the shelter. I did my best to ignore the noise and focused on forming the dirt into a small table. It took more effort for me than forming stone, but I had a usable table and a few beads of sweat on my brow. *Not long ago, I couldn't have made much at all with dirt. Funny what you learn trying to survive.*

"I'll get food," Bior said.

"Chairs will be ready by the time you get back," I said, wiping my forehead. "Bring extra water."

He bowed and fought to control the tent flap against the wind.

Light faded fast as I formed two chairs from the dirt. My tent opened as I tested the first seat.

My steward stuck his head in. "M'lord, the scouts helped carry our food and asked if they could report to you in person."

"I don't mind them joining us, but the table's a bit small, and we don't have enough seats," I said.

Bior entered with the scouts close behind. They covered the table in baskets. Bior offered me two waterskins before dropping my saddlebags near my bed.

Throst took a couple of candles from one of the baskets. Energy rippled around my feet before the table grew larger. He pressed the wax towers into small holes near opposite corners of the table, and they burst into flame. "Anyone else need a seat?" he asked, turning to the other scouts. "I don't mind standing for a while."

"As long as I don't have to stand outside," Brondulf said. "Clouds are rolling in fast, and it's an ill wind blowing."

I nodded and took a long drink. "Everyone here is welcome to speak freely and stay as long as they like."

Thorvid spoke as I reached into the nearest basket for a roll. "The archers tried to argue their daggers would be better for close fighting. After I took the first one's blade from his belt before he could react, they all decided to listen."

I chuckled. "Well played."

Flashes brightened the tent from outside moments before thunder roared through the camp.

"Storm's getting closer," Brondulf commented.

I shrugged. "Nothing we can do but hope for the best and ride it out. Guards are posted and patrols organized?"

"Not without many complaints," Thorvid said.

"I don't envy the warriors out in this weather, but we don't know anything about the man you chased. It's best to act like he's not friendly."

"Aye, Sire," Brondulf said. "I gave him no reason to run, but he beat foot like a hunted rabbit."

I chewed a strip of meat until it was soft enough to swallow. The first drops of rain thumped against the top of my tent. "At least we know there's someone out there, and we can prepare for whatever may come."

Everyone nodded as I took another drink.

Brighter flashes almost made the candlelight seem dim before thunder shook the ground. Rain hammered on the tent.

"Would the runner try anything in this storm?" Hallkel asked.

"I don't know the man, so ..." I shrugged.

"He doesn't seem desperate," Thorvid said. "Otherwise, he would have tried to raid our supplies or thin our ranks already."

I shook my head. "We haven't given him much opportunity and, provided—"

Someone outside cut me off, yelling loud enough to be heard over the howling wind and the drumming rain. It wasn't close enough for me to understand what was said, but it sounded closer than the edge of our camp.

I raised my eyebrows. "I don't like the way that sounded. Thorvid, take your fellow scouts, find out what's going on, and assist as best you can. Bior, guard the door. I think it best I put my armor back on."

"I was thinking the same thing," he replied, drawing his sword.

Chapter 18

"Stop!" Thorvid bellowed. "One more step, and you won't live long enough to regret it."

"I offer no threat!" an unknown man hollered. "I wish to speak with your leader!"

"Hands up! Drop your hood so I can see your face!" someone ordered.

"I have information — important information — for your commander!"

"Identify yourself first," Brondulf said.

I got to my feet. "Bior, I hate to ask you to go out in this storm, but as my personal guard, I need you to go assess the situation while I prepare for a possible meeting."

His head bobbed before he swiped the tent flap out of his way.

A cold, damp wind blew in, shaking the fabric walls. *At least the roof's keeping me dry.*

I pulled my armored pants on. The top of my armor slid over my shirt easily.

"Do you know how I get an audience with the camp commander?" the man asked.

Reaching back, I made sure my hammer was in place.

"Through me!" Bior replied. "Who are you?"

My helmet thumped quietly onto my head.

"An ally!"

I stepped back to the table.

"You're not Varian!" Thorvid bellowed.

"No!" he yelled. "I'm Croian!"

"Bior!" I called out. "Bring him to me!"

"Yes," Bior answered.

"Move too fast, and I'll drop you in your tracks," Brondulf said.

Bior backed into my tent, holding the man at sword point.

The mysterious visitor, standing about a head taller than my guard, held his arms away from his sides, fingertips peeking out from the long sleeves of his cloak.

Lightning flashed, giving me a glimpse of my soaking-wet men standing outside. I noticed the stranger's cloak shed water easily.

"Stop," I said. "Lower your hood. Prove you are Croian."

"Are you the king?"

"I am. Who are you?"

He shook his head. "Not with an audience." His shoulders sagged. "I beg you. Lives depend on my secrecy."

"Is that a threat?" Bior demanded, squaring his shoulders.

"On your knees, stranger," I ordered.

He slowly knelt on the ground.

"Bior, out."

"But —" my guard argued.

"Everyone is right outside the tent, and I *can* take care of myself."

He glanced back at me. "If you are certain, m'lord."

"I am."

Bior circled the man, sword at the ready as he moved. "Remember, we are right outside."

Tapping on my hammer's handle, I spoke, "I have no doubt you're a strong stonesyth. If I feel even a trickle of energy, I'll call for the men outside. If you move too fast for my liking, I'll call for my men. If I see a weapon, anything that looks like a weapon, I'll cry out before I attack. Any sign of misbehavior or mischief, you will die on your knees. Do you understand?"

"I do."

"Slowly lower your hood."

His head dipped below the tabletop as he brought his arms up to push the cloth back. He raised his lightly tanned, smooth, bald head, showing me his eyes. A quick look at his complexion and the shape of his face showed he was telling the truth. *Not even a hint of gray to his skin. He's Croian.*

His blank expression gave nothing away as I studied him. The longer I looked, the more I got a creepy sense of familiarity. *Perhaps I've seen him before?* "What is your name?" I demanded.

His upper lip quivered. "I'll gladly answer all your questions if you would do me the favor of removing your helmet so I can see your face."

"This is not a negotiation."

The increasingly familiar man closed his eyes, forming deep wrinkles at their corners, and bowed his head. "I apologize for disturbing your camp this night and ask to be released with your word for my safe exit. Do this, and I swear on my life, you will never see me again."

Something about the way he spoke made him seem even more familiar. *Little things. I feel like I should know this man.* After removing my helmet, I placed it on the table. "Who are you?"

His eyes opened wide as he raised his head. "The useless windbag wasn't a complete liar," he said quietly. "Fitzeirick, son of Sar'sa. Is that you?"

An uncomfortable burning formed in my gut. "How do you know me — my mother?" I demanded.

"Your Majesty. My family shared meals with your mother before she was with child. My wife and I were there when you were born. My son taught you to be a man." He shuddered. "Have you seen my boy? Do you know if Roi still lives?"

My heart pounded in my chest, its beat drumming in my ears as I reached for my hammer. "Rorec!" I roared. I gripped the handle, pressing my fingers against the smooth, green stone under the metal. My talent flashed into the shiny, black stone in the hammer's head and pressed a spike out of the face. "My half-brother may have branded me, a traitor but you... You rode with the Satran army as they invaded my skati, slaughtered fellow Croians ... my people. Why should I spare your life?"

Rorec raised his hands. "Mercy! Hear me out. If death is the sentence for serving my homeland as best I could, at least hear the truth of my deeds."

I live with a well-practiced liar. Should help me decide if he's telling the truth. I rested the hammer on my shoulder in a less threatening but still ready-to-strike posture. "Speak your truth. Explain how riding *with* our enemy, wearing their armor, is not a traitorous act that should cost you your life."

Rorec dropped his arms and shifted to sit with his legs crossed in front of him. "Eirick made a treaty with Satra before your birth. He paid them to protect the south of Croy. I was sent as an ambassador to ensure they kept their end of the bargain. Eirickson." He spat. "The short-sighted fool poured honey in the ears of Satra's ruling clan. His hatred for all things Varian burned so hot he offered Satra your land — to remove all traces of Varia from his country — in exchange for stopping the payments. I did everything I could to convince the Satran chieftain your half-brother was trapping them. The lure of even more land was too tempting when he proposed an alliance to capture and divide Varia."

I glared at him. "Having failed at your task, you chose to ride with them ... why?"

"I was forced to ride in the invasion. My wife, Asfrid ... you probably don't remember her, would have been killed, or worse, had I refused. I suspect Sifet, Satra's chieftain at the time, expected me to die in the fighting. Instead, I did everything I could to help Croians escape."

The ground trembled as my anger poured into it. "Yet my mother died. If you knew Sar'sa and truly cared about her, why did you not help her?"

"I mourn her death to this day," he said, closing his eyes.

"And my fiancée? Aesa suffered at the hands of a general before he sold her as a whore. You could do nothing to save her?"

"I didn't know of her and couldn't reach your hall ahead of the Satran advance. Who told you she was taken by a general?"

"Eirickson. He didn't live much longer after."

"He was a foolish, stone-headed man-child." Rorec spat again. "What do you know of Satra and its people?"

"Only what every civilized person knows."

Rorec smiled weakly. "Do you trust me enough to explain how the country works?"

"No." I narrowed my gaze. "But I believe you've told the truth so far. Enlighten me."

"I must tell you how it was before the sons of Eirick upset the balance, so you understand the damage wasn't suffered by Croy alone.

"The Satra your father knew was divided into four clans. The League ruled the nation. Their word was law, absolute, and never questioned by the lower clans. The Legion, Satra's ruthless fighting force, led by Field Masters who drive their men hard, often treating them no better than slaves."

"Why would fighting men willingly endure such abuse?" I asked, interrupting him.

He held up his hand. "Let me finish, and it will be easier to understand. The Devoted are Satra's lifeblood. Farmers, builders, workers, and the like supplying the nation's needs. Last, and by far the least in their society, are the Bane. Outcasts. Satra's sickly, malformed, insane, or those banished from higher clans.

"You asked why their soldiers tolerate ill-treatment. Because if they don't, their families become Bane. The ablest of the Bane are servants or slaves. The rest beg. Groveling out a short, hard life. This has been the model of Satran society for longer than they have written history."

I pressed my lips together tightly while considering his story. "Sounds like a horrible way to live. Why don't they join with other clans and revolt?"

"You see it as terrible; they see it as normal. Until recently, none of the Devoted dared raise a hand against their leaders. Any showing such aggression was forced into the Legion."

I scratched my chin. "You said, 'until recently.' What changed?"

"Your war emboldened a select few of the Devoted. Porsey's lies did even more damage. On his word, the League decided to wait for your fall after you turned back two, small incursions. Your successful attack on the western stronghold embarrassed some powerful men in the Legion and made them question the League."

"He won't be a problem as soon as we find him," I said.

Rorec laughed. "You won't find him. To placate the Legion's leaders, the League gave them Porsey. Soldiers strung him up by his ankles and ripped out his persuasive tongue. He bled to death, screaming gibberish until the end."

I shivered out of joy or revulsion...or maybe both. "He didn't know I had discovered the traitors in my army."

Rorec shrugged. "The damage was done. Suspicion turned into dissension. A bold leader from a secretive sect of the Devoted whispered into High Field Master Dejan's ear, offering the Bonetaker's backing, should the Legion want to overthrow the League."

I sat down as he spoke, standing my hammer on the ground. "Who or what is a bone taker?"

He motioned to the seat across from me. "May I?"

I nodded.

"The Bonetakers were spoken of as myths of scary men to frighten unruly children. Not long ago, I learned they weren't simply stories. It's a group secretly practicing sything techniques long considered taboo, even by the Satran. Zealots use strong stone and wood talents to somehow weave bone into their creations. They believe it gives life to their works. I've seen the statues they refer to as Stoneskins move. Never been able to figure out how."

I leaned forward to rest my elbows on the table and sighed heavily. "Another secret group to deal with."

"You know of other groups like the Bonetakers?" Rorec asked, eyebrows raised.

"No. At least, nothing like you describe. What else do you know about this bone-taking group?"

"Bonetakers," he corrected. "Not much other than they talked the Legion into dismantling the League. The ousted members of the ruling clan had two choices, die or fight against Croy. Many chose to die."

"The Bonetakers, are they on Croian soil?"

"No, they are gathering power in Satra."

"So, they had nothing to do with the open graves we found earlier today?"

"Directly? No," he answered. "They have the Legion march Bane to grave sites and force them to dirty their hands gathering bones."

"Do you know if those were Croian bodies?"

"I do not. Bonetakers don't care."

I sighed. "Disgusting."

He nodded. "Seeing as we've found common ground in our dislike of the Bonetakers, may I offer a proposal?"

I tapped my fingers together. "What sort of proposal?"

He turned his palms up and smiled. "An alliance between former League members and your army."

I spat at him. "I don't need aid from the losing side in this war. My men have triumphed at every turn. Satra's soldiers are running home with their tails between their legs, hoping we don't catch them."

Rorec shook his head. "You misunderstand the situation. The exiled League who chose to fight helped raise the wall here and stayed behind to slow your pursuit while the Legion and the Bonetakers forced their will on the Satran people."

"Are you saying my warriors haven't faced true soldiers?"

"Not since the earliest battles. Certainly not since the standoff at the wall."

I pursed my lips. "What would weak, disgraced rulers have to offer? I don't need their advice on how to win this war."

"You're preparing to enter lands you know nothing about. They could guide you through obstacles like the black sand sea. That knowledge alone would keep your advance from grinding to a halt."

"Let's say I consider the offer. In return for their service, they get ... what?"

"Their country back. Existing as a tribute to Croy, ruling under your guidance."

Heat rose from my chest, through my neck, and flared in my cheeks. I tapped my scar before scowling. "No. Never. So long as I draw breath. I have this brand because of the men who agreed to Eirickson's proposal. My mother and fiancée died horribly ... disgracefully because those men invaded my lands. Rorec, I always considered you a good man. Nothing you've said tonight changes my opinion. I can get you someplace safe and send a message to Roi on your behalf. He couldn't believe you were seen in Satran armor—"

"Roi?" Rorec interrupted. "My son. He's alive?"

"Yes. And doing well."

He bowed low. "Thank you for telling me. As much as I want to accept your offer, I cannot. Asfrid hides among some Bane. I won't abandon her in Satra and can't easily get her out as things are now."

"Understandable," I said. "I would do much the same for my wife ... or your son."

"Porsey claimed you'd taken a Varian wh—" He raised his hands. "Excuse me, a Varian woman, as your promised, but never mentioned you'd married her."

"He was in Satra when we wed. She's an excellent queen. I'd guess you'd like her." I rubbed my chin. "How can I help you, Rorec? My father sent you to Satra. My half-brother — fire take him — put me in a position to trap you there. How do I make this right by you and Asfrid?"

He smiled. "We can help each other if you let go of your hatred. There are some good, decent people in Satra. Many among the Bane are punished for simply existing, and most of the Devoted are forced to give everything — even their loved ones — as their rulers demand. Those people don't deserve your wrath. They deserve the liberation you can bring."

Pinching the bridge of my nose, I closed my eyes and considered Rorec's words. *My mother's dead because of Satra. Aesa, held captive in a brothel to be raped by soldiers, chose to chew her wrists open and bleed herself to death. How much Croian blood has soaked this land? How many of my people now live as Bane? Even worse, how many have died among the outcasts?* "No. The only liberation they will get from me, my army, is from their miserable lives. From the day I took control of Croy, I've done everything to prepare for the destruction of Satra. The debt they owe for what they did to my people, my family, and my life — I want the blood of every Satran, and I want them to bleed until they have none left."

"You would slaughter innocents, turn away those willing to fight to better their own future or even have a future?"

The table shook when I pounded my fist into it. "What if Roi had died in the invasion trying to protect Croians who couldn't fight back? What if Asfrid had to choose between a fate worse than death or taking her own life to spare herself endless torture?"

Teeth clenched, I pointed at him. "How would you act if this happened while you were locked away, deep underground, groping around in the dark until you found a way to escape? You emerge to learn your family is dead, and you failed everyone who looked to you for protection."

Rorec scooted back in the seat when I leaned over the table and ran my fingers through my hair.

"Would you ally yourself with the leaders who put this in motion?" I paused and thrust my pointing finger at him. My arm was rigid; it quivered in time with my pounding heart. "If so, you are a much, much better man than I."

Rorec wiped tears from his cheeks before covering his eyes. "No. I can't say I'd feel differently were I in your position. However, I'm not certain I'd be so quick to act. You consider Satra an uncivilized nation, and in their own way they are, but ... should you accomplish your goal, should you kill every man, woman, and child, are you not guilty of much savagery yourself?"

Easy to see where Roi got his sense of wisdom. I crossed my arms. "The dead can judge my actions. Those living under my rule will surely benefit when this is all over."

Rorec bowed. "I do believe we are at an impasse. Do I leave here tonight? As you said earlier, my life *is* in your hands."

Chapter 19

I rubbed my chin for a moment. "You offered no hostility entering our camp. As best I can tell, you spoke the truth as we talked and provided useful information. Because of this, and your history as a family friend, I give you my word. You will leave this camp without harm. However, I need a promise from you first."

He nodded. "Ask."

"Do not impede our movement nor aid Croy's enemy as we take this war onto Satran soil. I won't ask you to fight for us, but I do require a promise to not fight against us."

"I freely promise what you ask. Please try to rescue any Croians you find in Satra ... especially my wife."

"Already part of our battle plan," I said, offering him my hand.

He shook it. "Thank you ... Sire."

"Bior," I barked, releasing Rorec's hand.

Rorec pulled his hood over his face before the tent opened.

My steward rushed in, drenched. "Sire!"

"This man is free to go with my promise of safe passage. Escort him from camp and see that he remains unharmed until he is no longer in your sight. Have the scouts release the patrols; there is no threat this evening. Everyone should try to get some sleep. We move south as soon as possible after first light."

"Sire. If I may. Who is this man?" Bior asked, sheathing his sword.

Rorec twitched his head.

"A Croian and a friend," I replied.

"Understood," Bior said, before bowing and holding the tent open.

Rorec bowed low before leaving the tent.

Taking a deep breath, I held it a moment before going to the travel chest and taking off my armor again. Before laying down, I decided I needed to pass on some information Rorec had mentioned and searched my saddlebags for a sheet of parchment, a quill, and an ink pot. I glanced toward the table, where the candles were burning low, and dug through the bag again for my seal.

I jotted a short note directing the bargemen to look for anything they'd consider a black sand sea, explore it, and do their best to map it.

The tent flap opened as I finished folding the message. The rain had turned to a cold mist.

Bior stopped inside the entrance and wrung water from his hair and beard. "He's off into the night, Sire."

I nodded and dribbled a generous pool of wax for my seal. Pressing the stone into the cooling liquid, leaving an imprint resembling the brand on my face.

"Memory fails me at the moment. Did we bring any messengers?"

"No, m'lord," he said, pulling off his soaked overshirt.

I sighed and left the table to put everything away. "Shortsighted on my part. I'll send it when we reach the battlefront."

"What is it?" Bior asked.

I shrugged. "A request for the bargemen based on information I was given."

"Are you going to tell me who he was?"

"No. He put others at risk coming here. Keeping his secret may save lives. I can say we'll benefit from the information he shared. Are you sleeping in here tonight?"

A deep frown creased Bior's face. "No. Sleep well, m'lord."

"Before you leave, put out the candles for me. If you don't mind."

"Not at all. Good night."

The tent went dark before my knees hit the wet straw mattress. *How?* I ran my hand along the edges, finding a spot where the tent wall wasn't secured well. Wind-driven rain pushed under it, into my bed.

After a heavy sigh, I stumbled back to the table and sythed it and the seats back into the ground. After softening the dirt, I lay on it. *I've slept on worse.*

I slept but didn't get much rest. Visions of bodies jutting from the ground, tripping me as I walked, dominated my dreams. I woke when sunlight assaulted my eyelids. It felt like I'd just closed my eyes.

"Sire, are you well?" Bior asked.

I nodded, yawned, and opened one eye. "Well enough," I muttered.

"Why are you sleeping on the ground?"

I explained about the tent and my bed as I got to my feet.

"I'll make sure it doesn't happen again," Bior said.

"Don't worry about it. Provided nothing slows our travel, we should reach our army before dark," I said. "Breakfast?"

He handed me a woven sack and a tankard with something steaming in it. "Sweet rolls are getting a little hard. At least the tea's hot this morning."

"Another reason to get moving, the stronghold should have better food," I said.

"Aye, Sire. Men are moving slow this morning, and the sloppy ground isn't helping."

"Have you eaten?"

"How else would I know about the rolls?"

I nodded. "See to your things and get our horses ready. I'll find you once I've changed."

"Take your time, m'lord."

I raised a seat from the ground and dipped a roll into the tea, hoping to both soften the bread and sweeten the tea. My effort failed, leaving me with wet, hard bread and crumbs in my hot drink.

The combination of warmth in my belly and putting on clothes free of yesterday's dust and sweat improved my mood before dressing in my armor. Once my hammer clicked into place, I draped my saddlebags over my shoulder and set off to find Bior.

"Didn't expect to find you so far from camp," I said, finding my steward with the horses on the far side of the wagon corral.

He shrugged. "The horses huddled to this side, for some reason."

I nodded and secured my saddlebags. "Is he ready?"

"Yes, Sire."

"Remind me to recommend you for a promotion when we get home," I said, smiling.

Bior laughed. "Unless you expand the guard, there's no need for another lieutenant."

I pursed my lips for a moment. "Never know what the future holds."

Bior nodded. "As you say, m'lord."

Lifting my boot to mount Andale, I slipped and fell forward, pressing my face against the horse's shoulder. *Better than tumbling backward onto wet, sloppy ground.* Fueling my talent with frustration and embarrassment, I pushed my will into the slick mud, flinging it from my boots, and got into the saddle. "See the drivers get these wagons ready to go soon. I'm going to find the scouts."

Bior smirked. "Your words from my mouth, Sire."

After asking a few warriors on my way through camp, I found out the scouts had headed south to see if the storm had damaged the path. Putting my heels to Andale, I set off to catch them. From what I saw, the way looked clear—muddy, but nothing washed out.

The scouts had gathered a short ride from camp. I greeted them as I approached.

Thorvid waved to me. "Good morning, Sire. Are we on the move?"

"The wagons weren't ready when I left camp."

Throst looked over his shoulder. "Is there a problem?"

"Mud's slowing everyone down," I said.

"Any concern for our visitor last night?" Brondulf asked.

"Don't worry about him," I said.

"Who was he?" Hallkel asked.

"A Croian and a friend. Still, no reason to drop our guard, though," I said, looking from one man to the next. "There could be threats we don't know about. Like yesterday, ride three men to the west, one east, with at least one of you in sight of the lead wagon to pass along signals. Be extra careful around openings in the wall. No telling what might be waiting on the other side."

"Seemed to work well enough before," Thorvid said.

"One more thing," I said. "If you spot more open graves, I want to know about it immediately."

"Not to argue, Sire," Throst said, but I'm a fairly strong stonesyth. I could cover any we come across."

I shook my head. "Thank you for offering, but I want to honor the dead."

"As you wish, m'lord," he replied.

Brondulf squinted before running his fingers through his beard. "If I'm overstepping my bounds, please excuse me, but is there something you're not telling us, Sire?"

I took a deep breath. "I'm not going to lie, there is but —"

"If our king keeps something from us, we have to trust it's for good reason," Thorvid said.

I raised my hand. "I do have a reason. If it's good or not remains to be seen. More than anything, I want to avoid rumors which could damage warrior morale."

"Rumors usually aren't good anyway," Brondulf said. "If this one could be harmful ... best to keep the information to yourself, m'lord."

"Agreed," Thorvid added.

"Thank you for your trust," I said, bowing slightly. "I'm going to go check on the caravan."

"We'll wait here, m'lord," Hallkel said.

"Keep watch and be ready to ride when you see us," I said, before turning Andale back toward the camp. I reached the area — *hard to call it a camp when all the tents are down* — to find only a couple of wagons lined up. Bior's yells weren't doing much to motivate the men.

My first instinct was to drop to the ground and shout orders through the dirt, but I remembered the mud and decided it might not work. *Time for the personal touch.* Trotting among the scattered wagons, I barked orders at warriors taking their time getting their gear, and themselves, loaded. Several men complained about the mud. I ignored them and kept riding. Passing Bior for the second time, I told him to wait for me at the front.

Once I saw no one wandering around and wagons lining up, I gave the signal to move and turned to take my place at the lead. After a quick check to make sure the wagons were rolling, I shifted my focus back to the road ahead.

From what I remembered about this part of my old territory, the ground leveled off into a fairly flat prairie with a few groves of trees. The grasslands were still there, undisturbed, except for the farms and homes left in ruins. Most of the trees were gone. *Disgusting.*

Best I could tell, Rorec kept to his word and left us alone. The scouts kept a steady pace until the stronghold came into view. They stopped where two warriors stood watch and waved me forward. I sent Bior back to let the drivers know what was happening before trotting to the scouts.

I held my right arm across my chest. "Hope the day finds you well, men. A caravan of fresh warriors and supplies approaches. I, King Fitzeirick, request passage."

The men returned my salute. "Welcome, Sire. Please, continue on."

I bowed to him. "Thank you for your service. Scouts, with me."

"As you wish, m'lord," Thorvid said.

The watchmen signaled to men atop the stronghold wall. The gate swung inward, and someone waved us inside.

Chapter 20

Passing through the stone wall — *Looks like hornblende. There's plenty of it around here.* — brought a sense of comfort and safety.

"Welcome to Southold, m'lord. The stables are to the left," a warrior said, bowing. "I'll send someone to meet you there and take you to General Gudmann."

I thanked him and turned to my escorts. "Stay here and help with the caravan as needed."

"Of course, Sire," Brundolf said.

Warriors dodged as I rode along the edge of a wide street to a wooden fence holding a few horses.

A young man — *Is he old enough to be a warrior?* — hurried from a building attached to the wall. "Leave your horse with me. I'll see him taken care of."

I dismounted and handed him my reins.

Before I could wonder how long I'd need to wait, Commander Osvif jogged to me. Red-faced and breathing hard, he bowed. "Sire. General Gudmann's eager to meet with you."

"I have something to share with him, too," I said. "Send word to the gate. Let Bior know I said he is free for the evening."

"Of course, m'lord. Once I've taken you to the general, I'll gladly pass the message along."

As I followed the commander back the way I'd come, Bior rode toward us.

"Guess you won't have to return to the gate after all," I said.

Osvif chuckled.

"Consider your duties fulfilled for the day," I said, as Bior stopped and saluted. "You are dismissed until first light tomorrow."

"Thank you, m'lord, but I was hoping you'd include me in your meetings," Bior replied.

I raised my eyebrows. "Figured you'd enjoy spending the evening with your cousins, and surely you know more than a few warriors here. Take the opportunity to talk with old friends."

He nodded. "Aye, Sire. I am keen on spending time with friends and family, but they'll be busy unloading supplies and stowing the wagons for some time."

"He's right, m'lord," Osvif commented.

I looked at the growing crowd near the open gate. "Find someone to take your horse to the stable and meet us." I looked at Osvif.

"The large building near the center of the hold with two guards at the door. You can't miss it," he said.

"Be there before you know it," Bior said, before heeling his horse to a trot.

"Anything I need to know?" I asked, as we started walking again.

"General's been a bit under the weather the past couple of days, Sire," Osvif said.

"Nothing serious, I hope."

"Herbalists have treated him," he said, shaking his head. "I'm sure he'll be fine."

"Good," I said. "Winning this war's going to be hard enough as it is. Don't want to think about what we'd do without Gudmann's experience and leadership."

"You'll get no argument from me, m'lord."

Bior, breathing heavily and a little red in the face, met us as the building Osvif had described came into sight.

"No need to rush," I said.

"Didn't want to get lost," he said, huffing. "Or pressed into working."

"More of the second than the first, I'd guess," Osvif said.

"Bior does what's asked of him," I said, defending my steward.

"As you say, Sire," Osvif said, nodding.

Bior muttered something I couldn't understand.

Osvif hurried to the guards and spoke to them as we approached. "King Fitzeirick, and his companion, to see General Gudmann," he announced.

"Welcome to Southold, King Fitzeirick," a guards said, as the other opened the door.

"The general is in his quarters," Osvif said, as we entered a torchlit hallway. A few paces in, the hallway continued to the left of a staircase. We clomped up the stairs, following Osvif to a closed door. He knocked.

The door creaked as it opened just wide enough for someone to look out. "The general is resting. Go away."

"I was told he was waiting for me," I said.

"You were told wrong. I'm sure he'll send for you when he wakes."

Osvif cleared his throat. "King Fitzeirick is here to meet with General Gudmann."

"Oh," the man said, from behind the door before swinging it open. "Apologies, my lord. I didn't know it was you. Let me light some candles and wake the general."

"Hakon, I'm already awake," Gudmann said, from inside the room. "Let them in and be quick about it."

"Yes, General," Hakon said. Sparks flashed then a candle flame grew, lighting the way for us to enter. His green robes billowed with each step as he went around the room, lighting candles in metal holders mounted to the walls.

"Welcome to Southhold, King Fitzeirick," Gudmann said, getting out of bed. He wore a thick, woven shirt and matching pants that a warrior has under his armor. "Good to see you, Bior."

Bior saluted.

"Again, I apologize, my king," Hakon said, bowing low.

"You're dismissed," Gudmann said. "I'll send for you if I think I need someone to worry over me unnecessarily."

"I'd advise you to rest, General," Hakon said, still looking at me. "You may not recover as quickly otherwise."

"I've beat this before, and it won't best me this time either," Gudmann responded, scowling. "Off with you before I lose my temper."

Hakon nodded and hurried out.

"Have a seat, Sire," Gudmann said, gesturing toward a small table nearby.

"If you aren't well, you can lay down while we talk," I said.

"Nonsense." The general coughed. "This happens from time to time. A change of the seasons or a storm carries an ill wind, and I get tired easily for a few days. Been dealing with it my whole life. Nothing to worry about...but Hakon doesn't listen. Stubborn herbalist."

I took my helmet off and placed it on the table. "They can be like that," I said, nodding as I sat.

Bior took the chair across from me.

"Commander," Gudmann said. "See that our guests have rooms ready and their gear is delivered quickly."

"Glady, General."

"I trust your trip was safe," Gudmann said, sitting.

"We arrived safe and sound but had an interesting night before arriving here," I said.

He nodded. "You got some of the nasty storm that rolled through here?"

"We did," I said, "along with a surprise visitor."

He frowned. "A visitor? Who?"

"Before we discuss that," I said, "Are you aware of an open burial site along the road between here and the turn to the eastern pass into Varia?"

Scratching his chin through his beard, he furrowed his brow for a moment. "Nothing of the sort has been reported to me. Why?"

"We found one. Many bodies were exposed. Several had parts missing."

"No doubt predators in the area dug up some bones to gnaw on," he said.

"Had I not seen it for myself, I might agree. There were no tracks or other signs of animals."

He shook his head. "I don't understand."

I raised a finger. "Another question. How close of a watch are you keeping on Satra?"

He smiled. "We have men on the southern wall at all hours. Events are reported to me three times a day."

"And have they seen anything?" I asked.

Bior shot me a questioning look.

Gudmann nodded. "We've seen occasional movement, which we assume are patrols, near the edge of the forest."

"They saw movement but didn't see who was there?" I asked, tapping my finger on the table.

"No one leaves the woods except to attack," Gudmann said.

"I have reason to believe the bones were taken by Satran raiders."

Bior's eyebrows shot up. He leaned forward in his seat.

Gudmann shook his head. "Having seen the destruction left behind by Satra's invasion, I better understand your hatred. I can't say I feel the same, but I do understand. Regardless, why would they need bones? How would they get them with a constant watch on the border? Most importantly, what makes you think they did?"

"Information from our visitor," I said.

"I don't doubt your word, Sire, but I'm not hearing an explanation," Gudmann said.

"Before I continue, you two swear what you hear next does not leave this room," I demanded. "Croian lives may depend on keeping this information secret."

"I swear on my life," Bior said, wide-eyed.

"I will keep it in confidence," Gudmann said, "same as all other secrets revealed to me."

"The visitor was a Croian who delivered valuable information about Satra. How their society works. What happened since we drove them from their stronghold beyond the central forest. And more. For example, he told me Porsey is dead."

"Interesting," the general said. "I received no report of a warrior seeing him fall during battle. How does this man know our traitor is dead?"

Bior stared at me.

"Porsey's lies caught up to him. The visitor witnessed the execution. From what he described, it was barbaric. Much worse than what I would have done."

"And you believe this man?" Gudmann asked.

"Thanks to my wife, I'm good at noticing when someone lies. This Croian gave me no reason to doubt his honesty."

"Fine, you say his word is true. I believe you," Gudmann said, "but why would Satra rob graves?"

"A secret group of Satran use taboo sything methods, one which allows them to weave stone, wood, and bone together into statues, called Stoneskins, which can move. After our successful attack, these Bonetakers convinced the warrior clan to overthrow the sitting rulers of Satra.

"Those rulers were forced onto the battlefield, facing our advance while the Satran soldiers and the Bonetakers secured their power. The graves were opened by another group made of the sick and outcast. The soldiers forced them to do the disgusting work."

"Assuming I believe this." Gudmann crossed his arms. "I haven't heard how they got past our watches."

"I don't know." I shrugged. "Perhaps they snuck through before this hold was in place, or some of your watchmen aren't as vigilant as they should be."

Bior shook his head. "Sire, if I may, I wouldn't make such an accusation outside of this room ... not without solid proof."

"Having been falsely accused myself, I know the implication. I'm not saying anyone should be punished, but everyone needs to be mindful of their responsibilities. It's also possible the attacks were diversions."

"Agreed," Gudmann said, nodding. "I will speak to the commanders. Do you have any other concerns before I give my report?"

"Some good news. King Crum will send soldiers to man this hold for us when we push south. We'll send a messenger to the eastern pass when we leave."

Gudmann smiled. "Good. One less thing to worry about."

"Stones off my shoulders, too," I said. "What do I need to know about Southold?"

Gudmann frowned. "We have a bit of a morale problem. These men have sat, waiting, long enough for some to question your commitment. Rumor is you've decided getting your old skati back is good enough."

I leaned forward, resting my elbows on the table, and laced my fingers together. "I did *not* send our warriors to fight for anything less than a complete victory, ending only when Satra is no more."

"I've said the same thing every time I hear a complaint," Gudmann said.

"I'll be happy to speak to the men and make sure they understand. What else?"

He shook his head. "Since my last message—"

I snapped my fingers. "Sorry to interrupt, but your mention of a message reminded me; I have a parchment to send to the bargemen."

"I'll arrange for a rider."

"Thank you."

He nodded. "To continue, there was an unorganized rush for our southern wall at dusk two days ago. Between the crossbowmen and archers, all but a handful fell before they got close enough to become a threat. The rest retreated."

"So, the new Varian weapon is useful?"

"Somewhat, Sire," he said, shrugging. "They're too cumbersome to use in the field, but the longer range makes them ideal for defending the hold."

"Good to know. I'll have to thank Kurt when I see him again. What else?"

"Hungry?" he asked, raising his eyebrows. "I haven't eaten lunch yet. We could go to the warrior's mess. Might help morale if the men see their king has arrived."

"Sounds good to me," I said, grinning as I grabbed my helmet and got to my feet. "I could use a warm meal. Please lead us to the warrior's mess."

"Gladly, Sire," he said, making his way to the door.

Chapter 21

Bior followed me, and we paraded down the stairs and out of the building, trailing behind Gudmann. We wound our way through the stronghold into an open passage entering a large stone building.

The dull roar of conversations died down as men recognized the general had entered the mess hall. Gasps and the clatter of chairs scraping on the floor filled the room when they noticed I followed him.

"I'm not here to interrupt your meal," I said. "Sit, finish eating, and see to your duties."

Each man saluted. Several said, "Aye, Sire." before returning to their seats.

"Line starts there, m'lord," Gudmann said, pointing toward the far-right corner of the room where a few men stood holding bowls, waiting to walk down the serving line.

It wasn't long before I had my stone bowl full of a steaming, dark liquid. Chunks of something, I guessed carrot and potato, bobbed on the surface. I took a sniff and decided it was rabbit stew.

Near the end of the line, a server offered me a tankard. "Ale, Sire. First pour from a fresh cask."

I smiled, cradled my helmet in my arm, and thanked him before following Gudmann and Bior to the nearest table with empty chairs.

"Hope you find the food acceptable," Gudmann said, before taking a bite.

"I'll take anything warm and filling," I replied.

A warrior sitting nearby got my attention. "What brings you here, my king, so far from the capital?"

"I'm here for the next step in the war. I'll lead you men across the border, taking the fight into Satra."

The warrior smiled and raised his cup. Several others voiced their agreement, saying things like, "It's about time" and "More than ready."

If they knew what they may face, they might not be so eager. I raised my mug and looked around the room, meeting gazes and returning smiles.

"You promised Queen Tindra you wouldn't fight, Sire," Bior commented. "And she expects me to keep you safe."

"I can lead our army into Satra without getting involved in combat," I said, before taking a drink. "Any thoughts on how our newfound knowledge of Satran society might be used to our benefit, general?"

Gudmann's spoon clunked into the bottom of his bowl. "I'd like a chance to discuss it with my commanders. They often come up with better ideas than I do. Would you like a tour of the grounds, Sire?"

"Only if we can go to my quarters first so I can get out of this armor, drop off my hammer, and grab the message for the bargemen. My request could be crucial as the war progresses."

"Of course, m'lord."

Gudmann led us back through the stronghold to a three-story building.

"Guest rooms are on the third floor," he said, before knocking on the door.

"We can't just go in?" I asked.

He shook his head. "First two floors house commanders. We have guards posted inside."

I nodded.

The door opened, and we were allowed in after a short conversation. A spiral staircase rose to the right of the hallway. Reaching the top, we stepped out into a hallway with windows in the right-hand wall. "Let's see where Osvif put your things," Gudmann said, looking back and forth.

A quick search told us Bior was in the first room on the left, and I was in the next one down the hall.

I used the candle just inside my door to light a few others, looked around, and didn't see my saddlebags. "After I change, let's find my saddlebags so I can get the message on the move."

"Most likely, they're at the stable where you left your horse," Gudmann said.

"I'll find them, Sire," Bior offered.

"Thank you. General, go with Bior. Two people searching are often better than one."

"As you say, m'lord," Gudmann said, with a nod.

A wooden desk and chair sat against the right wall, not far from the door. The middle of the room was taken up by a larger wooden table and chairs, suitable for serving meals for four or five men or holding a small meeting. A straw mattress sat atop a stone platform on the opposite side of the room from the writing desk, and a tall, wooden wardrobe stood near the foot of the bed. I stored my armor and hammer in the wardrobe, put out the candles, and closed the door on my way out. Jogging down the stairs, I dodged a commander on my way out.

Gudmann and Bior stood near the stable fence, discussing something. Many more horses stood inside compared to when I dropped off Andale. Bior had my saddlebags over his shoulder. He noticed me and waved.

Continuing my jogging pace, I crossed the road.

"Sire, find your message. General Gudmann will take you to find a messenger and continue with the tour while I take your bags to your room and make sure nothing else is missing," Bior said.

So much for him getting the evening to himself. "Give me a moment," I said, reaching to open a bag. It didn't take long to figure out that one didn't have the sealed parchment. "Turn around." The message had fallen to the bottom as I rode here. After checking the wax seal was intact, I looked at Gudmann. "Take me to a messenger."

Bior turned back to face me. "After I've taken care of your effects, Sire, what else do you need?"

I scratched my chin. "Find your cousins and enjoy what's left of the evening."

He bowed. "Thank you, m'lord."

"Make sure you're available in the morning," I said, trying to hide my grin.

"Of course, m'lord," he replied, before turning left and hurrying toward the field where the caravan would be parked.

I nodded. "General Gudmann, I'm following you."

He swept his arm in the direction Bior headed. "This way to the barracks."

Setting off at a brisk pace, we made our way through the flurry of activity still going on around the wagons. "Gudmann, without much fighting going on lately, there aren't any wounded to travel back to the capital. What will you do with the wagons?" I asked.

"Send them back empty for the next round of supplies ... unless you have a better idea."

I shrugged. "Not sure it's better, but given the number of men we're planning to move into Satra, perhaps we should use the wagons to carry supplies. Seems to me we could move faster or march the warriors longer if they weren't weighed down carrying food, tents, and such."

"We could, m'lord, but it carries extra risk. More things to guard, horses to care for, and if a wagon breaks down ... what do we do?"

I nodded as he listed the concerns. "It's not an order. Simply a suggestion. Think it over. Discuss it with the commanders."

"Understood, Sire. We can consider the merits over dinner this evening. Unless you want to eat with the warriors again?"

"It would be better to meet with the leaders tonight," I said. "I'm eager to see the elimination of Satra."

He turned to look at me and frowned before nodding. Pointing to yet another dark stone building ahead of us and to the right, he said, "The barracks."

Weaving through warriors and workers going about their tasks, we reached the building.

Gudmann pulled the thick, wood door open, and we stepped inside to a chaotic scene.

Some men were dressing, others were getting ready for sleep. A few dug through packs, scattering clothes and supplies on their beds and the floor.

The general pounded on the wall. "Who wants to carry a message for King Fitzeirick? Step forward."

All activity stopped. Men looked our way and saluted.

Gudmann cleared his throat.

I held up the sealed parchment.

Several men stepped away from their beds. One shouldered his way to the front of the crowd. "Skuf, my king, and it'd be an honor to carry your message."

I looked at him, standing about half a head shorter than me. An angry scar from a recently healed slice across his scalp was easy to see. He placed his arm across his chest again, exposing still bruised knuckles on his hand. As I looked from his hand to his face, I noticed an older, faint scar on his cheek, a line near the right corner of his mouth ending below his ear. "Looks like you've seen more than your fair share of fighting," I said. "Are you asking for this assignment to take a break?"

"No, Sire. I always volunteer."

"Sounds like my kind of man," I said. "I don't expect much danger, but it will take commitment and no small amount of speed. Time could be of the essence, depending on what we face entering Satra."

Skuf straightened his back, standing as tall as he could. "I'm your man, Sire. Tell me what you need, and it will be done."

I handed him the parchment. "Take this to the bargemen training on the coast, south of the capital. If you're of a mind to learn, stay and train on the boats. By the time you arrive, it will be the fastest way to rejoin the battle."

"I'm not afraid of a challenge, m'lord," Skuf said, taking the message. "Hope to see you on the battlefield, leading us to victory, Sire."

I nodded. "I'd like nothing more, but I promised the queen I wouldn't get involved in the fighting. I will do my best to make sure every man knows he has my support as we advance, though."

"I know a little of what you mean. My mother didn't want me to join the warriors, but here I am, doing my king's bidding. What more could a simple man ask from life?"

I chuckled. "Doubt you're as simple as you'd have me believe. Make sure the quartermaster gives you any supplies you need for the trip. If he refuses, show him the seal and explain you're carrying orders."

Gudmann snickered. "Supplies won't be a problem, m'lord. Quartermaster Aron won't deny his younger brother anything."

"And if he did, I'd best him and take what I wanted anyway," Skuf added.

I laughed. "Use my seal to get the best horse."

"Aye, Sire," Skuf said.

"Be assured, you are seeing to an essential task. Travel safe and swift."

"I shall, my king. When the fighting starts again, strike hard and true," he said, before stepping around Gudmann and me to get out of the barracks.

"Ready to peer into Satra?" Gudmann asked.

"Yes."

We reached the southern wall with little delay. Gudmann led me up three flights of stairs to the top. I was breathing heavily by the time we reached the archers' walk and looked south to survey the lands of our enemy.

"Ever been here before?" Gudmann asked.

"Never came this far south."

He pointed. "Every charge has come from the forest, but we have no idea what lies beyond."

My heart pounded as I tried to catch my breath — *Why am I winded?* — and take in the view. A grassy prairie stretched out from the wall to a river, maybe ten or fifteen paces wide, cutting across the land shortly beyond where the shores made a natural choke point by pinching the land from both sides. Two intact bridges crossed the river along with the broken remains of three others. Fifty or so paces from the river, the edge of a forest concealed the land. Trees stretched to a distant, hazy range of mountains crossing the land from one side to the other.

"What happened to those three crossings?" I asked.

He shrugged. "Like that when we got here."

"Any idea how deep the water is?"

"Since you ordered us to stay out of Satra until you arrived, we haven't sent anyone to investigate. Given the bridges, I'd guess it's too deep to walk across."

I scratched my chin and stared at the water, noticing it sloshed back and forth as waves traveled to the shore on either side. "We'll find out when we get there. How soon could we have the army ready to cross?"

"Tomorrow evening or the morning after. If we decide to use wagons, add a day to get everything loaded."

"Let's get the commanders' opinions over dinner. I've seen enough. I want to lay down. This trip must be wearing on me; I'm growing tired."

"Of course, Sire."

Workers were still busy with the wagons as I followed Gudmann to my quarters. "You need help up the stairs, m'lord?" he asked, smiling.

"No." I returned his smile. "Have someone get me for dinner. It's time we prepare to head south."

He nodded. "Many here will agree, Sire. A commander will come for you before dinner is served."

I thanked him and headed to my room where I took off my boots and lay down to rest.

Chapter 22

Someone pounded on my door.

"One moment," I said, sitting up and pulling on my boots.

Commander Alrik stood in the hall when I opened the door. "Time for dinner already?" I asked.

"Will be soon, Sire," he said.

"After you," I said, pointing toward the stairs.

He led me out of the building, into the dimming light of evening, back to the building where I'd met with General Gudmann earlier.

We entered a large room where the general sat at the table with the rest of his commanders, as well as two who served under General Nothri before I had him executed. Everyone stood and saluted.

"Thank you," I said, returning their salute. "Be seated. We have several things to discuss."

"Of course, Sire," Gudmann said. "Our food will be here soon."

I nodded and walked to the other side of the table so I could watch the door.

Alrik sat across from me.

"What do I need to know?" I asked.

A commander on my side of the table cleared his throat.

I turned, craning my neck to look past the men sitting between us. It was Sturla, one of Nothri's men.

"My king," he said, "many of the men grow restless. Several under my command question your commitment to this war. There's talk of desertion."

"I'm aware," I said, nodding. "I'll call a meeting tomorrow after breakfast and address the warriors. I want everyone confident in my dedication, knowing I'm ready to lead them to victory."

"We can pass the word after —"

Several men came into the room, interrupting General Gudmann. Our dinner arrived with a couple of small casks. Bowls and spoons were passed around. The smell of warm bread filled the room.

While stew was ladled into our bowls, a couple of men filled mugs from the casks and sat our ale in front of us.

"As I was saying," Gudmann continued, after the servers left. "My commanders will pass the word to their companies. Do you want attendance mandatory?"

I grabbed a roll, took a bite, and considered the question while chewing.

If everyone's there, I only have to say it once, but if I'm forcing troublemakers to attend ... I swallowed and shook my head. "I'd like every warrior to hear what I have to say, but don't force anyone. Anything else we need to address before I speak?"

Alrik took a drink and nodded as his mug hit the table. "The southern wall's been quiet since the last attack."

"I understood the attackers were killed before reaching the stronghold. Correct?" I asked.

"Yes," he replied.

"What happened to the bodies?" I asked.

He shrugged. "Gone by sunrise."

"More often than not, a thick fog rolls in from the water as the heat of the day fades," Gudmann added. "I've seen it deep enough to hide the bridges. No one saw who took the bodies."

Sounds like ideal cover. I tapped my fingers on the table for a moment. "I need everyone here to make it clear to their warriors; from now until the war is over, no dead body — Croian or otherwise — is left intact in the open. If you cannot bury the body deep enough no one would think to look for it, smash every bone you can."

Several commanders shifted in their seats.

Alrik looked at me, wide-eyed. "Why must we stoop to disrespecting the dead? Are we not better than that?"

I closed my eyes and rubbed my temples. *Blind loyalty only goes so far. If they're going to follow my orders, they have to know why.* "I'm told there's a group of men, now ruling Satra, who practice forbidden sything methods. Weaving stone, wood, and bone into something resembling a statue, except it can move."

Several men scoffed. Someone blurted, "Impossible."

"None of us have been into Satra," Sturla said. "How did you come by this information?"

"You shouldn't question our king," Gudmann admonished.

"No," I said. "Considering who he once served under, I can't blame him for being suspicious. He's right to ask. There are Croians living in Satra —"

"I knew Porsey wasn't a traitor," someone commented.

"Whoever said so lied," I said, hitting the table. "If you came up with the idea on your own, you have no idea how wrong you are. Porsey was, yes ... he's dead now. He *was* a traitor and a liar. His lies caught up with him.

"As I was saying. As part of a pact between Croy and Satra, Eirick sent two Croians to live among the Satran League ... the *former* rulers. One of them came to me during the recent storm. He gave me valuable information hoping to broker an alliance between our army and the former Satran rulers. They offered to help us defeat the Bonetakers if I put the League back in power."

"Never!" Alrik barked.

A smile crossed my face. "Exactly. We don't need their help, and I will see them all dead. Now, and listen closely, here's another thing you need to tell your men. After their defeat in our central forest, the Legion pulled their soldiers from the field and forced the overthrown League members to fight. Our warriors haven't faced trained, dangerous soldiers since before they delayed our charge at the wall north of here."

"Can't be the case," Commander Gesta, the other of Nothri's men, said. "We fought them hard every day. Even with superior numbers, it was a battle."

"Overthrown men of the League were given a choice, die where they stood or fight on the battlefield so their families wouldn't be outcasts; banished to be Bane, the lowest of the low in Satran society. Their motivation wasn't simply living to fight another day. How hard would you, any of us, fight to keep loved ones from being treated worse than animals? Would any of you do less than fight to the last breath?" I stood. "We need to understand what kind of people we'll face when we cross into Satra."

"Uncivilized brutes," someone said.

"It's not so simple. As it was explained to me, every Satran — save the rulers — face a hard life. Their soldiers endure beatings and abuse unless they are of top ranks. Otherwise, their families suffer. Every day, Satra's craftsmen and farmers live with the threat of someone taking what they want, as much as they want. Not only taxes or tributes ... I'm talking about soldiers forcing young men to join their ranks so their family can keep their land ... their homes. Their leaders take food, goods, even flesh, at a whim, simply because they can."

"Why don't the people rise up, fight?" someone asked.

"I had the same question," I said, nodding. "They fear the consequences of losing more than they hate their treatment. Should they start an uprising and lose, they are disgraced and made Bane. To the average Satran, life may be hard, but living in the Bane clan ... most see it as a fate worse than death."

"Could we not take advantage of this divide?" Alrik asked. "Recruit these Bane, maybe the others you mentioned, to fight at our side?"

"The whole point of this war is to eliminate everything Satran, to remove the entire nation from the world. Satra's unprovoked invasion damaged Croy, spilled innocent blood, and"—I tapped the traitor's brand burned into my cheek—"left me with this. They must all pay the cost. If we're not committed to that task, why continue fighting? Does every man in this room stand with me in this effort?"

"Aye," Osvif said, raising his mug. "We do."

Gudmann stood. "Sire, we follow your orders, but I fear your need for vengeance could turn us barbaric. Some of our men...well, one specifically already seems to be taking that path."

I locked eyes with him. "Who?"

"Fastulf."

"What has he done?"

"He's taken to collecting trophies," Gudmann said.

I shrugged. "Men taking weapons from fallen enemies is not unheard of. Surely that's not bothering you."

"Taking teeth seems like it crosses into the territory of savage."

I squinted. "Taking — did you say *teeth*?"

The general nodded. "Ask any man in this room. The leader of the guides wears a leather cord around his neck strung with teeth he's ripped from his kills."

"Why am I only hearing of this now?" I demanded.

"Because we only learned the truth recently," Gudmann explained. "Most of us knew about his necklace, but we thought he was sything the teeth from stones as mementos. No one suspected they were real until he showed Commander Hottir how he put holes in them. Looking back, I should have mentioned it earlier, but given your requests when you arrived, it seemed like it could wait. I apologize if I was wrong."

As if I needed another problem to deal with. I blinked several times before sitting. "I'll speak to him tomorrow ... after addressing the warriors."

Gudmann nodded and sat. "Hottir, make certain Fastulf is available to meet with the king at Fitzeirick's convenience."

"Gladly," the commander replied.

I pinched the bridge of my nose. "I could use more ale."

Alrik reached for my mug. "I'll fill it for you, Sire."

"Thank you," I said. "Earlier today, General Gudmann and I discussed using wagons to carry supplies into Satra. On one hand, it would lighten the burden carried by our men. On the other, we'd have horses to care for. Anyone have any thoughts?"

"Are we leaving this stronghold empty?" Commander Ketill asked.

I swallowed a mouthful of stew. "Varia has men ready to secure this hold while we push south. They'll bring their own supplies."

"But will they have extras for any wounded we send back?" Gudmann asked. "Or for when we return, after the battle's won?"

"Good point," I said. "We need to send a resupply list back to the capital. How soon will the quartermaster have the list ready?"

Ketill's mug clunked on the table. "When do you want it?"

After taking a drink, I shrugged. "Once we send for them, the Varians will arrive in two days or less. A messenger can reach the capital in two days. A day or more to gather supplies and load ... say, three since they'll need to find wagons. Two days later, the caravan arrives."

"I'll make sure the request leaves before we do," he replied, nodding.

Pointing to Gudmann, I asked, "How soon could we be ready to go south?"

He tapped a finger on his chin and looked at the ceiling. "I'd say at first light the day after tomorrow if pushed—assuming we have to load the wagons. Sooner if we decide to carry everything on our backs."

I smiled. "Either way, let's aim for after lunch the day after tomorrow. I'll let everyone know during my address tomorrow."

He nodded.

Several other commanders voiced their agreement.

"Should help morale," Osvif commented.

"Anything I can do to help," I said, raising my mug before taking a drink. "Now, are we taking the wagons or not?"

"With less load on the men, we can move faster," Osvif said. "I say that advantage outweighs the need to care for the horses."

"Aye," Commander Hegg agreed.

"Then it's settled. We take the wagons into Satra. What else do we need to discuss?"

"General!" a voice boomed outside the room. "General! Movement!"

Gudmann jumped to his feet, knocking his chair over.

I hurried to stand and headed toward the door.

A red-faced warrior rushed into the room. "General!"

"I heard you," Gudmann said. "Another attack?"

"Not sure." The warrior pointed toward the wall. His chest heaved as he tried to catch his breath. "Fog. Fires glowing. Shadows."

"General." My heart thumped in my chest. "Let's see what Satra's doing."

Chapter 23

I followed Gudmann out into a night lit by the full moon. A general and the king leading a parade of commanders attracts attention. Gudmann gave orders, without breaking stride, sending his commanders to gather forces at assigned posts.

I bumped into the general when he stopped a couple of steps up the wall. "Osvif, stay here. Alrik, Hottir, come with us," he said, before climbing the stairs without waiting for a response.

When we reached the top, everyone peered south, weapons at the ready.

"Report!" Gudmann barked.

One of them pointed. "Another fire lit right before you arrived, sir."

A chill ran down my back as I looked at the three, bright patches glowing in the thick fog, creating halos around tree trunks. Shadows shifted back and forth as the flames flickered and danced.

Pulling my eyes away from the light, I found the bridges hidden by the moisture hanging in the air. It also covered most of the field between our stronghold and the forest. Mist swirled lazily around the upper tree branches as far as I could see into the dark forest.

A fourth fire flared farther back than the rest. *Must be firesyths out there.* A shorter shadow flitted across the scene before disappearing. *What are they doing?*

The wind shifted, carrying the smell of something, maybe pork, cooking or burning.

Putting both hands on the dark stone in front of me, I pushed my talent down the wall, hoping I could detect anything moving on the ground in front of us. The effort was futile. I got light-headed before even a trickle of energy reached the dirt. *Silly to even try. If this is an attack, we can't let them get to the wall unchallenged.*

"Thoughts?" I asked no one in particular, keeping a hand on the wall to stay balanced.

"It's not normal," Alrik said. "I've spent lots of time here, watching. Never seen anything like this. Their last attack came before the fog rolled in."

"But they must know the fog hides them," Hottir said.

"Except the fire gives us an idea of where they are," I countered.

"True," Gudmann said. "But we can't see what they're doing."

"But if no one's seen this before," I said, running my hand through my hair, "why tonight?"

"A celebration of some sort," Hottir said. "Maybe?"

"Decent guess," Gudmann replied, "but who celebrates within sight of the enemy?"

"Anyone else have an idea?" I asked. "Could they be preparing an attack?"

"We didn't know they were out there until they lit the fires," Gudmann said. "Who prepares to attack by letting the enemy know where you are?"

As soon as he finished talking, the fires went out.

Soon after, screams rose in the forest.

A cloud of squawking birds erupted from the trees.

Hairs on my arms stood as the flock flew toward us. Passing overhead, their calls filled the air. Any sounds from the forest were drowned out until the swarm passed.

"Keep your eyes open!" the general shouted.

What's happening? I peered into the deep mist for clues.

"Crossbowmen. Archers," Alrik barked. "Watch close!"

"For what?" someone asked. "We can't see a thing."

He's right. We're practically blind.

Screams rose again, closer.

"If you see anything moving, shoot it," I said.

"Aye," an archer to my right replied.

Something splashed in the water ahead of us.

Bows creaked as their strings drew tight.

Pointless. An army could cross the field, and we'd never see them. "Gudmann, we need men on the ground to make sure nothing reaches the wall."

More splashes.

"Big risk," he said. "Our warriors won't see an attacker until they're on top of them."

"It's an even bigger risk to let them open a hole in our wall," I countered. "Send our spear point; they won't be blind."

"Fastulf? Are you sure you want to send him, Sire?" Gudmann asked, scowling.

"I'll deal with him tomorrow, either way," I replied, crossing my arms. "We *must* defend the stronghold, and his group is our best choice. Put them on the field."

He frowned and nodded. "Alrik, send word. The king wants Fastulf and his crew, yes ... I know, outside guarding the wall. Tell Osvif I want extra warriors along the inside of the southern wall in case someone punches through before the guides take the field."

The commander turned to leave.

I grabbed his arm. "Tell Fastulf they are *guarding*, not hunting. Make sure he knows our bowmen may be shooting blind. I don't want our men hit."

"Your words from my mouth, Sire," Alrik replied.

"One more thing," I said, letting go of him. "Tell them I said to not leave bodies on the ground. Bring the bodies inside the stronghold once the fighting is over."

"I'll make sure he understands, m'lord," he said, with a nod, before hurrying down the stairs.

"Is it necessary to drag bodies in here?" Gudmann asked. "You honestly believe they're using bones?"

The distinct sound of stone grinding against stone came from the forest.

"Hear that?" I asked, pointing toward the forest. "Ever hear anything like it before?"

He chewed his bottom lip for a moment. "No."

"So, we know Satra is doing something we've never seen before. They have a weapon, be it moving statues or something else, unlike anything we know of. Is it not wise to take every precaution?"

"Aye, Sire," Gudmann said, nodding. "It is the safe choice, even if I find it distasteful."

I offered him my hand. "We'll treat their dead with more respect than they'd treat ours. You have my word."

He gripped it firmly and looked me in the eye. "I'll hold you to your promise. Speaking of wise decisions, if this wall shakes — even the slightest tremble — you get down as quickly as you can, Sire."

I glanced at the ground below, inside the stronghold. *A fall from here might not kill me, but I don't like my odds of walking away from the impact.* "I'll do my best."

"Open the gate," someone bellowed below.

I shifted my focus down the wall and to my left. A stream of men, clad in black armor and wielding swords or axes, poured out of the opening and quietly spread themselves along the base of our southern wall.

Hope Fastulf listened to my orders. My heart raced, pounding in my chest. *Now we wait for ... something.*

"Eyes sharp," Gudmann barked. "If something moves, call out before you release an arrow."

"This is like hunting rabbits in a briar patch at dusk," a nearby archer muttered.

To our right, someone on the ground cried out in pain. Everyone turned to look for the source.

I saw nothing but swirling mists.

More screams came from the base of the wall. This time close enough I thought I heard a blade cutting cloth as the blow struck. *Someone's attacking but how many?*

Something hit the wall with a hollow thump.

Gudmann raised his eyebrows. "Maybe you should head to the ground."

"That was a sound, not a tremble," I said, smiling.

He frowned.

"If it happens again, I'll go," I replied. "You have my word."

He turned, looked over the wall, and shook his head. "Can't see a thing."

The unmistakable sound of steel smacking flesh reached us.

"Open the gate," Fastulf yelled. "The attack's over."

Gudmann looked at me. "That quickly?"

"I'd trust him and his men to know if anyone was alive between here and the water."

"With him out there, I'd be surprised if anyone is alive," Hottir said.

I shook my head and hurried down the stairs.

Chapter 24

Bior was waiting for me. "Sire, is everything all right?"

I tilted my head. "I believe the situation's well in hand. You're welcome to join me and see for yourself."

He grabbed my arm. "Sire, first. Fastulf. There's something —"

"I already know. I'll talk to him tomorrow."

"Oh. Fine ... yes. Let's go."

The gate was closed and barred by the time I reached the ground. Warriors stood in a half circle; a few held torches, and the rest had weapons at the ready.

"Report!" I yelled.

"King Fitzeirick. Thought I saw you up there," Fastulf said. "Good to hear your voice, m'lord."

Men moved out of my way.

"From what I can tell, your defense was successful," I said, pausing to look over the short warrior hefting a wet, rag-covered body over his shoulder.

"This one's still alive," he said, smiling. "Found him huddled against the wall. Snuck up and knocked him out cold."

Bior sucked in a breath next to me.

I nodded. "How many others were out there?"

"We killed four, Sire," someone near him said, pointing to the bodies piled together.

"I need light," I said, taking a knee next to the dead.

Bior called for a torch and held it over the pile.

A quick examination showed they were all gray-skinned men wearing soaked, tattered rags. Two were barefoot. Their thick, black and gray hair was matted and tangled. *No doubt they're Satran.* Each had several scars on their face and, from what I could see, their arms. Here and there were fresh cuts, likely from running through the brush before they fell into the water. One man was missing an arm at the elbow; the jagged wound had healed long ago. "Any weapons?"

"Nothing we could find," someone said.

"They didn't fight?" I asked.

"Never had a chance," Fastulf said, bravado in his voice.

Bior scoffed.

I stood. "Bury the dead. Someone get General Gudmann for me."

"Already here, Sire," Gudmann answered behind me. "What do you need?"

"Secure this man. Get a herbalist to check him over and wake him, if possible. We have questions. Maybe he has answers."

"Any idea of his talent?" the general asked.

I turned to Fastulf and raised an eyebrow.

"He wasn't sything the wall, so I doubt he's a stonesyth, Sire. Otherwise, not a clue."

"You two," Gudmann said, pointing. "Bind his arms. Chain him to the wall in a cell. Someone fetch a herbalist to the jail. Osvif, arrange a guard detail. I want eyes on this Satran until he wakes. When he does, let King Fitzeirik and me know immediately."

After two men lifted the prisoner from Fastulf, I grabbed his shoulder. "We don't know what's happening in those woods. That could have been a diversion. We're going back up to watch. Gather your men at the gate. We'll send word if we want you on the field again. Warriors, back to your positions and be ready."

Climbing to the top of the wall took more effort than I expected.

Bior lagged behind, his limp slowing him. His breaths came in huffs when he reached my side. "What. Are. We. Looking. For?"

While trying to catch my breath, I looked out into the fog and saw nothing. *I don't like this.* "Gudmann, should we send them out?"

"What's going on?"

"I don't know," I said, "and that bothers me. When does the fog usually clear?"

"When it's this thick, well after first light."

I sighed and hit the wall with my fist. "Has anyone seen any movement?"

"No, Sire," one of the crossbowmen responded. "Not a thing."

"That rush earlier doesn't make sense," I commented.

Bior chuckled.

"Hard to fight an enemy we don't understand," Gudmann said.

"King Fitzeirick! General Gudmann! The prisoner's awake!" someone yelled from below.

I grabbed the general's arm. "Where are we needed more?"

He looked over the fog-covered field and sighed. "Feels like we're wasting time here. Let's see if we can learn anything from the Satran."

"Men, stay sharp. Raise an alarm if you see or hear anything. Have a commander send Fastulf out if you suspect anything is coming," he said, before turning toward the stairs.

Commander Sturla waited for us at the bottom. "The herbalist checked him over. Said he seemed unharmed. A splash of water in his face woke him. I came as soon as I knew he'd stay awake."

"Has he said anything?" I asked.

"Keeps asking everyone if they are the boss," Sturla said. "Won't look anyone in the eye."

Exactly what I'd expect from someone mistreated their whole life. "If he's waiting for a boss, maybe he'll talk to a king."

"Commander Sturla, you're in charge until I get back," Gudmann said, before leading Bior and me to a small building beyond the warrior barracks. He opened the door and announced our arrival.

Two men stepped out and waved us inside.

We entered a room big enough for no more than six people to stand in with a bolted door in the opposite wall. Gudmann slid the bolt back, opened the thick, wooden door, and descended the stairs leading underground.

My chest tightened.

I stumbled, hesitant to enter the dark opening. Touching the wall, I felt energy in the natural stone and drew a little into my body to ease my fear.

Flickering torchlight marked the bottom of the steps, leading into a hall wide enough for three people to walk shoulder-to-shoulder with six cells down the left side. A couple of steps in, I noticed the stale air smelled fresher than I expected and didn't carry the stench of a well-used dungeon. Two men stood at the far end, staring into the last room.

"After you, my king," Gudmann said, stepping aside.

I nodded and strode to the end of the hall.

Bior followed a few steps behind.

The odor of someone who had gone many days without washing hung in the air outside the cell. The prisoner's hands were bound in a metal ring attached to a short chain buried about waist-high in the back wall of the cell. He didn't look when I approached the bars.

"Are you Vos?" he asked.

"Vos?" I asked, shaking my head. "I don't know what that word means. Who are you?"

"I belong to Vos Sifet."

Must be the chieftain Rorec mentioned. "Look at me, and let's talk."

The prisoner raised his head, stared for a moment, and lowered his gaze. "The scar. You Vos Fitzeirick...no?"

I nodded. "I am King Fitzeirick. I'll ask again, who are you?"

"I am Bane," he answered, shoulders sagging. "Belong to Vos Sifet."

Bior cleared his throat. "My king asked for your name. Answer him."

Shaking my head, I put my hand on Bior's shoulder. "What do other Bane call you?" I demanded.

"Da'rin."

"Where is this Sifet?" Gudmann asked.

"With Friend Rorec, beyond —"

"Stop!" I yelled, and pointed toward the staircase. "Everyone out."

The guards shrugged and hurried past me.

"Why?" Gudmann asked. "What are you hiding?"

"I'm protecting someone from rumors," I said, grabbing his arm. "I'll tell you anything I learn to help win the war."

He scowled.

"I'm asking...nicely," I said. "Don't make me order you."

Gudmann turned, pulling his arm from my grip, and stomped away.

Bior nodded, turning to follow the general.

I followed my steward and tapped him on the shoulder before his foot hit the first step.

"A favor," I whispered.

"Yes, m'lord. What do you need?"

"A blade. Do you have one?"

"Why?"

"In case something should go wrong."

Bior looked at me sideways before reaching into his boot. "Here."

"Thank you. Please bolt the door and make sure no one interrupts me."

He looked over my shoulder and nodded before leaving.

Carefully tucking the knife into my belt behind my back, I waited for the thud of the bolt sliding home.

The Satran will talk ... one way or another. I took a deep breath and hurried back to the cell. "You'd mentioned Sifet was with Rorec. Continue from there."

"We wait for friend Rorec and others. We had to move friend Asfrid. Vos Sifet said to keep her safe."

Guess Rorec was telling the truth about why he was in Satra. "I want to make sure I understand. Sifet's with Rorec. Asfrid, Rorec's wife, is hiding with the Bane."

"Ya. Right."

I scratched my head. "What about the fires? Why light them in the fog?"

"Lel and Daro snared a pig. We cut it between us to eat. The meat smelled bad. We wanted to cook it. Thought we were safe. Stoneskins hadn't been here before."

My eyes opened wide. "You were attacked by Stoneskins?"

He nodded. "One smashed our hut. I put the fire out. We ran. Most died before we got to the water. Couldn't find a bridge so I swim. Stoneskins and water don't mix."

"How many Stoneskins were there?"

Dar'in shrugged. "Saw one. Heard others."

"Five of you reached us. How many Bane were waiting for Rorec?"

He closed his eyes for a moment. "Four groups of four. The dead ones never rest."

After scratching my chin, I pointed at him. "What do you mean?"

"Stoneskins take bodies to Bonetakers. Bonetakers build Stoneskins. Dead Bane never rest."

I closed my eyes and took a deep breath to fight shivering at the sight forming in my mind. "Are all Bane used to make Stoneskins?"

"Can't say."

I nodded. "Where is Asfrid?"

"Only Friend Rorec should know."

"I'm a friend of Rorec," I said, flashing Da'rin a smile and spreading my arms wide. "I met with him shortly before coming here."

"Vos Sifet keeps her safe. Friend Rorec keeps him safe."

I nodded and put my hands on my hips. "Sensible, admirable even. As king, I'm in a better position to get word to Rorec, *and* I can help keep Asfrid safe, too. Tell me where she is."

He eyed me before turning away and shaking his head. "Only tell Friend Rorec. Keeps Vos Sifet safe."

I'm done being nice. Pushing my will into the stone floor, I forced the ground up his legs, hardening as it passed his ankles. "You belong to me now," I growled. "I'm vos here. Tell me where I can find Asfrid. I give you my word, as King of Croy, I'll get her back to Rorec." *Roi would never forgive me if he found out his mother was alive, and I didn't do everything I could to save her.*

Through my connection with the stone binding the prisoner's feet, I felt the shiver rack his body. He swallowed a couple of times. "First village south of the sea of black sand."

"I need more details. Where should we look?" I asked, tightening the stone until I felt the blood pulsing in his feet. "Tell me everything."

He crouched, putting his arms in an awkward position. "Bonetakers ordered everyone south. Legion moved us at spear point. We came back —"

"Are your boats still there?" I asked, interrupting him.

"Boats?" he questioned, frowning. "No boats. We walk."

"Don't lie," I said, squeezing the stone around his feet until bone scraped bone. "You can't walk across a sea. Tell me where you hid the boats."

He drew a hissing breath. "No lie to Vos. No boat. No need. Walk the edge."

I relaxed the stone a little. "It was faster for you to walk around the sea than cross it?"

"Ya, Vos. Right. Easier to walk."

Good to know. "Then what?"

"Hid in the forest. Waiting for Vos Sifet, Friend Rorec, and the others."

"How long were you hiding?"

"More than a moon, less than two," he answered after a short pause.

"How many soldiers are in the forest?"

"None. Never saw Legion there."

"There were no patrols? No soldiers looking for you?" I asked, furrowing my brow.
He shook his head. "No, Vos ... none."

"Why did the Stoneskins attack tonight?"

"Who can say," he replied.

Sounds like even the Satran people don't know what their leaders are doing. "Back to
Asfrid. How do I find her?"

"Find Bane. Say Da'rin said to tell."

"Sounds too easy," I said.

"Ya, Vos. Just say Da'rin said."

"What else can you tell me? Is this village hard to find?"

"Harder to miss. South. Watch out for Stoneskins. Pass the mountains to black sand.
Cross. Another pass. Village."

As he explained, I had trouble imagining the path he described. "The black sand sea
is between two mountains?"

Da'rin nodded, before shaking his head. "Mountains all around."

I pursed my lips for a moment. "So, it's surrounded by mountains?"

"Ya, Vos. Right."

Sounds more like a lake. No wonder he could walk around it. "I need to know
everything. What haven't you told me?"

"Told all, Vos. No lies."

Time to cut him loose. "Good." I smiled and unlatched the cell door. "Because you've
been cooperative, I'll do you a favor."

"Serve you, like Vos Sifet? Yes."

The prisoner stood more than a head shorter than me. "No." I grabbed his chin,
tilting his head back to expose his throat. "I'm going to let you rest."

I reached for the knife and opened his neck.

Hot blood sprayed from the smooth line Bior's blade sliced in the Satran's blotchy
skin. The warm, sticky fluid coated the underside of my arm.

Pulling back, Da'rin freed himself from my grip. His mouth moved as he tried to
speak, but no words came out.

A coppery smell hit my nose as the wound's flow slowed. The scent brought to mind
the day I killed Eirickson. My chest tightened for a moment before I clenched my teeth.
Both men had more merciful deaths than they deserved.

The prisoner shuddered one last time before sagging against the chain binding him
to the wall. I ripped a piece of his tattered shirt from his back and used it to clean the
knife before wiping the blood from my arm. *One less Satran to deal with. Many, many
more to go before we're done.*

I strode to the top of the stairs and pounded on the heavy door. "Bior. It's done."

The bolt slid free of the wall, and the door opened slowly.

I handed Bior his knife. "Thank you. I need to talk to Gudmann."

"As far as I know, the general went back to the wall," Bior said, studying the blade.

"I'll find him. Send a stonesyth to the cell to bury the prisoner."

Bior bowed and moved to let me pass.

Chapter 25

Warriors were barring the gate as I reached the wall.

Fastulf stood near General Gudmann and a couple of commanders near the stairs, discussing something.

"All is well, general?" I asked, approaching the group.

"Yes. We're likely safe for the night."

I nodded. "Fastulf, you and your men get some well-earned sleep."

Fastulf saluted. "Thank you, Sire. Should you need us again, we'll answer your call."

"General, escort me back to my quarters. We can talk before I turn in for the night."

"Commander Osvif, you're in charge. Keep a few men near the gate until first light," Gudmann said.

Osvif nodded and pointed to Commander Sturla. "Gather men for the gate."

Sturla turned on his heel, hurrying toward the barracks.

"The prisoner was still talkative after you ran everyone out?" Gudmann asked, as we walked away from the crowd.

"Yes, he was helpful."

"And will he cooperate further, should we ask?"

I took a deep breath and glanced around, noting how many people were still within earshot. "Best we not talk where others might hear something out of context. I sent everyone out to avoid rumors, after all."

Entering my quarters, I noticed a small barrel with the tap installed and several cups sitting on the table. "You know anything about this?" I asked, pointing.

Gudmann shook his head. "Looks like a barrel of ale. You weren't expecting it?"

"Didn't ask for anything to be brought to my room." I pushed the container. It felt full. One of the cups held a small parchment.

To your continued good health, my king.

Hakon

"It's from your herbalist," I said, handing the note to Gudmann.

He glanced at it and took a seat. "An attempt to gain your favor, most likely. Mind if I draw a cup? Easier to talk when my throat's not dry."

I nodded and sat near him. "Fill one for me. I'd hate for you to drink alone."

The general smiled, offered the first cup he filled, and poured one for himself. "What did you learn?" he asked, before taking a drink.

The ale tasted more bitter than usual but went down easy enough. I gave the general a summary of what Da'rin had said, raising his eyebrows when I mentioned the lack of patrols until tonight.

He emptied his cup and sighed. "We missed an opportunity to enter Satra unopposed."

"Not necessarily," I said, before emptying my cup. "The prisoner said people were living in the forest until recently. No telling how much resistance they were willing to give."

"True, but now we have to face those stonemen —"

"Stoneskins."

"Stonemen, Stoneskins, whatever. Don't see why it matters what you call people who can crush huts barehanded."

"Not people. Think of them as moving structures."

"That doesn't help," he said. "Don't like the idea of telling our warriors to fight a moving wall."

I nodded. "We'll figure out how to beat them. At least we know they don't like water."

"Should we go to war carrying buckets?" Gudmann asked, grinning.

"Not a sound or reasonable strategy, if you ask me." I smiled at his quip. "Still, knowing water affects them somehow is a benefit. Could be we can use the sea I keep hearing about to our advantage, but it seems I sent the bargemen on a fool's errand when I told them to map it."

"Why?"

"From what the prisoner described, it's a lake surrounded by mountains. Doubt the barges can reach it, but we can travel around it, from what he said."

Gudmann rubbed his chin for a moment. "This Satran seemed all too eager to help. We should consider the possibility it's a trap of some sort."

"Bane submit as a way of life. I made him understand I was the authority here."

He snapped his fingers. "He can get us deep into Satra with little danger."

"No, he can't," I said. "He's dead."

Gudmann squinted and tilted his head. "He's — what did you do?"

"Slit his throat. He didn't suffer."

The general slammed his fist on the table. "Why?"

"Too much of a security risk to let him live. He'd seen inside the stronghold and could tell his countrymen about our defenses and forces."

Gudmann glared. "And he was Satran."

"That too."

"May I speak my mind?"

"I've always welcomed your honest opinion," I replied, after draining my cup.

He stood and pointed at me. "Your blind hatred is a problem."

"It's not blind hatred. It's payback for what they took from our country and from me."

"Hatred, payback, revenge ... call it what you will, but it all means the same thing. You and I both know there's no reasonable way to kill every Satran out there. Insisting on trying to do so is a waste of our men."

I crossed my arms. "Yet leaving them alive means we could fight this war again. If not in my lifetime, certainly in my children's. Seems like a bigger waste of men."

His jaw clenched, and he shook his head. "There's another way."

My eyebrows raised on their own. Pointing to the chair, I tilted my head. "Give me your suggestion."

Gudmann wiped his hand across his face and returned to the chair. "Pluck out and burn the Satran leaders and fighters. Convert the rest of the people to our way of life. This avoids future fighting *and* saves lives."

Rubbing my chin, I locked eyes with the general. "You've spent your whole life as a warrior for Croy. Why are you concerned with saving lives? Especially those who've inflicted so much harm on our country."

He narrowed his eyes, and his cheeks reddened. "I'm not as concerned with Satran lives as I am with the lives of those I command. How many warriors will die, killing men and women who might otherwise not fight? Surely these Bane would submit to your rule as easily as they do their current leaders."

I shook my head. "Eirickson ruled Croy as a tyrant. I refuse to rule as an oppressor."

"I didn't say you had to enslave them." Gudmann tapped his finger on the table before pointing at me. "One more thing to keep in mind. We can't fight on empty stomachs. How many supply caravans will it take before the war is finished your way? Killing every last Satran is an unnecessary waste of Croian resources."

I stood and yawned. "General, we could argue forever. It benefits neither of us to continue, plus I need sleep. I respect your opinion. It has merit, even if I don't agree with you. Ultimately, the decision is mine. I depend on you to carry out my orders. However, if you cannot, you are free to step down. I'm not *asking* you to resign. I don't *want* you to resign. Perhaps you should consider how important this issue is to you before we set foot on Satran soil. I'd hate to change generals in the middle of a battle."

His mouth opened and closed a couple of times as he stood.

I offered him my hand. "Sleep on what I said. I'd prefer you stay and lead the army."

He gripped my hand gently and shook it with a limp wrist. "You've given me much to think about. May you sleep well, my king."

Following him to the door, I bolted it after he left, cleaned my armor, and changed into nightclothes. It took a while to settle. Several times I wiped at my forearm, where it had been coated with blood before. When a knock on my door woke me, I felt far from rested.

Yawning as I got to my feet, I rubbed my eyes and shambled to the door. "Who's there?"

"Bior, Sire. I brought breakfast."

I opened the door and let him in.

He looked at me sideways when I pushed the barrel to the side of the table to make room for the basket he had brought. "A gift from Hakon," I said. "Not the best ale I've ever tasted, though."

He took a small stone pot from the basket, placed a couple of bowls on the table, and filled them with boiled oats before pouring a couple of cups full of dark, steaming tea.

I sniffed at the drink, got a noseful of sweet but pungent steam, and scowled. "Any idea what's in this?"

Chuckling, he shook his head.

I glanced at the barrel of ale before taking another spoonful of clumpy oats.

Bior laughed but didn't take a drink of the tea.

My resolve crumbled after swallowing the grains, and I took a sip. It had a tangy flavor I couldn't place, but it wasn't bitter. "Not terrible. I wouldn't want it every day, but I've had worse."

Bior nodded and took a drink. "Agreed. Might be a decent drink on a chilly night."

"I don't want to be cold enough for this tea to improve my situation. I assume you've been paying attention while spending time among the warriors here. What are you hearing?"

"About what, m'lord?"

I shrugged. "Anything. Everything."

Bior swallowed a spoonful of grains. "I'd say the general attitude is happy enough. An idle warrior is a bored warrior, but your arrival gives everyone the expectation they'll be on the move soon."

"I'll let everyone in on the plan this morning."

"Good idea, Sire. A couple of things you should know. Word of your contest with King Crum has spread, and the story gets better with each re-telling. To hear some, you could take on the whole nation of Satra barehanded, by yourself."

I chuckled. "It doesn't hurt for my army to believe I can take care of myself in a fight. What else?"

He tapped his cup on the table several times before taking a drink. "Fastulf, Sire. I know you chose him, but ... there's something wrong with him."

"I know. Gudmann told me about the necklace," I said, frowning. "Fastulf's talented, but that doesn't excuse his actions. I'm going to speak to him today. If he doesn't promise to stop, I'm sending him back to the capital to train new recruits."

"Sounds like a solid plan, Sire, but who will take him to the capital if we aren't returning any time soon?"

"He can do as he's ordered or sit in a cell until he changes his mind."

Bior laughed. "Or figures out how to escape."

"I would have to take that into consideration." Smiling, I raised my cup to him before emptying it. "Breakfast *and* wise council, hard to ask for more from a travel companion."

"Doing my duty the best I know how, m'lord." He returned my smile.

Someone knocked on the door.

"Come in," I called out.

Commander Sturla stepped into the room and bowed. "Apologies for interrupting your breakfast, Sire, but General Gudmann said you'd want to know the bridges were damaged last night."

An unexpected problem. Clapping my hands together, I pushed my chair back from the table. "Guess breakfast is done. Sturla, please have someone clear my table. Bior, let's see how bad it is."

"I can see to the mess," Bior offered. "Doubt I'll be of much help on top of the wall."

"Never know what you might notice," I said, standing.

Bior stood. "As you say, m'lord. Let's see what we can see."

Chapter 26

We dodged our way through groups of men moving about the stronghold on our way to the southern wall.

Bior followed close behind, slowed by his limp.

"Good morning, General."

"Morning, my king."

I followed Gudmann's gaze toward the bridges. They sagged in the middle as if loaded near their breaking point, but there was nothing on them. "No one saw what happened?"

"No, Sire. I'd guess it was sabotage covered by the fog. Would have been nice to see if our Satran guest could have told us anything else."

"He told me everything he knew. Bior, any thoughts?"

"Without a closer look, and assuming most of the wood left is in usable condition, they can be repaired, but it's going to take some new wood."

"Gudmann, how many builders do you have here?"

"We sent most of them back after the stronghold was built. Maybe a dozen stayed to address any further needs—emergencies and such. Mind you, Sire, they aren't warriors. If Satra attacks ..."

I put my hand on Gudmann's shoulder. "Send someone to gather the builders. Call a meeting so I can address everyone. Bior, bring Fastulf to my quarters after I finish cheering up the warriors. Gudmann, you and I will meet with the builders after I've spoken with Fastulf."

"I'll make sure he meets with you," Bior said.

"King Fitzeirick, where do you want to speak to everyone?" Gudmann asked.

He's still upset with me for killing the prisoner. Hope we can get past this. Turning, I pointed to the ground below us. "Why not there? I'll stand in front of the gates."

Gudmann turned and looked down. "Should be enough space. I'll get the word out."

Leaning against the wall, I let him pass and followed Bior down the stairs.

"The commanders will round everyone up. I'll find the builders," Gudmann said, as we reached the ground. "Whatever you're going to do to prepare, my king, I'd say start now. We shouldn't take long."

"I'll be ready to speak as soon as the crowd's gathered, general."

He nodded and strode toward the barracks.

"Sire, is something wrong?" Bior asked.

"Nothing you need worry about." *What happened between me and Gudmann stays between us.* "Everything's going to be fine. Make sure Fastulf is available."

"I'll find him now, m'lord."

Once a few warriors had passed, clearing the area near the gate, I moved to where I wanted to stand and looked over the open area. Pushing my talent into the ground, I made a small rise to stand on before reaching deep to pull a stone podium to the surface in front of me.

Watching as warriors and workers filled the area brought a smile to my face.

Fastulf led his men to the front.

Bior stood next to him.

Once I felt sure everyone had arrived, I gripped the stone before me tightly and pushed my voice through it. "I know you are all busy, so I'll try to keep this short. Last night, several Satran rushed the southern wall under the cover of thick fog. A company of brave warriors stopped the threat. Also, the remaining bridges were destroyed. If they thought their actions would change our minds and call off our plans to conquer their country...they are wrong.

"Yes, it will take some time and effort to repair the bridges before we cross into Satra, but that will not stop us. To you, the best army Croy has ever sent to battle, I say prepare your gear and yourselves ... we march into Satra soon. No doubt you are sick of fighting on Croian soil. I know I am. Soon, you will spill Satran blood on their ground. Rest assured, Satra's time grows short." Pausing, I swept my arm across the crowd. "Your skills and sweat will end it."

As cheers and battle cries rose from the men, I looked at Bior and nodded toward Fastulf.

My steward put his hand on the small warrior's shoulder. Fastulf looked at him and smiled.

Raising a hand, I called for quiet. "Thank you for your enthusiastic agreement. It does my heart well knowing you stand ready to fight for your country and your king. Now, go and prepare. You will be called on, soon, to do what you do best. Win. You are dismissed."

The warriors cheered and left the meeting with their heads held high.

"Well said, King Fitzeirick," Gudmann said, as he approached. "Where should I gather the builders?"

"I'm going to talk with Fastulf in my quarters. Plan to meet there. I'll send Bior after the lead guide and I are done. Fastulf's decision could impact our plans."

"I'll gather them in my meeting room and wait for word there, my king," Gudmann said, nodding before walking away.

Chapter 27

I let the crowd thin before walking to where Bior held Fastulf. When I reached them, I offered the guide leader my hand. "Thank you for what you did last night. Let your men know their effort made a difference."

He stepped away from Bior and took my hand. "We're always ready to serve, m'lord."

"I have something to discuss with you in private. Accompany me to my quarters. Bior will make sure we are not disturbed."

"Gladly, Sire," Fastulf replied, bowing.

"Bior, lead the way."

My steward nodded and turned to head toward my room. "Make way for your king!"

Bior opened my chamber door. "I'll stay outside and make sure you aren't interrupted, Sire."

Smiling at Fastulf, I motioned for him to go ahead. "Have a seat at the table."

The door closed behind us.

I looked at Fastulf after sitting across from him to see if he looked nervous or upset. More than anything, he looked excited to be in my presence. "We're here to talk about a rumor."

He crossed his arms. "I'm not one to spread rumors, m'lord."

I shook my head. "This one is about you."

Cocking his head, he shifted forward in his chair. "I've done nothing to warrant rumors. You gave me a job. My men do what I say. We've been above reproach since we took to the field. What's being said about me?"

"Whispers about a necklace are reaching my ears."

Fastulf relaxed and smiled. Reaching down the front of his shirt, he pulled a dark cord out. It ran through several yellowed teeth. "That's not a rumor; it's the truth. Impressive, wouldn't you agree, Sire?"

"I'd like a closer look," I said, reaching across the table.

"Absolutely," he said, pride clear in his voice.

I took it from him and ran my fingers over the ornaments, hoping to find they were fake.

By their shapes, most of them appeared to be front teeth, but a few were flatter, blocky rear teeth. *I'm pretty sure these are real.* Looking Fastulf in the eye, I frowned. "I don't know what to say. How did you come to do this?"

"M'lord, you haven't heard the story?"

Looping the cord around my thumb, I leaned forward to rest my elbows on the table. Lacing my fingers together, I dipped my chin toward him. "No. Enlighten me."

Fastulf took a deep breath. "It started the night we attacked. I cut down a couple of soldiers before we were noticed. Soon we were in an all-out brawl ... steel on steel and flesh on flesh. We couldn't kill them fast enough to prepare for the next attacker. I'd finished off a soldier. Someone grabbed my arm. No one around me could help, so"—he raised his left fist—"I punched him in the mouth. A sharp pain ran from my hand to my shoulder. He let go, and I made him pay for grabbing me. My hand continued to throb, hurting every time I moved a finger, but I had to keep fighting."

I nodded.

"It seemed like the battle would never end. Dead Satran lay everywhere. A few of our warriors were down too. Every warrior still standing bled from several wounds before our main force arrived. Then Satra couldn't stop us.

"Once the fighting slowed, I examined the injury. Fresh blood trickled around a bone sticking out between my first two knuckles. I ripped cloth from a dead Satran's undershirt, wrapped the wound tight to stem the bleeding, and fought on."

Wincing, I rubbed the back of my hand, imagining the pain. Fastulf must have noticed the look on my face because he nodded.

"By the time I could spare a moment to care for myself, the cut had scabbed over but still ached, especially when I moved my fingers. When herbalists arrived, I asked one to look at it. Cleaning the wound exposed a tooth." He lifted his left hand again and pointed to a spot on the back. "I have this scar to remind me. Kept that tooth and took one from every kill since."

I twitched my thumb, rattling the necklace. "How many?"

"Fourteen. Would be more if I'd started collecting at the first attack."

"No more." Slapping my hand on the table, I fixed Fastulf with a hard stare. "It stops. Now." I raised my eyebrows. "Understand?"

He froze for a moment before furrowing his brow. "My king. Why?"

"Because this is barbaric. Our enemies disrespect the dead; we are better than them. Our war is meant to rid the world of such distasteful behavior. Croy cannot afford for its warriors to become that which we seek to eliminate. Am I clear?"

His face reddened as he stood. "I did exactly as you asked, m'lord. I was your speartip. My blade, my hands, dripped with the blood of our enemy because that's what you sent me to do. What's wrong with taking small trinkets to count my personal victories?"

Keeping my eyes locked with his, I rose from my chair. "I was proud of your company, your leadership, until I heard about this." I shook the necklace. "You serve as an example. Your conduct sets the standard for what others can expect from your men. These trinkets soil your reputation.

"Had you been collecting blades or armor or cloth, so be it, but disrespecting the dead is *not* acceptable. Leave this necklace with me and stop taking trophies from bodies, or you will suffer for it. My army will be worse for the loss, but I'll do what I must."

The young man shivered and sank to his chair.

I kept my weighty stare on him, hoping it would hold him in place. "I don't want to punish you. If you listen to me and learn from your poor judgment, you'll be a better leader for it. Ignore my direction and lose your position. Those are your options. Which do you choose?"

Color faded from his cheeks. "Sire, must—" He swallowed. "Must I decide here? Now?"

"Did you take any time to *think* before deciding to rip teeth from the mouths of the dead?" I asked, shaking the necklace again.

He shook his head, turning more pale.

"Decide. *Now.* I need you. Croy needs you. We don't need this." I threw the necklace to the floor and ground it under the heel of my boot.

Chewing his bottom lip, Fastulf lowered his eyes. "My king...I'll stop. As you ask."

"Stand. Look me in the eye. Give me your word as a warrior," I demanded.

The young man rose, met my gaze, and shivered. "I will stop collecting teeth. You have my word. On my honor, I will make you proud again or..." He sucked in a shuddering breath. "Or you may take my life, Sire."

"No need to go to such an extreme," I said. "Rest assured, I have no interest in killing you. If you break your vow, you will be relieved of duty, escorted to the capital, and put to work under Captain Agrim's direct supervision. You will never see another battle."

He bowed. "Understood, m'lord. Thank you for your mercy. I will not let you down again."

"Good. Now, make sure your men are well rested. I suspect you will be called to action soon."

He looked at me, and his eyes lit up. "We're ready when you need us, Sire."

Pointing toward the door, I nodded. "You're dismissed. On your way out, send Bior in."

"Gladly." He bowed again. "And thank you again, my king."

"Oh. Fastulf. One more thing."

He stopped, hand on the doorknob. "Yes, Sire?"

"If any of your men have joined in this practice, I expect you to put a stop to it immediately. Should I catch word of such behavior from any of your guides, you will be sent home with the offenders. Am I understood?"

He turned to look at me. "I swear, I'm the only one, and it will never happen again."

"Good. You may go."

He bowed low before hurrying through the door.

Bior entered with a questioning look.

"I believe he understands his behavior is not acceptable. At the least, he gave his word not to do it again, even offered me his life."

Bior chuckled.

"I made sure he knew that was not my intention, but I did point out what would happen if he went back on his promise. Now, I need you to do two things for me."

"Aye, Sire."

"First, go to Gudmann's meeting room. Tell him I spoke with Fastulf and addressed the situation, though I would like the general to have someone keep an eye on our young collector ... to be sure. Let him know I am ready for him and the builders to talk with me. Second, have some tea brought here. If you can't find tea, water will do."

"If my king wants tea, he gets tea," Bior said, bowing.

"But I want it soon," I said, "preferably no later than Gudmann's arrival. Might be best to secure several pitchers and plenty of mugs. I don't know how long we'll be talking."

"With all haste," Bior said, turning for the door.

"Pushing my voice through the stone left me drained. I'm going to rest until the men arrive. Make sure Gudmann knows to knock."

Bior turned back to me. "Are you sure you want to meet now? I could tell Gudmann about Fastulf and let him know you're resting and will ask for him later."

I shook my head. "I want to plan for our advance as soon as possible."

"I'm sure you're not the only one, Sire. Rest well."

Chapter 28

I was nearly asleep when the door opened. *I told him to knock.* Something thunked onto the table. Rolling to face the door, I found Bior whispering to a couple of men holding pitchers.

Clearing my throat, I croaked out my thanks, startling everyone. Bior almost dropped an armload of cups.

"Sorry, Sire. Did my best to not disturb you."

I waved at him and sat up to pull my boots on and get something to wet my throat.

"Gudmann is on his way," Bior explained, as the men left.

Grabbing a cup, I poured it full of dark liquid and drained it in one gulp. "I'd like for you to stay for the meeting and share any suggestions you may have. Go ahead and change the candles. No telling how long this will take."

He nodded as I refilled my cup. "Sire, I noticed something earlier. I'm not sure it should be my concern, but I'm curious."

Stopping mid-drink, I nodded and swallowed. "Of course. What's bothering you?"

His hand wavered as he put a fresh candle in place. "General Gudmann. It seems there's a rift between you two. Maybe I'm wrong, but he wasn't as," he paused and scratched his chin, "polite, I suppose is the right word, with you this morning."

Lifting my cup, I stared into it. *If Bior noticed the tension, likely others did too.* "He and I have a difference of opinion."

"Over how you handled the prisoner?" Bior asked, rubbing his chin.

I frowned. "Well...yes. He questioned my reasoning. Accused me of being driven by blind hatred. I explained why it was in our best interest for the Satran to die and made it clear, though I don't want to replace Gudmann, the good general was free to step down from his command and go home."

Bior's jaw dropped. "I see."

"Second thoughts on your part now?"

"What? No. No, Sire ... not at all. You have no reason to doubt my loyalty. It's — Gudmann served alongside Hallfrid. He could've learned some of his tricks. Perhaps I should watch your back more closely."

Shrugging, I finished another cup of tea. "I don't believe Gudmann will cross me, but anything is possible. I expect you to act in my best interest. If you believe there's a threat, handle it. Don't wait for my approval."

He nodded. "Yes, m'lord. Thank you for your confidence."

"If I didn't trust your judgment, you wouldn't have come with me."

The sound of boots approaching echoed in the hall.

"Invite them in," I said, before filling my cup again.

He hurried to the door, looked out, and turned to me. "Sire, there isn't enough room for everyone at the table."

How many men did Gudmann bring? "We'll make do. They can stand or," I paused and looked around the room, "sit on my bed or wherever there's space."

He nodded. "General Gudmann, please, come in. King Fitzeirick is ready to see you."

I stood when the general walked through the doorway.

He nodded and strode to the table, leading in at least a dozen men. "King Fitzeirick, are you feeling better?"

"Much," I replied, smiling. "Thank you for getting so many men together."

With little more than a nod, he sat. "My king has needs. It's my job to fill them to the best of my ability."

"Builders, thank you for answering my call. There's tea, if anyone would like."

I waited until everyone who wanted a drink had one, then looked at everyone crowding the room. "There's work to be done, and the sooner it's finished, the better. I want to march into Satra soon. For this to happen, we need a way to cross the water between us and them. Last night, the existing bridges were damaged. This was the work of cowards. The Satran are afraid to face us. Frightened of what's to come. They think this will stop our advance and rob us of victory. I ... we know better. However, now we must check the bridges. Repair and make them stronger, if we can, or replace them if we must. I need to know you can do what's asked. More importantly, we need to know what you need to give me two solid bridges across the water."

A tall, thin man stepped forward. The skin on his willowy arms stretched tight over stringy muscles. Sunken cheeks made him look underfed. "None of us have seen the structures as they are now, my king. Without examining what we have to work with, I doubt we can give you an answer."

"What's your name?" I asked.

"Orri, Sire."

Smiling, I stood and offered him my hand. "Well met." His grip confirmed the strength in his hand. "We need, at least, two strong bridges. I think any work done should combine stone and wood, woven together, but you builders will know what's best."

Gudmann cleared his throat. "The structures stand, but they are visibly sagging. I'm no expert, but I'd guess they can be repaired."

The builder nodded. "There's stone aplenty around here. If we need to take some trees, we'll have to search for suitable ones. Regardless, this sounds like a lot of labor. How soon do you want this done, Sire?"

"Ideally? They were finished yesterday." I chuckled.

Gudmann grunted.

"Truthfully, I want to move quickly," I said. "As far as I'm concerned, manpower is not a problem. Whatever you need, ask. I'll put the wagons at your disposal to transport men or materials."

"Protection, m'lord," Orri said. "We're not fighters."

I glanced at Gudmann.

He raised his eyebrows and nodded. "You will be kept safe."

"The general and I will discuss your guard in detail after we're done here. But I agree, your safety is our top priority until the work is done and you're back inside the stronghold."

"We need to look at what's there and what needs to be done," Orri said, looking from Gudmann to me. "Would that be possible now?"

"How close do you need to be to get an idea?" I asked.

"So long as we have a clear view, Sire. We shouldn't need to dip our toes in the water yet." Orri smiled.

I returned his smile and nodded. "Bior, take Orri and however many want to accompany him to the top of the wall. Any builders not going to look should be planning. Expect to work like we only have one try to get these bridges rebuilt. Are there any more questions, or should we end the meeting now?"

"Who do I speak with when we're ready?" Orri asked.

"Contact General Gudmann. If he has any concerns, he'll bring them to me," I said, looking at the general again.

Gudmann nodded. "I will keep King Fitzeirick informed."

"Let's see what we have to work with," Orri said.

"Bior, make note of their needs and get the list to General Gudmann. Come see me when you're through."

"Aye, Sire," Bior said, getting to his feet.

General Gudmann and I waited for the room to clear.

"My king, what do you have in mind?" he asked.

"My biggest concern is protecting the bridges at night. I believe Fastulf's company is best suited for this duty."

He crossed his arms. "How am I supposed to keep eyes on him if he's in the field?"

"If he's going to take teeth again, it won't be so soon after being told to stop. Don't worry about it now. With the night watch covered, how should we protect the builders during the day?"

"Depends on a couple of things." He raised two fingers. "First, how many men do they need for labor? Second, how big of an attack could we face?"

Rubbing my forehead, I shrugged. "Don't know the answer to either question. Will the builders demand every man here act as labor?"

"No, but you gave them the wagons too. They'll need drivers."

I nodded. "Which we have. How about we plan on three companies for labor. Ninety men should be plenty."

"Agreed. Make sure most of them are stonesyths."

"Right," I said, nodding again. "And exempt any archers from working so they can be dedicated to defense."

"Yes. But how many other warriors do we send outside the walls?" Gudmann tapped a finger on the table. "We have no way of knowing what Satra could send our way. Maybe two companies on the field during the day? The warriors helping the builders can also fight if needed."

"Except a tired warrior is a sloppy warrior, and the laborers will work hard to finish the bridges quickly. How about two companies on the field with two more ready to join the fight."

His finger stopped short of hitting the table again. "Good point and a solid plan. We'll need another company ready to support the guides should something happen at night."

I shook my head. "Too risky. The guides know how to move and fight in the dark. No one will get past them without taking losses. It's better to double the gate guards after dinner should Satra launch an attack."

"Sounds like a good plan," Gudmann said, a wide smile spreading across his face. "One question. How soon do you want to enter Satra?"

"No more than a day after the bridges are ready. Have every spare warrior making preparations now."

The general shook his head. "We can't load the wagons if the builders are using them. Plus, the pulling horses will be exhausted."

Wiping my hand across my face, I closed my eyes and sighed. "To the fire with whoever damaged those bridges."

"It definitely delays our advance. Perhaps they are buying time, preparing for our attack."

"I'm afraid you're right. Still, I'll call them cowards in public. Better for morale, I think."

Gudmann grimaced. "Never knew you worried about morale."

I tilted my head and steepled my fingers in front of my chest. "I know what it's like to have nothing but hope as a foundation for my morale. Had I let my spirits fall, I'd be long dead. Can I still depend on you to do what must be done for Croy?"

He eyed me for a few heartbeats before giving a shallow nod. "Yes."

Pressing my fingers together, several knuckles cracked. "Bior knows you're upset with me. I'll allow you to speak freely to me in private, but you should consider how you address me in public. Bior won't say anything, but if he noticed the tension between us, others will too, and rumors will not help our cause. What would morale look like if my top general is sent back to the capital before we advance?"

"I'm staying for the men and because I do believe Satra is a continuing threat to Croy. I don't agree with your ultimate goal, but we lost too many Croians to Eirickson's scheming. I'll do my best to be civil toward you for the good of my country."

I offered him my hand. "Guess I can't ask for much more. You have a lot of planning to do, and the sooner things get moving, the better. Keep me updated, and let me know if I can help."

After gripping my hand for a moment, he got to his feet. "I will, to the best of my ability."

Chapter 29

After Gudmann closed the door, I held my head in my hands and sighed heavily. *Why does everything have to be so complicated? We have men, well-trained men, ready and willing to fight for Croy, and they're sitting here doing nothing. Obviously, it was wrong to order the warriors to wait for me to lead them into Satra. All I can do is make the best of the situation. Tindra said every scar is a lesson. I've learned a new one; pride leaves scars no one else can see. Too bad I had to leave my wife behind. I could use her insight.*

The door opened. "I was coming to let you know —" I lifted my head and saw Bior with a concerned expression. "Are you sick, Sire?"

"No. Frustrated."

He furrowed his brow and closed the door.

"I need a friendly ear." I pointed to the chair across from me. "Sit, please."

"I'm not much for giving advice, Sire, unless you need to fight someone," he said, taking the seat.

Tapping my finger on the side of my head, I grinned. "The fight's in here. I'm doubting myself. Second-guessing some decisions. Did I cost us a chance at a quick victory?"

His eyes opened wide. He sucked in a deep breath, pressed his lips together for a moment, and exhaled with a loud whoosh. "Well ... I mean ... I'm no expert ..."

"Take a moment. Gather your thoughts, and speak freely."

He nodded and wrung his hands together for a few heartbeats. "I guess I don't understand why you'd ask such a question."

"Thinking about the bridges and the effort we'll spend fixing them. Had I not wanted to lead the army into Satra myself, the fight would be well underway. Perhaps, victory could be close at hand now. Instead, we're delayed further and exhausting our warriors to get back to where we were before I arrived. Did I do the wrong thing?"

He smiled. "I don't think you did."

I chuckled. "You can speak your mind. No need to agree with me. I need honest counsel."

"Consider what you've learned by coming here. You met with a Croian living among the Satran. He told you more about their country than any of us knew. You interrogated the prisoner, knowing how to use his status to get more information from him. No one else could have. Not as easily, anyway. Plus, you know they saw through Porsey's lies and took care of him for us."

Imagining what the former Thane looked like, hung upside-down and bleeding from the mouth, sent a shiver down my spine. "Knowing the traitor's dead is a small load lifted from my shoulders, but none of the rest was necessary for us to destroy Satra. Their society won't matter when they're all gone."

"Think of it this way," Bior said, crossing his arms. "What makes for a more successful hunt? Going after beasts you know nothing about or tracking game animals you know well?"

"I get your meaning but —"

"But nothing," he interrupted. "The better we understand our enemy, the more successful we will be. As far as their society mattering, consider this. We know the new Satran leadership is inexperienced. That can only work in our favor. We know the Bane will crumble under the slightest pressure. It's unlikely they'll resist our advance, and our warriors can cut them down easier than a woodsyth dropping a dead tree. The Devoted are used to working for tyrants. Surely we can use them to our advantage until they are no longer needed."

"You think I want to be a tyrant?" I asked, blinking several times. "You believe I want to lord over people, force them to do my bidding?"

He chuckled and shook his head. "Not at all. Honestly, I'm certain you're not interested in such behavior at all. If you were, Hallfrid would still be alive, taking care of your enemies. That doesn't mean the Devoted can't be convinced otherwise. And it's better their labor benefits Croy for a while instead of continuing to support Satra throughout the war."

I sighed and tilted my head back, looking at the ceiling. "For someone who's not good at giving advice, you seem to have a pretty clear idea of what we should do. How long have you been thinking about this?"

"Not long." He chuckled. "I'm surprised you didn't put it together yourself."

I brought my chin back down to look at him. "I have a lot on my mind."

"True. And you're more focused on killing all the Satran than using them first."

Tapping my finger on the table, I glared at him. "Don't tell me you're on Gudmann's side."

Crossing his arms, he shrugged. "I'm on Croy's side. I firmly believe it's in my country's best interest to conquer Satra and eliminate the threat to our future. Contrary to General Gudmann, I don't disagree with your decision to kill the prisoner. Had he escaped, he *could* have given information to our enemy. It's good you gave him a clean, merciful death. Had you tortured him, you and I would've had words already. Still, the general has a point."

"One he and I don't agree on."

Bior nodded. "Think about it like this. Eirick used Satra. Eirickson used Satra. There's no reason you can't use them too."

My glare turned into a scowl. "I am neither my father nor my half-brother. If they did it, that's a good reason for me to never consider taking similar action."

He stood, put his hands on the table, and leaned toward me. "My king, don't be so stone-headed. They were selfish. You don't have to be. Croy can use the extra manpower to rebuild the war-torn lands. Using Satran labor to repair the damage they did only makes sense. Using the conquered enemy to benefit Croy leaves a far better legacy than that of your kin."

"Sounds a lot like slavery," I said, holding my angry expression.

"Not as such. Those who want to work, who can show they'll follow our laws, and who contribute to a prosperous Croy can join our society. Much like Eirick did with the Varians who chose to stay."

I opened my mouth.

Bior raised his hand, cutting me off. "Before you protest, his plan *worked*. Despite Eirickson's hatred of them, Croy was never damaged by the presence of the Varians. Remember, you, yourself, are a product of such mingling."

"I'll never forget my heritage," I said, closing my eyes. "What were you coming to tell me?"

"I left Orri and his assistants on top of the wall to discuss the challenges they see in completing your request."

"Thank you. Now, you've given me much to think about, but I'm tired. I'm going to lay down and rest."

"What about lunch, Sire?"

"Not hungry. Check with me before dinner."

"Should I send a herbalist?"

"No." I smiled and shook my head. "All I need is a nap."

"Aye, m'lord. As you wish." He turned for the door.

As I settled into bed, I called for him. "One more thing. See if there's a messenger available to leave for the capital tomorrow."

"Of course, m'lord. If I'm not overstepping, what do you need to send? I can write it for you now if you'd like."

I chuckled. "I doubt Tindra wants to read a message written by your hand."

He grinned. "Oh. Right. And I don't need to know what you're saying to the queen. I'll make the arrangements. Rest. I'll check on you later."

I thanked him and waited for the door to close before laying my head on the pillow.

Chapter 30

A low, grumbling noise disturbed my sleep, waking me enough to realize it was my stomach growling. *Guess I should eat. How long have I been asleep?* Looking around the room, I noticed all of the candles were burning low, a couple burned out. *Been out a while. Where's Bior?* Getting out of bed, I pulled my boots on and crossed the room to the candlebox near the door.

After replacing the candles, I noticed a basket on the table. The pitchers and cups were gone. Looking closer, my quill, ink pot, and a few sheets of parchment sat near the basket. *Maybe this is Bior's way of letting me know he found a messenger, but why leave a basket?* I rubbed the sleep from the corners of my eyes.

Opening the basket, I found a piece of parchment lying across something on a stone plate and a large mug filled with something.

My king,

You were deep asleep when I came to get you for dinner. I decided it best to leave you alone. Should you want to eat, I left two rolls with roast deer on them and a mug of water.

Gudmann arranged to have a messenger ready to leave anytime after first light tomorrow. I will report on the builders when I bring breakfast tomorrow.

Bior

I smiled and took a sip to wet my throat. While eating the first roll—it probably tasted better hot—I considered what to tell Tindra. Half the mug was gone before I inked my quill.

Tindra, my love,

Though I haven't been away long, I miss you. So far, the trip has gone well. A little excitement after we left Varia, but I should tell you the story in person. Don't worry, no one was hurt, but I got some useful information.

Crum brought great news. Jesca is doing well and with child. She's getting the life she deserves. Crum's going to be a father. I can hardly believe it. Will I feel the same way when we have our first child?

I found my old home, or where it once stood. Raised a large stone and fashioned a memorial for my mother and Aesa, with plenty of room for other names to be added. I'd like us to visit it together, once the war is over. The war. To be honest, I'm doubting myself or at least my decision to delay the advance. I could use your support and counsel. Bior's trying to help, but he doesn't have your experience or insight.

I interrogated a Satran prisoner and got valuable information from him before I killed him. Not sure if you'd be proud of me, but it was necessary. My decision put me and Gudmann at odds, but the general will do what Croy needs.

If everything goes to plan, I'll lead the warriors into Satra soon. Maybe around the time you receive this message. I know you believe I'm going to fight, but I have no intention of taking part in the battles to come. You have my word; I will watch from a safe distance with Bior at my side. I still have questions about the land we're going to take and want to see it firsthand.

I hope the castle construction is going well. I can't wait to return victorious and see our new home.

With Love,

Fitzeirick

I folded the sheets, coating the edges with wax from a nearby candle. After dribbling a puddle over the seam in the back, I pressed my seal into it and blew on the wax to help it harden. Convinced it wouldn't come open accidentally, I put the candle back and finished my dinner.

The door opened slowly as I swallowed the last bite. "Who's there?" I asked.

Bior's head came into the room. "Sorry, Sire. I didn't mean to disturb you."

"You didn't. I was eating and writing to Tindra. Do you need something? Come in."

He stepped into the room and closed the door. "Need something? No, Sire. I couldn't go to sleep without checking on you first. Worried, I guess."

"Appreciate your concern," I said, smiling. "I'm feeling better. No doubt I'll be back to normal by morning."

"Good to hear, Sire. Sleep well." He turned and reached for the door.

"Hold on," I said, waving him to the table when he looked at me. "You're already here. Give me a quick report on what the builders think about the bridges."

He nodded and sat across from me. "Orri wanted a closer look, so Gudmann sent half a company out with him to examine the area. I watched from atop the wall and met them at the gate when they returned."

"You saw no movement on the Satran side?"

"Nothing but grass and leaves blowing in the breeze."

I rubbed my hands together. "Either Satra has no scouts, or they are extremely patient."

He nodded. "General Gudmann had the same thought. Orri said the damaged beams are woven solidly into stone. His men can syth new wood to them and reinforce the span. Gudmann sent warriors north with a couple of builders to find suitable trees."

"Good. We can't waste time. When did they get back?"

"They were still out at sunset. Gudmann said if they aren't back by sunrise, he'll send men to find them."

Rubbing my finger on my lips, I frowned. "The Satran did take a lot of our resources. Perhaps it's harder to find the right trees. Anything else to report?"

Bior nodded. "Orri's concerned about the weight of weaving stone with the wood, how to properly support it over the water."

"But he has a plan?" I asked, tapping my finger on the table.

"Said he had a couple of ideas," Bior answered, shrugging. "He's worried about how solid the ground is near the bank and under the water."

I clapped my hands together. "So, we're waiting on trees and a plan to support the weight. Anything else I need to know?"

"No, m'lord. I believe that's a good summary of the situation."

"Thank you. In the morning, I don't want boiled grains for breakfast. Perhaps a light broth or thin stew instead."

"I'll make it myself if I have to."

I smiled. "Worst comes to worst, boil some dried meat and bring it to me."

Bior stood and nodded. "Hope you get the rest you need."

"Sleep well."

He bowed before closing the door.

I made my way around the room, blowing out all the candles but one, and lay down. I eventually fell asleep, but it was far from restful. I was mostly awake when the door opened and Bior looked into the room.

"Come in. I was about to get out of bed anyway."

"Brought you some rabbit broth. Boiled the dried strips myself. I'm not alone, m'lord. Hakon heard you weren't out and about yesterday afternoon and insisted on checking on you."

I sighed and sat up. *Doesn't this herbalist have anything better to do?* "He's welcome to come in, but I'm just road weary."

Hakon shouldered past Bior as the door opened wide, nearly knocking a bowl from my assistant's hand.

"Sire," the herbalist said, stopping less than an arm's length from me. "I don't mean to be a bother, but I want to be sure General Gudmann's illness isn't affecting you, too." He turned to Bior. "I need more light to work."

What's the hurry? I got to my feet and shuffled toward the table. "Bior, I'm hungry. Help me light the candles so Hakon can see I am well."

"Gladly, Sire." Bior 'accidentally' bumped into Hakon on the way to the table and didn't apologize for his clumsiness.

I lit the candle on the table and turned to face Hakon.

He stood near the table, glaring at my assistant.

"What do you want to know?" I asked.

Bior snickered from somewhere out of sight.

Hakon rubbed his chin and looked me up and down. "You're up and about well enough." He stepped closer. "Any pain, especially in your stomach, or nausea?"

"I'm getting a bit of a headache, *and* I'd like to eat my breakfast." *And I'm running out of patience.*

"Shouldn't be a long wait." He glanced at the dish on the table. "Bior told me you didn't want boiled grains this morning. I'd like to know why."

I glared at him. "It is wise to question me in such a manner?"

His face lost some color. "I mean no disrespect, my king. But if you are ill, a hearty breakfast helps you feel better."

I'm no longer interested in your experience. I took my seat. "Hakon, I assure you I am not ill. I'm hungry. If you have any more questions, you'll have to wait until I finish eating."

"Enjoy your meal, m'lord. Send for me if you don't feel well afterward."

Bior stepped to my side. "Your spoon, Sire. The rabbit strips are likely sitting on the bottom."

Hakon turned and stomped his way out, nearly slamming the door.

"Is it just me or —"

"No, Sire...it's not just you. It seems the head herbalist thinks too highly of himself."

"I have more important things to focus on, but if he gets too far out of hand, I'll do something about it. Too bad Tindra isn't here," I said, stirring the bowl's watery contents. "I'd love to see her correct his behavior."

"Aye, Sire. I'd consider paying a copper or two to watch."

I laughed before taking a spoonful of warm broth. "Anything I need to know since last night?"

He took the seat across from me. "Aye. Good news at first light. One of the warriors sent north with the builders came back and asked for a wagon and more men to load trees. Word is they should be back before dark."

"Excellent," I said, after swallowing another spoonful. "Sounds like the real work starts early tomorrow."

Bior shrugged. "Haven't talked with General Gudmann or Orri yet to see what they have to say."

"We'll find them after I eat. Afterward, I guess I should decide what to do with the rest of my day. A bath would be nice at some point."

"I'm certain you can stop by the bathing house any time you choose, Sire." Bior snapped his fingers. "Don't forget you need to meet with the messenger."

I swallowed a piece of rabbit and nodded. "Thank you for reminding me. Messenger, find Gudmann and Orri, clean myself, and go about the rest of my day. Sounds like a solid plan."

"It does. And speaking of plans, I need to see to some things in my room. Knock on the door when you're ready, Sire."

I stirred the spoon through the bowl again. "I won't be long."

Bior stood, bowed, and turned for the door. "I'll be ready when you are, m'lord."

After scooping all of the meat from the broth, I brought the bowl to my mouth and slurped the rest of the liquid. *Could've been warmer, but it hit the spot.*

I changed into fresh clothes, slipped the message into my shirt, and glanced at my hammer. *Shouldn't need it.* Making my way around the room, I blew out all but one candle before going to get Bior.

Chapter 31

As we entered the courtyard, the northern gate swung open, and someone yelled, "Make way!"

A team of horses pulling a wagon loaded with long, thick logs entered.

"I'm guessing, if we wait here, we'll run into Orri soon," Bior commented.

"Probably. There's nothing urgent in my message to Tindra. Finding someone to take it back to the capital can wait."

Orri, leading a line of builders, approached as men paraded through the gate.

"Well met, Orri," I called out, waving.

He stopped talking to his men and motioned us over.

"What do you think?" I asked, resting my hand on the end of a harvested tree.

He smiled. "If the rest of the wood is as good as this one, we'll have the repairs done ahead of schedule. Then we can work on adding stone for more strength."

"Sounds like good news," I said.

Orri cocked his head to the side. "Can't say until I check every log in this load. Any weak trees will be broken down into their useful pieces while the rest get sythed into what we need. Takes time and effort. Tired builders are sloppy workers. I get the impression you want our best work."

Raking my hand through my hair, I shook my head. "If time wasn't important, I'd insist on it, but I'm not sure we have such luxury. When will you have something sturdy enough for a company to walk across?"

"Only men. No horses?"

"Yes. Men, their armor, weapons, and a few supplies."

"What do you have in mind, Sire?" Bior asked.

Holding up a finger, I dipped my head toward Orri.

The builder grinned. "My king, if we get started soon, men could cross by dusk. But we cannot be interrupted by other requests or attacks from Satra."

"Bior, find General Gudmann. I want him here as soon as possible."

"Aye, Sire."

As Bior left, I offered Orri my hand. "You'll have everything you need."

He shook my hand before bowing. "Sire, I'm sure these woodsyths need food and rest before they get started. No doubt the stonesyths who helped load the wagons would appreciate the same. Of course, I'll also need more men to unload logs for the builders to work with."

Nodding as he gave his explanation, I clapped my hands together when he finished and smiled. "I'll empty the stronghold if necessary. Make sure you have the wood you need. Don't worry about muscle or protection."

"Thank you, m'lord." Orri bowed again before calling to a couple of builders looking over the wood.

Stepping back to stay out of everyone's way, I waited for Bior to return with Gudmann. While keeping an eye out for them, Orri approached. "Good news, my king. Work can start once I have what we discussed earlier."

I smiled at the news. "And you'll have it as soon as General Gudmann gets here. Have you seen him today?"

"No, Sire. I'm afraid I haven't," he answered, scratching his head. "Of course, he and I don't usually cross paths. We'll wait by the southern gate, ready to work once the men have arrived."

As Orri walked away, I looked around again. *I know I told Bior I'd be here, but this is taking too long. Where is he?* I decided the best course of action was to find someone who might know where Gudmann was and headed for the southern wall.

I asked the first warrior standing guard where I could find the general. He shrugged and told me Commander Alrik had climbed to the top of the wall recently.

Judging by how hard I breathed, there was no doubt my face was red from hurrying up the steps. "Commander Alrik," I growled, at the nearest man.

He stepped back and pointed to a group of men standing above the gate.

I nodded and tried to catch my breath as I walked.

Alrik noticed me when I got close. "King Fitzeirick, well met. What brings you here?"

"Looking for General Gudmann."

"Sorry, Sire. I haven't seen him today."

I sighed. "Any idea where to find him?"

Alrik frowned, scratching his chin while he looked across the hold. "He could be anywhere. I'm sure we'll meet sometime today. When I see him, I'll tell him you're looking for him. Where will you be, Sire?"

Closing my eyes, I shook my head. "Don't bother. I'll keep looking until I find him."

Alrik bowed. "As you wish, m'lord. Sorry, I couldn't be more helpful."

"I appreciate the effort. As you were."

"Sire, I hope you find him soon."

Me too. I could order men to help the builders, but Gudmann knows his warriors better than me. I'd hate to send a woodsyth to do a stonesyth's job. I nearly ran over Bior at the bottom of the steps and grabbed his arm to keep him from falling. "Where have you been? Where's Gudmann?"

"Bedridden ... sick, Sire."

"Orri's waiting at the southern gate. Let him know what's happened. Tell him it's going to take a little longer before men are provided. Maybe suggest they eat an early lunch. I'm going to tell Alrik what has happened and put him in charge of gathering men for the builders. When you're done, wait for me here. I'm going to talk to the herbalists."

"Aye, Sire. Too bad Tindra isn't here; I'm sure she could motivate them."

That got me to laugh. "You speak true. I'm certain she'd be perfect for this situation."

As tempting as it was to hurry up the stairs again, I knew I needed to be able to talk when I got to Alrik, so I climbed slower than I would have liked.

"Commander's over there." The archer I'd spoken to before pointed away from the gate.

Alrik had his back to me. The archer he was talking to pointed before I reached them.

The commander turned. "Didn't expect to see you again so soon, Sire. Did you find General Gudmann?"

"Not exactly," I said. "He's in bed, sick."

Alrik's eyes opened wide. "Oh. That's not good at all. Anything I can do to help?"

I put my hand on his shoulder. "Gather men to assist the builders. Mainly stonesyths to move logs into place. More importantly, I want two companies assigned to guard them as they work. They stay with the builders until they come back into the stronghold. Clear?"

Alrik nodded. "How many workers, Sire?"

"The more, the better. Only strong stonesyths, though. It's going to be a lot of heavy lifting."

"Understood, m'lord. When do you need them?"

Squeezing his shoulder, I chuckled. "Now. The builders are waiting near the southern gate. Send the men there."

The commander frowned. "Understood, Sire. Anything else?"

After chewing my lip for a moment, I nodded and let go of him. "Fastulf and his company are exempt from this duty. I have plans for them. Also, once you have men on the move, I want you to watch the field from here. If anything happens on the Satran side, raise an alarm. I'll get word to you about General Gudmann as soon as I can."

"Consider it done, m'lord. I hope he recovers quickly." Alrik saluted and hurried toward the stairs.

Turning my eyes to the border, I tried to envision warriors crossing the bridges on their way to destroying our enemy. All I saw were sagging platforms I'd be afraid to send a single man across.

I hit the top of the wall with the edge of my fist. My worsening mood must have been evident; the men gave me plenty of room to pass on the way to the stairs.

Bior waited at the bottom. "Orri didn't seem upset when I told him about the delay. He sent a couple of builders to get more water and said they'd be ready when the men arrived."

"Good to know he's an understanding sort. Now, take me to Hakon."

"Straight away, Sire. The look on your face should keep everyone out of your way."

I looked sideways at him. "Let's see what the herbalist has to say. I could use some good news."

Chapter 32

As Bior predicted, we reached General Gudmann's quarters with little delay.

I didn't bother knocking before opening the door. Few candles lit the room, but I could see Gudmann lying in his bed, eyes closed and a cloth covering his forehead. Someone I didn't recognize sat near the bed, grinding something in a mortar and pestle.

"Where's Hakon?" I demanded.

"I'm here, my king," he answered, from a dark corner to my right. His unbleached shirt looked sickly yellow in the candlelight. "What can I do for you, Sire?"

"How sick is General Gudmann?" I asked, crossing my arms.

"Much worse than he has been before, my king."

I pressed my lips together and looked at Gudmann. *How am I going to enter Satra without a respected general?* "How long will he be down?"

"I don't know."

My foot tapped on the floor. "What are you doing to cure him?"

Gudmann groaned, and his eyelids fluttered.

"The general needs to rest," the herbalist sitting at his side said. "Perhaps, m'lord, you could take this conversation outside?"

"He's right, Sire," Bior said. "No reason we can't talk in the hallway."

I glared at Hakon and thrust my finger toward the door.

He bowed and turned to leave.

I glanced at the other herbalist. "I want to know as soon as Gudmann awakes."

He nodded and went back to grinding the mortar's contents.

Bior closed the door behind me.

Hakon leaned against the wall opposite Gudmann's room. "To answer your question, my king, I'm trying to figure out why this is happening. I still believe it's bad ale but can't find a way to prove it."

I gestured toward Gudmann's door. "When's the last time he drank any ale?"

"I — I don't know, m'lord."

I moved to stand toe-to-toe with Hakon and brought my finger under his chin, forcing it up. "Don't you think that might be something important to find out?"

The herbalist shivered. "Yes. Sire."

"As far as I know, the only ale he's had came from the cask *you* had delivered to my room."

"I'm — I don't know if he drank any other ale since."

"*Yet,*" I barked. "You don't know *yet.*" Pressing harder with my finger, I forced Hakon to stand on his toes. "Do I need to remind you we are preparing to ride south to destroy Satra? I *need* General Gudmann healthy and ready to lead."

The herbalist tried to nod. "I'm aware, Sire."

"So, you do know *something*, but not enough to do your job." Twisting my finger, a warm trickle flowed down its side. "You will figure out what is causing this, and you will work non-stop to make Gudmann fit for duty. If I am ready to send warriors south and he's still bedridden, you will be among the first to cross into Satra. If I'm feeling generous, I'll let you have a blade in your hand before you go. Am I understood?"

His throat moved when he swallowed. "Yes, my king."

Dropping my hand, I grabbed his shirt and wiped the blood off my finger. "Good. Now, do your job ... much better than you have been."

He nearly tripped himself, rushing to return to Gudmann's room.

"Is he going to take your threat seriously, Sire?" Bior asked.

"He'd better. I've had enough of the rude, ineffective herbalist. Honestly, I can't understand why Gudmann allowed him to stay here."

"Perhaps the general found him useful," Bior said, shrugging.

"When Gudmann wakes, I may ask him."

Bior chuckled. "Where to now?"

"After I see if Alrik has men on the move, I want to talk to the rest of the commanders. They need to know what's going on, and I need to make sure this isn't going to cause more trouble."

Bior nodded. "Understandable, Sire ... all things considered."

Leaving the general's quarters, we hurried back to the gate and found Alrik watching a group of warriors leaving the stronghold. "This looks promising," I commented.

"Good to see you, my king." Alrik bowed. "Orri and I decided it best to send defenses out first." He pointed toward a group of men gathered on the far side of the yard. "The builders are over there, talking to the stonesyths I sent to help."

"Excellent progress," I said, grinning. "General Gudmann was asleep when I last saw him. According to Hakon, the general's much worse than he's been before."

Alrik shook his head. "That doesn't sound good, Sire."

"You wouldn't happen to know anything about Hakon?" Bior asked.

Alrik scratched his head for a moment. "Not much. I think he knows General Gudmann's family or something. Maybe one of his parents worked as a herbalist for them. Wouldn't swear to it, though. Could be thinking of someone else."

Interesting. "Keep up the good work and stand ready for an attack once the builders leave the stronghold. I'm going to talk with the rest of the commanders. Send word if you need anything."

"Of course, Sire," he replied.

"Until Gudmann's on his feet again, the commanders will be busy men. I hope you're up to the task."

"Wouldn't be fit for duty were we not, m'lord," Alrik bowed.

I smiled at him. "I'll send word if I hear anything about General Gudmann."

"May the rest of your day go more smoothly, my king," he said, before turning to climb the steps up the wall.

"I need to meet with the rest of the commanders," I said. "Have them join me in the meeting room. I'll check on Gudmann."

"May take some time to find them, m'lord," Bior said.

"I'm in no hurry."

"Aye, Sire," he replied, before turning to leave.

• • • • • • • • • •

I reached Gudmann's room and knocked once before opening the door. A single candle near the bed was the only light. A lone man knelt next to the bed. His body shook, but I couldn't hear him making any noise.

"Who's there?" I asked.

Commander Osvif turned. Candlelight shined off his wet cheeks. "You heard right, Sire. General Gudmann's dead."

"I —" My legs trembled, knees buckled. Disbelief raced across my mind. "I hadn't heard. When?"

"Not long ago. I sent Anakol to find you once we were certain."

"Who?" I asked, still not wanting to believe my ears.

"The herbalist tending to him. I came to check on my general when I heard he was sick. Anakol was here when I arrived. Not long after, General Gudmann stopped breathing."

I shuffled to a chair, flopped down, and hung my head. *My senior general's dead. What do I do now?* "Bior is gathering the other commanders for a meeting. I need you to go to the gate and send word to the builders and their guard. Work stops immediately, and they come back inside until we figure out what to do next."

"Not to argue, Sire," Osvif said, "but is that the best course of action? What would keep the Satra from destroying what's in place now, wasting all this time and effort?"

I glared at him. "General Gudmann's dead. We ... I can't enter Satra without solid leadership in place."

Osvif put his hand on my knee. "My king, I knew General Gudmann well. At the risk of sounding stone-hearted, one man's death shouldn't stop the fight for Croy's future. My fellow commanders and I, along with our sergeants, can lead our men into battle without our general."

Grabbing Osvif's arm, I stared at him for a moment, eyes wide. "How are you?"

"Having trouble believing my general's gone, but — I'm not willing to give up."

"Good," I said, squeezing his arm before letting go.

I glanced at Gudmann and sighed heavily. "If we're not calling the builders in, I need you to get to the wall and let Alrik know what has happened. After I speak with the other commanders, we'll spread the word of General Gudmann's death. For now, everyone needs to stay at their posts, tending to their duties. Make it clear, I do *not* want a crowd around this building. We'll bury him outside the northern wall at first light tomorrow."

Osvif rose to his feet and bowed. "As you wish, Sire."

After the door closed, I walked to Gudmann's bedside and looked at his body, lying still as stone. For a moment, I considered shaking him to see if he'd wake, laugh, and tell me this was an elaborate joke. I reached out and touched his arm; he was cold to the touch. Too cold to be alive.

I moved a chair next to his bed and took his hand. Tears flowed from my eyes. The lump in my throat made it impossible to speak. *You didn't deserve to die like this. If you weren't killed in battle, you should have died of old age. Happy knowing you secured Croy's future. My friend, I know we disagreed recently, but we both stood willing to do what had to be done. I will finish what we started.*

Using the blanket folded at the foot of his bed, I covered his body and turned the chair to watch the door.

Chapter 33

I must have fallen asleep because my head jerked up. Crust gummed my eyes closed until I rubbed it away. The candle had burned out, leaving the room in blackness.

"Sire." Bior's voice came from a silhouette in the open door. "Are you still here?"

"I'm sitting near the bed. Guess I nodded off."

"No problem, I'm sure the tinderbox is right here, somewhere," he said.

Sparks flashed repeatedly, giving glimpses of Bior's face as he tried to light the tinder. Before I could offer to help, he had a candle lit. "The commanders are gathered, Sire."

"How are they?"

"Sad, mostly," he said. "A couple look angry, but that's just my impression."

"Nothing from the southern wall?"

"Quiet, so far, Sire."

"Good," I said, nodding. "One less thing to worry about, for now. I know I sent you to gather them, but now, I'm having trouble focusing well enough to figure out what to do next."

"Meet with them. Discuss our options. Afterward, you need to send a message to the capital, to General Gudmann's family."

"The message!" I barked.

Bior tilted his head. "What's wrong, m'lord?"

Frantically patting my shirt, I found it lying across my stomach. "In all the confusion this morning, I forgot to get Tindra's letter to a messenger. You just reminded me. You're right—I must send word of Gudmann's death to the capital. I'll talk to the commanders, see if you can find parchment, quills, and ink...but disturb as little as possible."

"Of course, Sire."

"Otherwise, go to my quarters and bring my supplies here."

Bior nodded, lit another candle, and began his search.

I stopped at the door. "Stay here until I get back. I don't feel right leaving Gudmann alone."

"Aye, m'lord."

"And don't let anyone disturb him," I said.

"Sire, don't worry. Go meet with the commanders. I will make sure nothing happens to the general's body while you're gone."

"Thank you, Bior."

Though the meeting room wasn't far, it seemed like I'd never get there. My mind raced, unable to focus on anything for long, while my legs seemed to resist each step forward. *What am I going to say to make this better?*

The commanders stood and saluted when I entered. I returned the salute and asked them to sit. "I—" The words caught in my throat. "I want you to know I feel this loss as much as you. No doubt, you all feel a bit lost. Rest assured, I do too. You can come to me, at any time, with any concerns while we figure out what to do moving forward. At the same time, expect me to lean on you for support and be ready to support each other. We cannot do this alone."

"We're here for each other, Sire," Hottir said.

"Our men will have questions," Sturla said. "What do we tell them?"

I took a deep breath. "Tell them this will delay our advance, but it will not stop the war. Tell them I am willing to meet with anyone and listen to their concerns, if necessary."

He nodded.

"Where will we bury General Gudmann?" Ketill asked.

"Unless any of you disagree, I will find a place for him to rest. Once I have prepared the spot, I'd like you men to carry his body."

"No argument from me." Ketill said, looking around the table. "Anyone feel differently?"

Heads shook, and a few commanders voiced their agreement.

"Anyone who wants to speak at General Gudmann's funeral is welcome. Make sure everyone knows this."

"We'll pass the word, m'lord," Hegg said.

"I will send a message to the capital soon. If anyone wants to send anything to General Gudmann's family, write it out and get it to me or Bior as soon as possible."

Someone said, "Aye," and heads nodded around the table.

"Anything else to discuss? I fear the next few days will be difficult."

"I'm not sure any of us know what to expect or what may arise, Sire," Osvif said.

"Understood," I said, nodding. "Support your men and each other. Bring me any concerns you cannot handle yourself."

One by one, they stood and brought their right arms across their chests.

"We will get through this together," I said, returning their salute until they filed out of the room.

Returning to the general's room, I found Bior sitting near his bed.

"How was the meeting, m'lord?"

"Well as could be expected," I said, shrugging.

"I put a few sheets of parchment, a small ink pot, and a short quill on the table for you. How long are you planning on staying with him, Sire?"

"Hadn't given it much thought," I said, taking a seat. "Wanted to hand the messages to the rider in person, and I need to find his resting place, but I feel compelled to continue a vigil. An honor guard is the least Gudmann deserves."

Bior rested his hand on my shoulder. "I understand, m'lord. Let me get you something to eat while you write the message. I'll find warriors to stay with him once you're ready to leave."

"Good idea. On your way back, go to my quarters and get my seal. No rush. This may take some time."

"Aye, Sire." Bior bowed before closing the door behind him.

The quill. It was shorter than mine and a bit fatter. The balance was nothing like the one I used. It took several moments before I had a comfortable grip. Twice I wrote words before deciding they didn't carry the meaning I wanted. Taking a deep breath, I closed my eyes and rested my head in my hands a moment before settling on writing exactly what I wanted to say.

Captain Agrim,

It is with the heaviest of hearts and in the worst of circumstances I write these words.

General Gudmann has died, taken by an illness. Pass the word and make sure he is honored as he deserves. Let his family know he will be buried in Croian soil, north of the stronghold, and assign men to see to their needs while they mourn.

The commanders believe we should continue with our plans and preparations. They assure me everyone under Gudmann's command will function as expected. By the time you receive this, we should be entering Satra if all goes well.

When we meet with the barges, General Jomar will join us as planned, and we will remove our enemy from this world, root and stem, to secure lasting peace and prosperity for all Croian Citizens.

Victory!

King Fitzeirick

Bior returned as I read over the letter four or five times, making sure it contained everything I needed to tell Agrim. I had no doubt the captain of my guard would carry out my requests. After folding it, Bior placed my seal within reach beside a roll with some meat inside.

I lit another candle and dribbled wax on the page.

"Sire, I have four warriors waiting outside. Commander Osvif thought it would be best to have two men in the room and two more guarding the door."

I sealed the message. "Let's go."

Leaving the room, I saluted the men in the hallway. "Thank you for accepting this duty."

"It's the least we could do for our general, my king," one replied, as they saluted.

I gave them a weak smile, then turned to find a messenger.

Chapter 34

Most men we passed on the way to the barracks wore grim expressions. No doubt, the word of Gudmann's passing had spread.

More somber looks greeted us as we stepped into the barracks.

"I need a messenger to carry two letters back to the capital," I said. Raising the message for Agrim, I nodded. "This one is— It goes to Captain Agrim. The other goes to Queen Tindra."

Every man stood and faced me.

I smiled. "Know this. These need to leave as soon as possible. The warrior carrying these letters will miss General Gudmann's burial and will not be among the first to enter Satra when we move south in the coming days. Who is willing to give those things up to do this for me?"

A thin man, nearly my height, approached. Stopping a pace from me, he brushed his curly, blond hair out of his face and locked his deep, gray eyes on mine. "I grew up with General Gudmann's brother. It would be my honor to carry word of his death and be there to grieve with his family."

"Your name?" I asked.

He bowed low. "Hross, m'lord."

"Who do you report to?" I asked.

"Sergeant Sighadd."

"One of Commander Ketill's men, I believe, Sire," Bior added.

I nodded and handed Hross the sealed parchments. "I will make sure your leaders know you accepted this duty. Both messages bear my seal, see they reach the queen and my guard captain intact. Gather your things and the supplies you need for the journey—quickly. I want these on the road soon. I don't expect you would encounter any difficulty between here and the capital, but stay vigilant. After you deliver the messages, aid the general's family as best you can. When you're able to return, go to the shore south of the capital. Barges will depart from there, carrying men and supplies. They will be the fastest way for you to rejoin your company."

"Thank you for trusting me with this task, my king," he said, saluting.

"Travel swift and safe," I said, returning his salute. "The rest of you, prepare yourselves. We will enter Satra soon." I turned to Bior as the warriors bowed. "I want to see how the bridge repair is going. If it's far enough along, I need to get Fastulf and his company ready to cross this evening."

"I believe he's in the warrior's mess, my king," someone said.

"We'll check there first. Thank you."

Bior opened the door and led me out of the barracks.

"Do you trust him to keep his word, Sire? I mean, what if the heat of battle makes him return to his habit?"

"I made sure he understood continuing his collection would cost him his company and his honor. If I didn't believe he took me seriously, the young warrior would already be on the way back to the capital."

Bior grunted and set a fast pace to the wall.

Looking around as we crossed through the hold, it was easy to tell the general mood was subdued. Everywhere I saw men going about their duties with slumped shoulders and heads hung low.

"Commander, well met. Anything to report?" I asked.

Osvif leaned against the wall, attention directed toward the builders and their guards. He flinched when I greeted him. "Sorry, Sire. Didn't realize you were there. Been quiet since before I arrived, but if that storm makes it here, it could slow the builder's progress."

"Looks nasty," Bior said, nodding to the southwest.

I followed his gaze to dark clouds gathering over the water. "Remind me to ask Orri when the builders come in for the evening. We may need to adjust our plans."

"Aye, Sire," Bior said.

I looked back at the workers, watching them move about the structure. A long, thick plank sank into the ground near the edge of the water on Satra's side of the divide. Soon after, the builders connected another piece to the support and rested it on top of the grassy bank.

A warrior walked across and stabbed his sword into the ground. Cheers rose from builders and fighters alike.

The men around us bellowed in celebration and clapped each other on the back.

It's not finished, but men can cross. The guides can protect against Satran scouts finding the work and destroying it in the dark. "Good. Best sight I've seen since reaching Southold." I smiled and smacked the wall with my palm. "Bior, I'm going back to my quarters. Find Fastulf and send him to me."

"Aye, Sire," he replied.

"Commander Osvif, send word if anything of note happens."

He saluted. "Of course, m'lord."

After returning his salute, I returned to my quarters.

A well-lit room is more inviting, and I want Fastulf to feel comfortable. I lit several candles before taking my seat at the table and watching the door.

While waiting, I considered Fastulf's reputation and decided he could meet some resistance from the quartermaster when his company asked for enough supplies to be on guard duty for two or three days. Tearing a small piece of parchment, I signed it and imprinted my seal in a puddle of wax. *Should address anyone's concern.* The wax wasn't set when the door opened, and Bior, carrying a pitcher and cups on a tray, led my spearpoint into the room.

I stood. "Fastulf, welcome. Sit. Please. I have something to discuss with you."

Fastulf crossed his arms. "I've done nothing wrong, m'lord."

Bior snickered as he walked past the warrior and placed the tray on the table. "Figured you might be thirsty, Sire."

"Thank you, Bior. You're welcome to sit with us. Fastulf, no one said you've done anything wrong. I wanted you to discuss an opportunity to serve Croy again."

He nodded before taking stiff-legged, hesitant steps to the table as Bior poured water for us.

"An opportunity to serve again?" he asked, sitting in the chair across from me. "How?"

I nodded and took a drink of water. "You and your company can have the honor and glory of being the first to go south. Assuming you, and your men, are interested."

He emptied his cup. "How? I'd heard the bridges were damaged and not safe to cross."

"The builders are repairing them. I need your men to protect the construction overnight until the bridges are strong enough for the army to cross. How long will it take you to get your men ready to move?"

He filled his cup and took a drink. "My king, tell me where you need us, and we'll go."

"I may need you outside the walls for two or three days ... if not longer."

Fastulf flashed a toothy smile. "We could be the first to spill blood on Satran soil?"

"Yes," I said. "The guides will have a chance to draw first blood again ... but only if the bridges are attacked before the army crosses."

"We'll be glad to serve you again, Sire."

"You aren't serving me; you're serving Croy," I said. "And remember, no trophies."

Fastulf closed his eyes and nodded. "On my honor, Sire. Never again."

"Good to hear," I said, smiling. "One more thing, this assignment means you, and your men, will miss General Gudmann's burial in the morning."

After tapping a finger on his lips for a moment, he looked at me. "Where will he be buried?"

"Somewhere north of Southold. The marker will leave no doubt who is there," I said.

"We'll visit him when we return from Satra as victors."

"You're certain?" I asked. "I need your entire company over there, alert and ready to defend the bridges to the last man. Even one distracted warrior could be devastating to our plan."

"I promise. We won't let Croy down." He stood and saluted me.

I stood and offered him the parchment. "Take this. Should keep the quartermaster from delaying your departure."

Bior shot me a questioning glance.

"What's this?" Fastulf asked, reaching for the token.

"My signature and seal as proof you are asking for supplies at my order."

His face brightened as he looked at the parchment in his hand. "Thank you, Sire." He bowed. "I can't —"

"Don't abuse it," I warned.

Bior snickered.

Fastulf furrowed his brow and blinked several times before looking at me. "Of course not, m'lord. I'd never consider misusing your trust."

"Good," I said. "Now, go—and hurry. You have much to do, and I want you ready to cross before dark."

"And there may be a storm coming," Bior added.

Fastulf nodded. "We'll be ready, rock solid, regardless of the weather."

As he turned, I cleared my throat. "One more thing. Like last time, this is a guarding assignment. You are acting as a shield, not a spear, until I tell you otherwise."

"Yes, Sire." He faced me and bowed.

"Travel swift and safe. Should you need to fight, strike fast and true," I said.

"We'll make you proud, m'lord."

Bior watched him close the door and turned to me. "The boy's too eager to prove himself. He's either going to get men killed or go back to his savage ways."

I shook my head. "He's already proven himself, as far as I'm concerned. His company led the attack to get this land back, and his men stand with him still."

"What are you going to do if — when he makes a new necklace?"

"You heard him. He won't."

Bior shook his head. "From what I've been told, he was way too proud of it to give up the habit. What if he does it again and hides it? What will you do?"

"Exactly what I said I'd do." I slapped my hand on the table. "He knows the price for disobeying me. I trust he won't risk it."

"You trust —" Bior pressed his lips together and tapped his fingers on the table. "Sire, can you afford to be so trusting now?"

"How can I not?" I asked, glaring at him. "It wouldn't benefit anyone for constant suspicion to be my guide. Otherwise, I'd question why you *don't* trust Fastulf. Do you know something I don't?"

Shock spread across his face, and he shifted in his seat, leaning away from me. "Me? No, Sire. I'd never keep information from you. Remember, I brought word of Fastulf's gruesome hobby *to* you, m'lord."

I nodded and softened my expression. "I recall the conversation. Now, explain why my trust in him is misplaced?"

He shrugged. "A gut feeling. The way other warriors talked about him. How he showed the teeth off. Bragged about his kills. I'd bet my weight in gold doubles that he reveled in the brutality."

Tapping a finger on the table, I listened to his description of Fastulf and compared it to my impression. When I first met the young warrior, he wasn't a confident leader. Quite the opposite. He was shorter than most, but size isn't important when you have as much natural stonesything talent as he commanded. He learned quickly, listened to authority, and followed orders well. *Hard to ask for more in a warrior. Has his time on the battlefield changed him? Certainly, but I have to believe he's still stone-solid at his core.* "I hear you but still choose to believe in him. If my trust is misplaced, he *will* pay for it."

"I'm not trying to bend your view to mine, Sire. Thought you should know how some of his fellow warriors see him."

I nodded. "Gathering valuable information for me is one of your tasks. You seem to be doing a fine job."

Bior smiled. "Thank you for the praise, m'lord."

"Now, I believe we have an unpleasant task to complete before dinner. I want to find a suitable place to bury Gudmann."

"Should we get horses?"

My feet told me I'd done enough walking for the day. "Yes."

Chapter 35

Two stablehands bowed as we approached the corral. "I need Andale ready for a ride. Bior needs a horse, too," I said.

"What supplies will you need, my King?" one asked. "We can fetch them for you and load your saddlebags."

"We aren't going far," I said.

"Understood, Sire," the hand said, nodding. "We'll be right back with your mounts."

"Any chance we run into your mysterious friend while we're out looking?" Bior asked.

"I wouldn't be surprised if Ro — *he* is watching the stronghold."

Bior's sly grin let me know he noticed I almost gave him a name. "I heard the Satran say his name, Sire. It's obvious he means something to you. You insist keeping his name secret will protect someone. I know everyone you'd want to protect. The only ones who aren't Croian are your mother and your wife. I can't imagine the stranger branches from either of them. Roi, his family, and King Crum are the only ones left."

I grabbed his shoulder and squeezed. "Don't worry yourself about him. He's not a threat. Not to me and not to Croy. Once the war is won, I'll make sure he's properly rewarded for his service."

He grabbed my hand but didn't push it off. "Never said I was worried, as such. Simply working through a puzzle to pass time."

The stablehands we spoke with earlier walked our horses out to us, stopping the conversation. We thanked them, took the reins, and mounted up.

The guards saluted as we approached the north gate.

I returned their salute and held Andale to a walking pace. Stopping a short distance from the wall, I glanced at the grassy areas far from the road. "Somewhere near the hold or farther north, maybe near a stand of trees?"

Bior turned to me, lips pressed together, and looked around. "If it were my grave, I'd want it to be closer to trees. Someplace with some shade, should anyone want to visit."

"Spoken like a woodsyth, but you make a good point. Let's go farther north."

The tops of Southold's northern wall were still visible when we reached the nearest stand of trees well to the right of the worn path.

"Here?" Bior asked.

Stopping Andale a few steps away from the sparse group of trees, I dismounted and squatted to put my hand on the ground. Pushing my talent out, I searched for stones near the surface.

My breath came quicker as I worked. A bead of sweat ran down my forehead and tickled the side of my nose before I found a stone large enough to work into a grave marker. It rested around twice my height underground and far enough from the trees to keep roots from making raising it too difficult for any decently strong stonesyth.

"Grab Andale," I gasped. Wrapping my energy around the rock, I willed it to the surface. Both horses whinnied as the ground quivered, but neither bolted. I stopped when a chest-sized piece of rough, gray-and-black speckled stone rose a hand's width above the surface. "This will work perfectly," I said, standing. "Now to prepare Gudmann for his final rest."

Bior nodded. "I would be honored, m'lord."

"Thank you, but I feel the responsibility falls to me."

We returned to Southold in silence, returned our mounts to the stable, and made our way to the general's quarters.

The two guards outside saluted when I arrived. Inside, the two men sat in chairs on either end of Gudmann's bed. A single candle burned on the table, leaving most of the room in darkness.

"Men, let's find his armor, make sure it is clean, and get the general dressed. Bior, I want his weapon polished and sharp, as if he were riding into battle."

"Aye, Sire. His gear is stored in there," my steward said, pointing at an armoire in the back, left corner of the room. "I found it while looking for parchment earlier."

"Then, let's get to work," I said.

The warriors lit more candles while Bior and I retrieved the general's gear. I was relieved to see Gudmann kept his equipment in good condition. Bior set his sword on the table and examined it while the guards helped me dress their fallen leader.

His body was not yet rigid, but stiffness was setting in, making the uncomfortable duty take longer than I wanted. By the time we'd completed our chore, Bior declared the sword ready. I took it from him, slid it into the scabbard, and placed it on Gudmann's chest.

"Men," I said, turning to face the honor guard. "Thank you for your assistance. When should I send others to relieve you?"

"It was an honor, m'lord," one of them said. "Commander Alrik will send warriors to replace us soon."

I nodded. "Thank you for your service."

They saluted and moved back to their seats.

"I'm going to the southern gate to speak with Orri when the builders come in for the evening. Find warriors to syth a litter so the commanders can carry General Gudmann to his grave. We'll also need a likeness of General Gudmann to use in the ceremony."

"I'll make sure everything is taken care of, m'lord."

"Once you're done, I'd like to eat dinner in my quarters."

"Aye, Sire."

Chapter 36

Warriors watched me pass as I walked through the hold. Their stares weighed on me. *All I can do is hope they still believe in me. I'm not sure another speech would help anything.*

A crowd blocked the southern gate.

"What's wrong?" I asked a nearby warrior.

"Fastulf's gathering his men, Sire."

"Is he here?" I asked.

The warrior nodded toward the group.

"Fastulf, a moment, please," I called.

Men stepped aside and the short warrior hurried to me, saluting when he stopped. "I wasn't expecting to see you here, my king. What can I do for you?"

"I didn't think you would be here. I'm waiting for the builders to come inside so I can talk with Orri. How soon will you take the field?"

"I'm waiting for three men to arrive, and then we'll go out."

I nodded. "So long as you're in place to keep anyone from attacking the bridges tonight."

He smiled. "We have discussed tactics. Anyone approaching from the south will pay for their mistake."

"Sounds good."

"Open the gates!" someone called from above. "Make way for the builders!"

We hurried out of the way as they entered Southold. I called Orri's name and waved him over.

"My king, an unexpected surprise," he said.

"I wanted to get a report in person. How are the repairs coming?"

"Better than I hoped," he said. "Assuming nothing happens to them overnight, we should complete the stonework before sunset tomorrow."

I nodded. "The bridges will be guarded, but I have a couple of concerns. We bury General Gudmann in the morning. Are you and your men planning to attend?"

"It has been discussed, Sire." He looked back toward the builders still coming in. "If we can get guards, we'd rather continue our work tomorrow."

I gave him a weak smile. "I'll see what I can do. Second, there could be a storm coming. Will that cause any problems?"

He shrugged. "I've watched the clouds. So long as we can safely work, a little rain isn't a concern."

I offered him my hand. "Thank you for the effort. I'll leave the working conditions to your judgment. No doubt you are hungry and tired. See to your men and get a good night's sleep."

"Contributing to Croy's future is our pleasure, m'lord," he said, grasping my hand. "Once our work is done, the warriors' work starts."

I chuckled. "Right you are. Have a good evening."

"You too, Sire," he said, before walking away.

Fastulf and his men left while I was talking with Orri. I saluted the soldiers guarding the gate and left for my quarters.

Arriving to a dark room, I struck flint to steel until the tinder smoldered. With a few puffs of air, I had a flame and lit several candles. I watched shadows flit across the walls and pondered how the loss of my senior general might change our plans. As gloomy thoughts filled my mind, Bior arrived with a tray of sandwiches, a pitcher, and two cups.

"All is well, Sire?" he asked.

"Other than the obvious problem, yes...things are progressing better than I should expect. Orri doesn't think the weather will slow the builders, but I'll need to ask some men to stay behind tomorrow to guard the builders while they work."

Bior nodded. "I'd planned to eat with you, Sire, but I can take my dinner with me and speak to the commanders."

"If you wouldn't mind," I said, frowning. "It's likely I wouldn't be good company anyway. Gudmann's death is weighing on me. More than anything, I want to go to sleep and wake up to someone telling me it was no more than a bad dream."

Bior pressed his lips together for a moment. "We're all carrying that burden, m'lord. Don't think you bear it alone."

"I know," I said, reaching for a sandwich. "And yet we have much to prepare for. Bring me my breakfast early; I want to be in the courtyard, ready to lead the procession, before first light."

"Aye, Sire. Rest well. I'll see you in the morning."

When Bior reached for a sandwich, I grabbed his hand. "I'm sorry to lean on you so much. Your assistance is appreciated."

He looked me in the eye. "I'm glad to serve, m'lord."

I released his hand and let him get on his way before eating. The meal did little to distract me from my worsening mood. Once I finished, I left one candle burning on the table and went to bed.

Thunder rumbled through the wall as I fell asleep.

Chapter 37

The door creaking as it opened woke me from a restless sleep filled with visions of dead bodies and funeral processions.

"Sire," Bior said quietly. "I have some food and hot tea for you."

I sat up and stretched before getting to my feet. The candle on the table was nearly gone. "Hot tea?"

I saw him nod in the dim light. "Bad storm last night. Left everything wet and a bit of chill in the air."

Taking a seat, I sighed. "A bit appropriate, I suppose."

He set a basket on the table. "Meat strips and hard rolls. The boiled grains weren't ready yet."

"Anything's better than an empty stomach," I said, before biting into a roll.

Bior nodded and sat to eat with me after lighting a few candles. We looked at each other but didn't say anything. *No doubt the significance of what we're about to do is weighing on him too.*

"I need to change clothes and put on my armor," I said, after washing down my last bite.

Bior grabbed the last roll before standing up."

"I should meet with the commanders over dinner."

He nodded. "Not in here. Use their meeting room. Also, you should know that men are openly discussing leaving."

"That doesn't sound like a problem to me. I'm ready to leave for Satra too."

He frowned. "You misunderstand. There are warriors in our ranks who are no longer interested in following you south. They are talking about heading home."

I took a long drink. "And the commanders are aware of this?"

"Aye. I can't prove it, but I believe some of them are working against you because they blame you for Gudmann's death. You need to convince them that you're fit to lead. If they believe in you, their men will follow."

"And if the commanders have lost their faith in me?" I took another drink. "What then?"

Bior shrugged. "Make your case to the warriors and rally as many as you can to fight for our country. You are still king. Maybe some of them need to be reminded of that fact."

"Perhaps, but if it's as bad as you say it is... Have I already lost?"

"You won't know until you try, m'lord," Bior said, bowing slightly.

I stared at him a moment. "You've given me a lot to think about, along with preparing for the funeral. I'll get you when I'm ready to leave."

"Aye, Sire."

Good thing I could dress without thinking about the process because my mind was scattered. *Two problems, both equally important and both related. Do I say something at the burial to boost morale? Seems risky. I could cause more problems if anyone takes something the wrong way.* The comforting click of my hammer onto my back told me it was time.

Bior and I stepped out onto the muddy path through Southold and sloshed our way to the northern gate. Golden fingers stretched across the sky from the east.

Two torchbearers walked ahead of the commanders, carrying General Gudmann on his last resting platform. Behind them, two warriors carried Gudmann's likeness made woven from branches, vines, and grasses. Winding behind, mostly obscured in darkness, were the men attending the ceremony. The squishing of their footsteps in mud echoed through the complex.

I turned to face the men guarding the north gate. "Open the gate!"

They bowed and then shoved the wooden gate open.

"On me!" I yelled, without turning to look at everyone behind me. Bior fell into step at my left flank as I passed through the wall.

Someone in the line of men marching behind me sang a tune I didn't recognize, using our synchronized steps to keep time. When that song ended, another voice started a different, still unfamiliar, ditty. It repeated three times before another lament went up.

Bright light from a clear, blue morning replaced dim twilight by the time we reached the marker I'd sythed. The singing stopped when I knelt to open the ground to receive our fallen general. Wet dirt resisted my will. "I'm going to need help," I said, looking up at Bior.

"Stonesyths, help your king prepare General Gudmann's bed," he ordered.

Ten men rushed from the crowd, putting their knees on the ground near me. Together we opened a hole down to the boulder the marker had come from. Once it was large enough, we created stairs so the commanders could carry their leader to his final resting place.

"Any who want to speak may start now, as these commanders serve their general one more time," I said, moving to carve the marker.

Someone started talking as my finger sank into the stone. Focused on sything the grave marker, I didn't pay attention to what was said,

Inscribing memorials was a task I'd had too much practice in, but the words did not come easy.

This is the final resting place of General Gudmann
A respected leader, loyal friend, and honored warrior
He gave his life to Croy, asking for nothing in return

I stood as the commander's head sank below the grass. The warriors chanted Gudmann's name, and I joined in, my heart pounding.

One by one, the commanders exited the grave. I looked down at my senior general, part of me hoped he would stand and rejoin us...the rest of me knew he wouldn't.

After nodding to the men who had helped me, we willed the dirt over him.

Singing started again as the woven statue was placed at the foot of the grave.

Taking my hammer from my back, I stood it in front of me and rested my hands on its head. "The stone is an everlasting reminder of the great man who lays below the ground. Now, let the smoke from his effigy carry this memory on the wind."

Two firesyths started a flame at the base of the statue. As it rose, we chanted again and filled the smoky air with Gudmann's name.

With the fire burning to embers, men continued their tributes to the general. I stood, stone still, until everyone who wanted to speak had a turn.

I turned to face the grave and brought my hammer across my chest in salute before turning to the men. "General Gudmann was more than a respected leader. He was a great man who loved his country and wanted nothing more than to see Croy prosper. I feel this loss as deeply as you, and should anyone feel the need to talk to me, I am more than willing to listen. Each of us mourns today and prepares for tomorrow. We will all miss Gudmann, but we will not falter in our mission. Our victory will be a tribute to all who have shed blood securing Croy's future."

One by one, men raised their weapons and bowed their heads.

Clicking my hammer to my back, I said, "On me!" and headed down the muddy path back to Southold.

Chapter 38

It was near midday when we reached the hold.

"I'll take lunch in my quarters," I said, passing through the gate. "I need to prepare for the meeting this evening."

"Of course, m'lord," Bior said.

We parted ways when I headed for my room. After lighting more candles, I took off my armor and sat at the table. Trying to clear my head, I rested my elbows on the wood and held my head in my hands. "How have I messed things up this bad?" Of course, there was no one there to answer my silly question. *Doesn't matter. Find a way forward.*

Taking a deep breath, I focused on the problem at hand. Could I get the commanders to agree with me and get everyone moving as soon as the bridges were reinforced? *If they're ready to leave, let's get going. If they'd rather take their men and abandon me, what can I do to change their minds? I need a better reason than 'we're leaving tomorrow.' Do I dare use Gudmann's memory to motivate them?* I sighed.

Roi's wisdom would have come in handy, but I had left him with plenty of work to do in the capital. Tindra's insight would be welcome, too, though her suggestion would likely be to do whatever's necessary to manipulate the commanders into cooperating. Such tactics wouldn't work for long. *I need these men to believe in me.*

Leaning forward, I spread my arms wide, rested on the table, and tried to find comfort in the rough texture of the wood against my cheek. *If Gudmann were still here... We had our differences, but he'd throw his support to me.*

The door opened. "Sire...are you well?"

Looking up, I saw Bior holding a bowl with steam rising from it. *A hot meal, exactly what I need on this gloomy day.* I smiled and nodded before pointing to the chair across from me. "Sit," I said.

Bior shrugged, set the bowl on the table, and sat. "What's on your mind?"

"You have to ask? The commanders. How do I keep them on my side?"

Bior leaned toward me. "I'm not sure I can give you much advice on this matter."

"Their main complaint is how long they've been waiting here, right? Are there other issues I should know about?"

"Morale was an issue for their men, but they tried to keep it from getting too bad. Your speech helped, but when the bridges were damaged, doubt grew like weeds. General Gudmann's death broke the branch."

"Thank you for your insight, my friend," I said.

"I do what I can, m'lord."

I nodded. "I need to get word to the commanders and make sure everything is ready for the meeting. I want to be the first one in the room to make the right impression."

Bior nodded and got up. "I'll come get you when it is time, Sire."

The stew was warm, but I was too distracted to notice much else about my meal.

Thoughts and possibilities bounced around my mind. Tactics and strategies for convincing the commanders to follow me into Satra came into focus, then faded away. Everything came back to one thought; If Gudmann was still here, he would support me.

The door opened. "Sire, A fresh cask of ale is on its way to the meeting room, and food is being prepared," Bior said.

I crossed my arms and nodded. "Then I know what I have to do."

He cocked his head. "You're going to use his death to convince them to stay, aren't you?"

"I'm doing what I must."

"What you must?" Bior slammed his fist on the table. "You're King of Croy. You can do anything you want."

"Contrary to what you believe, being king is not about doing what one wants. I carry a responsibility to those I rule. I will do what's best for Croy's future, no matter what it takes."

An unfamiliar expression crossed Bior's face.

Standing, I followed him to the door. "Your support may be critical to getting their cooperation."

"That depends on what you're planning. If I agree with what you do, I'll do my best to sway their opinion."

"Remember, this isn't for me ... this is for our country."

He nodded stiffly, and we left for the meeting.

Chapter 39

The sun hung low in the sky when we stepped out of the building.

Someone yelled my name.

Looking around, I spotted a warrior running toward us. I slowed my pace, and Bior moved to stand between me and whoever approached.

"Sire." The warrior came to a stop and saluted. "Sergeant Sighadd sent me to let you know the builders have finished and are coming in the gate."

"Happy to hear it," I said, returning his salute. "Return to your sergeant and give him my thanks. Bior, find Orri. Give him my thanks and tell him I'm sorry I couldn't meet with him and the builders in person because I had to attend an important meeting. I'll let the commanders know the bridges are complete, and we have no more obstacles keeping us from moving the army south."

"Aye, Sire," he said. "If everyone arrives before me, please don't wait to eat."

"If you're late, I'll make sure there's food for you," I said.

Bior chuckled before turning for the southern gate as I continued on.

Approaching the building serving as the quarters for the commanders and General Gudmann, I remembered the first time I met with the leaders here. My arrival that day seemed to bring hope and happiness as we planned to enter Satra. Now, knowing Gudmann wouldn't be among us, a cold sadness gripped my heart as I climbed the stairs.

Candles lit the room from alcoves in the walls. A small cask, ringed by wooden cups, sat on a small table near the door. I tapped the barrel, filled a cup, and took a drink.

I placed an empty cup at the head of the rectangular, wooden table before taking the seat to the right. *I'll leave that place empty for General Gudmann.*

Commanders Hottir and Osvif were the first to arrive. I stood, welcomed them, pointed out the cask, and told them to sit anywhere but the head seat. They took seats facing me. Ketill, Alrik, and Sturla walked in not long after, with Alrik sitting on Hottir's right. The other two sat on my side of the table, well away from me,

I motioned for Bior to sit on my left when he entered. He filled a cup before taking his seat.

Commanders Hegg and Gesta walked in ahead of three warriors carrying large covered pots with bowls and spoons balanced on top. Both commanders chose seats next to Ketill, leaving space between me and them.

"Get me an empty bowl," I whispered, to Bior, as the pots were placed on the table.

He looked like he had a question before nodding.

Everyone watched him give it to me.

Bowl in hand, I placed it next to the cup at the head of the table. "A gesture in remembrance of General Gudmann. Taken from us before his time and when we needed him most. May we never forget him or his selfless service to Croy."

Raising my cup of ale, I bowed my head.

"Aye," Bior said, "to General Gudmann."

The commanders echoed my assistant.

Standing, I cleared my throat and looked from one man to the next. "We have important matters to discuss this evening. This is no time to hold your tongue or tell me what you think I want to hear ... I want honest opinions. Now, everyone, take a bowl and serve yourself ... as much as you want. Same with the ale. If the cask goes dry, I'm sure we can get another."

Some of them chuckled, but no one moved until I filled my bowl. I stirred the stew before swallowing a spoonful. "I know you are all busy, and it has not been a joyous day. Thank you for meeting with me on short notice."

"I find it's good to be around people on days such as this, my king," Osvif said.

Hottir and Alrik nodded.

I smiled before continuing, "I have an announcement to make before discussing plans for entering Satra. On the way here, I was told the bridges were completed. Nothing stands between us and Satra now. I want us to cross those bridges in the morning, as soon after first light as possible. Commanders, what say you?"

Hegg tapped his cup on the table. "At first light? And you're telling us now? I don't see —"

"King Fitzeirick told us to get ready," Osvif said, cutting him off. "We all knew the bridges were being repaired. Have you not been preparing your men?"

"Have you not been listening to yours?" Gesta asked.

"Of course, he has," Alrik said. "We all have. Warriors get bored and complain ... it's what they do when they aren't busy, and none of us have been busy enough."

"I didn't ask you here to argue," I said. "I'm sure General Gudmann —"

Hegg banged his fist on the table. "Don't bring him into this. And don't claim to speak for a man who can't speak for himself. While he may have respected your title, my king, he wasn't happy with you either."

Under the table, Bior tapped my foot with his. When I glanced at him, he was staring at me wide-eyed.

Pressing my lips together, I nodded. "As I said, we're not here to argue. Let us calmly discuss entering Satra as soon as possible. Though your general and I had our differences, I respected him and his deeply rooted devotion to Croy. Disrespecting a great man was not my intention when I brought him up. No doubt you all knew him better than I, but would he want us arguing right now? I believe General Gudmann would advise us to work together."

"You're not wrong," Osvif said. "But ... it's more ... complicated than you think."

"Complicated, you say?" I asked, raising my hands, palms up. "I'm aware some of you — most maybe — aren't happy. I know morale among the warriors is bad. There's talk of desertion, abandoning the war. Any other difficulties or challenges I should know about?"

"Those are the major complaints," Sturla said. Several commanders nodded their agreement.

"And everything stems from the fact you've waited here too long, which you blame me for?"

"You are right in your thinking," Sturla said.

Everyone flinched when I stood. All eyes were on me as I walked past the empty chair to refill my cup. After a sip, I nodded. "It's not complicated at all. We're here to work out a solution to the exact problem everyone is complaining about. We agree; our warriors have been idle too long. We *all* want to leave. Everyone expected to leave days ago. I'm asking you to have everyone ready to ride south early tomorrow. Can you meet this goal?"

As I returned to my seat, Hegg sighed. "It's not as simple as you make it sound."

"I think it is," Bior replied, before I could.

"You would take his side," Hegg accused. "It's your job."

Bior bristled.

"It isn't his job to simply agree with me," I said, sitting. "I want the truth. Bior tells me the truth. He challenged me before I arrived. Do any of you know why General Gudmann was angry with me?"

"He said it was between you and him," Osvif said.

"Perhaps it's time I tell you."

"How would any of us know if you were lying?" Hegg muttered.

"Bior could explain if you'd like to hear it from him," I said flatly.

"We'd rather you tell us, m'lord," Osvif said.

I nodded. "Then here's the truth. Fastulf captured a Satran the night they damaged the bridges, remember?"

Heads nodded around the room.

"I questioned the prisoner alone—gathered information which may prove vital to our victory. Once I determined he was no longer useful, I killed him. That's what angered General Gudmann, damaging our friendship."

"Why kill a prisoner?" Osvif asked.

"He told me everything he knew freely. If his tongue was so loose with information from his own country, what would he tell his leaders about us, about our defenses, if he escaped? I gave him a merciful death to protect everyone in Southold."

Hegg, Ketill, and Sturla looked away from me. Osvif's face paled. Alrik wore a blank expression, staring at me.

Hottir raised his eyebrows and cleared his throat. "I can understand why my general was upset, but I see your point too."

I nodded. "It was not an easy decision."

He pursed his lips for a moment. "Certainly."

Bior tapped my foot again.

"Did the general mention he offered to resign?"

"No," Osvif replied, brow furrowed.

"If I wanted only men who agreed with me, I would have let him. Instead, I told him it was best for Croy if he stayed. My decision complicated a vital relationship. What we do here this evening is not difficult at all. Can you have your men ready to leave early tomorrow?"

Osvif nodded. "I can."

"Will you follow me into Satra?"

Osvif stood and looked around the room. "Aye, my king. I will. What say the rest of you?"

Hottir stood, and Alrik joined him soon after.

Bior stood and put his hand on my shoulder. "You have my loyalty, Sire. I'll be at your side the entire way."

"Sturla and Gesta, I wouldn't be surprised if your objection is based on anger toward me. I ordered General Nothri's execution, and now General Gudmann has died. No one can fault you for feeling some resentment," I said, nodding to each. "Ketill, Hegg, your dissension is puzzling. What keeps you seated?"

Hegg looked from one of the seated commanders to the next. In turn, each nodded to him.

He crossed his arms and looked at me. "We, the four of us, have lost confidence in you."

"Hegg," Alrik growled.

"No," I interjected. "I gave everyone permission to speak freely. Let him talk."

Alrik sighed, glaring at his fellow commander.

"We're not sure we want to change our warrior's minds," Hegg continued. "*If* we decide to try, it will take more time than you want to give us."

"I admire your courage and honesty," I said, nodding. "I'd rather enter Satra with all my warriors, but I won't force anyone. Assuming you four are willing to talk to your men on my behalf, how long will it take to convince them?"

"My king, I truly have no way to know," he replied.

"What will you do if you don't come with us?"

Hegg's eyes opened wide, and he glanced around, finally settling on Ketill.

"No idea," Ketill said quietly.

I nodded. "Would your men be encouraged to follow me if they saw the rest of the warriors leaving for Satra?"

"It couldn't hurt," Hegg said.

"A compromise then. We leave midday. This gives you more time to convince your men to follow and more time for them to prepare. Those who decide to go south with us are welcome. Those who don't, regardless of rank, are no longer part of the Croian army. They may leave Southold as soon as the southern gate closes behind us. No one will be here to stop them."

"Free to go," Gesta scoffed. "They'll face no punishment?"

I shrugged. "I won't take a roll call once we enter Satra. Likely I won't know who follows me and who doesn't. However, their fellow warriors *will* know. Who can say what might happen when they return from Satra as victors and see men who decided to not fight for Croy's future? Who's to say what they might do to a deserter who abandoned them in their time of need?"

Gesta shivered and looked away.

"No, *I* won't punish them. But a decision to stay, to make yourself a coward in the eyes of your fellow warriors." I shook my head. "That's a penalty many may not want to live with."

Hegg's face lost a little color as I spoke.

I clapped my hands together and stood. "Men, I have a full belly, and I'm tired. Pass the word to your warriors; we leave midday tomorrow ... no later. For anyone who is undecided in their commitment, I advise you to make up your mind and do it quickly. Remember, you and your men don't fight for me; this war is for the future of your families and friends. Take up your arms and follow me into Satra because it's what Croy needs."

I paused and looked from one commander to the next. "Bior, please wake me early enough to pack my things before breakfast."

"Aye."

"Good night, men. Sleep well tonight. It may be the last time we rest under a roof for a while."

The commanders standing saluted me. Those seated bobbed their heads.

Stepping into the darkness outside of the building, I pushed my talent out to make sure no one followed me and made it to my room without incident.

A couple of candles still burned when I entered my room. I didn't bother to put them out before getting into bed. The meeting's events flooded my thoughts, creating fears and doubts which kept me awake. I had to believe some of the commanders still had faith in me, in this war, but knowing there were more than a few men ready to abandon me — even worse, ready to abandon Croy's future because my decisions caused an unexpected delay... It chilled me to the bone.

I tossed and turned, trying to find a comfortable position while calming my mind. The room was dark by the time I fell asleep. When I woke, I was far from rested.

I lay awake, wondering what the day would bring when the door opened. "Bior?" I asked.

"Didn't mean to wake you, Sire," he said, before lighting a candle.

"Not sure I really slept," I said, stretching as I sat up.

"Sorry to hear that. I'll leave your clean clothes on the table. Pack what you need. It will be light soon."

"Thank you," I said, sitting up. "And thank you for your support last night."

Setting the clothes on the table, he nodded. "You didn't tell the complete truth."

"No, I didn't. You could have spoken up...I wouldn't have stopped you."

He shrugged. "It would have served no purpose to upset anyone further. What happens when we leave today?"

It was my turn to shrug. "Haven't the slightest idea. I hope we're leading over a thousand warriors into Satra. It could be fewer than half if the doubters stay behind. Should that be the case, Satra's Legion may have us on the run until we meet up with the warriors coming by barge somewhere south of here on the western shore."

Bior chewed his lip. "Sounds like a good way to lose a lot of men. I guess we'll find out if anyone changed their mind after breakfast."

"Speaking of which, I want to eat in the mess this morning. It can't hurt to spend time with the warriors."

He gave me a crooked grin. "Good idea. Come get me when you're ready to go."

"Won't take long."

I changed clothes and packed everything but my armor and hammer. After dragging my travel chest near the door, I put my saddlebags on top and left to get Bior.

Brightening twilight was enough to see swarms of men moving about. It made a breathtaking sight. Passing the stables was an exercise in avoiding horses. The courtyard was a maze of wagons.

"By the looks of it, everything will be ready well before midday," I commented.

"Aye, Sire."

Dodging men carrying baskets and crates, we continued our short walk to an empty dining hall. The air carried the smell of burning wood, but no one was in sight.

"Well ... makes it easy to find a seat," Bior quipped, eyebrows raised. "Let me find out what's going on, Sire."

I nodded and sat near the end of the table farthest from the door. *No sense jamming men up as they come in.*

Bior returned carrying a couple of small bowls. "No one's here because nothing's ready yet. They soaked hard rolls in some warm milk for us. Boiled grains should be ready soon."

I nodded and took one of the containers. Two oval rolls sat in a milky puddle. Carefully lifting one, I let some liquid trickle out before bringing it, and the bowl, to my mouth. Warm was its most redeeming quality. *At least I'm not choking down a dry, crumbling loaf.* Before I could get the second one out of the bowl, a cook brought us steaming bowls of watery grains.

"Might want to let it cool a bit, my king," he advised, before walking away.

Bior stirred his grains, looked at the bowl of milk, and dumped it in along with the roll.

I watched, waiting for him to finish working on the concoction.

He took a bite and nodded. "Wouldn't want it every day, but they are better together."

Taking his advice, I mixed everything and took a spoonful. The milk added much-needed flavor to the bland grains, and the roll crumbled when you stirred, thickening the sloppy mess. "Not great, but better."

Bior chuckled, and we finished our meal in silence. Men were entering the building as we stood to leave. A few noticed me and saluted.

I took their greeting as a sign of support and smiled before returning their salute.

"Looks like we finished at the right time," Bior commented.

I agreed, and we hurried out as soon as there was a break in the line.

"What do you want to do now?" Bior asked, as we dodged men loading wagons.

"As much as I wonder what the four commanders have decided, we should get our trunks loaded and check on our horses."

"I'll see to the trunks. You go to the stables and wait for me," Bior said.

"I need to go back to my room and put on my armor," I said. "Come to my quarters once you're done with the trunks.

"Right. I'd best get my armor on too."

I had to shoulder my way past several horses before I got to the fence and caught a stablehand's attention.

"Yes, Sire. What can I do for you?"

"Ready Andale and a horse for Bior, and take them to the southern gate," I said. "I'd hate to hold everyone up by riding through the crowd when it's time to leave."

"Yes, Sire." He bowed. "They'll be ready for you."

I thanked him and returned to my quarters. Bior wasn't there when I arrived, but my travel chest was gone. Someone had moved the saddlebags to the table.

With my lower armor in place, I reached for the upper half, and the door opened.

"Where are the horses?" Bior asked. "I didn't see them outside."

"I asked for them to be taken to the southern gate."

He nodded. "Anything I can help with?"

"Carry the saddlebags when we leave," I said, grinning.

If he replied, I didn't hear what he said as I pulled the top of my armor over my head. The weighty combination of leather and metal caught me by surprise, and I stumbled sideways under the load.

Bior rushed to my side to steady me. "Something wrong?"

"I forget how heavy this is when I haven't worn it in a while." After shifting side to side a couple of times, everything settled into place. I reached for my hammer and clicked it onto the magnets in the back of my armored shirt. Lifting the helmet, I decided to carry it until I was ready to mount Andale. "To the southern gate."

Descending the stairs in armor required careful movements to keep my balance. Bior offered to walk in front of me in case I fell, but I told him to follow me so I didn't crush him if I took a tumble. Men walking past gave us a wide berth when we stepped out of the building.

"Are you going to visit the four commanders and get their answer?" Bior asked, as we entered the courtyard.

"I told them there would be no pressure. Talking to them armored, with my hammer on my back, might be seen as pressuring them."

"You do make an imposing figure, Sire," Bior commented.

"Exactly. I'm not going to look for them or their men. Either they leave with us, or they stay and face whatever consequences may come."

"Understood, m'lord."

Within sight of the southern gate, I noticed Osvif having, what looked like, a heated discussion with Hegg. Both men were red-faced and gesturing wildly. A circle of warriors slowly formed around them. *At least no one has weapons in hand.*

"This can't be good," Bior said.

I groaned. "I'd better get over there before it comes to blows."

My armor bounced against my shoulders as I jogged toward the building confrontation. *Must have lost some weight while I was sick.* "Commanders!" I shouted, shoving my way through the crowd. "What *is* the problem?"

Hegg thrust his finger at Osvif. "He won't help me."

Osvif crossed his arms. "Because you want to go directly against the King's orders."

"No. I don't. That's not what I said. Not at all," Hegg argued.

I sighed and grabbed Hegg's arm. "Explain it to me."

He nodded stiffly. "Sturla, Gesta, and their sergeants aren't letting their warriors decide for themselves. I asked Osvif to help me get any warrior who wanted to leave with us out of their barracks."

I tapped a finger on my chin and stayed quiet until Hegg squirmed under my gaze. "You said 'us.' Are you leaving with me?"

He chewed his lip for a moment. "Ketill and I talked long into the night. After meeting with our warriors, we decided it was best for Croy to go with you and defeat Satra. I let Sturla and Gesta know this morning. They both said Gudmann's death broke it for them. They blame you for keeping us here so long, and they're forcing their decision on the men serving under them."

Closing my eyes, I sighed. "They *are* right. I did keep you here too long, but Satra didn't give me much choice when they destroyed the bridges. Osvif, where are the rest of the commanders?"

"Making sure everything is ready for us to leave, Sire."

"Hegg. Any idea of how many of their warriors want to leave?" I asked.

"Their sergeants won't let us talk to them."

I turned to Bior. "Must be less than half. Otherwise, they'd fight their way out. Right?"

"Depends on what they were told, Sire."

Nodding, I turned back to the commanders. "Hegg, do you know what Sturla and Gesta said to their men?"

"No, m'lord."

"Then you don't know the warriors are being held against their will."

Hegg put his hands on his hips, "Sire, I don't believe every one of those three hundred warriors agrees with their commander's opinion. There must be at least one man who wants to keep fighting for Croy."

I believe you, Hegg," I said, "what do you want me to do?"

"Prove to everyone you're worthy of their trust as a leader. Confront Sturla and Gesta, make them let their warriors decide for themselves."

I hope this isn't a trap. After running my hand through my hair, I pushed my helmet on. "Osvif, I have two tasks for you. Find someone to ride to the far eastern passage and let the Varians know we're leaving. Pick a company on horseback and move them onto wagons and keep their horses near the gate. We'll need them for scouts."

"Scouts, Sire?" Bior asked.

"I'll explain later."

He nodded as I turned back to Hegg. "Lead me to the barracks."

Chapter 40

Bior and I followed Hegg to a cluster of long, rectangular, two-story stone buildings near the western wall.

"Those five barracks there," Hegg said, sweeping his arm.

"Do you know which one the commanders are in?" I asked.

"No, Sire."

Still not sure this isn't a trap. Either way, I don't want any bloodshed. "Hegg, wait here. Bior, I want you at my side."

Taking slow steps, we reached the door. I raised my fist to knock and whispered, "Keep a sharp eye."

Bior answered with a quick nod.

I struck the door three times. "This is King Fitzeirick! I'd like to speak with Commanders Sturla and Gesta! Send them out, please!"

"They aren't here," a muffled voice answered. "And wouldn't talk to you if they were."

"And you are?" I asked.

"Sergeant Galti."

"Good sergeant, will you talk with me?"

"My commander ordered me not to."

Bior sighed.

I nodded and whispered, "Patience," before continuing. "Sergeant Galti, I know Commanders Sturla and Gesta are upset with me, with the situation I put everyone in. I don't want us to be at odds here. I'm still your king, and I'd rather not order you out of your barracks, but I don't want to have this conversation through a slab of wood either. Come out, and let's talk. Face to face. Man to man."

Bior and I backed away when the door opened, and Galti stepped out, dressed in armor with a sword on his belt. Standing half a head taller than me, his black hair was cut short, almost shaved.

Looking into his dark eyes, I saw a flash of fear. *Maybe not all is lost.* Saluting him, I smiled. "I need to know what your objection is to leaving with the rest of the warriors."

"My commander said General Gudmann's death is your fault. Sturla refuses to follow you any longer and ordered us to do the same."

Blind loyalty. The same thing got General Nothri executed. Had he not stood by Hallfrid's side, Sturla and Gesta would still have their general. "A good sergeant sets an example by doing as his commander says, but what if their orders aren't in Croy's best interest?"

"I —" He paused and chewed his lip.

He's thinking ... good. "Satra must fall to secure Croy's future, would you agree? What about your warriors? What do they say?"

"Didn't ask."

Nodding, I offered him my hand. "Would you be willing to let them decide for themselves?"

"We were ordered to keep our warriors inside."

"But you didn't ask the warriors if they wanted to stay or fight?" I asked.

"No. We had orders."

"Now, your king is telling you those orders are wrong," I said, still holding out my hand. "I'm asking you to speak with your men, not for me but for their country...their people. Go back inside, and talk to them. I'll wait here for an answer."

Galti looked back to his barracks before shaking my hand. "I'll do as you ask, my king."

"Try. Any effort is better than blindly following a bad order," I said. "And remind them, the fight is for Croy and its future, not my personal glory."

He knocked on the door and stepped inside when it opened.

Bior tapped me on the shoulder. "We don't have time to play this game four more times, Sire. Assuming it works at all."

"If it's successful this time, we won't have to. I'll send whoever walks out to gather as many of the rest, and we'll be on our way."

"And if no one comes out?" Hegg asked.

I shrugged. "Try once more at the next building. I don't want to give up too soon."

Bior groaned.

Enough time had passed that I considered this group a lost cause and turned to walk to the next building.

Before I could take a step, Sergeant Galti led a group of warriors out of the barracks. He stopped in front of the building, and they fell into lines behind him.

I counted forty men.

"Impressive," Bior commented.

The sergeant drew his sword, kneeled, bowed, and offered me the handle. "These men and I swear loyalty to our nation. We agree to fight for Croy to our last breath."

I took the offered blade. "Stand. Look at me."

Galti rose to his feet, and we locked eyes.

"Take your sword. Use it to spill the blood of Croy's enemies. Where are Sergeant Eldrim and the rest of the warriors?"

"Eldrim, and most of his company, refused to listen. They will stay behind."

I nodded. "Though I am disappointed to hear that, I won't force them. You take orders from Commander Hegg now."

"Yes, Sire."

"Commander Hegg!" I yelled. "I have an assignment for you and your new company."

He rushed to my side. "Yes, my king?"

"What I did here, you do with the rest of the barracks. Talk to them. Those who wish to go with us into Satra and fight for their country will be welcomed. Those who wish to stay will not be forced out. Above all else, spill no Croian blood."

"Yes, Sire, of course. But Ketill and I together couldn't change their minds before."

"True, but Sergeant Galti reconsidered what was at stake and spoke with his men. He made a difference once, and I believe he can do it again. Is my trust misplaced, sergeant?"

Galti saluted me. "I will do my best, m'lord. For Croy."

The warriors behind him saluted, shouting, "For Croy!"

"I leave you to this task, Commander Hegg. Do your best but remember, time is short. If I must choose between leaving a few reluctant warriors behind or risk angering the rest of my army ..." I shrugged. "You will be following us on foot."

"Understood, my king."

I nodded. "Do your best. We leave soon."

Hegg smiled before saluting. "Thank you for your trust, m'lord."

I returned his salute and turned to walk back to the gate.

"Will this work?" Bior asked, after we were well away from the barracks.

"We have more men than if I hadn't tried. If Hegg and Galti do the same four more times, they could bring enough men to turn a battle or two until we join the warriors traveling by barge."

"I hope you're right, Sire."

Looking at the sky, I noted it wasn't long before midday. "Right or wrong, we will be moving soon."

"Can't argue with you there," Bior said, before chuckling.

"Did Hegg change his mind?" Osvif asked, when we got close.

"He's trying one last time. Sergeant Galti is helping."

Osvif raised his eyebrows. "He talked Galti into going with us?"

"No, I did," I said. "Galti convinced his company, along with ten warriors from Eldrim's, to join the fight. Hegg and Galti are working to get as many others as they can to join them."

"Sire," Osvif said, wiping his brow. "Assuming Sturla and Gesta keep themselves rooted, who will these sergeants and warriors report to?"

"I assigned Galti to Commander Hegg. You and your fellow commanders can figure the rest out. I don't need to make every decision."

He nodded. "As you say, m'lord."

"Bior, let's get mounted. I'll give the order to leave as soon as I see Hegg coming this way."

"Making them walk as punishment?"

"Given how long it will take us to leave Southold, they'll have time to catch up."

Bior smiled. "They better hope you're right."

Andale snorted and pawed, letting me know he was ready to move.

A small herd of riderless horses paced and stomped at the ground near the gate. Whinnies of restless dray horses washed over the crowd. Wagons creaked as drivers held the animals in check.

Warriors stood at the gate, ready to open the passage.

Bior shifted in his saddle as if he couldn't get comfortable.

"Once I'm outside, drive those horses forward as fast as you can...without running me over," I said.

"Sire, why use the guides as scouts?" he asked, looking sideways at me. "Isn't their strength operating on the ground, in the dark?"

"It is, but more importantly, they know how to work and fight together without direct oversight."

"Hadn't considered that, m'lord."

From horseback, I could see past most of the crowd well enough to notice Hegg leading a group of men. *Looks like better than two hundred. I don't see Sturla or Gesta with him, though. A shame.*

I raised my fist. "Open the gate!"

Cheers rose behind me as the way was cleared.

Thrusting my hand forward, I ordered, "Croian Army! South! To victory!"

Chapter 41

When I put my heels to his flanks, Andale practically leaped forward. *Finally, we're on the move.* The crowd roared as I exited Southold.

Topping the small rise, I looked past the bridges to Fastulf and his company, standing at the edge of the forest. Thundering hoof beats behind me kept me from slowing my pace.

The guides rushed out of their cover, cheering when I rode onto the bridge. Their yells were returned from the warriors riding behind me.

I stopped when I reached Fastulf. "I take it all's well."

"Well enough, m'lord," he said, "if not a bit suspicious. We've had no contact with the enemy. It's like they are drawing us in on purpose."

I nodded. "The horses behind me are for your men. I want your company scouting ahead."

"Gladly, m'lord, but what about night watch?"

"Plenty of warriors riding in wagons can guard our camp at night. Wait here for your horses."

"We need to gather the last of our supplies anyway. We'll catch you once we're mounted, Sire."

I saluted and rode slowly toward the forest.

Fastulf, a pack over his shoulder, jogged ahead of his men and met me at the edge of the trees.

"Did you do any scouting?" I asked.

"Beyond finding places to get out of the storm, no, Sire."

I nodded. "Considering the number of trees Satra took out of Croy, there must be a path through this forest wide enough for wagons."

"Not that we saw. Maybe their woodsyths made paths as they needed."

"Would be a waste of effort but, from what I know of Satra, they have little value for most of their people."

"Make way!" Bior yelled, as the horses got close.

I waved him over to get his thoughts on how best to get through the forest.

"Looks like the trees thin out closer to the shore. We could pass there," he said.

"Not sure I like the idea," I said, shaking my head. "Leaves us open for an ambush from the forest."

"I agree, Sire, but sything a path through the trees leaves both sides open for attack," he countered. "Not to mention having a fair number of woodsyths too tired to fight if we're ambushed."

"Seems we should have spent more time scouting and planning." Scratching my chin, I considered our options. *Fastulf's company needs to know where we're going. Decide.*

"Likely we would have if not for the unexpected delays," Bior commented.

That's putting it lightly. I nodded stiffly and glanced at the scouts to make sure they were mounted. "Fastulf," I called, waving him to me.

"Yes, my king?"

"Finding, or making, a path through the forest will take too long." I pointed toward the shore to our right. "Lead us there. Ride two or three wide. Keep a sharp eye out for movement in the trees."

"As you say, m'lord."

I nodded. "Bior, I want a mounted warrior or two between the wagons and the forest, so long as the shore is passable in that formation."

"Aye, Sire. I'll pass your orders to the caravan."

Following the scouts, I moved Andale closer to the shore. We rode along the erratic boundary, with dark soil to the left and sand on the right. Both gave a little under the big horse's hooves. Water filled the hoof prints left by the guides ahead of me.

The smooth, blue water on my right made an uncomfortable contrast to the dark forest lurking to my left. *Don't like being stuck between someplace I can't go and another I can't see into.*

After Bior returned, positioning himself between me and the trees, I felt a little better.

He whistled and pointed to the mountains ahead. "At least we have a nice view of our next obstacle. How long until we reach them?"

"I'm guessing sometime after midday tomorrow, at this pace."

He nodded. "And we have no idea if there's a pass or what waits on the other side."

"The prisoner said there was a pass."

"But we're riding along the shore because Satra didn't leave a path through the forest. Couldn't they do the same with mountains?"

Why did he ask a question I'd rather not think about? "If they did, we'll find it or make our own pass."

• • • • ● • ● • • • •

As we rode, I kept my focus on the trees, dreading what they might hide. Having forgotten what was going on around us, I flinched when Bior asked if I was getting hungry.

Tension had kept me from thinking about my stomach. "I could eat. What'd you pack?"

"Hard rolls," he said, offering me a waterskin.

Life on the road. "I should have guessed," I said, faking a frown while searching one of my bags.

Taking a drink, I noticed the sun sitting low. "Ride ahead and tell Fastulf to find a place to camp."

"We haven't passed any place where the trees thinned enough to hold all of us. What if there are no clearings?"

Nothing's ever easy. I sighed. "I'll talk with Fastulf; you gather a few commanders. Meet me behind the guides."

"Aye, Sire, but it may take a little time."

"The longer it takes, the fewer options we may have for being secure tonight," I said, before putting my heels to Andale.

Riding to the right of the guides put me at the edge of the water. Occasionally a wave would push far enough up the shore for one of Andale's hooves to splash me with salty water. I could tell he wasn't happy with it but didn't balk as I pushed him to the head of the line.

The guides looked back as I passed them. *Probably wondering what I'm running from.* I didn't slow Andale until I reached Fastulf.

"What's wrong, Sire?" he asked, looking over his shoulder.

"We're running out of light," I said, pointing toward the sun.

"I was thinking the same thing, m'lord. Where do you want to make camp?"

"Take a few men and ride ahead. See if you can find a clearing. Anything big enough to hold most of us is better than nothing."

He nodded. "And if we find nothing?"

I shrugged. "See what you can find quickly. Report back to me. Travel swift. We need an answer soon."

"Of course, Sire. Vikar, Garda ... with me." His horse whinnied when he poked its flanks.

The two men passed while I turned Andale to meet Bior. Even at a walking pace, he wasn't there when I arrived.

Splashing and hoof beats came at me from ahead and behind at nearly the same time. Bior arrived with Osvif, Alrik, and Hegg. As they slowed their horses, Fastulf joined us.

"Well, we're all here," I said. "Fastulf, you first. Did you find someplace for us to set up a secure camp?"

"We found two spots big enough for half our force each," Fastulf said. "Nothing to fit everyone together."

"Not ideal, but workable," I said. "Commanders, would you agree?"

"How far apart are these places?" Alrik asked.

Fastulf shrugged. "A hundred paces. A hundred-fifty at most."

"How deep into the forest? Will we have to steer the wagons through the trees?" Hegg asked.

"The wagons can stay near the shore."

I looked at Osvif. "Thoughts?"

"Plenty, Sire," he said, frowning. "Most of them about how we should have scouted the route better."

"Any suggestions beyond the obvious?" I asked, giving him a crooked grin. "We're here, and we need to get there." I pointed toward the mountains. "Before we do, we have to camp tonight."

Osvif nodded. "At least we can concentrate our guards on the forest side. No one's sneaking up on us from the water, m'lord."

"Good," I said. "Bior and I will camp at the second clearing. The commanders can decide how to split everything else between the two. Agreed?"

"We'll figure it out, Sire," Alrik said.

"Fastulf, how far away is the first one?" I asked.

"If I had to guess, the first of the scouts may be passing it now. If not, they're close."

I nodded. "Get to the front. Split your men so both clearings are secured until everyone arrives. Commanders, figure out how you're going to split everything and let everyone know where to go."

After voicing their agreement, they left to make the best of a bad situation. The guides sped up as Fastulf rode past them, shouting orders. Bior and I pressed our horses to keep pace.

Half of the guides turned left as we passed the first clearing without breaking stride. I glanced at the area. *Going to be one crowded camp.*

Not being bred for speed, Andale slowed a little as we hurried past the meager clearing. Bior rode ahead and pointed left when the rest of the guides turned.

Pulling on the reins, I brought my horse to a walk and relaxed in the saddle. Sweat trickled out of the back of my helmet, making an uncomfortable line down my spine. Andale was still breathing heavily when we reached the group.

Fastulf and Bior stood together, watching the scouts searching along the tree line.

"That was fun," Bior said, when I got close.

"I don't think Andale agrees," I said, handing Bior my helmet and reins. I wiped sweat off my forehead and took a long drink from my waterskin before dismounting. The ground squished under my feet. "What's going on?"

"They're checking the ground to see if we can pull a short wall at the edge of the trees, Sire."

"Be glad to help," I said. "Gives me something to do until our part of the caravan arrives."

He nodded, pointing toward the southern edge of the clearing. "Garda's working alone, m'lord. No doubt he'd appreciate the help."

"You two keep an eye out and be ready to help organize camp if anyone arrives before I'm done," I said, before jogging off without waiting for a response.

Hurrying to the border between the grass and trees, I tried to remember what I could about Garda. Nothing about him stood out from the other men I'd trained to use their talent to move safely in complete darkness. He was taller than Fastulf, but most of the warriors were and kept his dark hair shaved close to the skin.

His energy flowed under my feet as I got close. Before I could join him, Garda looked at me with confusion on his face. "Sire, there's something below us, but it's not stone."

Sitting on the damp ground, I pressed one hand into the dirt and pushed my talent down. Not far below, I found something more solid than packed dirt but, like Garda said, it wasn't stone. Everything under me felt long and thin. Some were jagged in places. I moved my talent closer to his and found similarly shaped pieces. Moisture hanging in the soil made it difficult to find any details. "Roots?"

He shrugged. "I don't think so. Maybe something the waves dropped. Let me push one up so we can see."

"I'll help," I said. "Ready?"

He answered by shoving energy into the ground.

Adding my talent to his, we seized the mysterious object closest to the surface and pulled.

Water seeped from the soil as we forced whatever the thing was through the dirt. Shadows from the low sun made it hard to see the dark-colored item when it broke the surface. I grabbed it and held it in the fading light. Long and thin, it didn't take long to realize it was a bone. *Probably from someone's arm.*

"Sire, is that a—" Garda's eyes flicked from the bone to my face and back.

"Yes, it is. Put it back underground. I have a feeling this could be a graveyard. I'm calling off the search."

As the bone sank into the dirt, Fastulf yelled, "King Fitzeirick! Come quick."

Chapter 42

I jumped to my feet, spotted the guide leader near the edge of the forest with a couple of his men, and ran. Bior reached him just before me.

"What's wrong?" I asked.

"Vikar found this," he said, offering me a broken skull.

Bior gasped. "Oh. That's not good."

"Garda and I found bones too. This must be a large burial site."

"How many were broken?" Fastuklf asked.

"Once we figured out what was down there, I had Garda put it back, and we quit searching," I said.

"Most of what they found were damaged," Fastulf said.

"Doesn't tell us anything useful," Bior muttered.

"It might mean Stoneskins were made here. How many bodies did you disturb?"

"I don't think they're whole bodies, Sire. This sat on top of bone shards, maybe shattered ribs," Fastulf said. "Also, there's nothing but bones, no cloth, leather, metal ... nothing."

"Satra buries their dead naked?" Bior asked.

"I wouldn't put it past them," I said, wiping my hands on my armor. "Put the bones back, and keep this quiet. Bior, ride to the other camp and see if they found the same thing ... discreetly, if possible."

"Aye, Sire."

The unmistakable sound of horses and wagons reached my ears as Bior hurried away.

"Fastulf, make sure this stays quiet. I'm going to find out which commanders are here and work out plans for securing the camp," I said, watching riders and wagons enter the area.

"Don't worry, Sire. We know how to keep quiet," Fastulf said.

As I walked across the clearing, I spotted Commander Hegg riding next to a wagon and picked up my pace. When I got close, I called his name and waved.

He turned and trotted in my direction. "Well met, Sire."

"Well met. Who else is assigned to this camp?"

"Ketill and Alrik. We agreed to have a few more warriors here since it's deeper into enemy territory, m'lord."

I nodded. "Find them and meet me over there," I said, pointing to the southern edge of the clearing. "I'll get Fastulf, and we can work out how to best defend the clearing tonight."

"With all haste, Sire." He turned and rode back toward the caravan.

I jogged back to Fastulf. "Commanders Hegg, Ketill, and Alrik should be here soon."

"The sooner the better, Sire," Fastulf said. "My men can make camp in the dark. Most other warriors can't."

"I know," I said. "Have your men gather firewood ... we're going to need it."

"Anything we can do to help, m'lord." Fastulf pointed toward the trees. "You heard King Fitzeirick, into the forest, men. Keep your eyes open for signs of anyone moving about, and watch for traps."

The guides saluted and hurried into the woods to get supplies.

With a quick tilt of my head toward where the horses grazed, I said, "While we wait, I need to find Andale and see what Bior did with my helmet."

"After you, Sire."

"How are we going to have enough room for the horses and tents?" I asked.

"We'll have to pack the tents tight or sleep under the sky, m'lord."

"Given the unpredictable weather, I'd rather be under some kind of cover."

He crossed his arms and shivered. "You don't have to say that twice."

My turn to chuckle. "Was it that bad?"

He nodded. "The thunder gave us enough warning to syth crude shelters, but Alfgeir's filled with water. He panicked and tried to get back to the hold. We yelled at him to stop, but I guess he couldn't hear us over the wind and thunder. Thought he made it until I sent Onem to bring him back when the weather cleared."

"No one saw him fall in?" I asked, as we reached Andale eating grass near the center of the herd.

"Garda and Onem tried to catch him. Lost sight a few paces from the bridge. They told me the wind blew waves high enough to splash the top of the beam. Best guess, he was washed off trying to cross."

Frowning, I took a drink from the waterskin and offered it to Fastulf.

He pressed his lips together and shook his head.

Bior had wedged my helmet under the flap of a saddlebag and tied it tight. Shoving it on my head, I heard hoof beats approaching and turned to see Bior, Osvif, Ketill, and Alrik trotting toward us side-by-side.

The horses around us moved away. Fastulf and I dodged and pushed our way out without being stepped on.

The riders slowed to a stop as we escaped the startled herd.

I motioned toward the sun. "It will be dark soon. We still have a camp to set up and secure. Bior, what did you find out?"

He frowned. "The guides found much the same things underground as here, Sire."

Alrik raised his eyebrows and looked at Fastulf. "Underground? What did you find?"

"Bones," I said.

"What kind of bones?" Ketill asked.

"People. Bodies," I said, scowling.

"Oh," he replied, face twisting.

I nodded. "Best we can tell, the clearings are burial grounds."

"Is that a problem?" Hegg asked, looking at each of us in turn.

"I'd rather keep it quiet so it doesn't become a problem," I said. "Don't want anyone to feel like we are disrespecting the dead,"

"So, we make camp and leave early tomorrow," Alrik said.

"Good." Pointing to the scattered wagons, I looked at Bior. "Get the wagons circled nearer the shore, as best you can, and help get the horses secured."

"Gladly, Sire."

"Commanders, how are we going to secure this clearing?" I asked.

"We discussed it on the way here, m'lord," Alrik said. "Put double guards between the tents and the trees. It's safe to station fewer men to the south and have ten or fifteen men patrol the edge of the forest."

Nodding as he explained the plan, I looked at the other two commanders. "You agree?"

"Yes, Sire," Hegg said. "If there's an attack, it's enough warriors to alert the camp and hold off an initial thrust until the rest join the fight."

Looking around the area, I scratched my chin before nodding. "Get the men in place."

The commanders saluted and left to give orders.

Fires flickered to life across the clearing. *The light tells Satra where we are, but at least everyone won't be stumbling around in the dark if we're attacked.*

I drained my waterskin while heading to the wagons to see where I might be needed.

Someone shoved a bundle of cloth at me. "Take this to the nearest group of tent poles and hurry back. Plenty more where this came from."

I wanted to help. With a shrug, I left to find a tent frame needing its cover. Dropping the bundle near a tent site, I headed back for the next load.

Bior, a pack over his shoulder, called my name before I was halfway back. "Sire, what are you doing?"

"Helping," I said, smiling.

"I've been looking for you. Figured your waterskin would be empty by now. Brought you another."

A warrior carrying another bundle dodged around us.

"Also, Sergeant Sighadd asked me to remind you we don't know how far the tides wash onto this beach."

I shook my head and traded my empty skin for a full one. "In other words, we should have done more scouting before leaving Southold."

"I didn't take that from his tone, Sire. He seemed more concerned about wagons getting stuck in the sand or washed away if it's bad enough."

I sighed. "Let's find a commander."

Most of the tents were raised before we found Commanders Osvif and Alrik sitting near a fire with their sergeants.

"Commanders," I said, "Bior brought a concern to my attention. Along with watching for the enemy, every man on patrol needs to watch for rising water."

Alrik nodded. "Sighadd mentioned it to us, too. We assigned him the task of spreading the word, m'lord."

"Good thinking," I said, before turning to Bior. "When and where are we eating?"

He patted his pack. "Dried meat and hard rolls tonight, m'lord. We can eat when and where you'd like."

I raised a couple of seats. "Here's good, as long as they don't mind the company."

"We've already eaten, Sire," Osvif said. "But you're welcome to share the fire with us."

Bior sat, put the pack between his feet, and offered me a thin roll along with a handful of dried meat.

Dropping my helmet to the ground, I sat, tore off a piece of meat with my teeth, sipped some water, and chewed.

"Why haven't we seen any soldiers yet, Sire?" Alrik asked.

I swallowed and nodded. "I've wondered the same thing."

"No obvious paths for men or wagons either," Bior added.

"Right," Osvif said. "It doesn't make any sense."

"We don't think like the Satran people," I said.

"Does anyone?" one of the sergeants quipped.

Most of the men smiled and nodded.

"Remember, they don't think like us either. Everyone needs to pay attention and stay on guard," I said, snapping the roll in half.

Osvif looked around the fire. "King Fitzeirick's right. A trap looks safe until it's closed on you."

"Hope for the best but prepare for the worst," I said, tapping on the upside-down T branded on my left cheek. "A lesson learned the hard way."

Bior yawned. "Time for me to find my bed. You coming along, Sire?"

Looking at what I had left to eat, I nodded. "I'll finish this while we walk. We should get in the habit of bedding down early and rising with the sun ... if not before. Commanders, Sergeants, thank you for what you've done so far. Remind everyone: the hard work is yet to come."

They stood with us, bowed, and wished us a good night.

Bior slipped the pack over his shoulder and grabbed my helmet.

I ate as we walked toward the center of camp, finishing the meal a few steps before Bior stopped in front of a tent.

"Given the small space, your regular tent wasn't put up. You and I are sharing one meant for four warriors, m'lord."

"Is such a luxury causing problems for anyone else?" I asked.

He held the flap open for me. "No, Sire. With the number of men on guard and patrolling, no one's sleeping in the open."

"Good." Stooping over, I stepped into the shelter. *Plenty of space for two; four would be tight.*

"No straw either," Bior said, tying the tent flap closed behind him.

"Sleeping on damp ground?" I shook my head. "Thorgault claimed this armor would be comfortable enough to sleep in. Guess I'll test it."

Bior shook his head and pointed to the back of the tent. "Lie there, m'lord. I'll sleep nearer the entrance in case we're attacked."

"Can you sleep in your leather?" I asked, standing my hammer on the ground and hanging my helmet on its handle.

"My worry, Sire, not yours. Sleep well."

Using my talent, I did my best to squeeze water out of the ground below us and leave the dirt hard. *Might be less comfortable, but better than trying to sleep when you're wet.*

Chapter 43

"Move the wagons!"

What? I sat up in the dark tent and wiped visions of mud and bones out of my eyes.

"Everyone up! We gotta move the wagons!"

"Sire," Bior said.

"I'm awake." Clambering to my feet — *this armor may be comfortable, but it's not easy to go from lying to standing* — I nearly knocked Bior over as he hunted for the ties to open the tent.

We stumbled out into near darkness. From the slivered moon's position, first light was still some time away.

"Stonesyths, to the beach! Woodsyths, gather the horses. Firesyths, get the campfires lit!" I bellowed, before jogging to help push wagons. Pulling strength from the damp ground along the way was a struggle, but there was little doubt I'd need all the help my talent could give.

Similar orders were carried across the camp as I reached the beach. Fires flared behind us as water washed over my feet, disrupting my talent.

Bior headed to help with the horses while I turned to push a wagon.

On dry, packed ground, it would be an easy task. On the water-soaked beach, my feet dug in. The wheels tore long troughs, piling sand against them, making it harder to push.

Someone harnessed a team of horses and set them pulling.

I sloshed to the next one without waiting to see if the horses could move the wagon. From the sounds behind me, the team needed help to get it rolling.

The thin moon hung low in the sky before our wagons were freed.

After wiping sweat from my brow, I cupped my hands near my mouth, "Tents down!"

"To the fire with the tents," a warrior near me said, "I'm exhausted."

I turned toward the voice but wasn't sure who said it. "No less tired than your king, but if this water climbs farther, they could get washed away, and we'll be sleeping under the sky for at least a few nights. Move!"

Groans rose from the men, but they followed my order. Bior and Alrik found me soon after.

"Sire, rest," Bior said. "Others can take care of the tents."

"The sooner they're packed, the sooner we move away from this mess," I said.

"We're sending a rider to the other camp, m'lord," Alrik said.

"Load a couple of wagons with stonesyths and send them along," I said, "in case they need help."

"Yes, Sire." Alrik saluted and hurried away.

"After we drop this tent, I need some water," I said.

"Pushing the wagons didn't get you wet enough?" he asked, a big smile visible in the firelight.

"Water to drink," I said. "Let's get a waterskin and see if we can get something to eat early."

"I still have a few rolls and some meat strips in my pack."

I shrugged. "Better than having to wait. Let's get back to our tent, or where it used to be, and get ready to ride."

Our tent was gone. Someone rested the pack and waterskin against my hammer.

I took a long drink while Bior retrieved our meal.

"Take this, Sire. I'm not hungry."

"You sure?"

He nodded. "I'll get more once we're moving. No doubt you'll be hungry again before midday, m'lord."

After grabbing my helmet and putting my hammer on my back, I took the food. "Time to find our horses and get everyone ready to go."

Bior glanced north. "Are you going to give the order to move before we hear anything from the other camp?"

"No, but if everyone's ready to go and they need help, we can get there faster."

"True," he said, nodding. "I expected to hear something by now, Sire."

"I doubt there was an attack. We *would* have heard fighting." I spotted Andale. "If we haven't heard anything by first light, you and I will ride to the other camp. Get on your horse, let the commanders know about our plan, and meet me on the northern edge of the clearing."

"Aye, Sire."

Andale stomped on the soggy ground, snorting as I approached.

"I know," I whispered, sliding on my helmet. "I don't like this place much either."

Settled in the saddle, I quickly ate and washed everything down with a long drink. Hunger and thirst quenched, for the time being, I turned north and asked Andale to walk. Men and horses moved as I passed through.

The rhythmic splashing of a horse galloping through water rose above the sounds around me. "Send more men!" the rider yelled.

Putting my heels to Andale, I hurried to meet the messenger. "What's wrong?"

"The north camp got more water than we did. Two wagons of men weren't enough help."

I spun my horse around and trotted to the center of camp. "Stonesyths! Drop what you're doing! Go help the north camp! On horseback or afoot, I don't care! *Move!*"

For a few breaths, nothing changed, and then others yelled for men to go north.

Nodding to myself, I smiled and continued north.

Bior found me before I reached the edge of the clearing. "Sire, you're not still going to the other camp, are you?"

Looking at him, I furrowed my brow. "You wanted to go before we knew what was going on. Why not go now? They need men. I can help."

"And if you get hurt, m'lord?"

"Our warriors fight on," I said.

He crossed his arms. "Sire, these men have no general. The commanders look to you for guidance now."

"Maybe it's time to promote one, in case the worst should happen."

"I swore to Queen Tindra to keep you safe, m'lord. There are plenty of men to go help. We should find the commanders and make plans for the rest of today."

We trotted across the clearing, looking for the commanders, and found Osvif eating with his sergeants near a campfire where the forest met the southern edge of our camp.

"Well met, Commander," I said, as we approached. "Where are your fellow leaders?"

He saluted. "Ketill and Alrik rode north to help, m'lord."

"I wanted to discuss travel plans for today," I said, returning his salute. "As we get deeper into Satra, surely we'll face some resistance."

His sergeants nodded as he looked at them. "We have discussed similar concerns among ourselves. Until we know the north camp's ready, all we can do is wait for the wagons to return so we can load them."

"He makes a good point, Sire," Bior commented.

I tapped a finger on my chin, trying to figure out what we should do. The eastern edge of the sky brightened. *It will be first light soon, and we're nowhere near ready to advance.* "So ... we wait." I sighed. *We're forced to do the one thing we shouldn't ... waste time.*

"Stay here, Sire. I'll get food for the road," Bior said.

I crossed my arms. "I'd rather help with preparations than stand around doing nothing."

Bior nodded. "I'll find you after filling my pack."

Following my assistant, I turned Andale toward the first group of men I noticed loading a wagon.

"Can we help you, Sire?" one asked, as I dismounted.

"I'm here to help," I said, smiling. "I can lift loads as well as the next man."

"Understood, m'lord," he said, bowing.

Working together, we stacked enough to load three wagons before Bior found me. Bright rays of light crossed the sky.

Before he could say anything, the sound of splashing hooves rolled through camp. We turned north to see horses pulling wagons heading our way.

"Let's see how bad it is," I said, then hurried to mount Andale.

Commander Alrik rode next to the driver.

"Anything to report?" I asked.

Alrik shrugged. "The wagons nearest the water were stuck fast, but nothing was lost, as far as I was told."

"And the men?" I asked.

"Everyone's alive, but ..." He chuckled and slapped his knee, spraying water. "Most of us are soaked to the skin."

"Good to know no one was lost," I said, grinning, "you'll dry as we go."

"Yes, m'lord ... we will."

I gestured toward the forest. "Lead the caravan closer to the trees to get out of the water. We'll ride ahead and get the wagons loaded."

Alrik saluted. "As you say, m'lord. The men on foot are moving slow."

Once we were away from the caravan, I turned to Bior. "I'm guessing none of them had a chance to eat. Tell the quartermasters to get food to the warriors as quickly as possible once we're moving."

"Aye, Sire."

I kept a steady pace and found Commander Osvif leaning against a wheel and sweating heavily.

"Osvif, are you well?" I asked.

"Just winded, m'lord."

"Take a moment to catch your breath and then get everything loaded quickly. Exhausted warriors can ride where there's room." Pausing, I glanced south. "I'd like to reach the base of those mountains before we stop."

Groaning as he stood, he saluted. "I'll pass the word to my sergeants, Sire."

Returning his salute, I thanked him.

As the sun peeked over the horizon, I watched warriors and wagons trickle in and line up.

Bior returned. "The quartermaster assured me everyone would eat soon, m'lord."

"Good. I'm heading to the front of the line. Let me know when it's time to move."

"Aye, Sire."

Men waved or saluted as I rode past. I made sure to nod or salute in return. *Respect is a two-way path.* Reaching the southern edge of the clearing, I found Fastulf talking with a few of his men.

"Morning, men," I said, before yawning.

Fastulf smirked. "An early one, Sire, but nothing we can't handle."

"Good to hear. Plan to stop at the mountains," I said, "I'm told tents from the other camp are soaked and need to dry."

Fastulf nodded. "Any objection to us searching for passes once we arrive, m'lord?"

"Sounds like a good use of your skills," I said. "Before you leave, make sure you get food for the road."

He patted a saddlebag. "Ready for anything, Sire."

"What about your men from the northern camp?" I asked.

His eyes opened wide. "I ... umm ... I don't know, m'lord."

I crossed my arms. "Not ready for *everything*, it seems. Go see to your men."

"Yes, Sire."

As they rode away, I snickered and shook my head. They weren't out of sight when I spotted Bior coming my way.

"Everything's ready, Sire."

"Almost. Fastulf is making sure all the scouts have food. Shouldn't take long," I said, turning Andale to face south.

Soon, the company of scouts arrived and hurried into position ahead of us.

"Let's move!" I yelled, pointing to the mountains in the distance.

Bior echoed my order, and we set a steady walking pace.

Chapter 44

We rode closer to the forest than yesterday to avoid most of the water. The sounds of horses and wagons behind me, combined with the small waves washing up the beach, set me on edge. *Perfect cover for an ambush.* Breezes off the water moved leaves and limbs in the trees. My eyes flitted to each movement, watching for an attack.

Bior approached, blocking my vision. "Remember, m'lord, I've got food for us. Let me know when you want to eat."

I nodded and held out my hand, shifting in the saddle to look around him. My hand closed on whatever he gave me while my eyes swept the shadowy forest.

"Nerves, m'lord?"

I flinched at Bior's words. "What?"

"We've ridden a ways, and you haven't taken a single bite."

"We haven't seen a single soldier, no signs of a force, since we crossed into Satra," I said, glancing at the dried meat clutched in my hand. "I hope none of us are feeling too calm."

"I'm not sure I'd call our travels easy, Sire. This morning was a challenge."

"Only because we chose the open route and camped near the water's edge. Why haven't we been attacked? Why haven't Satran soldiers done anything to slow our advance?"

He nodded. "I'll admit, I expected more fighting by now, too, but you're the one who said the Satran don't think like us, m'lord. Maybe they're still setting their trap, planning something we'd never consider."

"So, how do we plan for something we'd never think of?"

He chuckled. "My king, we don't ... can't. But we have a surprise of our own unless they spot the barges before our warriors can reach the shore. Let's hope we catch them in our snare before they close the loop on us."

"True." I nodded. "Still, make sure you remind everyone to stay alert."

"Of course, Sire."

· · · · •·•· · ·

We ate on the move, the sun high above us, but our destination remained distant. I've never understood why mountains seem to stay far off as you approach until you're nearly at their base. Unlike ranges back home, where the forest gave way to foothills before you reached the rocky slopes, the forest remained thick until it met the edge of an abrupt rise sloping steeply to a narrow, grassy plain ending at the wall of towering peaks jutting from the ground as if the world grew them out of anger.

"Bior, let everyone know we're stopping here."

"Aye, Sire."

I dismounted, grabbed my nearly empty waterskin, and walked to the nearest mountain. Taking a drink, I closed my eyes, put my hand against the stone, and pushed my talent out to see what I could learn. Galloping hoof beats broke my concentration. The waterskin hit the ground as I reached for my hammer.

"Sire!" Fastulf bellowed. "Sire! I found something!"

"What?" I yelled back, jogging toward his voice.

He appeared from behind one of the many stone outcroppings jutting from the ground near the mountains, slowing his horse to a trot when he saw me.

"What did you find?"

"A tunnel, my king. Maybe. But the stone around it ... it's like nothing I've ever felt. It's wrong."

The hairs on my neck stood. "What do you mean?"

"It makes me queasy when I look at it and —"

My stomach churned. "There's no energy in it when you touch it."

He shivered. "How did you know?"

"Where?"

He twisted in his saddle and pointed. "A short ride back that way, Sire."

"And your men?"

"Left them to guard it, m'lord."

"Go back and make sure no one enters. I'll come to you after I find Bior."

Confusion on his face, he saluted. "Yes, Sire."

Clicking my hammer in place, I hurried back and mounted my horse. Andale wanted to keep eating grass, but he moved when I put my heels to him.

Men were unloading the first wagon I reached. Bior was nowhere to be seen. I asked the warriors if they knew where he was.

One pointed north. "Last I saw, he was riding toward the rest of the caravan, m'lord."

Trying to ignore the faint pounding in my ears, I thanked him and put my heels to Andale again. It wasn't long before I spotted my companion talking to a driver, pointing toward the wagons ahead. "Bior! I need you!"

His shoulders slumped when he saw me, but he nodded and trotted in my direction. "What's wrong, Sire?"

"The scouts found something and —"

"A pass?" he interrupted.

"I'm not sure," I said, "it could be a trap. I want you with me when I go look" My stomach twisted as I spoke. "What Fastulf described — it scares me."

"Sire, I'm not going to let anything happen to you."

"I believe you'll do your best. Let's go."

He followed me back to the mountains. I expected Bior's presence to help me relax, but my nerves were still on edge when we turned left to find the scouts.

Fastulf and his men were on foot, watching the woods or the dark square in the mountain.

"What can you tell me?" I asked, dismounting before I caught sight of what I feared would be there.

Fastulf jogged to me. "Sire, the strange stone surrounds the opening two or three armspans into the rock around it. It lines the hole as deep as any of us can push our talent. No idea if it's really a way through or simply a strange cave."

Sounds a lot like the tunnels under the capital. My stomach clenched into a tight knot. Gritting my teeth against the pain, I nodded. "Stay close," I whispered to Bior.

My eyes locked on the hideous, dead stone as soon as it came into view. To anyone who hadn't experienced it, the opening looked like a man-made tunnel sythed into the side of the mountains. A large square, defined by an arm's length of green-black material surrounding the opening. What little light entered showed the horrible stuff continued as far as I could see inside. If my guts hadn't been knotted, I would have vomited my lunch. The hairs on my arms and neck stood tall. My legs stopped moving, freezing me in place. *No doubt it's the same stuff.*

"King Fitzeirick, what's wrong?" Bior asked.

Closing my eyes, I shook my head. Visions of never-ending darkness flooded my mind. I couldn't ignore the memories of endless walking with Sir and Mam, never sure where we were going or what threats waited as we traveled. *How many people did I kill to keep us alive?* A burn spread up my throat as I recalled meals of raw rat or snake.

Chills shook me as beads of cold sweat collected on my forehead. *No matter how hard I tried, Sir died so Mam and I could escape. To the fire with those tunnels and this place too. To the fire twice with whoever created this dead stone.*

"Sire. What is it?" Bior asked.

"Bad memories," I said quietly, opening my eyes and willing myself to move again.

"I don't understand, m'lord."

"Until you've been there, you couldn't."

"Been where, my king?" Fastulf asked, looking concerned.

No doubt I looked terrible, likely pale and covered in sweat. "I'd rather not talk about it right now."

Fighting my own body, I walked to the opening. It looked wide enough for a wagon to pass through with room to spare. I pressed my hands against the material I feared most. The smooth stone had the same glassy feel as what lined the walls of the hidden dungeon under Croy's capital.

Taking my hammer from my back, I sythed a point from one face, pulled some strength from the ground, and hit the wall as hard as I could.

Brittle fragments sprayed everywhere. Several small pieces struck my chest hard enough for me to feel through the leather and metal. A chunk bounced off my helmet and fell at my feet.

"Careful, Sire," Bior complained.

"Was that what you expected, my king?" Fastulf asked.

I grabbed the rounded lump and studied it. *It's the same sickening color and breaks all rounded and blunt.* "Any woodsyths or firesyths among your company?"

"A few with minor talents, Sire. Why?"

Turning, I clicked my hammer in place and tossed the stone to Bior. "Torches. We're going to need lots of torches. No matter how weak a woodsyth they are, send them into the forest to gather wood. Rest your firesyths. Every stonesyth needs to make picks or hammers. The harder, the better."

"I don't understand, m'lord," Fastulf said.

"Me either," Bior added, still looking at a piece of the dead stone.

I thrust my finger toward the hole. "No one enters alone, in case it is a trap. No one goes in without a torch and something to smash stone. Swords and axes aren't well suited for the job."

"But if this is a passage, why not walk through?" Fastulf asked.

"Treat it like a trap until we prove it isn't because this same material makes the walls of the maze of tunnels deep under our capital."

Bior's eyes opened wide, and he dropped the stone. "Oh!"

"Far be it from me to question you, m'lord, but I've never heard of any tunnels under the capital," Fastulf said.

"No," Bior said, shaking his head violently. "Drop it."

"Listen to him," I said, crossing my arms and glaring at Fastulf. "And consider yourself fortunate you don't know about them. I wish I didn't."

The scouts backed away from me.

Fastulf bowed low. "My apologies, Sire. I didn't mean to anger you. Mercy and forgiveness, please."

"Torches, picks, hammers. *Now*. I'll bring food for your company, and we can decide how to proceed."

"Of course, my king," Fastulf said. "Everything will be ready."

He shouted orders behind us as we mounted and rode away.

Chapter 45

"Should we send men to search for another way through or around the mountains, m'lord?" Bior asked.

I shook my head. "Assuming the hole isn't a trap, wasting time looking for another path would trouble me more. The longer we take, the more time Satra has to prepare."

He sighed. "If you insist, Sire."

We entered a sprawling, makeshift camp on the other side of the strange rise. Tents were laid out to dry. Small circles of wagons corralled the horse teams, and small cooking fires heated pots. The rest of the horses grazed on grass.

"Let's locate a commander, find out what's going on here, and let them know where we'll be," I said.

Bior glanced toward the nearest fire and nodded.

"Don't let me forget to get food to bring back to the scouts," I said.

Riding through the chaotic site, we found Commanders Osvif and Alrik eating boiled grains. They saluted when we stopped. "Hungry, Sire?" Osvif asked.

I glanced at Bior and grinned. "Thank you for asking. We'll eat soon enough. I'm more concerned about how long it will take to dry everything."

"That's why we're eating now," Alrik said. "We expect everything will be dry enough to use by the time everyone's had their fill."

"The scouts found something," I said. "A way through these mountains, maybe. I haven't let them search any farther yet. Preparations must be made first."

"Sire," Bior said. "While you discuss this, I'll get grains for us and the scouts."

"Go ahead. I'll meet you there."

"You mentioned preparations, m'lord," Osvif said. "Anything we can do?"

"Nothing more than you're already doing. This tunnel could be a trap. I don't want to lose men finding out. Right now, the scouts are making tools to break through the walls if necessary."

Alrik cocked his head. "Break the walls? Aren't they all strong stonesyths?"

"They are, but this isn't ordinary stone. Sything doesn't work on it. Smashing through with hammers or picks is the only way."

Osvif glanced at Alrik. "Never heard of such a thing, Sire."

"I've encountered it before," I said, crossing my arms to hide the shiver. "Didn't think I'd ever see it again. Once everything dries, load up, head toward the mountains, and turn left. If the pass doesn't get through, we'll send word. Now, I better find Bior before he eats enough for half a company."

They laughed before saluting.

Following the smell of boiled grains, I met a red-faced Bior before I spotted any cooks. "Did you have to work for the meal?" I asked, smirking.

"No, Sire," he said, frowning. "Had to convince the cook you sent me for a company's worth of food."

"I see."

"And he almost forgot to give me spoons," he continued, rattling a sack hanging from his belt. "But insisted there weren't enough bowls to go around."

"I'm sure Fastulf and his men have eaten from the same pot before," I said.

Bior looked over his shoulder and huffed before we left to check on the scout's progress.

We arrived to find the men sitting near piles of torches, hammers, and picks. A noticeable hole was scooped out of the mountain near the dead stone wall.

"We brought boiled grains," I said, motioning toward Bior.

The scouts looked at him and smiled.

"We have to share from one pot," Bior said. "But we brought spoons."

Fastulf took the grains, and we dismounted to sit and eat with his men.

Bior opened the sack and burst out laughing.

I cocked my head. "What is so funny?"

He pulled a fork out of the bag and laughed harder.

"You think the cook did it on purpose?" I asked, noticing several men giving us strange looks.

Bior nodded as tears formed.

I sighed and walked to the depression left when the scouts made tools. "Stone spoons it is."

"We'll help, Sire," Fastulf offered.

I shook my head. "Some of you look worn out. Rest. This won't take long."

Though well-practiced at working stone, it took longer than I expected to make enough spoons.

Bior shoved his into the grains, pulled out a sticky glob, and looked at me. "You should've let them help, m'lord."

"There's a lot left to do today; they needed to rest." I forced my spoon into the gloppy mess and stuffed a wad in my mouth. Barely warm and thick best described the grains. *At least it's easier to chew than dried meat.*

"Sire, what's our next move?" Fastulf asked.

"Scout the hole, see if it goes through these mountains. If so, what's on the other side? If not, we have a decision to make."

Fastulf scrunched his face. "What decision, m'lord?"

Bior chuckled.

"How long do we look for a pass before we syth a big hole through the stone."

"Oh," Fastulf said. His confused expression changed to a concerned look. "We can't tell how thick these mountains are yet. Some of us could start searching now, Sire, in case this doesn't go through."

"I advised the same thing," Bior said.

I shook my head. "It's far easier to hide a path through a forest. Any decent woodsyth can, with little effort. I refuse to believe Satra syths a pass every time they come north. Hide it behind a thin cover, maybe, but that would be easy to find."

"How do we proceed, Sire?" Fastulf asked, looking in a near-empty pot.

"You know your men better than I, but no one enters alone. I'd say groups of five or six, at least two torches among them and each carrying a tool to bust through the dead stone if it blocks their way."

He looked at his men sitting nearby. Each nodded. "A sound plan, m'lord. Guides ready?"

The men slowly rose to their feet, several groaning on the way up.

"What will you do while we search, Sire?" Fastulf asked, approaching the piles of tools.

"Wait here for word of what you've found."

"Should I leave a few men as guards, my king?"

I shook my head. "Bior's staying here. Between the two of us, I should be safe enough until the rest of the army arrives."

Bior tapped his sword hilt. "Rest assured, no harm will come to our king."

Fastulf smiled and nodded. "Understood. Men group up and grab tools. Firesyths, get torches too. Let's see what we find." Hammer in hand, he led the first group toward the hole. Pausing before he stepped inside, he turned and saluted. "See you soon, my king."

I noticed there were several hammers and picks left, along with a pile of torches. "Be safe," I replied, returning the salute.

He led his men onto the smooth stone floor.

Bior and I moved to watch as the scouts moved deeper into the hole. It was easy to see the passage led straight for several paces before curving right, taking the torch flames out of our line of sight.

"What do you think they'll find?" Bior asked, sitting near the opening.

"No idea, honestly. Nothing the prisoner told me makes sense."

"What did he say? Maybe I can figure it out."

Shrugging, I tried to remember what the Satran prisoner had said, if anything, about the mountains. *Did he say a sea was inside them? Maybe he meant the waters beside them, and I misunderstood. There should be a village on the other side ... I think.* I raised a seat for myself, took a deep breath, and told him what I remembered from the conversation.

He furrowed his brow deeper and deeper as I spoke. "You're right. Not much about that makes sense. I mean, a village on the other side of the mountains ... sure. But a sea in the middle? How?"

"Assuming this is a pass, the guides should find the village. We'll know if the prisoner was telling any truth when they return."

"And what do we do while we wait?" Bior asked.

"Stay vigilant."

"Aye."

Chapter 46

Closing my eyes, I pushed my talent into the ground and let it spread around me. When it touched the dead stone, my stomach quivered. *This horrible material is in Croy and Satra. Who put it there? How did they do it? Where did it come from?* Forcing my mind toward more pleasant thoughts, I shifted my focus to the ground in front of us and the edge of the forest beyond.

The rise hid a jumble of rocks, shoved in random angles before time covered them in dirt. Pushing farther, I found places on the other side with long rods of stone angling deep into the ground. *Curious. I've never found anything like that before.*

"Sire," Bior said. "Wake up. We're supposed to be watching for threats."

"Horses are heading our way." I pointed to our right. "At least one wagon isn't far behind."

"Our warriors?"

"Would be my guess."

"My King!" someone yelled, behind us. "We found something!"

The dead stone muffled the voice, so I couldn't recognize it. Turning, I saw Fastulf running with a torchbearer struggling to keep pace.

"While I see what Fastulf's excited about, have everyone start setting up camp within sight of the opening. Keep them on this side of the rise. I don't want anyone wandering off through the forest and getting lost or worse."

"Aye, Sire, but it will be tight quarters."

"That could change, depending on what Fastulf found," I said.

He nodded and hurried away, shouting orders soon after he was out of sight.

Fastulf breathed heavily when he stopped next to me and bowed. "The tunnel —"

The way he said the word brought a shiver down my back, tightening my chest. "*Don't call it a tunnel anymore.* Call it a pass. Call it a hallway. Call it a big hole, for all I care ... anything but a tunnel. Do you understand?"

He bowed again, deeper. "Yes, my king. Deepest apologies for offending you. Please, forgive me."

I nodded. "What did you find?"

"It passes through the mountain to this." Frowning, he held a closed fist toward me.

It was my turn to squint in confusion. "What have you got?"

When he opened his fist, I wanted to look away. "A huge area of black sand, Sire, surrounded by mountains."

"The black sand sea," I whispered. *It's not water at all. This is what Rorec and Da'rin spoke of.* Touching the grains, I found them smooth, dry, and nearly round. My talent told me this was the same material as the walls in the pass and under the capital. *How would you make this solid?*

Wagons, men, and horses passed close by as I stared at the sand. We stepped toward the entrance to give them more room.

"What? I couldn't hear you, Sire."

I shook my head. "Nothing. There are no obstructions in the passage? No traps?"

"No, m'lord. We searched the entire length. The strange stone is perfectly uniform and smooth for about two hundred paces and then dumps into this sand."

How far to the other side of the area?"

"About a day's walk, if I had to guess."

"So, we can reach the other mountains before dark with an early enough start? Good."

"No. We may not be able to cross at all. Garda stepped out and sank past his knee before we pulled him back. No doubt a horse or wagon would sink too." He shook hard enough for me to see. "I'm not sure there's a bottom, Sire."

"That can't be right," I said, rubbing my chin. "Surely the Satran army brought supply wagons when they invaded Croy. Find out how they crossed." *Da'rin said he walked around the sea.* "Check the edges but be careful."

"We'll do our best, Sire." He frowned before hurrying back into the pass.

Looking into the dark hole made my heart thump in my chest. *I have to enter sooner or later. Or there's another way, and we haven't found it.* Grabbing my hammer, I slammed it to the ground and growled.

"What's wrong, Sire?" Bior asked.

"Frustrated," I grumbled. "We're missing something. Please, tell me you have good news."

"Not sure if it's good, but we found a way to corral the horses, m'lord, but then there isn't enough room for everyone to camp where you said."

I looked at the growing lines on either side of us and wrung my hands together. Turning to the pass, I gritted my teeth. *It's dry, has open space, is easy to secure, and Fastulf said it's safe. No matter how much I don't like it...it's best for my men.* "We have another option." I gestured toward the hole. "As many as possible can sleep in there. The rest can put their tents between the corrals."

Bior drew a hissing breath. "Are you willing to spend the night on that stone?"

My stomach fluttered. "I'll do what's necessary."

He stared at me and frowned before nodding. "I'm sure you will, Sire. What can I do to prepare?"

"Send woodsyths to collect firewood. I want the passage well lit."

He bowed. "Consider it done, m'lord. I'll find you before dark."

Osvif and Alrik found me while I watched men leading horses into the corrals to distract myself from what was coming.

"How are you doing this evening, Sire?" Osvif asked, saluting.

"Well. You two?"

"Doing fine, my king," Alrik said. "We wanted to discuss plans for tonight's patrol and guard assignments."

"Maybe I can make your jobs a little easier. The bulk of our men will be inside the pass. Post a few guards at each end of the corrals, patrol the hilltop."

"Sire, we aren't sleeping in the forest?" Osvif asked, looking toward the trees.

"There's too much we don't know about those woods." Pointing into the passage, I continued. "This empties on the other side of this mountain range. No reason most of us can't sleep in there. The rest can camp here. Bior's leading a group to gather firewood. Seems like the safest option we have. Do you not agree?"

"Depends, Sire," Osvif said. "We're fairly sure these woods are empty. Could we risk an ambush from the other end of this pass? What's waiting for us on the other side?"

"Sand," I said. "A large field of loose, deep sand with more mountains beyond."

"Sounds like a workable option," Osvif replied. Alrik nodded his agreement. "We'll tell our men about the change."

"See to your duties. I suspect we'll face more challenges tomorrow."

"No doubt, Sire," Alrik commented.

The commanders saluted and jogged away.

Taking a deep breath, I stared into the hole. My stomach knotted as its darkness filled my vision. *The way is safe. Fastulf made it to the other end and back.* My legs locked stiff as stone pillars, rooting me in place. *I must overcome this fear.* My heart pounded. The harder I tried to force myself to take a step, the more my body resisted.

Bior called my name behind me.

I flinched, lost my balance turning to look at him, and stumbled toward the pass.

He was at my side in an instant. "My king, what's wrong? Sit. I'll get a herbalist."

"No need," I said, patting his shoulder. "I'm not sick. It's nerves. Firewood gathered?"

"Aye, Sire. They're stacking it over the hill to save space here."

"Good," I said, with a slight smile.

"I take it you'll want to sleep out here tonight, m'lord."

"More than anything." Crossing my arms to hide my tremors, I shook my head. "But if I don't go in there now, I might as well leave for the capital. Letting fear guide my actions won't help anyone, least of all me. What kind of leader am I if I can't enter a place I know is safe?"

He moved to stand between me and the source of my dread. "Listen to me. Every man has his limits, Sire. From strongest king to lowest servant, no man is completely fearless. A little fear keeps us alert ... might save your life."

"What you say is true enough, but fear mastered is bravery. In order to be a good king and leader, I must be brave."

"Be careful you don't confuse being foolhardy for brave, Sire."

My hand went to the traitor's brand on my cheek. "A lesson I'll never forget. Seems like a lifetime ago, the last time I made that mistake."

"Oh. Sire. I didn't mean —"

"I know," I said, nodding, "and took no offense. Grab a torch and walk by my side. I want to see this black sand sea."

"Aye, Sire. If you're sure."

"It's now or never, and I'd feel better with someone I trust at my side."

He smiled and nodded. "Wait here while I get a light, m'lord."

Turning, I noticed men unloading supplies and took half a step back. Even knowing the feared hallway was behind me, I needed to make room.

Bior approached, carrying a lit torch. "Ready, Sire?"

"No. But it must be done." Turning to face my fear, I squared my shoulders. *If I don't go in now, this war is over.*

Chapter 47

Facing the opening, it seemed to grow smaller with each step. I stopped walking and wiped my eyes, trying to convince myself the mountain wasn't going to close behind me and lock me inside another tunnel of dead stone. *I'm not alone. I can do this. My people, my country, depend on me overcoming this challenge.*

Bior grabbed my arm. "I'm here. Both ends of the pass are open." A grin spread across his face. "I'll hold your hand if you'd like."

I glared at him before letting myself grin in return. "Won't be necessary. Plus, what would Queen Tindra say?"

He nodded. "She'd thank me for doing my job well." Before I could say anything else, he took a step. "Now, walk with me. Warriors will bring firewood into the passage soon. We don't want to be in their way."

I focused on him, not on where we were going. Stepping onto the smooth stone, my foot slipped, causing my chest to tighten around my pounding heart.

Bior grabbed my arm. "Steady, Sire. Walk carefully."

Nodding stiffly, I took another step. With both feet on the dead stone, instincts took over. Panic pushed my talent out so hard and fast, my head swam, the world tilted, and flashes of light popped before my eyes. "Wait," I whispered.

He squeezed my arm. "You don't have to do this."

"Yes," I hissed, "I do, but I need a moment to get control of myself."

"We have as long as it takes. I won't leave your side."

Grinding my teeth, I forced myself to slow the flow of energy my frightened mind dumped into the floor. *I'm safe. I'm not alone. I can leave anytime I want.* Several deep breaths later, the only light in my vision was the torch's flickering flame. "Go slow."

Using measured steps, Bior led me deeper into the passage. Without the torch, darkness would have engulfed us when we entered the curve. The unnerving lack of echoes raised memories of endless shuffling in the dark with Sir and Mam.

"This place isn't right," Bior mumbled.

"You have no idea," I said.

Anxiety kept me from counting my steps, so dim light flickering in the distance as the curve straightened took me by surprise. Torchlit shadows, barely visible against the dark stone, stretched toward us as Fastulf's men moved about near the exit.

With the opening in sight, we walked a little faster. *No doubt Bior wants out of here as much as I do.* Several guides greeted us when we reached the group standing a few steps inside the pass.

A thin layer of sand littered the floor, making for unsure footing as we got closer to the exit.

"Where's Fastulf?" I asked.

The warrior pointed to the far right. "We found a solid path, to the right of the exit, under the sand, Sire. He took some men and went exploring. We lost sight of him when the sun dropped below the peaks."

"Show me," I said.

Men moved to let Bior and me through to the end of the horrible stone.

Bior held the torch high, but it didn't do much to pierce the night.

I could make out mountain peaks against the twilight sky but not much else. Kneeling, I pushed my hand into the loose material beyond the hard floor. *Cold and lifeless, like the dead stone.* The sand offered no resistance, easily rising past my elbow as I groped for something solid. Finding nothing, I leaned back to keep from falling into the dark field. *Who knows how far I'd sink?*

"You're sure there's something under there?" I asked, sitting back and brushing grains off my armor.

"Yes, m'lord. There's a ledge, maybe wide enough for two men to stand shoulder-to-shoulder, a short stride to the right. It lays almost elbow-deep below the surface. Fastulf insisted on leading a small group to see where it ends."

Must be what the prisoner was talking about. Still doesn't answer how Satra moves horses or wagons through here. "Hope we haven't lost them. Bior, before your torch burns out, head back and get fires arranged through the pass. I'll wait here in case anyone returns."

"Are you sure, Sire?" he asked.

"I have men with me," I said, nodding while getting to my feet.

Bior smiled. "I'll be back soon, m'lord."

I followed him a few steps back into the pass. "Bring the commanders with you. We need to discuss options for tomorrow."

"Aye, Sire."

After Bior's torch faded around the curve, I stood my hammer on the floor, hung my helmet on the handle, and sat with my back against the wall near the group of men.

One of them knelt nearby. "Not to disturb you, m'lord, but I'm worried about Fastulf."

I nodded. "Understandable, but he's resourceful. I trust he'll return in due time."

"I meant my leader no disrespect, Sire. I mean, I'd follow him to the fire if he said that's what we needed to do. But maybe this was the trap you were worried about." He looked out into the darkness.

Offering him my hand, I smiled. "I'm sorry, you look familiar, but I can't remember your name."

"Gavid, my king," he said, taking my hand.

"Well met, Gavid. I share your concern. How many men went with him?"

"Five."

I could tell the others were listening to our conversation. *Must choose my words with care.* "While I share your concern, I trust your leader's judgment, or I wouldn't be in here now. Considering what we face now and in the coming days, it's unwise to send another group to search for your fellow guides. No doubt, six of you are a formidable force should they encounter any threats. He's resourceful and quick when it comes to solving a problem. More than anything, I believe he won't knowingly endanger any of you.

"When the commanders arrive, we'll discuss how we proceed tomorrow. Finding Fastulf and the others will be part of the conversation. Assuming they don't return before."

"Of course, m'lord. Thank you for listening to me."

"Gavid." I paused and slid up the wall to my feet. "This goes for everyone here. I am always approachable ... within reason, of course."

Several of them chuckled.

Resting my hand on my helmet, I continued. "I try to be the best ruler and leader, I can, but it's not always easy or fun. If I don't talk to you, I can't know what needs to be done to better Croy. That is the legacy I want to leave. Nothing would please me more than knowing I'm remembered as the king who did what it took to make Croy the best it can be."

Gavid nodded before turning to stare out into the darkness.

I sat again to avoid losing my nerve to the uncomfortable thoughts filling my mind. *To the fire with the horrible people who figured out how to do anything with this vile stone.*

A flicker inside the pass caught my eye. I turned to see sharp shadows on the wall and watched until I figured out it was men stacking wood. The fire flared shortly before a few men carrying branches came into view.

Bior stepped out of the curve and pointed to a spot near the far wall. "Next one here. The exit is just ahead. Once this fire is lit, go get enough wood for five more campfires and finish. King Fitzeirick wants to talk with the commanders."

As he said, the commanders came into view soon after Bior removed a pack from his back and leaned against the wall to my right.

"Sire," Osvif said. "Bleak setting for a meeting."

I shrugged. "Could be worse. Sit. I need to let you know about a few things before we decide how to proceed."

"Are you hungry, m'lord?" Bior asked, patting his pack. "I brought meat strips and hard rolls for everyone. Couple of waterskins too."

"Good thinking. Pass it around. No reason we can't eat together."

"Aye, Sire."

Once seated, Hegg looked out into the dark. "What's on your mind, m'lord?"

I pointed. "Out there is a huge field of black sand. I'd heard about a black sand sea in Satra. Now we know what it is and where. That's the best of bad news."

"M'lord, knowing where we are can't be all bad," Alrik commented.

"Trust me, it gets worse. I feared this pass was a trap but never thought it would lead to one. The sand is loose and deep. Step out of this pass in the wrong place, and who knows how far you'd sink. I easily pushed my arm in, past my elbow, with no sign of a bottom."

"Assuming there isn't another path around these mountains, Satra must have sent men and horses across," Hottir said. "Seems obvious to me, m'lord. They sythed the surface."

Patting the floor, I let out a heavy sigh. "That sand and this stone are the same ... and I can't syth either one. There must be a way, but *we* don't know the secret. There may be a path around the edge, but we won't know until Fastulf returns. Problem is, we lost sight of them when the sun sank below the mountain tops. It's possible we lost six men to a rumor ... or a lie."

"Stinking Satran," Hottir barked, slapping the floor. "More likely to lie than anything. To the fire with them all."

"To the fire with 'em," Alrik and Hegg repeated.

"I agree, but we still won't know anything until Fastulf returns."

"How long are we going to wait, m'lord?" Osvif asked.

"No one steps onto the sand in the dark. Once we can see, we'll decide how to proceed. One thing is certain, without figuring out how Satra crosses, it's likely we're going the rest of the way on foot."

A new fire flared to life nearby as Hottir crossed his arms. "Without wagons and horses, Sire, how are we going to bring everything we need?"

"I've been led to believe there's a village somewhere on the other side. If so, we capture it and hope it's got horses and supplies."

"More information from the prisoner, m'lord?" Osvif asked.

I nodded and took a drink of water. "He told me we'd find this sand. I suspect there's another pass somewhere and a village beyond."

"The Satran told you about the sand but not how to get an army across," he scoffed.

"He wasn't in the Legion. It's likely he didn't know," I said. "Barring something unexpected, we're walking for a while."

Another fire lit next to the wall across from where we sat.

Alrik coughed. "Sire, we'd better give our sergeants the bad news so they can prepare the men."

"You have my leave. Perhaps the morning will bring an answer."

The commanders stood and saluted.

"Sleep well, Sire," Osvif said, before leading them away.

"Bior, I want one more fire at the exit. Bright enough for Fastulf to notice."

"Aye, Sire. I'll see it done."

"I'll likely be asleep by the time you get back."

Bior smiled. "Rest well, my king. I'll be at your side should you wake and need anything."

As my back touched the floor, haunting words from my time trapped under the capital came to mind; *only the dead lay down.* Heeding the stern warning, I sat up, closed my eyes, and let exhaustion take me.

Chapter 48

I didn't sleep well. My rest was fitful, at best. The feeling of snakes slithering across my legs and the sounds of rats squeaking lurked in the background of somber dreams.

Something stirred next to me. Trying to move away, I found my right arm pinned to the wall. My heartbeat raced as I tried to free myself.

Someone mumbled something I couldn't understand.

Opening my eyes, it took a moment before I could see in the dim light of the nearly dead campfire. Looking right, I found Bior leaning against me. My arm rested across his shoulders, his neck pressing against it.

Reaching across, I gently tilted his head forward to free myself.

He sighed and smacked his lips but didn't wake as I moved his head back and slipped away.

"What was that?" someone whispered, near the exit.

It took me a moment to recognize Vikar's voice.

"I didn't hear anything," a voice, I didn't know, replied.

"I disturbed Bior," I said, stepping closer.

"No, Sire, that wasn't it," Vikar said, quietly. "I felt you moving behind us. I saw something out there along the edge."

"You sure it's not wishful thinking tricking your eyes?" I asked. "How long have you been awake?"

"Garda woke me before the fire burned to embers. It was my turn to watch. Athal woke a little later and joined me."

Can't blame tired eyes. "Let me look," I said, peering into the darkness.

"Nothing to see out there," Athal mumbled, moving to give me room.

"Hush," Vikar said. He swept his outstretched arm along the right wall of mountains, stopping to point. "Over there."

Reaching for his elbow, I nudged his arm to give me a clear view into the darkness. Something shifted at the edge of my vision, closer than where he'd pointed. When I looked directly at the spot, I saw nothing. *What I wouldn't give for a lantern. Even a torch and a mirror would be an improvement.* Out of habit, I pushed my talent out through the dead stone. Finding everyone around me was easy, but when my energy hit the sand, it scattered and told me nothing. With a sigh, I looked again and caught another shift in the darkness. "I think there *is* something there."

"Maybe." He wiped his hand across his eyes and looked again. "Not at that spot now — Closer to us ... I — Sorry, Sire. I'm not sure."

I patted his shoulder. "It's fine. We're all worried about the men who left. Could be we're tricking each other into thinking something's moving this way."

"There is," Athal said. "Saw it too, m'lord."

A shiver ran through me as I stepped back to get my helmet and hammer. "Wake your men in case it's a Satran. I'd like them taken alive, if possible."

"Vikar, keep watch. I'll wake the others," Athal said.

After slipping my helmet on, I tapped Bior's boot with mine. "Wake up. We might need your sword."

He mumbled something before yawning.

I tapped harder. "On your feet."

He nodded and rubbed his eyes. "What's wrong, Sire?"

"Something's moving this way from the sand."

"Something's ... Oh!" He blinked and leaped to his feet.

A shrill, two-note, warbling bird call came from outside.

One of the guides cupped his hands near his lips and gave a long whistle.

"What's going on?" I asked.

"That's Fastulf's call, Sire," Vikar said.

"Sounds like he's not far away," Athal said.

"Bior, change of plan. Bring at least one of the commanders here."

"Aye, m'lord."

As Bior hurried away, the call repeated, varying slower this time.

"He's alone," Vikar said, frowning.

Garda let out a pattern of quick chirps.

Fastulf replied in the same pattern.

"He's unhurt," Garda said.

"Sounds promising," I said, clicking my hammer to my back and leaning against the wall to wait.

Fastulf saluted after stepping onto the solid floor. "Good to see you, Sire. I bring news ... strange news, I suppose."

"I've sent for a commander," I said, saluting him. "Where are the men who went with you?"

"They stayed behind to secure the entrance to another pass on the other side of the sand. It's lined with the same stone but takes a straighter path through."

"You found a way across?" Garda asked.

"The solid ledge continues along the mountains. It's safest to walk one man ahead of the other, but you might fit two side-by-side if you're willing to risk someone falling into the sand."

Bior returned with Commander Osvif at his side.

Fits with what the prisoner told me. "Am I safe in assuming you scouted beyond the pass?"

Resting his hands on his hips, he cocked his head. "Wouldn't be worthy of my duty if I didn't, Sire. We found a village. That's where the strange begins. Every building's made of this dead stone."

Rorec said the Satran used some strange sything techniques. "You're sure?"

He nodded. "Even the fence around the corral. No wood in any structure we could see, Sire."

"Doors? Shutters?" Bior asked.

"Same stuff," Fastulf replied.

"How many are in the village?" Osvif asked.

"More strangeness. Didn't find anyone. Not even a sign of people around the well."

"You said there was a corral. Any horses?" I asked.

"No, Sire. I'd guess the corral held goats at one point, but we saw none in our search."

"Obviously, the village was abandoned for some reason," Garda said.

The prisoner claimed Asfrid was in that village with a group of Bane. If it's abandoned, where is she? "Any sign of fighting? Perhaps Satra's Legion killed everyone and took the belongings for themselves."

"If they did, it's the cleanest battlefield I've ever seen. Sire, the place is spotless."

"What's beyond the village?" Osvif asked.

"A hill, same as this side, a good-size field on the other side, for farming, I'd guess, then forest, Sire."

After chewing my lip a moment, I nodded. "How long will it take for us to reach the village?"

"Us, who, Sire?" Bior asked.

Pointing down the dark hall, I cleared my throat. "Everyone. The entire army."

"What about the horses and wagons?" Bior asked. "We still can't get them across the sand."

"Fastulf, did you see an obvious way to get anything bigger than men to the pass?" I asked.

He looked back at the field for a moment. "While a horse could walk on the ledge, if it spooked...even a misstep ... That's a big risk."

I turned to Bior and rested my hands on my hips. "We'll leave the horses behind. Stuff packs full. Syth the wagons into as many two-man carry racks as possible and load them. We'll take the village and use it as our base. Fastulf, how long will it take for us to get there?"

He looked out. "Dawn's coming soon, Sire. Loaded men move slow. Anyone not used to moving carefully in the dark is in danger of taking a wrong step once the sun sets. It's possible everyone could make it to the other pass, but we'd best be done before dark. The safest option would be to get about half the men across today and the rest tomorrow."

"I'd rather not wait," I said, frowning.

"But rushing ahead could cost us men," Osvif said.

"If we can't get everyone across safely, they still need to be ready to go. All of you, wake everyone. There's work to do and not much time to do it."

"Aye, Sire," Bior said. "You heard the king. Let's move!"

The group passed me in a hurry. Shouts followed soon after as they went about waking men who would rather sleep.

I stared out of the pass and watched the sky change from dark to slowly brightening dawn. *No doubt, the men will need to eat before much work gets done. At least it won't be breakfast on the move today.*

Chapter 49

"Preparations are finally underway, Sire," Bior said, handing me breakfast and a waterskin.

"Anything I need to address?" I asked.

A couple of the quartermasters weren't happy having their wagons torn apart. Commander Ketill and I stepped in before an argument came to blows.

"I see."

"I'm going to fill my pack, but I'll be back before it's time to leave," Bior said.

I nodded and munched on dried meat strips.

Tinges of blue streamed into the sky from the east. Darkness faded slowly from the imposing danger between us and the rest of Satra.

"Shoulder-to-shoulder," Fastulf said, behind me, "line up against the right wall."

"How soon will we be ready?" I asked, turning.

"Soon, Sire. Can I have a word with you?"

"I'm listening."

"While we were waking everyone, Garda and I talked about how to get everyone safely around the edge of the sand. My guides have experience leading groups around obstacles; we can help the warriors stay on the narrow ledge. Especially the men carrying heavy loads between them."

I smiled. "Direct your men to help where they think best."

He nodded. "One more request, my king."

"Go ahead."

He bowed before looking me in the eye. "Sire, I would like to personally see you safely to the other pass."

"You may lead the way once everyone's ready to go. Find Bior. Get warriors lined up."

He clapped his hands together. "With all haste, my king. Thank you for the honor."

"You've earned it."

He bowed low before turning to run through the pass, calling for Bior as he went.

Instead of continuing to frustrate myself by watching the sky, I turned to watch warriors lining up. Soon the ranks stretched back to the curve.

My shadow stretched long into the hallway when Bior, Fastulf, and Garda stood nearby. "Ready, Sire," my steward said.

"Warriors!" I yelled. "This journey will not be safe, but it is necessary. The way around this field is narrow. Be mindful of your steps. If you walk off into the sand, we may not be able to rescue you. Watch the man in front of you. If he steps away from the wall, correct his path before he leads people to their deaths. Listen to the guides, and we will all make it to the other pass. Satra waits on the other side. Let's make them pay for what they did to our people and our nation."

Even the dead stone couldn't dampen the roar of acknowledgment.

Bior handed me a full waterskin.

I tapped Fastulf on the shoulder. "On your lead."

He turned to Garda. "See you on the other side."

His fellow guide saluted and followed us to the exit.

"Step where I do, Sire, and everything will be fine," Fastulf said, taking a long stride out of the right side of the opening.

I stepped into the slowly brightening field of sand. My heart pounded when my foot left the stone. Breakfast threatened to come up as sand flowed over my boot, stopping above my ankle when my foot landed on something solid. "A bit unnerving," I muttered. Carefully, I took my other foot from the stone floor and stepped forward. It, too, sank below the surface as my weight shifted.

"Follow his footsteps, Bior," Garda said, behind me. "Keep your right shoulder to the mountain, and you'll be fine."

"The first step might set you on edge," I said.

Fastulf snickered. "It does take getting used to, m'lord." He set a plodding pace, placing each step with care and making sure of his footing before moving forward again.

I did my best to keep my nerves under control and match his movements. Part of me wanted to look back and see how others were doing. The more sensible part decided it was best to keep my eyes ahead, focused on the path and Fastulf.

An eerie quiet dominated the area, broken only by the faint scraping noise of sand scrubbing against our boots and the hissing of the grains filling our empty footsteps. Much like the dead stone, this material muffled sound in ways nothing else I'd ever encountered did.

The sun was fully visible, leaving the field well-lit by the time I reached the halfway point of our trek. Taking a drink, I was surprised the container felt more than half empty. Running my hand over the skin showed it was dry. *No leaks. I must have been drinking without realizing it.* "Bior, still back there?"

"Aye, Sire."

"Everyone behind you doing well?"

"Don't know, m'lord. Too afraid of losing my balance to look back."

"Makes two of us," I said, nodding.

Fastulf let loose a short, shrill whistle, and I nearly stopped in my tracks.

"What's wrong?" I asked.

"Nothing, Sire. Checking with the other guides."

"What?"

"We'll soon know if there are any problems, m'lord."

Similar whistles repeated behind us.

A few heartbeats after the calls stopped, Fastulf nodded. "Sounds like everything is fine, Sire."

"How do you know?"

"I counted twenty-four 'all clear' chirps. No one signaled an alarm."

"I take it you worked out these calls with them," I said, trying to calm my nerves.

"We did. Safest way to pass information in the dark, Sire."

"I see. But doesn't it let the enemy know you are there?"

"Only if they are worried about birds being about, my king."

"Clever."

He gave a warbling whistle similar to the one I heard before dawn.

"What was that?" I asked.

"Checking on the scouts securing the other pass, Sire."

A reply came several moments later. "Sounds like everything's clear."

I nodded and kept plunging my boots into the sand, one slow step after another.

A dull rumble crossed the field. The sun shined bright over our heads. Glancing at the sky, I looked for clouds and found none. The next boom left no doubt there was a storm somewhere close. "Judging by the thunder, it's about to go from bad to worse," I said.

"Wonder how slick this sand becomes when it's wet," Bior commented.

"No clouds in sight, Sire," Fastulf said. "Likely the storm's a ways off. Could be we can get under a roof before it hits."

"Bior, you still back there?" I asked.

"Aye, Sire. Why?"

"You hearing this? What Fastulf said about the storm?"

"Most of it, m'lord."

"In your time acting on my behalf, did anyone mention he was annoyingly optimistic?"

"No, Sire. Can't say I've heard such a thing before."

"Fastulf, I suspect you're not who you claim to be," I said. "At the least, you're not the shy, reluctant youngster I put in charge of the guides. Perhaps, I'm following a well-disguised Satran spy into a trap."

Fastulf laughed. "I'll take your words as praise, my king. If I were a turncoat, don't you think my own men would have found out long before now?"

"True, they should have. Still, what would you say to convince me otherwise?"

"I am doing your bidding as best I can. It was you who told me to change my ways, Sire, lest I pay a harsh penalty."

"I did, and it seems you have."

Chapter 50

Trudging on, I nearly jumped off the ledge when Fastulf gave a loud, twittering whistle. "A little warning next time," I commanded, willing my heart to stop pounding.

"Sorry, Sire. Wanted to let them know we're getting close."

"Not saying it was a bad idea. I wasn't expecting the outburst."

He nodded. "Get ready for one more, m'lord."

Before I could answer, he twittered again. *At least I knew it was coming.*

A shrill sound answered, long and dropping pitch until it faded away. "All's clear, Sire."

"Good. Too bad we can't safely walk faster."

"I agree, m'lord. At this pace, it will be nearly dark before Garda reaches this side. Assuming nothing goes wrong, of course."

Assuming. "All good back there, Bior?"

"So far as I know. Steady but slow going, Sire."

"Keep at it," I said. "We'll be on solid ground soon enough."

"You know exactly how to make a person happy, Sire."

I smiled and kept moving, ignoring a growing ache in my legs. *If he's doing well enough to be grumpy, he's doing fine.*

"Not far now, Sire. Look!" Fastulf pointed.

Following his finger, I looked and saw no change in the rock to show where the pass opened. I shaded my eyes against the glaring sunlight and noticed where the dead stone had a slight contrast against the dark mountainside around it. "Step lively, Bior. We're nearly there."

"Good to hear, m'lord. My legs are near giving out, and my back needs a rest."

"Push on. We'll rest soon."

"Aye, my king. I won't stop until you do."

I caught myself staring at the opening instead of watching Fastulf and swayed when one foot stepped near the edge of our path.

"Careful, Sire," Bior cried out. "If you fall, we can't save you."

Nodding, I hurried back toward the wall and wiped beads of cold sweat off my forehead. "Lost focus for a moment. Won't happen again."

"Easy to do out here, m'lord," Fastulf said.

"A lesson I won't forget," I said. "At least after my heart quits trying to pound its way out of my chest."

Continuing the trek, taking each step with care, I heaved a sigh once both feet were on solid ground again ... even if it was more dead stone.

Fastulf's men saluted. "Good to see you arrived safe, Sire," one said.

"Glad I made it. How far is the village? I want to see it for myself."

"It's not far, m'lord, but I'd suggest you wait for enough warriors to arrive so you have a guard," Fastulf said. "We *are* on enemy soil."

"Listen to him, Sire," Bior said behind me. "There's wisdom in his words."

"Bior, join me down the hall."

"Aye, Sire. Anything to get away from that sand."

"The rest of you, do what you can to help our men get here safely," I said.

"Yes, m'lord," Fastulf said, bowing.

Bior walked by my side into the darkness of the pass.

"I need to search the village. It *can't* be empty like Fastulf claims," I said, looking ahead.

"I'll admit it doesn't make sense to me either, Sire, but what makes you so certain?"

"The prisoner told me Bane were here waiting for someone and hiding another Croian. If the village is abandoned, the situation is much more complicated than I'd like."

"Is it someone I'd know, Sire?"

"Not likely, but she's important to someone I know well."

"She?"

I said too much. Grabbing his arm, I pulled him toward me until we stood nose-to-nose. "Not long after I was born, my father sent two Croians into Satra as part of an agreement to protect my lands," I whispered. "The man I met with and his wife. That's all you need to know. Do you understand?"

He tried to back away, but I held him in place. "Answer me."

"Sire. I don't —"

"Answer," I hissed.

"Aye, Sire," his voice wavered. "I understand. But if they were supposed to convince Satra to guard the border, why are we at war now?"

"Something else Eirickson messed up," I said, releasing my grip. "Keep your eyes and ears open while we search the village. If you see or hear anything, let me know immediately."

"Of course, my king."

"King Fitzeirick," Fastulf called. "Everything's going well here, and it's about to get crowded. You might want to move farther into the pass. Also, Commanders Alrik and Hottir are about to arrive. Should I send them your way?"

"Thank you for the update," I replied. "Tell the commanders to gather a company of men and find me."

"As you say, Sire."

"Bior, let's move out of the way and eat."

"I wondered if you'd forgotten what it was like to be hungry," he said, chuckling as he handed me a couple of hard rolls and some meat strips.

We walked past the point where the hall curved left. A hint of light from the exit ahead calmed my nerves.

The commanders arrived while I had a mouth full of food. "Hottir will be here soon with the men you asked for, Sire," Alrik said.

"In case you haven't heard, this passage leads to a village that may be abandoned. I want to look it over. Bior will stay with me. Have the warriors patrol until everyone arrives. If they see or hear anything, I want to know."

"Why not wait for everyone to cross, m'lord?" he asked.

"Because it's easier for me to search the area before it gets crowded."

"Should I leave orders for everyone to wait for your permission to enter the village, my king?" he asked.

"No. The more eyes we have looking, the better, but keep them in groups. I don't want anyone to get lost or captured."

"Understood, Sire."

As he walked away, I pushed enough energy into the floor to track Alrik.

Bior stuffed my empty waterskin into his pack and offered me another. "I know how hot you get when you do a lot of sything, Sire."

"Thank you."

Alrik walked out of my sight and stopped near a group standing too close together for me to count. I pulled my talent back when he turned to lead the group our way. "Put on your pack. Won't be long now."

Alrik and Hottir led the warriors toward us, stopping when I stepped into the middle of the path. "Everyone has their orders?"

"Of course, m'lord," Alrik said.

"On me." Turning to face the light at the end of the pass, I took a brisk pace because I was more than ready to get outside. Bior fell a step or two behind but stayed ahead of the commanders.

When sunlight hit my face, I glanced around for threats and headed into the village, stopping near a well.

Bior joined me, breathing heavily.

"Feeling unwell?" I asked.

He shook his head. "Trudging through the sand took a lot out of me, m'lord. Let me catch my breath, and I'll be fine."

I nodded and looked around. As Fastulf said, everything was made of the sickening green-black stone. To our right was the corral. Beyond the enclosed area stood rows of square buildings on either side of a path. On the left, more of the same buildings in the same orientation. A large, rectangular structure sat a few paces ahead and ended at the hill separating the village from the rest of Satra. Every wall was smooth, the dark color camouflaged doors and shutters.

The commanders saluted as they passed, as did the warriors that followed. Splitting their ranks in half, they veered toward opposite sides of the building ahead, climbed the hill, and spread out to start their patrols.

Two companies would have been better, but the day grows shorter by the moment. "Ready, Bior?"

"Aye, Sire. Lead the way."

I headed for the big building in front of us. The door opened easily, with complete silence.

Following the daylight inside, we found four rows of long stone tables with ten matching chairs around them and nothing else except a small fireplace and a second entrance.

"Maybe a dining hall?"

"If so, the meals must be prepared elsewhere," I replied. "There's nowhere to cook for this many people."

He shrugged. "At least we can eat under a roof."

"True. I don't see anything of interest here. Let's check some of the smaller buildings."

Turning left as I walked out, Bior followed me to the nearest structure. It was nearly square, with the door not quite centered on the wall facing the path. As before, it opened with a gentle push. There wasn't enough light to make out most of the room.

Bior opened the shutters covering a window to our right.

It was obvious this was a home. Like the first building, everything was made of the horrible dark stone—the low shelf near the fireplace I took to be a bed, a small table, and a few chairs scattered about. But as Fastulf had reported, no sign of people living here. No clothes, no baskets, no weapons ... nothing. *What are we missing?*

We hurried to the next home and the next, each laid out the same and lacking signs of life. An itchy unease crawled up my neck. *We're overlooking something obvious.* "Bior, find the commanders who have arrived. Have them gather their sergeants and meet me in the dining hall."

A questioning expression flashed across his face. "Aye, Sire."

Returning to the hall, I stood my hammer on the floor, pulled out a chair, and sat. Perching my helmet on the hammer's handle, I held my head in my hands. *Nothing about this place makes sense.* My frustration escaped as a loud groan. The unnerving lack of echoes from the unnatural stone made the room feel even more lonely.

"Commanders Osvif, Alrik, and Hottir, as you requested, Sire," Bior announced, entering the hall.

I stood and waved them in.

"Our sergeants have yet to arrive, m'lord," Osvif said, sitting.

"But all is well?" I asked.

"No losses to report so far, m'lord."

"Anything from the patrols?" I asked.

Alrik shook his head. "All's quiet, Sire. Have you found anything of interest?"

"Nothing. Every building we checked has no signs of anyone living here ... ever." I spread my arms wide. "Houses all around but no clothes nor cloth to make them. No bedding. Fireplaces empty. Not even ashes. We found no food nor anything to cook." *Da'rin told me Asfrid was here. I'm not sure anyone's ever been here.*

My frustration boiled over. The commanders flinched when I slapped the table. "Does any of this make sense to any of you?"

Again, they looked at each other for an answer before shaking their heads. "No, Sire. I see no reason in anything you're saying," Osvif said. "But, does it matter? We have enough room to house everyone and places to store our supplies. What we need to do is plan our next move. Where do we go from here?"

"We head west, to the coast, and watch for the rest of our force coming by barge. Once we meet them, we set about conquering the land. Having the sea at our backs takes away a weakness too. Satra can't sneak up on us from behind."

Alrik nodded as I spoke. "Hottir and I discussed much the same strategy while crossing the sand, Sire. Seems like our best option, do you agree, Osvif?"

He stared at me while scratching his ear. "I recommend we spend some time scouting the area, given how little we know about where we are and where we're going."

"We're on foot now," Hottir said. "We walk west until we come to a reason to turn south again."

"But we won't be able to travel as fast. Especially with men carrying our supplies," Osvif countered.

"Assuming anyone ever lived here, they left for a reason. Staying any longer than we must is a risk I'm not willing to take. When herbalists arrive, have them check the well water. If it's safe, we can replenish our waterskins before leaving. Rest here a day, two at most, then push west. Surely we'll find horses sooner or later," I said.

"Until then, we move slow and keep our eyes and ears open," Osvif said.

"Yes," I said. "Unless you three have anything else to discuss, I give you leave to check on your men. Let them know we have a plan."

"I have nothing else, Sire," Osvif said.

Hottir and Alrik shook their heads.

"Perhaps the news might boost morale. That would be a nice change."

They stood as one and saluted. "We'll do our best, m'lord," Osvif said, before they turned to leave.

Chapter 51

After putting on my helmet and sticking my hammer in place, I motioned for Bior to follow me outside. "I know it's likely a waste of time, but I want to search a few more homes. There has to be something here."

"You're worried about the woman."

"Shh! I don't need someone to overhear something they don't understand. A rumor would do nothing but cause problems." I glared at him before nodding. "Everything else the prisoner told me turned out to be true. If she's not here, I want to know where she went."

He returned my glare before moving inside, away from the door. "No one's close enough to hear. Do you have an idea of what we might be looking for? Scattered searches aren't likely to uncover much except by happy accident. Assuming we find something, how will we know it means anything or leads anywhere?"

I rested my hands on my hips. "I don't know."

"Did the prisoner tell you anything else?"

Closing my eyes, I took a deep breath and tried to remember the conversation. The smell of blood came to mind first, followed by the feel of the Satran shivering as he drew his last breath. *I did what had to be done ... what was right for Croy.* With some effort, I pushed the memories away and focused on what the prisoner said. Nothing new came to mind. "I've told you everything ... more than I told General Gudmann. If someone was waiting here for Da'rin, and they left, there must be something here telling him where to find them."

"Makes sense to me." He shrugged. "Pick a building, and let's look."

"We searched houses to the left. Let's go right this time."

"Lead on, my king," Bior said, with a smile and a nod.

Glancing toward the pass, I saw several sergeants near the exit, directing warriors.

The corral acted as a barrier, keeping the path clear until we passed it. We dodged tired-looking men dragging their feet on the way to the hill.

Reaching the first house, I opened the door. "Check this one," I said, "I'll check the next."

This home was the same as the others, empty and clean. Sitting on the low shelf, I ran my finger across it. *Not even dusty. That's what's been bothering me. Dust happens. Why are these places so clean?*

"Find anything? Anything at all?" Bior asked, from the door.

"Nothing's dirty."

"Well, if no one lives here, how would it get dirty?"

"No, I mean there's no dust. Wipe your finger along the tabletop."

He did as I suggested and, after staring at his finger for a moment, his eyes opened wide. "There's no dust. How?"

I shrugged. "Dust gathers when there's no one around to clean. If no one lives in this village ..."

"Why is everything inside spotless?" he finished my thought.

"Let's check another," I said, getting to my feet.

"Right behind you."

"To arms!" someone yelled, as we stepped outside. "Movement in the trees!"

Bior wore a confused look. "Did someone say movement?"

My heart raced, blood pounding in my ears. Without thinking, I grabbed my hammer and turned to leave the house.

Bior grabbed my arm. "No! Stop! You promised the queen you wouldn't fight."

"I can't lead unless I can see what's going on," I argued, turning to face him.

"You have commanders. Trust them to do their job."

Something hit the back of my armor with a faint tap. I ignored the impact until it happened twice again, close together.

"What was that?" I asked, turning. "Something hit me. Do you see anyone?"

"Nothing. We're alone here," Bior said.

"Ouch!" Something stung my neck below my helmet. Grabbing at the bug, I found a stiff, metal spine with cotton fluff on the end. "What's this?"

"What?" Bior said.

As I turned to show him, the wound itched and burned.

"Get inside, Sire!" Bior ordered, concern clear in his voice. "I've got to keep you safe."

Twice more, my armor was struck by an unseen attacker. The metal sheet sandwiched between thick leather kept me from getting hit again.

The burning spread, flowing into my chest and my shoulder as I stepped back inside.

Bior shoved the door closed and pointed toward the bed shelf. "Sit."

I nodded, shivering as smoldering discomfort continued through my body, leaving a trail of tingling numbness behind. "I need a herbalist," I mumbled. My jaw wasn't working right.

"What?" Bior squawked.

"Poison!" Slumping to one side, I flopped down and tried to stay calm. "Get help," I muttered, fighting to stay awake.

"I can't leave you, Sire. I can't."

"Go ... now."

"Fine, but I'm sending the first warrior I see to protect you."

Everything looked blurry as he stopped near the door. "Don't die, Sire ... please."

The door closed.

I lay alone in the dark.

My heart raced.

My eyes closed, and my head lolled onto the hard, unnatural stone.

Someone grabbed me. Hands pulled me through the floor. My body ignored my mind's command to fight.

Despite trying to force my eyes open, my eyelids didn't move.

Someone, at least four someones, carried me by my arms and legs.

My head flopped back.

More than anything, I wanted to free myself from the unseen captors, but my body gave up.

Somewhere along the way, I fell into a deep sleep.

Chapter 52

I woke to darkness, bound to a hard, flat surface. Something covered the poisoned wound on my neck. *Where am I? A cell. A tomb.* The surface under me didn't feel cold enough to be stone, but I pushed out my talent to check. After more effort than it should have taken, a trickle of energy left my body and told me nothing. *I must be strapped to a wooden table.*

Wanting to sit up, I struggled against the wooden bands holding me in place but didn't have enough strength to break free. My joints ached. Every muscle throbbed with deep soreness.

I tried to yell, but little more than a rasping groan escaped my dry throat. *Bior failed. I'm captured.*

The air smelled musty … or maybe it was me. I wasn't wearing my armor or my clothes. My captors dressed me in rough, woven cloth. The band across my chest forced the prickly garment into my skin. Stiff, sharp fibers scratched me with every beat of my pounding heart. *Are my men looking for me? Were we defeated?*

"Bior," I croaked, hoping someone would answer and let me know I wasn't alone.

I swore I'd never let myself be captured again. How will I escape? Visions of imprisonment, torture, and execution forced their way into my head. My breath came in short rasps, my heartbeat speeding up to match. "I won't tell you anything," I said, hoping to prompt a response. "No matter what you do to me."

The silence deepened my anxiety.

Panicking won't help. Closing my eyes, I focused on remembering the faces of those I loved: my mother, Aesa, Roi, Crum, Tindra. Trying to calm myself, I pictured each person and constructed apologies I worried might go unsaid.

Muffled sounds from the other side of the room broke my concentration.

Chapter 53

After a faint scraping sound, a red haze shined through my eyelids.

"Still breathing," a gruff voice said.

I wanted to open my eyes and see who it was but decided it was safer to act like I was asleep.

Something warm and wet brushed across my face.

I opened my eyes and quickly closed them against stabbing candlelight.

"Good, you're finally awake," a woman said. She didn't sound like the others. Her voice had a vaguely Croian accent and a soothing gentleness that almost made me forget my predicament. "I'd feared the worst."

Asfrid?

"I wasn't sure we drew out the poison in time," she said, taking the covering off my wound. "Always imagined you'd be strong-willed. Knowing your father, you had to be."

My eyes flew open, ignoring the discomfort from the candle flame. Glare hid her face. I tried to talk, but my voice caught in my parched throat.

"I'm sure you're thirsty. I'll be right back with help to get you up."

I looked around as best I could. The walls and ceiling were dark. *More dead stone?* A small table stood little more than an arm's reach from where I lay. It held several stone bottles. A mortar and pestle sat near the edge.

"Stand him up so I can give him some water," she ordered, entering the room.

"Waste of time. Take him to Vos Borik. Get rewarded."

That was a different voice than the one I heard before.

"Velimir, stop talking like that." Her matronly voice reminded me of my mother. "Fitzeirick will help us once he has his strength back. You and Muncel stand his bed against the wall. He needs water."

Velmir mumbled something about 'useless Croians' as my bed rose before leaning at a steep angle. I slumped against my bonds, legs too weak to push me back up.

"Thank you," she said. "Go. I'll call you if I need you."

"I can stay. Watch."

Muncel was likely who I'd heard before.

"I'm sure Fitzeirick will be more comfortable if I'm the only one in the room."

Silhouetted by the light coming through the door, I still couldn't see her face, but she had long, silvery-gray hair.

Has to be Asfrid.

She lifted a cup to my lips. "Drink."

I looked from to cup to her and then to the bottles nearby.

"It's only water ... I swear."

My lips cracked when I parted them. At first, the water stung the raw, split skin, but relief for my dry throat made the discomfort worth it.

As she took the cup away, I cleared my throat. "I ... I have questions."

"Let me treat your lips first."

I kept my eyes on her while she retrieved a small pot from the table. Turning back to me, she rubbed something slick across my lips. "They'll feel better soon. I would have treated them before, but I didn't want to waste salve on a dead man."

It had an oily texture and filled my nose with an unfamiliar scent. Overall, it wasn't unpleasant, especially compared to my circumstances.

Given my inclined position, it was hard to judge much about my caring captor. She was shorter than me, maybe shorter than Tindra. Her soft voice gave the impression she was old, but a steady hand held the cup for me. "Where am I? What happened to my men?"

"You're bound for your own safety. As a captive, I can convince those who see you as a threat that you are not dangerous until they understand you could be our ally."

"Who?"

"Before I tell you anything, I need to know something. On your way here, did you happen to see or speak with anyone unexpected?"

Closing my eyes, I tried to shrug and grimaced at the pain in my arms. "You'll need to be more specific."

"Did you happen across an older, Croian man in your old territory?"

She means Rorec. "Asfrid?"

"That would be a strange name for a Croian man. Perhaps he —"

"I know who you are," I said, "and you're asking about Rorec, your husband. Yes, I met with him. When he left my camp, he was alive and well. Now, tell me where I am. Where are my men?"

"Did you meet with Sifet?"

I shook my head. "Had he entered my camp, he wouldn't have left alive."

"Friend Asfrid," Velmir called, from the hall. "They sent for you."

"I'm busy," she said, without looking back.

"Important, Friend Asfrid."

Sighing as she stood, she pushed the chair toward the table and turned to leave.

"What are you going to do with me?" I demanded.

She kept walking.

You will *talk to me.* "Roi," I said. "Your son."

She stopped mid-step.

"Answer my questions. Free me, and I'll tell you about him."

Without turning back, she said, "I must go."

"Asfrid!" I yelled, straining against the wooden bonds holding me fast. "Let me go!"

She closed the door, leaving me alone in the darkness.

I stopped myself from yelling again and relaxed to conserve what little strength I had for when I'd need it.

A good friend once insisted if you couldn't see the sun or the moon, time didn't move. *No sun, no moon, no stars, no time.* I knew she was wrong, but it's hard to argue with the notion of time passing differently in complete quiet and darkness.

While I waited for Asfrid to come back, my legs cramped. I cried out in pain, unable to do anything else. Some of the candles had burned out, leaving the room dimmer than before. "Help!" Despite knowing it was useless to yell, I needed someone to hear me and relieve the pain. "Hey! I need help!"

My heart raced when the door opened.

Asfrid stopped less than an arm's length from me. "What's wrong?"

"My legs," I said, through clenched teeth, "muscles knotted."

"Hold still. This will get worse before it gets better."

Before I could ask what she meant, she touched the table and released me.

My bare feet hit cold stone, and I collapsed, unable to hold myself upright.

She caught me, leaned me against the table, and helped me slide down until I was sitting with my legs straight out. "Don't try to get away. Velimir is listening for my call."

Glaring at her, I frowned. "Doubt I could move anyway."

"From the poison, most likely, though I figured you would've recovered by now. Maybe we *were* too late."

While she searched through the jars on the small table, I rubbed my legs to get rid of the pain.

Asfrid offered me a wad of leaves and a tall container. "Swallow this and drink everything in the cup."

I cocked my head. "What is it?"

"Neither will hurt you," she said. "I didn't keep you alive to kill you now."

Typical herbalist answer. I took the leaves, shoved them in my mouth, and swallowed after chewing as little as possible. They tasted like bitter peppers. The tonic was much worse. It was a slimy mixture of bitter, sour, and salty ... strong enough to make my eyes water. *At least it took my mind off my legs.*

"You should feel much better tomorrow."

"Where am I?"

She slid the chair over and sat. "I'm keeping you safe. Best I can do, for now."

I sighed. "Were my men killed in the attack when you captured me?"

"First, we — The Bane here did not attack you. Those were Legion soldiers. We rescued you."

"If you insist," I said, crossing my arms. "Is my army dead? Did we lose the war?"

She chewed her lip a moment. "Some fell, but your warriors drove the Legion away. From what we know, the force arriving at Buzvat was little more than a patrol. No real match for your men, except by surprise."

"Am I the only one you rescued?"

She nodded, and my heart sank.

"Is Bior dead?"

"I don't know who that is."

"Why me? How did you know I was there?"

"The first Croians to enter the village almost caught Plamen, but he got away and told us what happened. Rajoe tracked your movements from underground. You caught his attention as a strong stonesyth. His friends helped him open the floor to watch from the house next to the one you hid in. He —"

"How?" I asked, slapping the dead stone beneath me and interrupting her. "Stronger stonesyths than I have tried working this stuff and ... nothing."

She frowned. "Groups of Bane stonesyths can."

"Would they tell me how?"

"I can't speak for them," she said, shrugging.

I nodded. "Please continue."

She smiled. "He knew someone needed help, so he brought you to me. He couldn't save anyone else. They fell outside...in the open. No one knew who you were until we took off your helmet to get at the wound on your neck. Bad place to take a poison dart, I'll have you know. Anyway, everyone had heard of the branded king from Porsey. Fire take him for the trouble he caused."

I chuckled. "Many agree with your opinion of him. Since we're talking like friends, are you going to let me go?"

She shook her head. "Keeping you safe keeps the rest of us safe."

"Why?" I asked, frowning.

"Your warriors stayed, searching for you for a couple of days before deciding the fleeing soldiers had taken you. They were going west, last we knew."

"The plan was to go to the western sea from the village," I commented.

"Why?" she asked, furrowing her brow. "There's nothing but trees and grass between there and the beach."

"The men with me weren't the entirety of my army. A larger force traveled across the water. The two forces will meet on the western shore."

"Oh..." Her eyes widened, surprise evident on her face. "Wait here."

Crossing my arms as she stood, I put on my best defiant glare. "You won't bind me without a fight."

She smiled. "You might be able to walk, but I doubt you can run. Velimir is between you and the others. He will stop you. Besides, you have the opportunity to do the right thing for Croy *and* Satra."

"The right thing for Croy is to destroy Satra."

"No, it's not. Just wait. You'll understand soon enough." She hurried out of the room.

Alone and confused, I took a couple of deep breaths to focus. *I'm still alive. How do I get free?* I looked around for anything I could use. A small table with a couple of chairs sat nearby. My talent flowed better than before, but I couldn't push it to the walls without getting light-headed. All I learned from the effort was the open door in front of me was the only way in or out.

Someone bigger than Asfrid blocked the light from the hall.

Velimir might kill me, but he'll get hurt before I go. Gathering my strength, I braced against the wood behind me and tried to stand.

Chapter 54

"Wasn't sure I'd see you again, Fitzeirick."

Warmth flooded my tired body. "Rorec?"

"Yes, my boy ... it's me. Asfrid's still worried about you, but I insisted any blood of Eirick's would pull through." He lifted me to my feet, supporting me with an arm over his shoulder. "Vos Sifet wants to speak with you."

My jaw clenched. "He's here?"

"Yes, and wanting to meet with you."

"Why? Surely he'd rather kill me."

"There is more at play here than you know."

"Do I have any say in this?" I asked.

The doorway was a squeeze to get two men through, but the hallway was nearly as wide as the room. Depressions in the walls held candles to light the way.

"You know you aren't in control here, right?"

Even though I had no doubt as to my status, I couldn't help but shiver at his words. "Obviously. I'm a prisoner."

"Close enough. Keep acting like a captive, and things will go smoother for everyone."

I took slow, measured steps. My muscles resisted as if they hadn't moved in weeks. "What does he want with me?"

"He's offering you a seat at his table. Isn't that how leaders do business?"

"Isn't Sifet an exile? He has no power in Satra, right?"

"All I can say is keep an open mind."

I nodded, deciding to save my breath for whenever I could get my hands on Sifet.

We continued at a plodding pace past barely visible dead stone doors and a couple of branching passages before stopping at a pair of wooden doors. Rorec knocked.

The right door creaked as it opened inward. A thin, Satran boy, wearing patchwork clothes, stepped in front of us. "Friend Rorec and another Croian, Vos."

"As expected," an unseen voice—Sifet's, I assumed—replied. "Let them in."

Rorec and I walked into a large room with a round, wooden table in the middle. Dead stone lanterns hung from the ceiling, lighting the area in a muted glow. Five, older-looking, Satran men sat on the far side. The man in the middle stood and nodded to us. "Welcome to my table, Rorec. This is Croian King Fitzeirick, yes?"

Rorec put his hand to his chest and bowed. "It is, Chieftain Sifet."

The dethroned ruler was bald, with a heavy brow and rows of deep wrinkles across his forehead and scalp. It was hard to make out his build, though, as he wore a dark, purple robe. His voice carried a noticeable strength. He pointed to a chair across from him. "Please. Join us as equals, in peace, so we can talk."

Rorec nudged me.

Peace...how long will that last? I nodded and stumbled toward the seat. My legs supported me until I could sit.

Finally, I was in the same room as the man who was the focus of my hatred and anger. The man who killed my mother, took my first love, and conquered my skati.

I stared at him.

Had I been healthy, he would already be dead, along with the men sitting with him. My stomach churned. My heart ached. Unarmed, I couldn't split him open like I had Eirickson, couldn't splatter his blood onto the walls and spill his guts on the floor. If I got close enough, I could wrap my hands around his throat, slowly cutting off his breath, relishing his death, and making sure my face was the last one he saw. Despite my deepest desire to kill this Satran, I was too weak to be a threat. *I'll observe tradition only because I can do nothing else.*

"This is the remnants of my League," Sifet said, still standing. "My dearest friends and advisers. Without them, I'd likely been long dead."

I kept my eyes on Sifet. "It's good to have friends you can depend on."

Rorec cleared his throat.

"I considered Jarl Eirick a friend," Sifet said, returning to his seat. "His son, not so friendly. You are Eirick's *brach*, correct?"

"I don't know that word," I said. "But Eirick *was* my father."

"As I had heard," Sifet replied. "So, can we be friends, or are you more like his true son?"

"Neither," I said. "Eirick's blood runs in my veins, but I am my own man."

He raised his eyebrows and smiled. "If I were to guess, I would say you are more like your father. We will see in time. Rorec told me you hate my people. You consider us *dikari*, barbarians, and want to kill us all. Am I correct?"

Putting my hands on the table, I squared my shoulders. "Yes."

Rorec grabbed my wrist. "Careful."

"Is it not uncivilized to carry so much animosity?" Sifet asked.

"Put yourself in my place," I said, raising a finger to my brand. "I wear this because of your actions. You sent raiders into my skati. You killed my mother. Cost my fiancée her life. Slaughtered my people. Took my territory. What would you carry in your heart had that happened to you?"

Sifet stood and glared at me. "Let me tell you what your actions cost me. Though I do not carry a visible mark, I am forever scarred. Because of you, King Fitzeirick, my people questioned my strength. A perceived weakness empowered the schemers who turned my country against me. My own Legion executed my wife and sons at the order of a Bonetaker usurper. Men, women, and children who are treated worse than beasts are now my family."

"Is this supposed to make me feel better? Or help me understand why you slaughtered untold numbers of innocent Croians?" I asked.

Cocking his head, Sifet sat. "I don't care if you feel better or not. I revealed all to you so you can see we are almost truly equals now."

"So, you want ... what? A truce? You'll free me if I promise to take my men home while the Bonetakers strengthen their hold on Satra and prepare another invasion?"

The chieftain looked to the man on his right. "Youth makes one shortsighted. Does it not?"

"Right, Vos," he replied. "Wisdom comes with age."

Pressing his lips together, Sifet nodded. "Young king, I have a problem. One I cannot solve by myself, but I believe we can resolve together ... should you agree to listen."

Flexing the muscles in my legs told me I couldn't do much running, if any. *Escape is not possible right now. I have no idea where the exit is or what waits outside should I find it.* "You invited me to your table in peace and have made no threat. It would be disrespectful for me to ignore tradition without cause. I'll listen."

"Surely, by now, you understand we share a common enemy," Sifet said. "Though I doubted your ability to defeat the Legion."

"My warriors proved their worth storming your fortress in the central forest. From there, your soldiers did little to stop me from taking back my territory."

"Victory through surprise is no cause for celebration. Nor is weakening the enemy through deception. But now is not the time to debate tactics. This time is better spent discussing how we can help each other."

I sat back in the chair. "If you doubted my warriors before, the fact we're talking now tells me you've changed your mind. Obviously, Asfrid told you I have more men coming.

"She said you have men traveling across the sea. What makes you so sure they will arrive?"

Why would he ask such a question? "Is there something to keep them from reaching Satra's shores?"

"The sea itself," he said. "It devours men."

His advisers bowed their heads.

"I don't understand," I said, glancing toward Rorec. He too had bowed.

"Generations ago, a powerful vos sent a legion force to sea searching for new lands," Sifet explained. "Days passed. Then seasons. No word and no sign of the men returned. No Satran has been willing to needlessly give their lives to the unknown since."

They fear the water. I nodded. "My men have well-built barges and have trained for the trip. They will arrive. Soon. When they do, they will go on the attack. Doubt me at your peril."

Sifet cocked his head at my challenge. "Your words carry confidence. You believe the trip will be successful. If your forces do survive the journey, I must believe they have a good chance at victory."

"If I have a superior force, what do you have to offer?"

"My followers' knowledge," Sifet said. "These Bane know every field, hill, brook, and pass. At my word, they can guide your men through seemingly unpassable obstacles."

"But will they?" I countered. "At least one of your people isn't shy about voicing his dislike for Croians."

"Bane follow orders," he smiled. "It's how they stay alive."

I shrugged. "Fear and respect may produce the same results initially, but long term, only one leads to success."

Sifet nodded and locked eyes with me. "Do you fear me, King of Croy?"

I didn't look away. *What I wouldn't give to have Tindra at my side.* "I fear few things. You are not among them."

He leaned forward. "Do you respect me?"

"I respect the power you hold over my situation. I respect your offer of peace ... while we talk. Before you ask, no ... I do not trust you."

Sifet sat back. "You are alive because of my mercy. Does that not warrant some amount of trust on your part?"

"Mercy which comes at a cost is not mercy at all. I'm alive because you want something, Chieftan Sifet. I do appreciate the efforts spent saving me, but what do you want from me?"

"I, we, want you to do what you set out to do when you started this war." He paused. "With one difference. Spare my people."

"Wound the mountain lion but let it live to attack my cattle later?" I asked. "Doesn't seem like a wise decision."

"While I find the comparison flattering, in truth, I'm a bit of a toothless lion at this point. The real threat was your half-brother and those who shared his ambitions."

"Did you not share his goals?" I countered.

Sifet shook his head. "I was fooled by his poisoned promises. His saz-tongue blinded me to his true plan." The chieftain smacked his fist on the table. "Your father and I once had an agreement benefiting both nations. I care enough about my people to make another agreement with you. Should you destroy the Bonetakers and reinstate me as vos, I will bend my knee to you and order my people to follow your will. Your word will be the law of this land as it is in Croy. As I said before, I am without an heir. When I pass, you will select the next vos, setting your power in stone for generations. With time, Satra will simply become part of Croy. Much like your father once did with the Varian lands to our north."

I don't believe him. "How do I know you aren't speaking with a saz-tongue?"

Rorec coughed.

The large Satran to Sifet's left growled and stood, towering over his countrymen. "You dare insult Vos Sifet at his own table?"

Sifet grabbed the big man's wrist. "Sit. King Fitzeirick offered no harm. He is a guest in peace welcome to speak his mind."

Glaring at me, the broad-shouldered, fuzzy-haired brute huffed before pulling his arm free and returning to his seat.

"Why doubt my honesty?" Sifet asked. "As you can see, I honor my word of peace. Were we as barbaric as you believe, I would have let Mecik defend my reputation until he was satisfied."

I nodded, scratched my chin, and pointed at the chieftain. "Perhaps I chose my words poorly. You have kept your word, but I have no way of knowing if others will, in fact, follow you in subjugation to my rule."

Sifet snapped his fingers before pointing at the floor behind Mecik. "Cesci, here. Now."

The boy ran, sliding to a stop behind the large Satran. "Yes, Vos."

"Take two steps back, so our guest can see you."

Ordering a servant around proves nothing.

"Right, Vos," he said, backing into view.

"Bare your neck for Dalibor."

I leaned forward, resting my forearms on the edge of the table.

The servant turned to face a beady-eyed Satran sitting on Mecik's left. Standing rigid as a stone pillar, the boy tilted his head back until he stared at the ceiling.

"Cesci, my most favored. I love you like a son," Sifet said. "Would you die for me?"

"Right," the boy said, swallowing. "Yes, Vos."

No. He can't —

"Dalibor, surely your blade thirsts for blood."

"Yes."

My heart raced as I understood what was about to happen. "Stop!" I slapped my hands on the table and leapt to my feet.

Rorec grabbed my arm. "Sit."

"I will not sit and watch an innocent's senseless death at the whim of an overthrown tyrant."

Sifet laughed.

Everyone near him, except Dalibor, joined in.

This isn't funny.

"Well done, my servant," Sifet said. "Return to your post. You will be rewarded later."

"Yes, Vos," the boy replied, smiling wide and walking away as if nothing had happened.

"Sit and listen," Rorec said, squeezing my arm before letting me go.

After slumping into my chair, I turned to look at the young servant boy again. He stood motionless near the door, showing no concern that his life was nearly ended.

Sifet snapped his fingers again. Cesci's head turned faster than mine.

"Fitzeirick. Do you understand we, you and I, feel the same way? You asked for a demonstration and then interrupted it to save one, as you said, innocent life. I offer a way to save a multitude."

My mother's ghost told me not everything I believed was true. Is this what she meant? Sifet used a child to corner me with my own words. I had to admit, he'd set an effective trap. I wanted to slap myself for not seeing it coming. *If I disagree, I am no better than him but agreeing leaves me open to further manipulation.* "Did you care about sparing the innocent when you conquered my skati?"

Lacing his fingers together, he rested his hands on the table. "I did not, but I see things differently now. Perhaps you do too. For one who swore to kill all Satran, you stopped me from killing one now. Is one young Bane life more important than the rest of my nation?"

"No," I grumbled. "But I will not send my army home, leaving the Bonetakers in power and the Legion intact. If that is a condition of my release ..." I shrugged.

Sifet's toothy smile returned. "I believe we can find common ground, but we must reach an agreement before your men spill too much blood."

I tilted my head. "What do you propose?"

Sifet whispered something to the man seated on his right.

In turn, that man tapped the next on the shoulder and stood. "Branko. Mecik. Come with me."

As they left the room, Sifet led Dalibor around the table, stopping a few paces from me. Sifet bowed his head and dropped to one knee. His suspicious adviser stood behind him, hand near a slender knife handle.

"I beg you," Sifet said. "King Fitzeirick, have mercy on the innocent among my people and those I can sway to your cause. You have my word. We will follow you into battle and after. Satra will welcome Croian rule once the Bonetakers are gone. Dismantle the Legion. Put your army in place to enforce your will and protect Croy's new land. I willingly bow to you, ready to enter a blood pact to save my people."

Chapter 55

Though Sifet's action caught me off guard, I wondered if he was setting a trap to be sprung by the adviser standing behind him. Before deciding what to do, I considered how much of a threat Dalibor presented.

His dark eyes darted between me, Rorec, and Sifet. The sharp features of his face, framed by tightly coiled black and gray hair, reminded me of a rat. Even his arms were rodentlike, short and thin.

Rising to my feet, I took a step toward Sifet.

Dalibor's shoulders tensed as he wrapped his hand around the knife handle, watching me closely.

"I'm unarmed and weak," I said, glaring at him. "The biggest threat I pose is losing my balance and falling on him."

The rat didn't let go of the knife, but his shoulders relaxed.

"Sifet, look at me," I said. "Put your promises and demands in writing. Give me time to look them over and consider your offer. I may require changes or ask for compromises before agreeing to a binding oath."

The chieftain craned his neck. "If your warriors arrive from the water, time will quickly grow short. You must be open to my ideas."

"Time grows short for you and your people. Once my army is on dry land, they will proceed with or without me leading them. Unlike the Satran soldiers, beaten and serving out of fear, my warriors do not fight for me. They fight for Croy and the future security of its people."

"I will do as you ask, but you must understand time is of the utmost importance. Any delay reaching an agreement could cost innocent lives," Sifet said, rising to his feet. "Rorec, see our guest to his room. I believe he'll find it more welcoming than the sick room."

"With pleasure, Vos. King Fitzeirick, follow me, please."

Cesci opened the door as we approached. "Good evening, friend Rorec and Croian King Fist-er-rick."

Looking down at him, I frowned at the young man. *Does he not understand what I told Sifet about my army's orders? I may have saved him from Dalibor, but my warriors won't hesitate.*

"Do you know what Sifet is planning?" I asked, after the door closed behind us.

"In detail? No, but I don't expect him to ask for anything more than he already discussed with you. I am sure his offer will benefit both nations if that's what you're asking."

Rorec's voice reminded me of Roi. *What would he advise? Caution and restraint, no doubt.*

We turned away from the hall we'd come from before and kept walking.

"What if I asked you to take me to the nearest exit and point me in the direction of my warriors?"

He shook his head and put his hand on my shoulder. "I doubt you'd live to see your men again if I turned you out. Coming to an agreement with what's left of the League is best for you, Croy, and Satra. Think on this. I gain nothing by lying to you, but you gain invaluable aid in coming battles and a society that will quickly become productive once you have won."

"Your room is near where Asfrid and I sleep," Rorec said.

I pushed his hand away. "And Sifet gets his power back, putting him in charge of a nation that poses a threat to Croy. One I swore to eliminate."

"I've known the chieftain about as long as you've been alive. He doesn't enter blood pacts often."

"What's a blood pact? I think I should know what Sifet is asking before I agree to it."

He nodded. "After two sign the agreement, your palms are cut. You grasp hands over the parchment, dribbling your mixed blood on it as a binding seal. Breaking the pact carries a penalty of death if caught."

"So, he thinks an agreement between us is worth risking his life for?"

"Don't doubt Sifet's devotion to his country. Though he hungers to lead again, living as Bane has changed him. He recognizes his power is no longer absolute. Also, his time is not long. Before you know it, you will have the opportunity to appoint a new leader here. A skald of your choosing. That alone should eliminate any worry for the future."

"Croy no longer has skalds; I did away with the office. I have much to consider, and I'm tired. How much farther to my room?"

"Not far."

As we continued, my thoughts turned to understanding my current situation and what may happen both soon and in the near future. *I'm alive. Rorec seems to think Sifet has changed. Doesn't mean either can be trusted, especially not the desperate tyrant.* I needed to keep my suspicion of the chieftain in mind at all times. He'd already outmaneuvered me once. I couldn't let it happen again.

"You sleep here. Asfrid and I are across the hall," he said, pointing.

I nodded. "Good to know. Doubt I'll be much of a bother. I need lots of rest."

"Should be a candle and flint to the right as you enter." He pushed the door open, stepped aside, and waved me in. "You've noticed some don't like your presence here. Don't wander the halls alone. Someone will bring you food in the morning."

I stepped inside, not knowing what to expect.

"Sleep well," Rorec said.

I lit the single candle on a small table and looked around the room before closing the door. My quarters were slightly longer than wide and empty except for a short wooden structure piled with straw for sleeping. It creaked when I sat. Pushing my hands through the bedding, I found ropes crossing back and forth, holding the straw from falling to the floor. After a long yawn, I lay down. Trying to figure out what course I should take, my thoughts drifted to what other people in my life would tell me. Tindra wants me to pay attention and survive. Roi would recommend caution and restraint. Undoubtedly Crum would make light of the situation, proclaiming it would make a great tale. Sar'sa's ghost spoke the loudest, reminding me some long-held beliefs aren't based on truth. She insisted my people needed me to find the truth.

A knock on the door woke me. The candle had burned out, leaving the room black. Sitting up, the coarse robe scratched me. Unsure of where the door was, I called out, "Come in."

Asfrid's face was lit by the candle she carried. "Oh, did I wake you?"

"Yes, but if it's important, that's fine."

"Rorec and I would like for you to eat with us, but I can leave if you need to sleep longer."

"I could use a meal, and I'd rather not eat alone." Turning to hang my legs off the bed, the stone was cold as ever when my feet touched the floor.

She smiled, making me feel warm and comfortable. Offering her hand, she said, "Come with me."

I walked with her to the room she shared with her husband. Lanterns lit their living space from sconces in the walls. It was larger than my quarters. A long table, piled high with leaves, flowers, pods, and other things I didn't recognize, along with a collection of herbalist's tools, took up most of the extra space. *Wonder what Sefit's room looks like.*

"Good morn, King Fitzeirick," Rorec welcomed, from his seat at a square, wooden table toward the back of the room.

"Have a seat. I'll get our meal," Asfrid said, motioning to a chair across from her husband.

She closed the door behind her as I sat. "Good morning, Friend Rorec," I quipped.

He grinned. "See. You're picking up the Bane's manner of speaking already."

I raised my eyebrows. "I need to know where your loyalty lies."

His grin faded as he nodded. "With Croy, always."

"With my father's Croy or with mine?" I asked, locking my eyes on his and tapping a finger on the table.

He didn't wither from my stare. "I am loyal to the people of Croy, as is my wife. What's best for them is what I want."

"And you think aiding Sifet is what's best for Croy?"

"Our country benefited from an agreement with Satra until Eirickson decided to twist it to his favor. You can repair the relationship and save innocent lives at the same time."

"You swear you're telling me the truth?"

"On my life." He nodded.

"Not good enough. Give me your word on Asfrid's life and Roi's. Would you risk your family if I find out you're lying to me?"

He sighed but didn't look away. "Yes."

"Tell me about Dalibor," I said, crossing my arms.

"You don't want to know about Sifet?" He asked, looking confused.

"I've dealt with men like Sifet enough to have a feel for him. He's desperate. Regaining his lost power is his only motivation."

"But he's forcing you into an agreement."

I nodded. "Didn't expect him to back me into a corner with my own words. Won't happen again. The chieftain's rat is a bigger concern."

"He's the one I know least about. Calling him secretive isn't enough."

"Seems he has no problem slitting throats."

Rorec glanced at his hands. "He's spilled more blood than I, or at least that's the impression I get."

I nodded again. "I'm guessing he provides the same service as a Varian spion. Gathers information, finds people, eliminates problems ... that sort of thing."

The door opened behind me.

"I'd say that's a good way to think about him," Rorec said. His expression changed, a narrow smile telling me our conversation was over.

Chapter 56

Asfrid placed a tray, holding mugs and plates, on the table. The plate she sat in front of me had a stack of thin, roughly round patties. Next to the food was a small bowl with a thick, dark liquid.

Waving my hand over the plate, I asked, "What's this?"

"The Bane call them kartblin. Think of it as flattened, roasted potatoes," Rorec explained. "The cup holds a sour grape paste to dip them in."

"It took me some time to adjust to the taste," Asfrid said.

"And the drink?" I asked, sniffing it.

"A tart wine," Rorec said. "I'd guess you've never tasted anything like it before."

After a sip, my lip twitched.

"It, too, takes some getting used to," Asfrid added.

I nodded and tore off a piece of kartblin. Alone it tasted like salted, roast potato. With the paste, the flavor changed. It wasn't offensive, but I wasn't in a hurry to acquire the taste, either. "During my stay in Varia, I met a Satran man who ran an eatery in the capital. His food tasted nothing like this. It was more herbal in flavor."

Rorec nodded and gave me a sad smile. "Had we met before the Bonetaker uprising, you would have eaten the food of the upper clans. The Bane, and most Devoted, survive on humble meals."

"Better times," Asfrid added. "Happier times for all of Satra."

"Even the Bane?" I asked.

"Don't question what you don't understand," Rorec advised.

"I understand being mistreated," I said, pointing to my brand, "and I understand injustice."

He lowered his eyes and muttered something I couldn't hear.

"I can add something to your drink to help you regain your strength if you'd like," Asfrid offered, as she lifted her mug.

"Will it make it taste better?" I asked.

She frowned. "It shouldn't make it any worse."

"It's been my experience that not all herbalists' remedies are as helpful as they claim. You'll understand if I'm concerned about what you add to my drink."

"I didn't spend so much time and effort saving your life to poison you now," she replied, a matronly tone adding weight to her words.

I chuckled. "If it will help me, go ahead."

She grabbed my mug and took it to her bench.

I munched on a piece of kartblin and watched Asfrid select various ingredients.

Rorec sighed heavily. He had a look of contentment as his wife ground something in a mortar and pestle.

She patted the mixture with her finger and tasted a bit. Shaking her head, she plucked two leaves from a small jar and ground them into the remedy.

I'd nearly finished my first patty when she tasted the mixture again, smiled, and nodded.

Asfrid scraped the contents of the mortar into my drink, stirred it with a thin rod, and hurried back to the table. "You probably won't notice anything immediately, but it will help."

I took a sip and tried to hide my reaction. *Didn't know you could combine sour and bitter so each made the other worse.* After several blinks and a shake of my head, I tilted the mug toward Asfrid. "I'll take all the help I can get." I turned to Rorec. "Getting out of here and touching real stone would be even better."

"Sifet will decide when it's best to leave," Rorec said.

"Can we not discuss such matters over our first meal together?" Asfrid asked.

"What would you like to talk about?" I asked.

"Tell me about my son and his family."

"There's a lot to tell. Do we have time?" I asked.

She nodded.

I gave her a big grin and started the story at the Trader's Cup Inn, where Roi and Geri reunited and we met Grima and Einns for the first time. Leaving out the grim details of my time in the tunnels under the capital, I quickly got to finding Roi in Swinter and his devotion to his promised and her son.

Asfrid's smile grew wider as the tale was told. She nodded when I told her about him coming to the Croian capital to serve as my top adviser and grasped Rorec's hand when I mentioned he made a home in one of their old safe houses. Tears down her cheeks when I finished with the story of two marriages, first Roi's to Grima, then mine to Tindra in the home they had made together.

Rorec put his arm around his wife and pulled her close. I looked away and ate quietly as they shared the moment. I considered taking my meal and finishing it in my room when Rorec cleared his throat. "Your families are close, I take it."

"Roi and I are as close as ever. Tindra and Grima became fast friends, but Roi and Tindra ..." I shrugged. "Call it a truce."

"Why?" Asfrid asked, wiping her cheeks.

"He doesn't like what Tindra is — was. He doesn't trust her because of her past."

"What's in her past?" she asked.

"She was one of King Ander's spions. Made a good living manipulating people, and worse."

"Much like you distrust Dalibor," Rorec said.

"Point taken," I said, nodding. "How about a more pleasant subject? Will you come back to Croy when the fighting is over and we've won?"

Rorec turned to his wife. "We haven't discussed much of the future. Too much uncertainty to worry about what may come." He looked at me. "Would we be welcomed back?"

"Of course," I said. "Why wouldn't you be?"

"We've been here so long," Asfrid said.

"And you told me Roi knows I wore Satran garb during the invasion," Rorec added.

"Which can be explained. I'm sure he would welcome you both with open arms."

We jumped when someone knocked on the door.

"Come in," Rorec called.

The door opened as I turned.

One of Sifet's advisers stepped into the room.

"Branko, you're welcome to join us," Rorec said, standing.

He was one of the men on Sifet's left. His dark, oily hair was pulled back, exposing his thin face and small eyes. He wasn't overly muscled and stood no more than my height, maybe a bit shorter. "I can't. Vos Sifet sent me to get our guest. His room was empty, so I came here hoping you might know where he was."

"I'm here, enjoying a meal with friends," I said, rising to my feet. "What does Sifet want?"

"He has his offer written out, as well as his demands. Come with me," Branko said.

"I'd rather not be the only Croian in the room," I said, looking over my shoulder.

"I'll go with you," Rorec said, before bending down to kiss his wife and grab a potato patty.

"Lead the way," I said, motioning toward the hall.

Rorec and I followed Branko back to the large dining room we'd met in before.

Vos Sifet sat in the same chair with Dalibor on his right. The chieftain stood when we entered, welcomed me, and asked me to sit to discuss the agreement.

I nodded and led Rorec to the far, left side of the table.

"I'll see you are not disturbed," Branko said, closing the door after he left the room.

As soon as I was seated, Sifet pushed a scroll toward me. "I believe you will find this agreeable."

"If nothing else, it gives us a place to start negotiations," I said, unrolling the page. Dalibor grunted.

"We do not have time to draw this out, young king," Sifet said. "I believe my offer far outweighs what I ask for in return."

I glanced at him, pursed my lips, and took my time reading the proposed agreement.

The writing was tight, tilted to the right, and difficult to read until I turned the page slightly. Even then, I had to start over several times before I could make out the words.

It began with Sifet's offer. I would have the support of every Bane and Devoted loyal to him. *Interesting he did not put a number to his followers. Does he know how many support him? Considering I have yet to meet anyone I could tell was Devoted, I suspect few skilled people are among them.* His advisers would serve me as they do him. *I think the Bane will be more useful. I doubt Sifet's most trusted will be eager to do as I ask.* Finally, he pledged loyalty to me once he regained his rule and swore I would choose the next leader of Satra upon Sifet's death.

His expectations followed: Destroy the Bonetakers and Legion while sparing all Satran citizens who swear loyalty to him or me. Direct my men to do as little damage as possible to buildings and animals while battling the usurpers. Assign Croian forces to protect Satra as it would be part of Croy upon our victory.

The document ended with an agreement for both of us to keep the peace between our people and work toward future benefits for both nations.

After a second read, making sure I hadn't overlooked some detail meant to trap me. "You left out one important detail," I said, sliding the scroll toward Rorec. "Would you agree?"

Sifet squinted. "I don't know what you mean. This is a simple agreement, after all."

I smiled. "What happens should you fall before my army topples the Bonetakers? Suppose you die in battle?"

"I have no intention of being involved in the fighting," Sifet said.

"I hadn't planned on being poisoned and captured." I spread my arms. "Yet here I am. Life has taught me to consider many unexpected possibilities. Give me a quill and ink. I will correct your oversight after Rorec gives his opinion."

"He is correct, Vos Sifet. There is nothing binding the agreement should either of you die before victory is complete," Rorec said.

"Give me your words; I'll add them to the page," Dalibor offered.

"My words will be in my hand. Quill and ink, please."

The rat grumbled something before pulling what I asked for out of his robe. He placed them in front of Sifet, who slid them to me.

After removing a cork from the small inkpot, I dipped the quill and added a line to the page.

Once signed, this agreement is binding to the leaders of both nations until such time as it ends by mutual agreement in front of witnesses.

I offered Sifet the page, unrolled. "I believe that covers either of us dying before our time. You'd better hope I live, though. My wife is not as agreeable as I can be."

The chieftain took the document, glanced at my addition, and gave it to Dalibor.

His shifty-looking adviser's eyes moved back and forth several times as he read the sentence in detail. "I see nothing wrong with the addition, Vos."

Sifet took the page back and looked at me. "King Fitzeirick, would you prefer to sign first?"

I slid the pot toward him before offering the quill. "It's your proposal. I believe it customary for you to sign first."

He bobbed his head and took the quill. Using swooping motions, Sifet signed the agreement. "Your turn."

I took the quill and added my name next to his. "What now?"

"We seal it with our mixed blood. Dalibor, your knife."

He drew a long, thin blade from the sheath on his belt and placed it on the table in front of Sifet. It reminded me of a knife I'd seen a fisher carry when I first visited the beach south of my capital.

Sifet sliced his palm. Blood pooled in his hand as he offered me the blade.

I opened my palm before setting the knife on the table.

We grasped our bleeding hands over the page, dribbling large drops of sticky, red fluid onto our names.

"Do you men recognize the commitment made here and agree to abide by the pact or forfeit your life?" Dalibor asked.

"For Satra, I do," Sifet said.

"For Croy, I promise."

Dalibor nodded to Rorec. Together they said, "May you be bound to this agreement which is sealed in freely given blood."

"It is done," Sifet said, releasing my hand.

And ties Croy's future even deeper to my survival and our victory. Hope my men understand. The stinging cut across my hand brought me out of my thoughts.

Chapter 57

"You insist time is short," I said, "when do we leave?"

"We expect word soon on where your men are and where the Legion is," Dalibor said. "Once we have that, we can prepare."

"I need my armor and hammer," I said.

"Rorec will see you get your things," Sifet said.

"Of course," Rorec said behind me. "Fitzeirick, come with me. Asfrid can tend to your hand while I get your belongings."

"One moment," I said, nodding. "Sifet, I know there are men among your followers who dislike me. Now that we are allies, should one attack me, I will protect myself."

"Yes, young king. Don't worry." He turned to Dalibor. "Tell everyone we are bound by a blood pact, and he is now Friend Fitzeirick."

"Of course, Vos. Your word will be heard and followed," Dalibor said, bowing.

"I'd hate for a misunderstanding to endanger our new alliance," I said, bowing to the Satran men. "Rorec, let's go."

"Yes, right ... Friend Fitzeirick." He chuckled. "You better get used to that."

I shook my head and smiled. "It's going to take some time."

Sifet laughed behind me. Dalibor didn't make a sound. Rorec opened the door and let Branko know the meeting was over. The Satran man smiled and offered me his hand.

"Sorry," I said, showing my palm, "I'm still bleeding."

He raised his eyebrows. "Hope you heal quickly."

The walk to Asfrid seemed shorter this time. *Maybe her tonic is working.*

Rorec let me into their room. "Fitzeirick needs your care. Blood oath."

"Silly tradition," she said, looking up from her work table. "Come here. Let me see how bad it is."

Rorec patted me on the back. "I'll find your things and take them to your quarters."

I nodded before crossing the room so Asfrid could inspect my cut.

She turned me to face the table and placed my hand over a bowl. "Don't move."

"Yes, ma'am."

After filling a small cup from a pitcher, she grabbed a cloth. "Have to clean it first," she said, before pouring the cup over my hand.

The sting I expected never came. *Guess it was plain water.*

I flinched at the pain racing up my arm as she wiped the cloth across my palm.

"Hold still."

"Sorry."

Another wipe. More pain, but this time I was ready.

"Not too deep. Don't think it needs stitches. It should heal on its own, but plaster and a bandage will help. Give me a moment."

"Whatever will help me heal faster," I said. "I want to be able to take care of myself when we leave."

She smiled and shook her head before searching through jars and baskets, tossing things in the mortar as she found them. With a nod, she poured something from a jar into the mortar and stirred it with a slender rod. "It's ready," she said, placing the stone bowl next to the small dish under my hand.

The mortar held a dark, green mixture resembling boiled grains gone horribly wrong. It had a pungent, unfamiliar smell.

"Likely this will burn," Asfrid warned. "But it's your own fault that I have to use it."

"Sifet's idea, not mine," I said.

"You agreed to enter a blood pact, so it's your fault."

I clenched my jaw and waited for the pain.

From the moment the paste touched the cut, it burned. Not the pleasant heat of a spicy meal but an uncomfortable stinging pain.

Drawing a hissing breath, I grabbed my wrist to hold my hand steady.

She applied a second coating, and the burn continued. I hissed again as she wrapped a bandage around my hand tight enough to force the paste farther into the wound.

"Sorry," she said. "It works best if it sticks the cloth in place."

Nodding, I tried to focus on anything but the sting in my now throbbing hand.

"There. Done. Best if you don't use your hand for a couple of days and leave it wrapped."

Raising my hand, I looked at the wrapping and thanked her. *Not sure how I'll manage not using my right hand for a while.*

"Thank you for treating me. I hate to be a burden."

She grinned. "Hardly a burden, especially compared to what it took to keep you alive."

"Why did you save me?" I asked. "Maybe the real question is why did Sifet let you?"

She put her hands on her hips and gave me the look a mother gives an irritating child. "Vos Sifet does not control who I treat and who I don't. He didn't know you were here until after I applied the paste to draw the poison from your wound. Like I told you before, the Bane knew someone was hurt and needed my help."

Not sure I believe her, but she has no reason to lie. "What do you know about Dalibor?"

She shrugged. "Not much. Seems like he's always near Vos Sifet, whether you see him or not. Otherwise, he keeps to himself. Most of the Bane call him *tene'yas*. It means something like 'a rat in the shadows.'"

"Good name for him," I said, grinning. "May I have some water? My throat's dry."

"Of course." She filled the small cup and handed it to me.

Compared to the sour wine I'd had, the water was sweet. As I put the cup back on the table, Rorec entered the room.

"Your clothes are in your room," he said. "That armor's heavier than it looks. I don't see how you can move in it, much less fight. And the hammer ... impressive."

"Hammer was a gift in Varia. Took a lot of practice to use it effectively. The armor has metal plates between the leather. The heft takes some getting used to, but it's worth it. And it's comfortable enough to sleep in."

"I pulled four darts out of the back," Asfrid said. "Likely, it saved your life."

"See. Worth it," I said, smiling. "Now that I've got my clothes back, I'm going to change. This cloth's rough on the skin."

Rorec chuckled.

"Make sure you rest," Asfrid said. "I can tell you're feeling better, but believe me, you're not fully recovered yet."

"Best if you stay in your quarters or come here. I know what Sifet said, what you made him say, about your status, but better safe than sorry. The hall's clear now," Rorec said, stepping away from the door.

I thanked them both and, heeding Rorec's advice, hurried to my room. My clothes sat, folded, on the bed. He'd piled my armor in the corner with my hammer resting on top.

I let the robe drop to the floor. *Would make a better sack than clothes, but I guess beggars, or Bane, can't be picky.* Compared to the rough cloth, my shirt was the finest silk. Pulling on my pants showed I'd lost weight while recovering from the poison. Being cautious with my tender hand, I struggled to cinch my belt. With my boots on, the floor no longer chilled my feet.

I looked at the pile of armor, and Asfrid's warning about resting came to mind. *I'll rest for a little while and put it on later.*

*   *   *

Something tapped my shoulder.

I brushed it away and grumbled.

A woman called my name.

I looked toward the voice and blinked before shading my eyes against the glare of a candle flame. "Who's there?"

"It's Asfrid. Rorec asked me to look in on you after you slept through lunch. Are you well?"

I yawned and stretched. "I feel fine. Didn't know Rorec had come in. Guess I was more tired than I thought."

"I'm not surprised. The poison takes a lot out of you. Sit up and drink this."

Sitting up, I rubbed my eyes before reaching for the cup. The sour smell hit my nose about the same time the bitter taste crossed my tongue. *Shouldn't be surprised. Don't complain either; it seemed to help earlier.* I handed her the cup and wiped my hand across my mouth. "Thank you."

She nodded. "I do what I can to help. Let me tell Rorec you're awake. Would you mind if he came to visit?"

"Not at all," I said, smiling. "Any word on when we're leaving?"

Asfrid shook her head before turning. She put the candle in a holder near the door as she walked out.

I moved to the small table and sat to wait for Rorec. *Why didn't she invite me to their room?*

Rorec entered carrying something. He closed the door before sitting across from me. "Water," he said, placing a mug in front of me.

I thanked him and took a long drink. "Why are we talking here instead of in your quarters?"

"Some topics I don't discuss in front of my wife. She worries enough without hearing about things that don't involve her."

"Understood. What's on your mind?"

"It's likely you'll be invited to join Sifet and his advisers for dinner. I'll accompany you if you'd like, but I want to know what you expect from me."

"Assuming you were telling the truth when you said your loyalty is with the Croian people, I expect you to support me until I win or I fall in battle. Along the way, guide me when you think I need help. Can you do that for your country?"

"I can. Provided you will listen to me."

"Much like I've told Roi, if I don't do what you advise, it wasn't because I didn't listen. Is there something I need to know now?"

"You won't be adding much of a fighting force to your army when we leave here. Most Bane don't have the will to fight. Those who do are brutes with no sense of tactics. Don't expect them to follow orders in the heat of battle."

"They have to be useful. Otherwise, why add them to the pact?"

He nodded. "They are servants and laborers. The braver among them can act as scouts. One thing all Bane have perfected is going unnoticed by the other clans. Survival learned through harsh lessons."

"How many Devoted are among Sifet's followers?"

"I haven't seen any since the exile." Rorec shook his head and shrugged.

"But he must have some," I said, frowning, "somewhere. Otherwise, why mention them?"

Rorec's frown matched mine. "He doesn't tell me everything, but I think you're right."

"What else is on your mind?"

"A favor," he said, looking away.

"I can't make any promises, but I'll do what I can for you. Ask."

"I know you said Asfrid, and I would be welcomed back to Croy. Let us choose whether we return or not."

I squinted. "Why wouldn't you want to go home?"

"Home?" he questioned. "Croy hasn't been our home for most of your life."

"Look at me." I tilted my head. "Are you doing this to avoid Roi?"

"Partly," he said, locking eyes with me. "But also because this nation is all we know now, and I can do you some good here. Work for you like I did your father."

"I see. If you want to stay, you can stay. What if Roi wants to come see you or Asfrid? I won't stop him. Family is important."

"It is, but we're hardly family now," he replied, looking away again.

"It's likely he'd come and bring his family ... at least once."

"I'm sure Asfrid would want to meet them."

"Or she could come to Croy for a visit."

Someone knocked softly on the door.

"Who's there?" I asked.

"Asfrid. Branko's with me."

Rorec shrugged when I looked at him.

"Come in," I said.

Asfrid led the Satran into my, now crowded, room.

"You're never where I expect to find you," Branko said.

I raised my eyebrows. "Me or him?"

"You, King Fitzeirick," Branko said, with a shallow bow. "Vos Sifet has information to share."

"What sort of information?" I asked.

"All I know is my vos wants to talk with you."

"Interested?" I asked, pointing to Rorec.

He nodded.

Standing, I looked at Asfrid. "Roi's wife is used to me interrupting their plans; I hope you don't mind when the same happens with Rorec while I'm around."

She smiled, but her eyes showed a hint of sadness. "I knew who he was when we married. He belongs to his work as much as he belongs to me."

"Thank you," I said, bowing to her. "Your service will be rewarded."

She laughed, shook her head, and left.

"Branko, after you," I said, nodding toward the hall.

Chapter 58

Branko set a fast pace on the way to the meeting room.

Opening the door, he waved us into the room but stayed outside.

Must be important if he's guarding the room again.

Sifet greeted us with another adviser, who resembled Branko, standing to his right.

I looked for Dalibor but didn't see him. *He's always near Sifet. Just because I don't see him doesn't mean he's not around.*

"Are you strong enough to travel, young king?" Sifet asked.

"Where am I going?"

"*We* are going to meet your army," Sifet said.

My eyebrows raised on their own. "We? You and me?"

He spread his arms wide. "All of us. You, me, Rorec, Asfrid, my advisers, my followers ... everyone."

My heart sped up. "You found them? Did Bior survive the attack?"

"I don't know who that is," Sifet said. "Bojan, did anyone mention any Croian names?"

"No," the adviser answered.

"He's one of my warriors. About my height. Walks with a limp."

Bojan shook his head. "Don't expect such details from Bane. We know where they were recently and have a good idea of where they are going."

"So, they're on the move?"

"Heading southwest," he said. "A Legion force left the area recently, but more could arrive soon. It would be best for everyone if we reach your men before the next battle."

"Do you know if the barges reached the shore?" I asked.

"For certain? No. But I'm told your army is large," Bojan said.

What's a large army to the Bane? I nodded. "When do we leave?"

"Preparations are underway," Sifet said. "Expect to eat on the move and travel at night."

"I should tell Asfrid to pack her things," Rorec said, pushing his chair away from the table.

"Branko should have told her already," Sifet said.

"I have to make first contact," I said. "Any Satran who approaches will die before they reach the camp."

Sifet nodded. "You will be among the Bane who guide us through the dark. Are you sure your men won't attack anyway?"

"My warriors know what I look like," I said, pointing to my brand. "Also, I doubt there are any other Croians in Satra carrying this mark."

"True," Sifet said.

"This seems too easy," I said.

"We'll be less than half a day behind a Legion force," Bojan said. "I doubt they'll have much of a rear guard, but we have to step with care until we reach your army."

"You said everyone is leaving. How many are going with us?" I asked.

"Sixty-three in total," Sifet said. "Why?"

I let out a low whistle. "Two companies worth of people less than a day behind battle-ready soldiers. How many of your followers are trained to fight?"

"I told you the Bane know how to move about unnoticed," Rorec said.

"A few, maybe, but any group this large will attract attention," I said, turning to him.

"We know how to survive, young king," Sifet said. "Do you?"

Whipping my head around, I glared at him. "I can take care of myself."

"Yet, you are here," Sifet said, smirking. "Many, even myself once, discounted the Bane and their survival skills. Overlooking them may be what tips the scales in your — our favor. Stay close to Rorec, so we can find you when it's time to leave."

Rorec clapped his hand on my shoulder. "Let's go help Asfrid pack."

I nodded. "I'll need to stop by my quarters first."

"Whatever you need to do, be quick," Bojan said.

I nodded and followed Rorec back to my room.

"Go help your wife," I said, raising my bandaged hand. "It may take a little time for me to put on my armor."

He chuckled. "You know where I'll be when you're ready."

"See you soon." The pants slid on easily, but cinching them tight enough to stay up was a challenge. Putting on the top went smoother than I expected. Gritting my teeth against the ache in my palm when I grabbed my hammer, I clicked it in place on my back. Carrying my helmet, I left to see if Rorec and Asfrid needed any help.

Normally the heft of my armor was reassuring, a comforting load. Now, the extra weight had me breathing hard after walking to their room. *Maybe I'm not ready to leave. We have to take the opportunity to go while it's safe, but what if Sifet, or one of his people, sees me as weak? I don't want to trust him, but the blood pact should secure my safety.*

"Are you sure this is only the essentials?" I heard Rorec ask through the open door. "I don't know how much help we're going to get for carrying our supplies. Best to pack light."

"I have to be ready to tend wounds and deal with a saz-dart attack," Asfrid said. "Not my fault it requires so many reagents."

"Put much more in that pack, and it will take two men to carry it."

"Anything I can help with?" I asked, stepping into the room.

Asfrid's table was all but empty. Bulging sacks and several backpacks sat on the floor in front of it.

Rorec had a sack tied to his belt, an axe tucked against his right hip, and a pack hanging from his shoulders. "Not with the hammer slung on your back."

"And not while you're still recovering," Asfrid added, holding a cup toward me. "Drink."

The sour-bitter flavor went almost unnoticed. *Not something I want to grow accustomed to or dependent on.*

"I can take a small pack," I offered, handing Asfrid the empty cup.

"By the look on your face, you're loaded enough as it is," Rorec said, motioning toward the table. "Sit. I'll find some help."

Asfrid continued stuffing leaves, flowers, and jars into sacks as Rorec left. "Are you excited?" she asked, staying focused on her task.

"Nervous."

"Not looking forward to rejoining your warriors?"

"Of course, I am, but I'm not sure how they'll accept a crowd of Satran entering the camp. They were told to kill every last person in the nation. Most of my men follow orders well. I'm surprised you're not upset at having to leave on short notice?"

After tying a bag shut, she turned to me. "To be honest, I'm ready to go."

I furrowed my brow. "It's this your home?"

"If I stay in one place too long, I end up gathering too much stuff." She patted a nearby sack and gave me a sad smile. "I've lived most of my life on the move. I think the adventure keeps me young. It will be nice to see more Croian faces, too."

"Where will you settle after the war?"

"I don't think too much about the future anymore." She shrugged, sniffed at a jar, and put it back on the table.

"You're welcome to live in Croy's capital. I'm sure Roi would like to see you ... introduce you to his family."

She smiled again. "Rorec and I will decide when the time comes."

"What will we decide?" he asked, leading four, large Satran men into the room.

"Where we'll live after this mess is over," Asfrid said.

He glanced at me. "We'll discuss it after the war is over. Is everything packed?"

"Those are ready to go," she said, pointing to the pile of sacks and backpacks. "I can carry the few things left."

"We'll take them, Friend Asfrid," a Bane said, before approaching the stack and handing loads to the others.

"Be careful. Some of those are breakable and not easy to replace," she said.

"Treat it like it was ours, Friend Asfrid," he replied, with a wide smile.

Each man took two backpacks, one over each shoulder, and four sacks before leaving the room.

I sat and watched the couple secure the last of the herbs and tools into a small sack.

"Ready?" Rorec asked.

"Between us, I'm wondering if I'm strong enough to make the trip," I said.

"I'll stay nearby, ready to help if you need it," he said.

Asfrid patted a sack hanging from her waist. "And I have plenty of tonic at hand."

Their reassurance made me smile but didn't remove my doubts. "Rorec, do you have any idea how long we'll be traveling?"

He cocked his head. "If I knew where we were going, I could give you a fair guess. The coast is two, maybe three days' walk. But we don't know if your men have joined with the rest of your army or not."

I nodded as my smile turned into a frown. "Assuming we're heading south or southwest of where we are now, what obstacles lie in our path?"

He shrugged. "Nothing like crossing the black sand. Assuming the Legion hasn't destroyed bridges at the river crossings, the biggest challenge is avoiding patrols and watchmen."

I looked at my bandaged hand. "I can't fight with only one working hand. If we're discovered, will you protect me?"

"Of course," Rorec said. "Returning you, alive, to your army is the most important thing right now. Convincing your men to spare innocents and focus the fighting where it needs to be will save lives, end this war sooner, and put the Satran people on a path to a better life."

"Is putting Sifet back in charge the best option?" I asked.

"He has bound himself to your will. Though he may resist making broad changes, things will change. And when he passes ..."

"I choose who leads Satra, I know. But there will be resistance—you even said as much."

"And you insisted you could make it go away," Rorec countered.

"Aren't you putting the cart before the horse?" Asfrid asked. "Once we reach your army, you must convince them you've changed your mind before they attack us."

"Some disagreed with killing all Satran anyway."

"But they would have?" Asfrid asked.

"Enough so the ones who didn't wouldn't matter."

Branko stepped into the room. "Everyone ready to leave?"

"We are," Rorec said, turning to look at him.

"Come with me."

I stood, squared my shoulders, and did my best to look like I wasn't burdened by my armor.

Chapter 59

Neither Rorec nor Asfrid looked back as I followed them out of the room.

Interesting, considering it could be the last time they see this place.

Branko led us farther down the hall than I'd ever been before. It ended at a room larger than the meeting room, filled with people.

"Make way for Croian King Fitzeirick," Branko announced.

The crowd parted so we could pass.

Sifet and his advisers stood near the far wall.

"You look winded, young king," the chieftain said.

"Lasting effects of that horrible poison," Asfrid said.

"Don't worry about me," I said. "I'll do what I have to."

"That's what we're counting on," Bojan said.

"When do we leave?" I asked.

"Soon," Sifet said, turning to look at the wall. "Those Bane are preparing to open the way now."

Behind him, a group of five men crouched near the wall. Three had their hands pressed against the dead stone. The other two joined hands between them, holding their free hands against the wall. "Release now," one said.

The three men grunted, then the wall hummed as they poured their talent into it.

Working together, the two in the middle moved the stone to make an opening.

Part of me suspected it was some kind of trick. My ears told me it wasn't. The humming changed as the dead stone moved. Though tempted to send my talent toward them, I held back to keep from accidentally disturbing their efforts. *Better to get out than mess everything up by trying to learn how they are doing this.*

Once the hole opened wide enough to let three men pass together, the humming faded. The five Bane leaned on each other, breathing heavily.

"Amazing," I whispered. "I can't believe they can syth this dead stone."

"Yet it happened," Sifet said.

"How?" I asked, as the Bane stonesyths entered the hole.

"I cannot tell you," Sifet said. "I'm a fire worker. All stone is dead to me."

The floor trembled as the Bane stonesyths moved material behind the wall.

"I wish I understood how," I said.

"If you get the opportunity to ask, they may tell you," he said, "if they decide they can trust you with their knowledge. Now, unless I am mistaken, the way to the surface will be open soon. Best get ready."

Looking over my shoulder, I called for Rorec and pointed to the new exit.

"After you," he replied. with a nod.

"Sifet, where will you be?" I asked, after taking a step.

"We travel in a group of Bane for safety," he said, "but do not worry, we won't be far behind."

I slid my helmet in place and headed to the exit. Twitching tremors rolled under my feet from the opening ahead, telling me the Bane stonesyths were still hard at work.

A staircase, carved from natural stone, started its steep climb into darkness a few paces beyond the opening in the wall. Keeping my hand on the left wall, I pulled some strength from the stone to help me up the stairs. As I climbed, the Bane ahead weren't keeping their energy contained, so it was easy to follow as I plodded ahead at a steady pace. Footsteps echoing off the smooth walls let me know Rorec was not far behind me.

Stepping through a large boulder, I found myself on level ground. Moonlight made it easy to see the Bane stonesyths spread out a few steps away. I kept walking until I was well away from the stone, then sat and used my talent to pull more strength and stamina into my body. In the fresh air, the smells of grass and trees filled my nose. *Funny what you notice after being underground for a while.*

Rorec stopped nearby and asked how I was doing, concern evident in his voice.

"I'll be fine. Are these men leading the way? Given how much sything they've done, I'm surprised they're still standing."

"Let me find out," he said, before approaching them. I didn't try to listen in on their conversation, choosing to focus on preparing myself to keep going when it was time to walk again.

Rorec came back. "We're with the group behind us. These Bane stay behind to close the way underground and cover everyone's tracks."

I nodded. "Sounds like a solid plan, the more hidden our passing is, the better."

"And waiting lets you rest."

"That too."

He chuckled. "I'll wait by the stone for our escort."

As he walked away, I continued drawing stamina from the ground until my muscles tingled from the extra energy. *That might be enough.*

Looking around, I felt exposed, alone, in the clearing. Staring into the dark trees, my neck itched where the poisoned wound had healed. *Anyone could be hiding out there, watching ... waiting to attack.* I tapped the handle of my hammer to make sure it was still there. *Not that I can do much with it.*

Keeping my talent pushed out told me a group approached from behind. I turned to see Rorec and Asfrid walking with some Bane.

"You ready?" Rorec asked, stopping near me as the group continued on to the southwest.

I nodded and got to my feet.

"Follow them," he said, pointing at the group.

We joined them at the edge of the clearing, getting into the middle of the cluster as we entered the dark woods.

Watching our guides dodge trees and branches made it easier to avoid obstacles hiding in the dark, so I could use my talent to maintain my strength. Even being careful, I thought we were making too much noise. The snap of every twig and scrape of branch against rough cloth sounded louder than I thought it should.

Ahead of us, someone said, "Friends. Wait here. Yes."

"What's going on?" I whispered to Rorec.

"Not sure," he said. "Something ahead must have gotten their attention."

"May be near a footpath," Asfrid said, "if we are where I think we are. I have kartblin if you're hungry."

"I'll take one," Rorec said.

On the road, you eat when you can. "I'll have one too, please," I said, though I wasn't hungry.

Even eating slowly, I finished mine before the Bane returned.

"Can I have some water?" I asked.

"The Bane have our water," Rorec explained.

"So, if they get caught or lost, we go thirsty?" I asked.

"They won't get lost," Rorec said.

"And there should be a river not far south of here," Asfrid added.

"Assuming *we* don't get lost ... or worse," I said.

"Patience," Rorec said. "As long as we don't move too far from where they left us, the Bane will return when it's safe."

"You're asking for a lot of trust," I said, shaking my head.

"They've kept me safe so far," Asfrid said. "After the Bonetakers — I'm not sure I'd have managed to stay alive on my own."

Rorec put his arm around his wife. "You have skills many don't. I'm sure you would've made it fine."

She shrugged before leaning into him.

Watching them comfort each other brought Tindra to mind. *Does she know I'm missing, thought captured, or dead? Will she join the fight to avenge me?*

One of our guides came into view from the black around us. "Safe. Clear. Friends. Come with me. Yes."

"Do you happen to have some water?" I asked.

"Friend Fist-er-rick, share with Friend Rorec and Friend Asfrid, yes?" he replied, tossing a bulging skin to me.

I sighed. "You may call me Fitz, and I will be glad to share."

He nodded.

Pulling the plug from the container, I tilted my head back and squeezed a stream of warm water into my mouth. After a second drink, I offered it to Asfrid.

Shook her head. "I'm fine for now, thank you."

"Rorec, catch."

He grabbed the tossed skin from the air, took a long drink before hanging it around his neck, and nodded to the Satran. "Ready to go."

The Bane turned south and set a quicker pace than we had walked earlier. He led us to a worn footpath outside the trees and turned west. Bright moonlight shined on us, casting shadows at our feet.

"How far are we traveling tonight?" I asked our guide.

"Don't know yet."

Rorec answered my questioning glance with a shrug.

I sighed but kept my eyes on the guide while using my talent to watch for threats around us. *Where are the other Bane?*

Our guide stepped off the path into the trees without slowing. I followed, unsure of what awaited ahead and steadily growing more concerned.

"Where are we going?" I demanded.

Instead of answering me, he made odd, sloppy, clicking noises with his tongue.

A similar sound answered from somewhere ahead of us.

"There," he said, before clicking again.

Like Fastulf and his whistles. Maybe all guides work out sounds.

An owl hooted overhead, as if asking who dared invade its territory.

Other Bane joined from behind trees as we kept walking through the woods until the group was back together.

"River's not far," one of them said. "Cross the bridge. Yes."

"And enter the woods on the other side, right?" Asfrid asked.

"Right, Friend Asfrid. Yes."

Sounds like Asfrid knows where we are. That's a relief.

We kept a fast pace through the trees, exiting onto a broad road leading to the bridge.

"Friends. Wait here. Yes." one of the Bane said.

I didn't want to stand still, exposed on an open road, but I had to believe they knew best.

Two of our guides padded carefully across the wooden structure spanning the river. It looked strong enough to hold a loaded wagon and didn't make a sound as they crossed. Safely on the other side, one turned and waved to us.

Still concerned about being seen, I moved as fast as I could while still staying quiet. When I reached the road on the other side, the pair pointed to trees on the other side of a small clearing. "Friend Fist-er-rick, wait there. Yes."

I nodded, jogged into the forest, and rested against a tree.

From the east, faint streaks of light pushed into the night sky. *How much longer can we move about and stay unnoticed?* Somewhere above me, an animal hissed, letting me know I wasn't welcome.

Asfrid and Rorec joined me before I could spot the upset creature. Our Bane guides weren't far behind. They passed the three of us without pausing, and we followed them deeper into the woods, stopping at the edge of a field.

One of the guides pointed to a small house on the other side of the clearing. "We go there. Stanimir'll keep us until we can go again. Yes."

"Who's Stanimir?" I asked.

"A blacksmith," Asfrid said, "loyal to Sifet. He hid me for a while. We should be safe."

I patted one of the Bane on the back. "Let's go."

He nodded, and we made our way to the house.

The men ahead of me veered away from the front of the building when we got close, walking toward a small workshop behind the home.

There's no way this group's hiding there. And where's Sifet and the rest of the Bane?

Two men approached from the back of the house. One of our guides and a tall, broad-shouldered, heavily muscled man.

Must be Stanimir ... I hope.

I thought he was bald until he got close enough for me to see his hair was cut short.

He looked me up and down. "Hope you're not afraid of the dark." His voice was deep and rough, like rocks tumbling downhill.

I shook my head.

He smiled and turned to look at Asfrid. "Gonna be crowded when the rest get here, but you'll be safe."

"All that matters," she said.

Energy rushed through the ground toward him as he entered the lightless shop.

Something heavy slid across the ground. "Getta move on."

Asfrid took her husband's hand and led us into the darkness.

I followed them to a hole in the floor. Next to the opening stood a large, wooden block topped with an anvil.

Eyebrows raised, I looked at the smith. "Where does this go?"

"Someplace safe," he rumbled. "No one will know you're there."

"How will you know when to let us out?"

"Same way I knew you'd arrived. Everything's going to plan ... don't worry."

"Seems like the best time to worry," I argued.

He chuckled and pointed to the hole. "Go. Down the ladder. Rest easy."

I stared into the darkness and considered my options. *I can be locked underground, trusting this man will keep us safe and let us go, or I can run and take my chances. Don't know where I am. Don't know where my army is or what danger waits between here and there.* My body shook again before I knelt to find the ladder he mentioned.

I almost laughed, remembering the last time I'd been on a ladder. Memories of Mam chanting, "Hand, hand, foot, foot," as she climbed into a hiding place on our way to Varia. *Feels like so long ago. So much has changed so quickly.* After descending long enough that I began to wonder where the bottom was, my foot hit solid ground.

Someone grabbed me before I could let go of the ladder.

Chapter 60

"Turn around and walk straight," Rorec said. "Asfrid's waiting for you at the door."

"Maybe give me a warning before you touch me next time," I said, my heart pounding.

"I'll keep that in mind," he said, turning me.

I pushed my talent into the floor to get a sense of where I was and decided it was a storage room. Rows of something stood between me and the walls on either side. As I walked, I got whiffs of leather and coal and stale air. *Why hide the entrance under an anvil?*

Like Rorec said, Asfrid stood near an opening when I reached the other side of the room.

"The way narrows as you go," she said, "but don't worry, you'll fit. When you get to the room on the other side, turn right and wait in the corner. After Rorec and I make sure everyone's here and knows where to go, we'll join you."

"You're sure we're safe?"

"Completely." I could hear the smile in her voice.

I shook my head but followed her directions. Like she described, my shoulders brushed the walls before I reached an enormous empty space. *At least it's not dead stone.*

Following her directions, I found the corner. Deciding I might as well get ready to stay a while, I took off my hammer and helmet and sat, back against the wall, to wait in complete darkness.

Time crawled.

I must have nodded off because I didn't know anyone else had arrived until I heard a murmured conversation. After looking around in the pitch black, I shoved energy into my surroundings, searching for the source.

A group of five or six stood about halfway between me and the far end of the room. More entered as I considered moving closer to listen in on the group. *Asfrid said they would find me in the corner. No one's bothering me. Safer to stay put and keep my back to the wall.*

Closing my eyes again, I tried to relax while keeping my talent pushed out far enough to let me know if anyone came close. Boredom and fatigue got the better of me, and I slept until Asfrid woke me.

"Eat a couple kartblin before we leave," she said.

"Could I have a little water first?" I asked, rubbing my eyes.

"Certainly," she said, dropping a full skin in my lap.

Taking a sip, I swished it around my mouth and swallowed. "Thank you. I'm ready to eat now."

"Best be quick," Asfrid said, after I took them from her. "Vos Sifet wants everyone to get moving soon."

"Unless the anvil's out of the way, we won't be going anywhere," I quipped before stuffing the first patty in my mouth. *At least they seem to travel well, and they're easier to eat than hard rolls.*

"No doubt Sifet spoke with Stanimir before joining us," Rorec said.

I got to my feet, devoured the second patty, and stretched before taking a long drink. After hanging the skin around my neck, I put my helmet on and snapped my hammer in place. "Ready. Where are our guides?"

"Heading for the ladder," Asfrid said.

"Hope they wait for us," I said, turning toward the small opening. "Don't want to get lost."

"I know where we are," Asfrid said, "but I'm not sure where we're going."

"A sure way to get lost or captured," I said, brushing the narrow walls.

Our guides waited for us in the moonlight outside the smithy. "Lead the way," Rorec said, as we walked out.

"Yes, Friend Rorec," one said, before turning southwest.

Again, we made our way through trees and shrubs, disturbing a few, small animals along the way.

I wanted to ask Rorec about Sifet but wasn't sure how close we may be to a Legion force, so I kept silent to stay safe. *If only the wildlife knew the importance of staying quiet.*

The men ahead turned east at one point before heading directly south.

Do they know where they're going?

My frustration lessened as we curved back to the southwest. After crossing a couple of narrow creeks, the Bane stopped. One turned and waved for me to come to them.

"What?" I whispered.

He pointed to our left. "Friend Fist-er-rick's warriors. Yes?"

Looking where his finger led, my breath caught in my throat.

Two men wearing Croian armor stepped into the moonlight.

My heart pounded. "Yes," I whispered, afraid to speak out loud. "Wait here."

He nodded.

I turned and waved Rorec and Asfrid to me. "Those are my men."

Rorec nodded and put his arm around his wife. "Fitzeirick. Be careful."

I flashed him a smile before turning to approach the guards.

Walking slowly, I held my hands up, well away from my sides. "Well met, brave guardsmen. I'm not a threat."

"Movement!" one of them yelled. "Archers!"

Bows creaked in the darkness ahead of me.

Freezing in place, I raised my hands higher. "Hold. Please. I beg you. I'm King Fitzeirick."

Drawing swords, they stepped back into the night. "Sure you are. Walk toward us. Slowly. Any sudden moves, arrows fly."

I nodded and took slow, deliberate steps until he ordered me to stop. My heart pounded in my ears. Beads of sweat formed on my forehead. "Stay your hands. Hold your arrows. Let me prove my claim."

"You don't sound Satran. Who are you?" someone asked.

"You can see me clearly … yes?"

"We can. Answer the question. Who are you?"

"I am your king. Let me remove my helmet and show you."

Whispers passed between them. "On your knees. Keep your hands where they are."

After an exaggerated nod, I fell to my knees with all the grace I could manage.

"Use your left hand to take off your helmet and keep well away from that handle."

I nodded again before slowly reaching for the front of my helmet. It was more awkward than using both hands, and I scraped my right ear, but my head protection came off. I dropped it and rested a quivering finger under my scar.

Gasps burst ahead of me.

"Sire...How?" someone asked.

"Get Bior and General Jomar ... *now!*" another guard ordered.

Bior's alive. I couldn't help but smile at the good news.

Running footsteps thudded away, quickly fading into the night.

While I waited for people to come and confirm my claim, I worried my escorts might get restless. *How will the next group know to stop if this takes too long?* A muscle in my neck twitched, and I almost turned to look over my shoulder but caught myself and stopped. *If the guard noticed, he might order a search. That would be bad.*

Heavy footsteps told me several men were running toward us. *Guess they aren't worried about being quiet.* They stopped short of where I could see who it might be.

"It's him!" Bior blurted.

Before I could react, he sprinted out of the darkness and tackled me. "How did you survive? Where do you go? Where have you been? How did you find us?"

My hammer pressed uncomfortably into my lower back. "Let me up," I grunted. "I'll answer all your questions soon."

"Help him up, Bior," Jomar said.

"Oh. Yes. Sorry, Sire. I ... uh ... couldn't help myself," Bior stammered, before rolling off me and pulling me to my feet.

"It's good to see you ... you have no idea," I said, hugging him tightly. "Jomar, order the men to relax. There are people in the woods behind me, and I don't want anyone hurt."

The general shot me a questioning look but gave the command for everyone to stand down.

I waited for the guards to put their swords away before calling Rorec and Asfrid to join me. "Two Croians," I said, "living among the Satran as part of an agreement between my father and the Satran rulers. They are not hostile. Treat them with respect."

"Sire?" Bior questioned, as they came into sight. "Is that the man you met with in camp?"

I nodded. "Now. Everyone listen. This is of utmost importance. We didn't travel alone. There are about sixty men, women, and children on their way here. They saved me and brought me back to you."

"Where did you find that many Croians?" Jomar asked.

"They're Satran."

"What?" the general bellowed.

"Save it," I said. "I signed an agreement with the exiled, Satran ruler, Vos Sifet. Those I arrived with are our allies. They pose no threat and mean us no harm."

"Sire, your orders —" Jomar argued.

"I know what my orders *were*," I said, crossing my arms. "Things have changed. I'll leave Rorec and Asfrid here to identify every Satran who approaches as ally or enemy. Speaking of which, do you know there is a Legion force east of here?"

"No, m'lord. I did not."

I nodded. "They're likely less than a day away. Are you prepared for battle?"

"Aye, my king," Bior said. "We are."

"Good. Now, how do we arrange for the safety of our new allies?"

Jomar scratched his chin before nodding. "Bior, escort King Fitzeirick to your tent. Send Commanders Ottar and Alrik, along with Fastulf and his company, to me. Once I have their cooperation, I'll join you and the king to discuss matters further."

"Sire, are you sure about this?" Bior asked.

I raised my bandaged hand. "Sure enough to make a blood pact with the exiled chieftain."

"A what?" he asked, confusion clear on his face.

"I'll explain later."

He frowned. "Come with me, Sire."

"One moment," I said, grabbing my helmet. "General, I owe these people my life and promised my support. They *will* be safe in our camp. If not, my punishment will be swift and painful. Am I clear?"

He bowed. "Understood, my king. It's good to have you back with us."

"Lead on, Bior."

"Hope you're ready to answer lots of questions," he said, turning to leave.

Chapter 61

As we walked, he looked at me several times. *Guess he's trying to convince himself I'm really here.*

Approaching the camp, smells hit me like a physical blow, slowing me for a few steps. Each breath brought something new: smoke from burning wood, mouthwatering stew cooking, fragrant oiled leather, and other scents nearly brought tears to my eyes.

Since I hadn't been there when the warriors arrived by barge, I also wasn't expecting to see so many men waiting to witness my reappearance. Salutes, bows, and cheers greeted me. I waved on the way to Bior's tent.

He held the flap for me. "Have a seat. Once I've sent the men to General Jomar, we'll talk."

I took the chair on the far side of a small, wooden table, so I could face the entrance. Putting my hammer on the ground and my helmet on the table, I sat. "Does Tindra know I went missing?"

"No, Sire. Jomar and I discussed sending me back on a barge to tell her but decided it would be best to wait until we knew if you were alive or dead."

"And you didn't want to face her wrath when she found out."

"That too, m'lord," he said, frowning.

I nodded. "Before you go, did I smell stew cooking?"

"From earlier. I'm sure I could find some if you're hungry."

"Would be welcome," I said, smiling.

He nodded. "It's good to see you again, Sire. I'll be right back."

"It's good to be here," I said. "Pass on Jomar's orders first. I'm not going anywhere."

He chuckled, looked me over again, and closed the tent.

I didn't need my talent to know he sprinted away. Judging by the sounds after he left, men crowded around the tent. *No doubt they want to hear the story.*

Leaning forward, I rested my head on the table.

"Orders issued, m'lord," Bior said, breathing heavily as he entered the tent.

Sitting up, I smiled at him.

He put a large bowl in front of me and placed a mug next to it. "It's not as hot as it should be, m'lord, sorry."

"I'm sure it will be fine. Before we trade stories, you might advise the men around us to put up more tents."

His eyes opened wide. "Oh. Good idea. But where, Sire?"

"The edge of camp. On the side you and I entered, perhaps."

He nodded. "Give me a moment."

Bior's raised voice wasn't muffled by the cloth walls around me. I couldn't help but grin as he shouted orders so fast men couldn't respond before he ended by telling one of them to let the general know about the plan.

I'd eaten several spoonfuls of stew before bothering to consider the temperature or the taste. Warm and filling. *Best stew I've had in a while.* The mug was filled with ale. It, too, was warm but a welcome luxury compared to sour wine.

"We thought you'd been captured, m'lord," a red-faced Bior said, stepping back inside. "I couldn't explain how. I knew no one got past me at the door. What happened?"

"Some of the Bane can syth the dead stone."

His jaw dropped as he sat across from me. "How?"

I shrugged. "All I know, for certain, is it takes several of them working together. Regardless, they knew we were there. I don't fully understand how they knew I was hurt — poisoned by the dart — but one of them did. Asfrid's a herbalist and knows how to draw the poison from the wound. She saved my life, but it took a toll on my body. I'm still not fully recovered."

He glanced at my half-empty bowl. "Did they not feed you, Sire?"

I chuckled. "I slept most of the time I was there. What did I miss?"

"The fight at the village was chaotic. Both sides were surprised the other was there. We lost several men to the poison. Too bad we don't know how to cure it."

"I'll ask Asfrid to share her knowledge with our herbalists."

He nodded. "I'm sure they would appreciate the help. Anyway, our warriors fought like never before once they heard you were hurt, Sire. They could have killed twice as many soldiers. Then we couldn't find you. Gone with no trace. Nothing telling us where you went or how. Fastulf was convinced we — I — missed an attacker and they took you away in the confusion. He wouldn't listen to reason ... drove his men to search for two days non-stop. Commander Alrik finally forced him to call it off."

I shook my head. "How is he doing now?"

"I'm not sure he's forgiven us, but he's behaving well enough for Jomar to trust him again."

The general entered. "Why are you talking about me?"

"Bior was explaining about Fastulf," I said. "Join us. We need to talk."

"Oh. Yes. He lost himself for a little while," Jomar said, frowning.

"Almost cost us more men in the process," Bior said.

"I'll talk to him later. Right now, we need to figure out how to spread the word. Plans have changed," I said.

"My king, who swore to destroy everyone alive in Satra, disappears for days before appearing in the middle of the night, leading a group of Satran." Jomar shook his head. "Something's changed. No question. More than a few men are going to want an explanation. Once they're over the shock, and elation, of your return..." He pointed at me. "You have to admit, Sire, it looks suspicious."

I nodded. "Rightfully so. I want to make it clear, if not for the Satran's aid and care, I'd likely be dead."

Bior sucked in a hissing breath.

"Asfrid got me healthy enough to meet with the former ruler of Satra, a man named Sifet. He's the chieftain exiled by a secretive group called the Bonetakers. Porsey caused a lot of trouble which ended in a coup. The Satran with me are loyal to their dethroned leader. They still call him Vos."

"What?" Jomar asked.

"Think of it as their word for king."

Both men nodded.

"He explained why the invasion started. It was Eirickson's fault at the root. Not all Satran are the uncivilized brutes I thought them to be. Because of what I learned, I've agreed to spare the innocent in this country and return Sifet to power. In exchange, he will lead his people under Croian law. When he dies, I choose who leads Satra as part of Croy. All we have to do is slaughter any who fight against us."

"My king, how do you know he will keep his word?" Jomar asked.

I turned my bandaged palm up. "We made an agreement, sealed with our blood. The Satran call it a blood pact. Breaking it is a death sentence."

"You did this willingly, m'lord?" Bior asked.

"I did ... because it's what's best for Croy. Pass on my new order. From now on, do not harm any Satran if they pose no threat. Members of the Legion clan, Bonetakers, or any who attack us—they all die. Make sure everyone understands."

"Yes, Sire," Jomar said. "I will make your direction clear."

"Now, we discuss the next issue of importance. There's a large Legion force, not far away, heading this way."

"I'm guessing this disgraced king, Sifet, told you this," Jomar said.

"Yes."

"How would he know?" Bior asked.

"The Satran dressed in rags—they are from the Bane clan. Because they are considered the lowest of the low, they're often ignored and move about unnoticed. It's a survival skill learned through painful lessons. Most are cowards, but a few are brave enough to act as scouts. They got the information for Sifet while trying to find you."

"The only Satran who approached us before tonight lie dead, my king," Jomar said.

"Yet, these Bane easily led me here," I said, cocking my head.

He chewed his lip.

"Does the approaching force know where we are, m'lord?" Bior asked.

I shrugged. "I'd say we'd best prepare like they do but hope we catch them by surprise."

"Sound thinking," Jomar said. "May I have permission to leave and spread the word, Sire?"

"With haste."

He stood and saluted. "It's good to have you back with us, King Fitzeirick."

I drank the last of my ale. "It's good to be back with my men."

"Yes, m'lord."

Bior tapped a finger on the table, looking like he wanted to say something.

"What's bothering you?" I asked.

"With all due respect, who forced you to make those promises?"

"No one," I said. "There came a point where I understood my beliefs were wrong. My actions were making me a barbarian. Once I reached that conclusion, I chose to save the innocent."

"But they killed so many Croians, including your mother. They took your first love. M'lord, are any of these people innocent?"

I stared at him until he squirmed. "My time among the Satran exiles showed me that some things I believed were not true. Consider the Bane. Most of them live their entire lives treated worse than beasts. Every day is an exercise in avoiding punishment, or worse, simply because they exist. Are they not innocent and deserving of a better life?"

Looking away, he chewed his lip for a moment. "Aye, Sire. I'd say it's likely they are."

"If we kill them simply for being Satran, aren't we as bad, as barbaric, as their oppressors?"

"Worse." He slapped his hand on the table. "At least they can live under their current rulers."

I nodded. "It's not much of a life, but yes. Once I control Satra, everyone will have a chance at a better life."

"A noble goal, but this is a severe change in your attitude toward the Satran."

Closing my eyes, I pinched the bridge of my nose and sighed. "Sometimes a little suffering helps you see things with more clarity. All I've ever wanted was to make Croy better. Even as a skald, my first concern was improving the lives of the people in my skati. Saving innocent Satran, and letting them learn to flourish under Croian rule, means both nations benefit without our people having to settle lands they know nothing about. This is best for all concerned."

Bior yawned. "Maybe it's because I'm tired, but I doubt it will be as easy as you say."

"Nothing's as easy as I think it should be. Now, where can I sleep?"

He pointed over my shoulder. "Back there. I'll sleep near the door. Someone has to keep you safe."

"You did such a fine job before," I said, smiling.

"Not my fault the Satran knew tricks I don't," he protested. "You didn't know they could syth that stone either."

I nodded before turning to walk to my bed. "Right, and I don't blame you. The whole situation was chaos. It could have turned out much worse."

He sighed. "Yes, it could've. It's good to have you back, my king. Sleep well."

Chapter 62

Bior's raised voice woke me. "For the last time, Satran, I don't care who you are or who sent you. King Fitzeirick is sleeping, and I'm not going to wake him. I will ask him if he's willing to meet with you once I know he's awake. Until then, go back to your camp and wait."

Must be Sifet, come to discuss our next moves. Hope he understands when I defend Bior's response. "I'm awake! Let him in!" I rose to my feet and hurried to sit at the table before the tent opened. *Need to remember to thank Thorgault for making armor I could sleep in.* The man following Bior wasn't Sifet. It was Dalibor. *Why is here?*

"Would you like breakfast now, Sire?" Bior asked.

I nodded, raising my eyebrows. "Dalibor, have you eaten?"

He bowed his head. "I have, kind king, and don't want to take much of your time anyway. I know you have much to plan for."

"Thank you for your consideration. No doubt you're right. I'm sure I have a busy day ahead. Please, sit. Bior, looks like I am the only one eating."

"Understood, Sire," he said, bowing. "If anyone else asks to join you, what should I say?"

"Use your best judgment."

"Aye, m'lord. Be back soon."

"Interesting," Dalibor commented, a look of amusement on his face.

"What?"

"The amount of trust you place in your servant."

I shook my head. "Bior's no servant. He's a friend, as well as my personal attendant and guard."

"Yet he does as you command without question."

"Surely Vos Sifet didn't send you to debate the difference between our cultures," I said, raising my eyebrows. "What brings you this morning?"

"I have a proposal." His expression went blank.

"Tell Vos Sifet I want it in writing first."

"This does not come from Vos Sifet. It remains between us. Spoken only."

I pushed my talent into the ground to see if anyone stood close enough to hear us. "You advise him, correct? Do his bidding?"

"I serve Satra. My father arranged for the koron to sit on Sifet's head; when the time was right. Neither of us saw the Bonetaker's treachery. Malibor gave his life so Sifet and I could live. Sifet's time is over. To willingly bend a knee to you, even in private, shows he knows his time is short."

Did he just — No. I must have misheard him. Crossing my arms, I leaned back in my chair. "Are you saying Sifet is dying?"

Dalibor shrugged. "I am no herbalist, but he seems no closer to death now than any of us."

I must be missing something. "Then, what makes you say his time is short?"

"No vos has ever humbled themselves in front of a foreign king on Satran soil. Sifet did so out of a desperate need to spend what time he has left clinging to the illusion of power. When the usurpers fall, the koron will rest on another head."

"And you want it?"

"Me?" He placed his hand over his heart and shook his head. "Oh, no ... not at all. I do not rule; I serve...as all my ancestors have. As the agreement sealed with mixed blood says, you will choose who wears the gold and silver circle. I offer my continued service to my nation as a way to make your task easier. This is my responsibility, passed on to me by those who held my position in the past."

"I'm not interested in evaluating who is fit to lead now. Once Sifet passes, I would welcome your counsel when making my decision. Though you must know, I'll likely choose a Croian to lead."

He nodded before lacing his fingers together. "Yes, wise king, I recognize the possibility. As I said, I serve ... I make things happen. Much like my father before me. With your permission, I will remove this problem for you and help you rest the koron on the right head. When the time is right ... of course."

What I wouldn't give to have Tindra here for this. Resting my hand on my hammer's handle, I locked eyes with the Satran. "I'd hate for there to be a misunderstanding between us. You're offering to remove Sifet before I place the symbol of Satra's power back on his head."

Dalibor pressed his lips together tightly for a moment. "To be blunt, yes. You understand perfectly."

"Why not kill him when he bowed to me?"

He shook his head. "Had I acted then, my action would have been misunderstood. Everyone would have accused me of treachery. I would have disgraced my family name. That is not the legacy I will leave."

I felt footsteps approaching the tent. "How do I know this isn't a trap or some kind of test?"

"Do I look like a man who plays games?" he asked, placing his hands on the table. "Vos Sifet trusts me. Whether you do or not is for you to decide. I made an honest offer. Take it, and I make your life a little easier. Don't and — We'll see how things turn out."

He's asking for trust I'm not ready to give. "This is a lot to consider, and we won't be alone much longer," I said, nodding. "I'll need to think over your offer. You'll know as soon as I've made a decision."

"Understood." Rubbing his hands together, he dipped his chin. "One more thing to consider, King of Croy. Time is not something you have much of. Decide sooner so plans can be made. Wait until the last moment, and things could get messy."

"I'm aware," I said, standing.

Bior stepped inside carrying a large bowl and a mug.

Dalibor stood and bowed. "Good day, King."

"Good day. Please tell Sifet I hoped he slept well."

The adviser nodded as he turned to leave.

"Boiled grains, Sire. Sorry it took so long. They had to make a fresh batch."

"No worries. It gave Dalibor and me more time to talk."

"Why did Vos Sifet send him?"

Shaking my head, I lifted a spoonful of steaming grains and blew on it to cool. Taking time to savor the hot food, I waited until I was sure Dalibor was far enough away to not hear our conversation. "Don't worry about why he was here. Once I'm finished, I want to meet with Rorec. Afterward, send Fastulf to see me. If Jomar, or any of the commanders, need to see me, they take priority."

"Of course, Sire. And if Dalibor returns? Or one of the other Satran wants to meet with you?"

"With the exception of Sifet, everyone else can wait. I doubt Dalibor will come back anyway."

"He doesn't make much of a good impression if you ask me, Sire."

I nodded. "Keep your eyes and ears open when he's around, and mind what you say. His own people don't seem to trust him much. From what I know, they call him a rat in the shadows ... or something of the like. Always watching, even when you can't see him."

Bior's eyes opened wide. "And I left you alone with him? Why, m'lord?"

"He knows better than to attack in the open. If the queen were here, I'd let her play with him. Would be fun to watch."

He chuckled. "I believe you are right, Sire."

"Any problems I should know about?" I asked, after swallowing another spoonful.

"Nothing to speak of." He shrugged. "The Satran seem to keep to themselves. Some of our men insist on keeping a close eye on them, but no conflicts so far."

"Not surprised the Bane are staying away from our camp. And hearing our warriors aren't bothering them is exactly what I wanted. I've promised to keep the Satran safe. I'll need you to help make sure they are. Any rumors or threats by our men, I want to know, but if you can't get word to me first ... make sure nothing happens to our guests."

Bior glanced toward the group of tents. "Aye, Sire."

"And don't neglect the rest of your duties."

He sighed. "If I didn't like you so much, Sire, I'd say I was happier when you were missing."

"I'll be sure to let the queen know when I see her again. I'm sure she can find a better assignment for you."

He smiled and raised his hands. "I joke, m'lord. A jest, nothing more."

As I scraped the last spoonful from the bowl, I couldn't help but laugh. "I know, and don't worry. Your position is rock solid. Take this and find Rorec for me."

"Aye, Sire. Gladly."

As he walked away, I focused on what I should tell Rorec about Dalibor's offer. *If I say too much, will it get back to Sifet and cause trouble? Does Sifet know his rat may be more trouble than he's worth?* Lost in thought, I didn't notice two people walking toward the tent until Rorec spoke. "You sent for me?"

I flinched. "Yes, come in. Sit. Do you mind if Bior joins us?"

"Not at all," Rorec said, sitting across from me.

"Bior, come in," I said.

Turning to Rorec, I smiled. "Hope you slept well."

"I did, but not long enough. Took a while to get everyone settled."

"I could have slept longer myself, but sometimes, kings get early visitors."

"Especially when the king went missing for days," Bior commented.

Rorec chuckled. "What can I do for you, your Majesty?"

"First, I need a favor from Asfrid. I'd like for her to meet with our herbalists and teach them what she knows about the Satran poison and how to treat it."

"I'm sure she'd be glad to spend time with them. She loves to teach. Given half a chance, she'd take over as leader of your healers."

"Probably be an improvement," Bior muttered.

I smiled at him and nodded. "Now, I need your honest opinion as well as an oath to keep this between us."

"I have no reason to lie, but..." Rorec frowned. "You can't ask me to give my word without telling me why."

"I promise you it's for the benefit of Croy and Satra."

He shook his head. "That's vague. Can you give me anything else?"

What's the worst that can happen? "Is Vos Sifet the best choice as a leader?"

Bior coughed.

Rorec's eyes opened wide. "Fitzeirick, you made a blood pact to put him in charge of Satra again. Don't take it lightly. His men won't."

"I know what I did and will honor my vow."

"Good," he said, rising to his feet. "Breaking a binding pact would not benefit either country. I'll ask my wife to spend time with your herbalists when she can."

I got to my feet and bowed. "Thank you."

Bior sat quietly as Rorec left.

"M'lord, dare I ask what that was about?"

I shook my head and looked at him. "It's best you don't know. Find Fastulf. After you send him to me, get a report from Jomar. We need to prepare for the coming battle."

"I'm sure Jomar's getting everyone ready, Sire."

"You don't need to hear what Fastulf and I will discuss," I said, frowning.

"Now is not the time to keep secrets ... especially from me."

Leaning toward him, I put my hand on his shoulder. "I trust you, Bior ... I swear I do, but the fewer people who know about this, the better."

"This has something to do with your Satran visitor this morning, doesn't it?"

"Of course, but —"

"But nothing," he interrupted. "He told you something about Sifet, and now you doubt your decision."

"Not exactly, no. You don't need to worry about it. Get Fastulf for me."

"Yes, my king." His sullen tone matched his expression.

It's not his job to be happy with my decisions. He'll get over it anyway. My biggest concern is figuring out how to keep an eye on Dalibor without him knowing he's being watched.

Fastulf's smile announced his arrival. He bowed low before sitting across from me. "I'm overjoyed to see you, healthy and whole, my king, I didn't want to call off the search, but Commander Alrik reminded me we had a job to do."

I grinned and nodded to him. "Time and again, you've proven your value and your loyalty. Your dedication to me, to Croy, is admired and appreciated. Sit. Let's discuss another task."

His smile grew bigger, which didn't seem possible. "Of course, m'lord. Name it and consider it done."

"Don't be so quick to promise success." I shook my finger at him. "This won't be easy."

"You wouldn't call for me if it was, Sire." he countered, his expression not wavering.

I chuckled. "You're right. There is a Satran, one of Vos Sifet's advisers. I need him —"

"Say no more, m'lord. I have no doubt we can catch him alone and dispose of the body without anyone noticing. It may take some time, but ... it's a war. People die."

"No, I don't want him killed. I want him watched, but you must be careful. If this man knows he's being watched, I don't know what might happen."

"Did he threaten you, Sire?" Fastulf asked, eyes wide.

"No. I suspect he may be up to something, but I'm not in any direct danger."

He nodded as I explained the situation. "Give me a name and a description."

"He's smart and dangerous. You must keep this secret. The fewer people who know, the better."

Fastulf shook his head. "Smart and dangerous makes a bad combination. I'll be careful. Who is it?"

"His name's Dalibor. He has a distinct look about him. He's one of Vos Sifet's trusted advisers. You'll know him as soon as you see him. You're going to have to spend a lot of time among the Satran. Will that be a problem?"

He shrugged, smile waning slightly. "I do what I'm told, Sire."

I nodded. "Pick four or five of your best men. I'll send you to the Satran camp to meet with the Bane and learn what you can about sything the dead stone."

"What?" he blurted. "No one can work that stuff."

"Some of the Bane can," I said. "Saw it myself. It takes several working together to do it. Can't say I understand what little I've been told, but if you're there to learn ..."

"I can move around their people more freely and find this adviser."

"Yes. At least, I hope so."

He nodded. "How long do I watch him, and what am I watching for?"

"Try to find out who he spends time with. Outside of Sifet, of course. Be friendly, and keep your ears open. Once the Bane feel comfortable with you, no telling what they might mention."

"I'll do my best, but I'm not a spy, sire."

"I know, but you're my best option out here," I said, smiling. "Even doing your best, we may not learn anything more about Dalibor, but I have to try."

"Of course, Sire. When do I start?"

"Pick your men and go find Rorec. Tell him I want you to study with the Bane. He can introduce you to the right people."

He stood. "Happy you're back, my king. We were all worried."

"I appreciate the concern. Rest assured, I am fine ... thanks to Asfrid and our Satran allies. Now, move with haste. We don't have much time."

"Yes, Sire." He bowed and hurried from the tent.

If only Tindra was here ... Dalibor wouldn't know what hit him.

My wife's face appeared in my mind, and I closed my eyes. *How I miss her. I wonder what she's doing now. How's the castle shaping up? Are she and Roi getting along at all?* With a heavy sigh, I shook my head to dismiss such thoughts. Having her here would have caused more trouble than it solved when I went missing. *Time to find Jomar.*

Chapter 63

An unnerving quiet dominated the camp. Many of my men gathered closer to the Satran tents, often glancing their way while going about their assigned tasks. *Can't expect everyone to see them as allies overnight.* When someone noticed me passing, they smiled and saluted or bowed. I made sure to return their greeting. I found Jomar and Bior talking with a guard near the western edge of camp.

"Anything to report?" I asked.

Jomar turned and saluted. "All's quiet here, m'lord."

"There's a Satran force heading this way," I said. "Keep an eye out for scouts."

"My orders, exactly, Sire," Jomar said. "Though I want to move a small force into the forest. They can flank any soldiers traveling on the path. If we've had no contact before our warriors finish breakfast, the main force will start east, with the rest of camp following soon after. What about our new allies? Where will they be?"

"I'd expect them to trail behind us, but I need to speak with Vos Sifet to be sure. Like I said last night, the Bane aren't fighters; they are survivors. Once our men are comfortable with them, we can use them as porters and servers, but I doubt they will take up weapons and join the battle."

"Shame," Jomar said. "I noticed several of them looked well-muscled when they arrived. Even a handful more men would be welcome."

"I'm not fighting next to a mindless, gray-skinned brute," a nearby guard said.

"Like it or not, they saved my life, and their knowledge might save yours at some point," I said.

"I'd rather die."

"Watch your tongue," Bior barked.

Jomar nodded. "You are speaking to your king. You'd do well to remember that."

"General, I'd rather hear the truth. I asked you to spread the word that those Satran are welcome here as allies. Sounds like you have more work to do."

"Aye, Sire," he said, bowing, "it does."

I stared at the guard. "All the same, men keep a sharp eye out. A force is coming. We'd best be ready."

"Of course, my king," the guard said, saluting.

"Bior, come with me to find Sifet," I said. "I want him to know who you are in case I need you to work with him."

"Of course, Sire."

Crossing through camp, we made our way to the scattered tents housing the Satran. "Any idea where Sifet slept?" I asked Bior.

"No, Sire. I wasn't here when they chose tents."

I nodded and walked close to the nearest tent. "Well met. Hello. Is anyone in here?"

"Friend?" a woman asked, from inside.

"Yes. I'm Friend Fitzeirick."

Bior snorted behind me.

"Right, yes. What do you need?"

"I'm looking for Vos Sifet. Do you know where he is?"

"No. Ask Friend Cesci."

"I will. Thank you."

"Yes. Bye, Friend Fist-er-rick."

I shook my head but didn't bother correcting her.

"What was that about?"

"If the Bane know you, they call you Friend. It's an honor, from what I can tell."

"Can I call you Fist-er-rick?"

"No."

He chuckled for a moment. "Who's Cesci?"

"A young boy. Serves Sifet."

"And you know where this boy is?"

"No, but I wasn't going to bother asking her. Let's walk a little deeper. If I don't spot him, I'll ask someone else."

"I'm following your lead, Sire," he said. "Are we safe in here?"

"Yes," I said, deciding not to mention Velmir's dislike of Croians.

"Doesn't feel like it," Bior muttered, looking around as we continued deeper into the Satran camp.

Passing another jagged row of tents, I still didn't see anyone. Cupping my hands next to my mouth, I yelled for the servant.

Bior looked left and right before shrugging.

As I took a breath to yell again, the boy responded from somewhere ahead of us. "Yes, Friend. Coming."

Bior sighed. "Why didn't you yell for Sifet instead?"

"No need to be disrespectful. I'm sure the chieftain heard my voice and knows I'm here."

"Of course, Sire."

Cesci stepped around a tent and stopped in front of me. "Here, yes, Friend Fist-er-rick. Good to see you."

"Nice to see you too. This is Friend Bior. Take us to Vos Sifet, please."

He bowed to Bior. "Right, yes. Hello new friend, Bior."

As we followed Cesci, Bior looked at me like he didn't know what to say.

"Greet them as you would anyone," I whispered.

He nodded.

We stopped at a large tent near the far edge of the group. "Wait here, yes?"

"You may announce us," I said, nodding.

The boy stuck his head inside the tent. "Vos Sifet. Friend Fist-er-rick and Friend Bior are here."

"Thank you, Cesci. Let them in."

The boy stood up straight and waved us into the tent.

Sifet sat alone on a low seat raised from the ground. "Welcome, young Croian King Fitzeirick and —" He paused, looking over my steward. "Adviser Bior."

Interesting that his men, especially Dalibor, are nowhere to be seen.

Bior bowed. "Pleasure to meet you, Vos Sifet."

"What brings you here, King of Croy?"

"I wanted you to meet Bior. He is my right hand and often speaks for me. Also, while meeting with my general this morning, a question was asked. When we leave, where will your followers be? Do you plan to combine forces, or would you rather stay separated?"

"Is there enough trust between your men and my people to mingle without a conflict?" He steepled his fingers and cocked his head. "I doubt it, but you are sworn to our safety. Do you believe we would be safe in your ranks, young king?"

Bior scooted to the edge of his seat.

I glanced at him and shook my head. "Your safety is a concern though not all of the animosity would be from my men. Lest you forget, a number of your followers don't care for Croians and could cause trouble should tempers flare at the wrong time."

Sifet nodded. "It seems the best choice is to stay apart."

"Yes, it does," Bior grumbled.

I glared at him before turning back to Sifet. "But I do have another concern. We are moving into unknown territory. It would be beneficial to have guides who know the land. Might some of your people know the best route to your capital? And would they agree to join the front ranks of my advance?"

"I will ask." Sifet tilted his head again. "How did you plan to address this issue before our agreement?"

"Our scouts have gotten us this far," Bior said.

"But knowledgeable guides could help us travel faster," I added.

"Would your scouts trust them?" Sifet asked, staring at Bior. "Assuming any Bane are willing."

"I sent some of my most powerful stonesyths to learn how to work dead stone," I said. "Perhaps they are building trust, too."

Sifet nodded. "I am aware you have men visiting our camp, young king. After they leave, I'll speak with the Bane involved. We'll see what happens."

"I'll speak with my men, too," I said, smiling. "Cooperation and familiarity breed understanding. Hopefully, the two groups have moved us in the right direction."

"Again, you have wisdom beyond your years. However, the Bane are a suspicious clan. Being wary and untrusting helps them survive. It would say a lot about your men, should they gain their trust quickly," Sifet said.

"I agree. Is there anything you need from me?" I asked.

"We've been forced to depend on ourselves for so long, I am hesitant to ask for anything you have not already agreed to, your Majesty."

"Your situation will change soon enough. For now, I offer any assistance we can provide," I said. "If you find a need, get word to myself or Bior. We'll do our best to help."

Sifet bent at the waist, resting his hands on his knees. "I will keep your generosity in mind, honorable king. Your visit was most appreciated. You are welcome anytime, as is your ... adviser."

"And you are welcome in my tent, honorable Vos," I replied, standing before bowing low.

Bior stayed quiet, bowing before turning to leave.

Judging by his stomping, Bior wasn't pleased. Combined with his pace, there was little doubt he was in a hurry to leave the Satran camp. I had to walk fast to keep up with him. He didn't say anything until we returned to our tent.

"Why did you put up with such treatment?" he demanded.

"What do you mean?"

"Don't tell me you missed his complete disrespect."

"Oh. I should have warned you. He sees everyone who isn't a ruler as beneath him."

"He talked down to *you* the entire time. How could you miss it? If he called you 'young king' again, I was going to take his head," he said, resting his hand on his sword's hilt.

"I *am* young, much younger than Sifet. He respects me and what I represent. Trust me."

His eyes narrowed. "Didn't sound respectful."

I shrugged. "The Satran have a different way of speaking."

"Right, yes, and friend whoever," Bior said. "Seems like it would get on your nerves."

"Those are common phrases among the Bane, from what I can tell." Smiling, I raised my eyebrows. "One could argue everyone constantly calling me 'sire' or 'm'lord' would quickly become annoying."

"But you're the king. Other than sire or the like, how would someone address you without using your name all the time."

"And I'm considered a friend of the Bane, most of them anyway."

He pointed at me. "But they still used your name."

"As is their way. Even if Sifet's being rude on purpose, I'm not going to endanger Croy's future by responding. Remember, I have a binding agreement with him. My honor, and possibly my life, is at stake if I don't do my part."

Bior nodded, but his expression didn't change.

"You don't have to like it or even understand it, but don't make trouble. Once we're home, you never have to come back to Satra. No one will call you Friend Bior again." Glancing sideways at him, I chuckled. "Assuming I don't decide to do it."

I caught a mischievous gleam in his eye before he bowed. "Whatever you desire, young king."

"Young enough to best you," I said, shaking my fist.

"While I might not agree, Sire, I find myself unwilling to find out. Now, we could keep poking each other until one of us says something we'd regret, but I doubt that's what you had in mind for the rest of your day. What else do you need to do before lunch?"

I looked at my bandaged hand. "Where are the herbalists camping? I'd like someone to look at my hand and make sure it's healing properly."

"Say no more, Sire. Follow me."

Chapter 64

Bior led me to a long tent, open on both ends. A group of men gathered near a table, watching Asfrid prepare something.

"Again, it will turn into a paste but keep grinding until it becomes a powder. If you don't, it won't soak up the bad blood," she explained.

"Is the paste used for anything?" Hakon asked.

The pestle kept moving as she shrugged. "Can't imagine an ailment or injury it would help with, but you're free to try ... so long as you don't make the situation worse."

"I believe that goes without saying," Hakon replied.

"When you've spent as many years doing this as I have," she said, smiling, "you'll find someone always finds ways to make a situation worse while trying something new."

"No one here doubts your experience, Lady Asfrid," Varmond said.

Good to know Hakon's contrary attitude hasn't changed.

"Well met, everyone," I said, hoping the distraction would stave off a possible conflict. Everyone turned to look at me.

Hakon's eyes opened wide. "King Fitzeirick," he said, through a forced smile. "Good to see you looking well. What can we do for you?"

I raised my bandaged hand. "Lady Asfrid treated me recently. I wanted to get it looked at, make sure nothing was wrong."

She waved me over. "Is it bothering you? Hurting? Fevered?"

"Not hurting, as such. Still tender when I move my hand."

She nodded.

Hakon stepped toward me. "Let me check it for you, Sire."

Asfrid raised her eyebrows and tilted her head but didn't say anything.

Hakon unwrapped the bandage and shook his head. "Water. I need to rinse this muck off."

"It's not muck," Asfrid said. "It's —"

"Quiet," Hakon snapped. "I'm working on my king's hand and need to concentrate."

Pressing my lips together, I watched Asfrid's face turn red.

Someone handed him a cup. He poured the water into my palm and used the bandage to wipe away the partially dried paste. Pain flared as he pressed the cloth against the wound.

I flinched, my hand pulling away on its own. "Easy."

"Sorry, m'lord, but this must be cleaned so I can see how it's doing. Hold still."

My arm jerked twice more before he was finished.

To me, the cut looked good. The paste had wrinkled my skin, but there was no redness along the wound's edges.

Hakon looked at it, shook his head, and clicked his tongue. After sniffing the bandage, his lips curled. "What did you use?"

Asfrid squared her shoulders. "A paste of garlic, onion, and turmeric."

He chuckled. "Turmeric? Never heard of it, but garlic and onion? Were you planning to cook it? This needs a honey paste. Varmond, grind some cat's claw and dandelion."

Asfrid put her hands on her hips. "I was treating wounds before your parents knew they wanted a child. You know nothing of the plants in this nation. Yes, your mixture would work, given enough time, but it is not the best choice when you have more effective herbs available. Fizeirick, may I see your hand?"

To anyone who was paying attention, the tone in her voice made her annoyance clear. Hakon spun to face her. "He is *my* king. *I* will determine his treatment."

Bior grunted.

I cleared my throat. "Hakon, Asfrid was there when I was born. You *are* the head herbalist in our camp, but dismissing her wisdom and experience is not the mark of a good leader. She's here, at my request, passing on what she's learned during her time in Satra. A little respect and goodwill would be appreciated."

Stepping aside, he turned to me and bowed. "Of course, Sire. My concern for your well-being overtook my good manners. I apologize to our guest. Please, Lady Asfrid, share more knowledge with us."

Bior mumbled something under his breath.

She glanced sideways at the rude herbalist and huffed before approaching. Cradling my hand in hers, she looked at the cut. "It looks about as good as I'd expect. Tenderness will stay another couple of days, most likely." She turned to Hakon. "Cat's claw would be my choice if it's fresh. Is what you have still green?"

"No, my lady. We planned to replenish our stock from what grew here," Hakon said.

"Doubt you'll find it. I haven't seen any of the vine in years. Now, if the wound were red and fevered, dandelion and honey would be an excellent treatment. Given how it looks now, my advice ... bandage the hand and keep it dry."

Hakon grumbled something.

"What say you, Hakon?" I asked. *Diplomacy.*

"Covered and dry is a good method. Varmond, don't bother grinding anything. Bring some bandage cloth, please."

"Yes, sir," the herbalist answered. It didn't take him long to deliver a roll of cloth to his leader.

Hakon took it and, to my surprise, offered it to Asfrid. "Would you like to wrap it? Perhaps you have a different method than we use."

Her snarling smile made it clear Hakon crossed the line, but the arrogant herbalist didn't seem to notice. "So long as the cut is well covered," she said.

Bior's chuckle got a glare from Hakon before he went to work.

I steadied myself, expecting rough treatment, but he surprised me again, applying the bandage carefully.

After thanking him, I looked at Asfrid. "I apologize for interrupting your lesson. You're here as a favor to me, and I appreciate your effort. Hakon, is there more to be gained by Asfrid continuing?"

"Surely there is new information to be learned, Sire," he answered, dipping his chin. "If nothing else, the different plants and such we could come across in this new land."

I nodded, smiling as he spoke. "I suggest you ask her nicely to share her knowledge."

"Of course, Sire," he replied before bowing so low I thought he'd fall over.

I dipped my head to Asfrid.

She winked and mouthed, "Thank you."

"Bior," I said, turning. "I believe it's time for lunch."

"As you say, m'lord. I'll bring your meal to the tent."

Returning to the tent Bior and I shared, without getting lost, I had barely sat when he entered carrying a small pot and two mugs.

"Water and boiled grains for lunch. They were out of bowls. We're sharing the pot."

I shrugged. "Good thing I like you."

He laughed and took the seat across from me. "Dig in."

As I lifted the spoon to my mouth, I heard yelling from the eastern side of camp. Bior furrowed his brow.

"Soldiers!" someone yelled. "Warriors! Form ranks! Prepare for an attack!"

A shiver ran down my back. I dropped the spoon and leaped to my feet. Pain flared in my hand when I grabbed my hammer. "The Satran force is here. Let's go."

"Wait!" Bior's chair fell over as he jumped from it. "You promised Tindra you wouldn't fight."

"I know, but I have to do something, and let's be honest, we both know there's no way I get home without getting my hands bloody sooner or later."

Bior grabbed my arm. "There are no guards assigned to the herbalists nor the injured they're treating. With our warriors engaged in battle, the healers are vulnerable."

I nodded. "And Rorec will skin me if I let his wife get hurt."

Bior smiled at my answer and hurried out of the tent.

Metal struck metal.

Bowstrings twanged.

Screams of pain mixed with angry roars.

The unmistakable sounds of fighting flowed through our camp.

Gooseflesh raised on my arms. I hesitated before turning to follow Bior away from the fight, against the stream of warriors running to do battle. *I'd rather go with them, but if the front lines fail, we'll be fresh and ready to back them.*

We reached the healer's work area. Asfrid stood in front of our herbalists, knife in hand, watching for threats.

"Fitzeirick, what's happening?" she asked, as we approached.

"Sounds like the Legion made it here before we expected," I said. "Come with us. We'll get you to Rorec."

She shook her head. "I can take care of myself. He's likely doing what he can to keep Sifet safe."

"Your husband would protect Sifet instead of making sure you're safe?" Bior asked.

"After so many years together, doing what we do, he trusts my abilities."

"Even so, I'd rather you were at his side," I said. "I have a responsibility to Sifet and his people too. Please, come with me."

She looked at the herbalists behind her. "They aren't trained to fight. I'd hate to leave them alone."

I followed her gaze to Hakon. The arrogant man's face was pale, covered in large beads of sweat.

"Bior will protect them," I said, tilting my hammer toward my steward. "Hakon, make sure your men listen to him."

He shivered and nodded. "Y-Yes, my king."

"Keep yourself safe, Sire," Bior said, saluting.

I returned his salute and then hurried toward our ally's campsite.

The sounds of battle continued, but I couldn't tell if the fighting was any closer.

I heard Rorec shouting orders well before we arrived at the exiles' camp. Branko and Mecik, both bloodied, stood near several broken tents.

"Everyone safe?" I asked.

The big Satran pointed east. "A small scouting party caught us off guard. Killed a couple of tents full of Bane before anyone realized what happened. Rorec and Bojan rallied enough Bane to slow the attackers, and your warriors helped cut them down."

Wasn't sure if Fastulf would stay here or head for the front lines. "Where are my men now?" I asked.

"Guarding the eastern edge of camp with Bojan, last I saw," Mecik said. "Some Bane are with them, raising a wall."

I nodded.

"Where's Rorec?" Asfrid asked.

Branko pointed deeper into the camp. "Somewhere near Sifet's tent, trying to get everyone organized."

"I'll find him. Keep yourself safe, Fitzeirick."

As she hurried into the camp, I turned my focus back to the advisers. "What else do I need to know? Is Vos Sifet safe?"

"Dalibor is with him," Mecik said. "I suspect a few Bane will rally around Vos as well. He should be safe unless your warriors fail to hold off the main force."

"If my army fails, all is lost. Do what you can to protect Vos Sifet."

"Once we're sure this area is safe, we'll go to his side," Branko said.

"I'll leave the decision to you two. I'm going to find Fastulf."

I hurried toward a wall rising into sight. The smell of blood hung in the air as I passed another row of sliced, broken tents. Slowing my pace, I watched for attackers.

Fastulf and his men crouched near the wall not far from a small group of Bane. Bojan stood near the edge of the structure, glancing beyond. All were panting and soaked with sweat.

"You shouldn't be here, Sire," Fastulf said.

Bojan turned and looked at me.

I nodded to the Satran adviser.

"Your men do you proud, King of Croy," he said. "I don't see any Legion. I'm going for waterskins."

"I saw no soldiers on my way here. Your path should be clear," I replied, before turning my attention back to Fastulf. "I had to get Asfrid back safely and was told you were still here. What happened?"

"We heard a commotion. My men and I recognized the sounds of fighting and jumped into action. Rorec and Bojan raised the alarm before we got here. We killed a handful of attackers, but if we hadn't been here or if it had been a larger force — I hate to think about what could have happened, m'lord.

"Most of these people won't defend themselves. Even the ones who decided to stand up and protect others weren't very good. We each killed two or three soldiers for every one the Bane dropped, Sire. Once the attackers turned and ran, these Bane started raising this wall. We stayed to help so our flank would be covered."

"Saving Satran lives couldn't have been an easy decision for you...but it was the right one."

He smiled. "M'lord, you said they were our allies. I couldn't leave them to die. Given how long it took to get any of them to be comfortable having us here...it would have been a waste to let them get killed."

"Did you learn anything?"

"Once the Bane understood we mean them no harm, we'd made some strides toward learning how they syth that horrible material. Of course, we don't have any here, so..." He shrugged.

Bojan returned, leading a few Bane women and children carrying water skins. They rushed to their own kind first, then brought water to my men and scurried away.

"How are your people?" I asked.

"I need to go back and get more Bane working to secure our area, bury the dead, and clean up the mess."

"Go," I said, nodding. "No telling when Legion soldiers might return."

He bowed and hurried away.

"Fastulf, you did well jumping into the fight," I said. "Take a moment longer to rest, but the battle isn't over. I'm sure you and your men would be appreciated at the front."

He nodded and looked toward a nearby Bane. "Zivek, you will fight if they get past the wall, yes?"

One of them smiled. "Right, yes. Friend Fast-elf. We will fight."

Shaking his head, Fastulf turned to his men. "Ready?"

They answered by getting to their feet.

Fastulf stood and smiled. "After you, Sire."

Bior must have been watching for me because he ran up to me soon after I entered the main camp. Fastulf saluted him and continued on.

"All is well, m'lord?" Bior asked.

"Some Bane were killed. Sifet and his advisers are safe, as far as I know." I looked toward the battlefront. "Now, let's see how we can help our men."

"As you say, Sire."

The sounds of fighting diminished well before we reached the edge of camp. Cheers rose ahead of us.

"I'll take that as a good sign," Bior said.

"Agreed," I said. "Let's find General Jomar."

"He likes to lead near the front," Bior said.

"As I would expect. Hard to move men where they're needed when you can't see what's going on."

"Which would be much easier from horseback," Bior commented.

"We could move faster, too," I said, "but we have to do without until we capture some."

Passing through our camp, I didn't see any damage. *Scouts must have spotted the Legion early enough to keep them out. Wonder how many men we lost.*

"It's likely the general's over there," Bior said, pointing to a gathering of warriors.

Some were covered in blood. I couldn't tell if it was theirs or the enemy's, but everyone seemed to be standing. "If not, someone should know where he is."

We jogged toward the group. Their muddled conversations grew louder as we got closer.

Chapter 65

"Enough!" Jomar's voice rose above the noise. "I'm open to suggestions, but not all at once."

"Wait for me to hear the options before we decide," I said, raising my voice.

Everyone turned to look my way.

Jomar saluted. "We welcome your opinion, my king. I heard you were nowhere to be found after the fighting started. Some feared the worst. Good to see you're unharmed."

"We weren't the only ones surprised by the attack," I said, glancing toward the Satran camp. "If I hadn't sent Fastulf and a few of the guides to train with the Bane, their entire camp might have been lost."

"Their safety isn't much of my concern anyway," he said. "As long as they don't get my warriors killed, Sire."

"We can use their help," I said. "Don't overlook a useful resource."

"I hear you, my king, but I have yet to see them be useful."

If the Bane teach Fastulf how to syth dead stone, that will be enough. "What were you discussing before I arrived?" I asked.

"What we should do now that we have the enemy on the run," Jomar said.

"I say we regroup and go after them in the morning," Commander Alrik said.

"While they prepare to attack again tonight," Bior commented.

"I'm afraid you're right," I said, looking at my steward.

Jomar nodded. "Me too."

"Pursue them now," Commander Ottar offered. "They're on the run; let's keep it that way."

"Which leaves the camp, and everyone in it, unguarded while they prepare to move," Jomar argued.

"Agreed," I said. "If some of the Legion sneaks by, they could do a lot of damage here if we rush ahead."

"They know we're here. Best to set our defenses against another attack while the camp gets ready to move. Leave as soon as everyone's ready, even if it means traveling at night," Commander Ketill suggested.

"I'm not sure it's a good idea to move this many people in the dark," I said. "Your opinion, General?"

"If we knew the area, moving at night would be fine. As things are now...an ambush could be a devastating blow."

"Would the exiled Satran help?" Bior asked. "Surely they know their own country."

I shrugged. "I asked Vos Sifet for some Bane to act as guides. After this attack, they may be reluctant. Several of their clan were killed before Fastulf could act."

"If they won't help us, they shouldn't expect us to help them," Alrik commented.

"I find myself agreeing," Jomar added.

Ignoring their remarks, I tried to keep everyone focused on our next move. "Ketill is right. It's not safe to stay here any longer than necessary. Getting our army moving quickly is our best chance at victory," I said, rubbing my hands together. "Bior, find Fastulf and have him gather his men. If we aren't ready to break camp by sunset, they'll guide us and watch for ambushes, with or without help from the Bane. General, have your commanders spread the word; we're marching into battle—pack only what's needed. Everyone carries their own load. If a warrior can't carry it, he doesn't need it. As for the exiles helping, Sifet and I have a pact. He's obligated to give what aid he can."

"Understood, Sire," Jomar said. "I'll leave the diplomacy to you. Commanders, you heard your king. Get moving and pass the word."

"What of our wounded, Sire?" Bior asked.

I didn't think of them. "General?"

He frowned at me for a moment before nodding. "I'll assign a company to guard the herbalists and help with the wounded until they can move."

"Hate to leave men behind," I said.

Jomar nodded. "Any who can't fight will be helped back to the barges and wait there to return home, Sire. The warriors who recover will rejoin the fight once the herbalists are free to move. The company will keep them safe until we're all together again."

"Agreed. Bior, make sure to grab something we can eat on the move, then find me in the Satran camp."

He smiled. "Consider it done, m'lord."

"General, time is not on our side today. Move with haste but stay alert; we don't know when another attack may happen," I said. Turning toward the exile camp, I clicked my hammer in place and jogged away.

I hadn't made it halfway when the effort and the hammer bouncing on my back wore me to the point I had to walk. A line of Bane men stood at the edge of their camp. "Well met, friends. I need to speak with Vos Sifet."

One turned and pointed. "Right, yes. In his tent, friend."

"Thank you."

He smiled at me as I passed.

The amount of activity I had to dodge around surprised me. *Maybe getting help from Sifet won't be too hard.*

Bojan and Branko stood watch outside of their leader's tent.

"Vos Sifet is safe?" I asked.

"He is," Bojan said.

"I need to speak with him. We're preparing to move soon."

Branko opened the tent. "King Fitzeirick of Croy asks to see you, Vos Sifet."

"Let him in. I'm sure we have much to discuss."

Branko nodded. "Enter."

Dalibor sat at Sifet's right. Mecik stood on his left.

"Vos Sifet, it seems you guessed we'll be on the move soon," I said.

He nodded. "I have. What is the plan?"

"We want to move fast, try to catch the Legion force off guard."

"How do you know they aren't ready?" Dalibor asked.

"I don't but sitting and waiting for them to attack us again is not a good strategy," I said, crossing my arms.

"I agree," Sifet said. "What do you need from me?"

"The Bane who worked with my men today, I need them to help us travel safely through the lands on the way to the capital."

"I will speak to them," he said, "but I will not force them."

"Make sure they know they'll be with Friend Fastulf. That may convince them to help."

He nodded and turned to Mecik. "Find them and bring them to me."

"Yes, Vos. Right away," the big Satran said.

"What else, young king?" Sifet asked, as Mecik passed me.

"We are traveling light, leaving everything one can't easily carry. Our wounded will stay behind to recover. There won't be many guards. Have your people ready to move soon and impress upon them the need to keep pace with us for their safety."

"I will make your plans clear, young king. Dalibor, spread the word...it's time to move again."

The adviser eyed me, tapping his fingers on his knife's handle. "Yes, Vos. I will pass along the Croian's advice." There was an edge to his voice that made my skin crawl.

Should I tell Rorec how much of a threat Dalibor is to Sifet? Would he believe me? Rorec claims he's loyal to Croy, but I don't know what he might say to Sifet...or anyone else. I waited until we were alone before speaking again. "Vos Sifet, the Bane's aid will go a long way toward securing our victory and returning you to power."

"I understand," he said, tilting his head. "Rest assured, I will uphold my end of our agreement."

"As will I, but the more cooperation Croy gets from your followers, the easier it is to keep you safe."

He smiled. "Again, I understand, young king."

"We both have much to do. I appreciate you sparing a moment for me. May today bring us a quick victory."

"Agreed," Sifet said, as I turned to leave.

Bojan and Branko nodded as I walked past. Along the way, I looked around for Bior. He called my name before jogging toward me as I neared the border between the two camps.

He patted a sack hanging over his shoulder. "Sorry I'm late, Sire. Stopped by the tent and took the pot back. The cooks weren't happy about the wasted grains, but I have enough hard rolls, dried meat, and water to get us to nightfall. Did the Satran agree to help?"

"We'll talk while we make our way to the front," I said.

· · · ● · ● · · ·

The smell of blood and death hung in the air where the fighting took place. The unpleasant odor turned my stomach, diminishing my appetite.

Bior stopped. "This is far enough for now, at least until more warriors gather. Want to eat, m'lord?"

A line of men stood guard around twenty paces ahead of us. Hands rested on weapons as they swept their gaze across the land in front of them.

I sythed seats for us from the ground and waved my hand in front of my nose as I sat. "I'll wait until we're away from here."

"I'm hungry enough it doesn't matter," he said, before gnawing on a hard roll.

He's seen more fighting than I have. Makes sense this wouldn't bother him. While he ate, I told him about the meeting with Sifet. As I finished, a company of warriors approached.

"Hold." The lead man saluted. "Sire, I wasn't told you'd be here."

"Doubt many know where I am," I said. "Ready to go?"

"Almost, m'lord. Sergeant Bolverk sent us to relieve the guards so they can prepare to leave."

"Best be on your way. The longer we wait, the more prepared the Legion can be."

"Understood, Sire. Move on, men."

Each warrior saluted as they passed.

The guards—Fastulf and his men among them—hurried back into camp.

"Are you scared, Sire?" Bior asked.

"Concerned, mostly, but sure … I'm a little scared. What if we've underestimated our enemy? Tindra worried they were setting a trap for us … for me." I shrugged. "Maybe she's right. All things considered, our invasion has gone pretty easy so far."

"Easy as a baker making sweetbreads, as long as you ignore needing to repair the bridges, crossing the black sand, and you getting captured." He scratched his chin for a moment. "Still, this doesn't feel like a trap, but it's hard to plan for an enemy who seems to like to hit once and run away."

Groups of warriors passed as we talked.

"On their own ground, no less." I nodded. "Their strategy does make you wonder, doesn't it?"

"Aye, Sire … it does. Have you asked Vos Sifet about it?"

"No. Considering his attitude toward the Legion, I doubt he has anything useful to say about them."

Bior cocked his head. "Or he's keeping secrets to trade for his own gain later."

I nodded again. "Possibly, but I doubt it. Plus, the Bonetakers lead the country now. No doubt they dictate the Legion's actions."

"Which could explain why their tactics don't make sense," Bior commented.

"Let's make our way closer to the front. At the rate men are arriving, we'll be leaving soon."

"After you, m'lord."

"Sire! King Fitzeirik!" Jomar yelled, somewhere behind me.

I turned and looked for him in a moving crowd of warriors.

The men parted, and General Jomar jogged out of the group. "A moment, my king!"

"What's wrong?" I asked, crossing my arms.

"Nothing's wrong, Sire. I wanted to let you know the wounded are with the herbalists, and I have a guard posted for them. The cooks and porters heard about their arrangement and asked to have a company assigned to them. Considering we could be ambushed along the way, it made sense, so I have a company keeping them safe."

"Good. We should be ready to leave once Fastulf and his men arrive. I don't know if any Bane are coming."

"Understood, Sire." Jomar nodded. "I know you said they are allies, but they need to act like it if they expect our help."

"Agreed," I said, nodding. "And I told them as much. We'll see how serious Vos Sifet takes his vows."

"I'd rather you not walk with the first group out, m'lord," Jomar said. "Should we come under attack, you're at greater risk."

"I'm here to lead my army into Satra."

"And I'll be at his side," Bior said. "King Fitzeirick's safety is my responsibility."

"Yet he was captured while your back was turned," Jomar countered.

"Bior and I are both more aware of the threats we face now. We'll be more careful," I said.

"As you say, Sire. Still, I'll ask you to stay toward the back of the formation."

"I appreciate your concern, general. I'll do my best to stay out of danger."

He smiled before saluting. "On to victory, my king."
Bior and I returned his salute.
"To victory," I replied.

Chapter 66

A commotion came from behind me. I turned to see Fastulf leading his men and a small group of Satran wearing Croian armor.

"Of all the stone-headed ideas," Bior said.

"They *are* helping us," I said.

"This still could cause some trouble," Jomar said.

"I'm sure he has a good reason," I said, before waving Fastulf over.

As a group, they jogged to us.

"Yes, Sire," Fastulf said, saluting.

"Why are these —" *Bane, Satran, men ... how do I say this without being insulting?* "Why are our Satran allies wearing Croian armor?"

"These brave Bane wanted to help but were worried about their safety. I promised to protect them if they aided the Croian army. To show I would keep my word, we gave them some spare armor. Should lessen confusion when the fighting starts. I'd expect my fellow warriors to attack any Satran on sight, but they shouldn't turn their weapons on anyone wearing our armor."

I found myself nodding as he spoke. "Sensible. Any questions, General Jomar?"

"No, m'lord, but many concerns. Commanders, make sure you let everyone know about this."

"Yes, general," Alrik said, before the leaders turned to leave.

"Move quickly," I said. "We march as soon as the guides are ready."

Jomar shook his head. "Fastulf, I hope you haven't caused more trouble than you solved."

I cleared my throat. "Considering I agree with Fastulf, any who disagrees with this can speak to me about it."

Bior snickered.

Jomar bowed. "Of course, Sire."

"Fastulf, get your men to the front. Be ready to go."

"Glady, Sire." Fastulf saluted, before shouting, "On me!"

"At least he's not collecting teeth again," Bior commented.

"True," I said.

"Collecting teeth?" Jomar asked.

"Long story," I said. "Not worth telling now."

"As you say. Unless you expect more surprises, m'lord," Jomar said, as the last of the group passed, "I'd best be on my way, too."

"Doubt there'll be anything else," I said. "At least, nothing I can't handle."

"As you say, m'lord." Jomar saluted and hurried away.

"Sire, you wore Varian armor at one time ... correct?" Bior asked.

"I did."

"Did it upset any of the Varian soldiers?"

"Not as much as Tindra wearing their armor."

He raised his eyebrows. "What? Why?"

I nodded. "Some of the men we rode with didn't like having a woman in their ranks. It's beside the fact she was a better fighter than most of them."

"I'm guessing she set them straight."

"No. She allied herself with their sergeant. He made sure no one threatened her."

He whistled. "Hiding behind someone doesn't sound like her at all."

"Spilling countrymen's blood over a petty disagreement would have caused her more trouble. She's smart and resourceful. One of the reasons I married her."

"Good reason, Sire, though I can see how she could rub some people the wrong way," Bior said. "I probably shouldn't have said that out loud," he added a moment later, looking away from me.

I laughed. "I'm not saying she's perfect. Far from it. She irritates me too, from time to time."

He eyed me for a moment before joining my laughter.

We'd gotten ourselves back under control shortly before General Jomar returned. "Word about the armored Bane is spreading. Doesn't seem to be causing any problems so far. Are you ready to go?"

"Yes, General," I said.

"Good," he replied, before cupping his hands near his mouth. "Croian army! Form up!"

Cheers filled the air, blending into a roar.

Warriors ahead of us hurried to line up.

The general took a deep breath. "Fastulf! Forward!"

"If the Legion didn't know we were coming before, they do now," Bior said.

"Maybe they'll run scared," I said, standing quickly as the rows ahead marched. Glancing back, I couldn't see if the exiles left with us or not. *Sifet knew we were leaving soon. Not my fault if he couldn't get the rest of his followers ready.*

The land reminded me of my old skati. Open fields bordered by forests. Occasionally, I noticed structures resembling houses or barns well off the path, but I never saw any people moving about. *Perhaps they're afraid of us or the Legion ... or both.*

• • • • • • • • • •

The sun was setting and I was eating another roll when a warbling whistle came from somewhere ahead. *Don't know what that means, but I bet it's not good.*

A shrieking whistle sounded from the right edge of the formation, and the men in front of me shifted toward it.

Shortly after entering a nearby forest, Sergeant Sighadd approached me. "Sire, Commander Ketill sent me to tell you the path runs through a village ahead. The Satran guides said we shouldn't go in. My commander sent me to tell you while they discuss options."

"Tell the general I'll talk to Vos Sifet and see if I can get them some information."

"Yes, m'lord." Sighadd saluted before jogging away.

"Do you know where he is?" Bior asked.

"I hope he's behind us."

"I'll stay here, Sire, in case anyone else comes looking for you. Travel swift."

I wove my way around groups of warriors, through clumps of trees and bushes, to the back of our formation. The crowd of Bane stood well back from my warriors. "Where's Vos Sifet?" I asked a barefoot woman.

She lowered her gaze before pointing to the group.

I spotted Mecik standing head and shoulders above everyone.

Men, women, and children all moved out of my way as I waded through the crowd to the big Satran. "I need to speak with Vos Sifet," I said.

He moved aside.

I nodded and stepped past him to find Sifet standing behind Bojan and Branko, talking with Dalibor. "Vos Sifet, a moment of your time."

He looked at me, smiled, and cocked his head. "Of course, young king. What can I do for you? I assume it has something to do with why we've stopped."

"There's a village ahead. The Bane guides say we shouldn't enter it. My leaders are discussing how to proceed. Perhaps you can let the villagers know we aren't a threat."

He shook his head. "They were right to stop you. We're outside Sosniok. I'm not welcome there."

"So, they aren't innocent?" I asked.

"It isn't so simple, young king. Families in Sosniok are known for raising strong sons. I sent the Legion to recruit here often. No doubt, you understand why they wouldn't look favorably on me."

"I do. What would you recommend? I'd rather not spill blood unless we have no other choice."

He nodded and scratched his chin. "If our presence angers the Devoted living here, peace may not be an option. Dalibor, you can be most persuasive. Take two or three Bane. Meet with the Sosniok elder. Explain our situation. Ask him to allow the army to pass in peace."

"As you wish, Vos."

Sifet still trusts him. Maybe his offer to kill the chieftain was a test. It probably won't help to send a warrior with him, but having other Satran accompany him could discourage the rat from conspiring against us. "If the villagers may be hostile, shouldn't you send men to protect him?"

Sifet patted his frail-looking adviser on the back. "King of Croy, should Dalibor succeed, no blood will be shed. Should he fail, a few guards will not matter."

"Then, let's hope he's able to convince them to let us through without trouble. I'll let my men know, and we'll wait for word."

"Thank you for seeking my advice. May our continued cooperation help victory come swiftly, young king."

Dalibor cleared his throat. "Wise king, would you like to accompany us? You could make your intentions known to the elder in person."

"I doubt the presence of an armed and armored Croian would convince anyone we mean them no harm. I'll leave you to select your escorts and wait with my leaders for word of your success. If we don't have an answer by midnight, we'll assume you failed and prepare to fight if they confront us."

"Sound reasoning, young king," Sifet said.

"Should things go in our favor, I will return to you straight away," Dalibor replied, before bowing.

Why do I have to trust our safety to the man who offered to kill his ruler?

Chapter 67

As the daylight faded, warriors settled into groups instead of moving about. Though they were no longer an obstacle, I had to use my talent to avoid running into trees or tripping over exposed roots while making my way back to Bior. "I need to talk to General Jomar and Fastulf."

"Are the exiles going to help?" he asked.

"They're going to try. Come with me so I don't have to tell the story twice."

"Aye, Sire."

We found Jomar sitting with the commanders, Fastulf, and several of the guides.

"Anything to report?" I asked.

Jomar shook his head. "No one has reported any movement. If it wasn't for the smell of stock pens and hearth fires, I'd say the place was deserted."

"I spoke with Vos Sifet. It seems he has an unpleasant history with this particular village and felt his presence would do more harm than good. He's sending an adviser and some Bane to speak with the elder. Dalibor is supposed to let them know we mean no harm and ask them to let us pass through peacefully."

"Why Dalibor, Sire?" Fastulf asked.

"His power of persuasion," I said.

Bior chuckled next to me.

"We don't have long to wait, m'lord," Jomar said. "I have to believe Satra's soldiers are regrouping, preparing for another attack. At the least, sitting here makes us easier to find."

"I told Dalibor if he hadn't sent word of success by midnight, we'd prepare to fight our way through, if necessary."

"And raid the village for supplies," Commander Osvif said.

"Which would delay us longer. Also, that's not the impression I want to leave with a group of people I hope to rule after our victory," I said.

"So, what do we do while we wait?" Bior asked.

"Eat," I said. "Rest. But make sure we have enough men on watch to avoid being surprised."

Jomar nodded. "Commanders, pass the word. No patrols. Men can sleep as long as someone is on watch."

The leaders stood and saluted before slipping into the deepening darkness.

"Fastulf, keep your men alert. If anyone's going to notice someone approaching in the dark, it's them," I said. "And keep our allies with you. Don't want any accidents."

"Of course, Sire. Guides, you heard him. Spread out, stay out of sight, and pay attention."

It was a little eerie watching the group move away in almost complete silence.

"And now we wait," I grumbled. "Bior, I'll take a hard roll and a waterskin before I find a tree to rest against."

"Aye, Sire."

Snack in hand, I found a tree where I could sit, look up, and see a portion of the slivered moon to keep track of time. After washing the last of the crumbs down with warm water, I lay my head against the tree, closed my eyes, and wondered what was going on in the village. Other than the occasional whispered conversation and a few quiet snores, the forest was quiet, peaceful, and calming. *Regardless of Dalibor's success, life will be hectic soon enough.*

• • • • ● • • ● • • • •

A shrill whistle startled me.

"What was that?" someone nearby asked.

"Those guides talking like birds again," someone else answered.

Opening my eyes, I noticed the moon had nearly crossed the small opening above me. *Are we moving on or fighting? Guess we'll know soon.*

Two sharp tweets came from where I'd left Bior.

Stretching muscles in my back made me groan as I got to my feet.

Men stirred as I made my way toward the last calls I'd heard.

Bior stood and stretched as I approached.

"What's going on?" I asked.

Another whistle sounded in the distance.

"People approaching from the south, Sire," Fastulf said.

"Do we know who or how many?" I asked.

"There are two, m'lord."

Dalibor was supposed to take several Bane with him. Would he return with only one?

"We'd best be ready for anything," I said.

"Of course, Sire," Fastulf said, before giving three slowly rising whistles.

"What was that?" Bior asked.

"Getting my men ready. They can wake the warriors around them in time to face any threat headed our way."

"Good thinking," I said, resisting the urge to send my talent into the ground around us.

Two chirps followed by three long whistles came from the south.

"Athal's made contact. He's leading them to us," Fastulf said.

"Thoughts?" Jomar questioned.

"Why are they coming from the south?" I asked.

"Who knows why any of the Satran do what they do," Bior commented.

"Maybe there's a good reason," I said. "We'll have to wait and find out."

It seemed like everything stood frozen while I watched for movement from the south. My eyes swept from one clump of darkness to another on their own. Though the night was cool, large beads of sweat formed on my brow. I reached to lift my helmet to wipe my forehead, but a branch snapped, reminding me the unknown was approaching.

Athal stepped out of a shadow. He had Dalibor's forearm in his grasp. Another Satran was not far behind. They weren't dressed like Bane, as best I could tell.

"My king," Athal said, bowing. "General Jomar, Fastulf. Dalibor asked for my help finding you."

"Thank you, Athal," I said. "You may return to your watch."

He saluted and walked back into the darkness.

"King Fitzeirick, this is Traiko, son of Sokol, the Sosnioki elder," Dalibor said, gesturing toward the Satran.

He stood tall, close to Roi's height. Some sort of gown, possibly leather, hung from his broad shoulders. A long braid of black and silver hair draped over his right shoulder. His left arm was missing below the elbow.

"Welcome, Traiko," I said. "What can we do for you?"

"My father sent me to make sure you honor the agreement."

"Which is?" I questioned, looking at Dalibor with my eyebrows raised.

"Safe passage to the south, so long as we stay outside their lands, King of Croy."

"Exposing our flank to the Legion," General Jomar said.

"And slowing our progress," Fastulf added.

Both valid concerns. "Traiko, it would be best if we could pass through your village."

"Give us Sifet."

As I considered his demand, my hand throbbed where I'd cut it. Dalibor eyed me while I considered how best to respond. "I cannot do that," I said, showing him my bandaged hand. "He is under my protection. But you have my word that we will move quickly and do no harm."

The Satran adviser gave me a quick nod.

Traiko crossed his arms. "You may be king elsewhere, but your word has no value here, and what is best for you means nothing. My father offers no resistance to you passing outside our lands in exchange for the payment given."

"Payment?" I turned to Dalibor again. "What does he mean?"

"I traded a few women and children for our safety. Surely a king knows how such deals are made," Dalibor said.

Bior growled.

"What? No! I don't trade people for anything." I glared at Traiko. "What are you going to do with them?"

He shrugged. "We will use them as we see fit. Servants, laborers, brood mares... Why do you care? Were some of them yours?"

"Disgusting," Jomar said.

"Dalibor, did Vos Sifet know you were doing this?" I demanded.

He nodded. "Why else would I take Bane with me?"

"I don't like it," Fastulf said.

"It doesn't sit well with me either," I said, "but —"

"But? There is no but, Sire," Bior interrupted. "If those people are our allies, this is inexcusable."

"Wise king, if I may," Dalibor said, bowing.

"What?" I snapped.

"Bane are traded all the time. This is the way of Satra. Once you have control of the country, things may change ... in time. For now, and if you lose this war, this is how things are."

"Doesn't mean it's right," Bior said.

"It's not," I said. *What have I done? Now that I know, it will never happen again. As soon as I can, I'll come back and make sure those Bane are freed.* My stomach churned. "Traiko, does the offer of safety include not telling the Legion where we are?"

"Dalibor asked for safe passage, nothing more. Know this; we hate the Legion. Honor the agreement as it was made, and none among us will speak of your presence."

"We will not bother your village," I said, offering Traiko my hand.

He looked at it for a moment, then said, "We will be watching," before walking into the dark woods in the direction of Sosniok.

"Dalibor, let Vos Sifet know we are going south."

He bowed again. "As you say, King of Croy."

After he left, I glanced toward the Bane who were helping Fastulf guide us. *Did they know what Dalibor was doing? Why didn't they say anything?* "General, wake everyone. We need to get moving quickly."

"I'm not comfortable exposing our flank to the Legion, Sire, and it's a risk marching on their capital with them behind us."

I nodded. "Our position isn't ideal, but we don't have any better options. As long as those villagers are good to their word, the Legion won't know where we are. If we're careful, we can attack on our terms and draw blood before they know what's hit them."

"Let's hope everything works out so well, Sire," Jomar said, saluting.

"Nothing ever works out that well," Bior commented.

Jomar chuckled. "Commanders, let's get everyone ready to move. Order them to keep distance between them and the village."

The leaders saluted and hurried out into the dark forest.

"Fastulf, gather any men you have north of us and get ready to lead the way around Sosniok."

"Yes, Sire. Gladly." He saluted before turning north and giving a pattern of tweets and. whistles.

Anxious to get underway, I watched as about half his company trickled in, gathering around their leader and the Bane who stayed within sight of him.

Jomar arrived and let me know everyone was ready.

"Fastulf, on you," I said. "Remember to stay well away from the village."

"It will be slow going, but we'll do our best to guide everyone through the woods, m'lord. Men, stay sharp and keep our warriors safe."

Chapter 68

Bior groaned as he joined me. "How long is this going to take, Sire?"

"No way of knowing since I don't know how big the village is."

I kept glancing through the trees, trying to watch for villagers as we made our way around Sosniok. Thick undergrowth blocked my view and hindered my talent. *They may hate or fear the Legion, but I doubt they care much for Croy, either. Never know when someone might decide to attack.* We exited the forest and crossed a narrow path heading south. *They've been true to their word so far.*

I looked back when my foot hit the hard-packed road and couldn't see the village through the trees. *Guess the road curves somewhere between here and there.* Realizing we'd passed the village without incident so far made me smile despite my growing fatigue.

Out of the woods, our pace sped up, and soon, I was breathing heavily. *Rushing headlong toward the next clash with the Satran Legion.* "Bior, can you jog ahead and get Fastulf for me?"

"Why, Sire?"

"Maybe it's our surroundings, but I'm getting worried about stumbling into a trap. I'm going to have him send a few of his men farther ahead so we don't want to stumble into any Legion soldiers."

"I feel much the same, m'lord. Let me fetch him for you."

Our pace slowed a little before Fastulf reached me. The Bane followed him like ducklings. "You sent for me, Sire?"

"I'm growing concerned about finding the Legion or them finding us. Send a few of your men ahead so we don't blindly walk into a trap."

He glanced over his shoulder at a smiling Bane woman. "Jitka and I were talking about where the Legion could be, Sire. She believes they could be camped near a river not too far ahead. If we can keep this pace, we might get there near sunrise."

"Right. Yes, Friend Fast-elf," she said, nodding enthusiastically. "Water and food from the river."

"Assuming she's correct, we'd best make sure the way is clear. Send a couple of men ahead to make sure."

"Of course, Sire. We'll do our best."

He turned and made a series of twittering calls before raising his hand over his head and motioning forward. "They'll be well ahead of us by the time I return to my position, m'lord."

"One day, you're going to have to teach us what those mean," Bior said.

"But not today," I added. "You have enough to worry about, Fastulf."

"Yes, Sire," he said, saluting before hurrying away, Bane in tow.

"Do you believe her, m'lord?" Bior asked.

"They're here to help us with the lay of the land. If anyone should know, it's them. Plus, it doesn't hurt to prepare as if she's right."

"I don't trust them, Sire. Why would they help us against their fellow countrymen?"

"The exiles are loyal to Vos Sifet. By aiding us, they support their leader."

"If you insist."

"I'm not asking you to blindly trust them, Bior. Let them work, and we'll see how it turns out."

"Aye, m'lord."

As we continued, I watched for unexpected movement. Searching with my talent was pointless when surrounded by loose lines of warriors. For a moment, I envied Fastulf and his company; they only had to worry about what lay ahead, using their skills to avoid surprises.

A faint warbling call drifted back from somewhere well ahead of us.

More signals were exchanged before the rows of men ahead of me slowed, turned off the path, and entered the trees on our right.

Fastulf and Jomar rushed back to me. "Sire, the camp is no more than two hundred paces ahead," the guide leader said.

"My king, if we move quickly, we can attack before sunrise," Jomar added.

"I like your plan, but quick and quiet are hard to achieve together," I said.

"Will they fall for another sneak attack, Sire?" Fastulf asked.

I shrugged. "Who knows? What do you have in mind?"

"M'lord, five of my men have the camp in sight. Me and the rest can join them, sneak in, and attack while our army makes its way through these woods to take the fight to the Legion in the confusion."

"Any guards or scouts?" Bior asked.

"I don't know," Fastulf said. "But I'd expect us to kill lone fighters easily without making much noise."

"General Jomar ... your opinion?" I asked.

"It might work, but we're risking a number of valuable men," he said. "What about your Satran friends, Fastulf? Will they fight with you?"

"Some might, but we haven't talked about it."

"Bad idea to take them," Bior said.

The guide leader glared at Bior.

"I say leave them behind, but the decision is yours, Fastulf," Jomar said. "You've spent more time with them than any of us."

"I'd be surprised if they fought at your side. If they don't, they're little more than a distraction," I said. "Like the general recommended, leave them behind."

Fastulf looked from the general to me. "If they are our allies, Sire, shouldn't they decide if they want to fight for us or not?"

I crossed my arms and stared at him for a moment. "Ordinarily, I'd say yes, but this is far from a typical situation. They have no experience doing anything other than avoiding punishment as they live their lives."

"Good point, m'lord," Fastulf said. "Who do I leave them with? I doubt Bane wearing our armor would be well received by their people."

"I'll be too busy keeping you out of harm's way to watch them, Sire," Bior said.

"And I need to focus on the battle and giving orders," Jomar said.

"None of us needs the distraction," I said, nodding, "Fastulf, tell them to stay out of the way, behind the archers."

"Yes, Sire. I'll make sure they know where to stay, m'lord."

"How far to the camp?" Jomar asked.

"General Jomar, count to one hundred once you lose sight of me," Fastulf said, turning to point into the woods, "then advance through those trees."

He saluted. "Understood."

Fastulf returned the salute, nodded, and hurried into the forest.

"Told you those exiles would be a problem," Bior said.

"As long as they don't get in the way, they won't be," I said, "and if they do, I'll take care of them myself."

The ranks ahead of us moved forward.

"You swore to protect the exiles, m'lord," Bior said.

"So long as they help us win this war, yes. If they hamper our efforts, the situation changes."

"No argument from me, Sire. I hope you can get Sifet to see things your way."

"Considering he knowingly traded some of his followers for our passage, I'm sure he already does."

"Good point, m'lord."

We watched Jomar for the signal to move. His head bobbed several times before he raised his hand over his head and then pointed for us to advance.

Reentering the forest, my skin prickled under my armor, my heart beating faster in anticipation of the coming fight. I hadn't seen battle since the poisoned dart nearly killed me, and I was ready to do anything to avoid a repeat of that happening. The trees and brush seemed to reach out, grabbing at my arms and legs as I advanced. Each brush of a branch or briar grew louder as if the plants were announcing our arrival. Yet my feet sank deeper into the dirt with each step, muffling the sound of our approach. *Fastulf's doing? Or is it because we're getting closer to a river? Is the softer ground an advantage or a hindrance?* My body quaked as I prepared to face our enemy.

Chapter 69

"Bior," I said quietly, "keep your eyes open. We can't stay undetected much longer."

He nodded but kept his focus ahead.

Shortly after hearing the faint sound of running water ahead, I thought I heard three or four dull thumps. *Are they in the camp already?* My heart urged me to run ahead of our advance and watch Fastulf and his company in action. My brain told me it was best to stay behind and let my warriors do their job.

Two more thumps.

Jomar snapped his fingers then motioned for the archers to advance.

Two rows of men ahead of us hurried through the trees.

Someone yelled.

Horses whinnied and neighed.

"Archers, loose arrows at will," Jomar said.

Bowstrings twanged.

"Warriors! To battle!" Jomar roared.

My army bellowed its response before men ran past me.

The archers played their one-note song of death again before the first clash of metal striking metal rang. Soon after, a shriek of pain pierced the air.

"Archers! Hold your arrows! Take cover!" Jomar ordered.

"I have to see," I said, to Bior. "Let's make our way to Jomar."

Horses cried again. Their distress rose above the steadily growing sounds of battle and chaos. Hoof beats rumbled in a thundering rhythm. Water splashed soon after.

As we reached the general, someone barked orders in the camp.

I looked past our archers to a group of tents. Edging closer to the treeline, I found the ground sloped away gently. The Satran camp spread across a floodplain below.

In the slowly brightening light, this camp could easily be mistaken for one of ours, except they kept their horses corralled closer to the center. Big mistake. Several of the spooked animals had knocked tents over, trying to escape the commotion. A few of them fled to the other side of the river behind the Satran camp.

My gaze swept across the scene. A few Croians were down, and many more Satran lay motionless. I couldn't find Fastulf.

A stiff breeze rose, blowing the smell of blood into my face.

Near the fighting, a tall Satran raised his sword and yelled for his soldiers to attack.

"Archers!" Jomar yelled. "Aim carefully!"

An arrow lodged in the tall man's armor near his gut. More bowstrings sang. Three more arrows hit before he went to his knees. A warrior finished the soldier with an axe to the back of his head.

A fallen tent, writhing as soldiers tried to free themselves from the cloth, caught my eye.

Without anyone saying anything, it became the next target to sprout arrows. Red spots spread where they found flesh.

A blade thrust outward from the canvas, slit an opening, and a Satran stumbled out. Blood ran down one arm, hanging limp at his side. He ran as more arrows sought him and his fellow soldiers. After a wrong turn, two warriors stabbed him, and he fell to the ground.

Smoke rose from the southern edge of the camp before a tent burst into flame. Before I could say anything, it jumped and lit two more.

"General!" I barked.

Shouts of "fire!" added to the confusion in the camp.

"We need to end this before we lose more men to that fire than we do to the fight," Jomar said.

"Order firesyths to put it out," I said.

"They'd have to quit fighting and concentrate," he said. "Too risky."

"Bior. Go to the exiles. Get firesyths to help."

"Me, Sire?"

"Yes... you. What else are you going to do, stand here and watch Croians cook?"

"Aye — I mean, no, m'lord. I'm not going to watch our men burn."

As Bior hurried away, one of the Bane guides shuffled toward me, head down. "Friend Fist-er-rick."

I recognized the voice. It was the woman who told Fastulf about the river.

"What?" I snapped.

She licked her lips before glancing over her shoulder toward her people, huddled behind a large tree.

"What do you want? Speak quickly."

"Right, yes. Vos King Fist-er-rick ... we —"

"Spit it out, girl," Jomar said.

She nodded. "We can help, yes."

"You've been helping," I said. "But need firesyths."

"Right, yes. We can put the fire out," she said.

"What?" Jomar barked. "How?"

"We can help, yes, Vos King Fist-er-rick?"

"We don't know how long it will take Bior to find firesyths and get them back here," Jomar said.

"You're sure you can put the fire out?" I asked.

She looked at me and smiled. "Right, yes. Watch."

Turning to face her fellow Bane, she dropped to her knees and pressed her hands against the ground. "Hurry, right!"

The others spread out in front of her, on their knees with hands to the ground, and hummed. Soon the ground quivered in time with the humming. Energy, lots of it, rushed under my feet.

"What are they doing?" Jomar asked.

"Don't know," I said.

Her head dipped, and the energy shifted, rushing through the ground, like a flooded stream, toward the flaming tents.

I pushed my talent into the ground to track what they were doing. There was a resistance where my will brushed against theirs. *Strange.* The harder I pressed, the more their energy fought back. *What are they doing?* Wanting to learn anything I could about their technique, I shoved energy out and willed it to mix with theirs. The backlash hit me like a physical blow. Lights floated in my vision. My knees buckled, but I stayed on my feet.

The flood stopped near the fires. The ground groaned before a wall of dirt rose between the burning tents and the rest of the camp.

"Well ... at least the fire can't spread," Jomar commented.

I shook my head. "They're still working."

"Wh—" Jomar couldn't finish his word before everything stopped.

The ground above their flow shook. Tents near the firebreak collapsed before the wall fell, covering the flames in dirt and stone.

The fighting stopped as everyone, Croian and Satran, turned to gawk at the cloud of dust and smoke rising from the southern edge of the camp.

I took off my helmet and wiped my hand across my face.

"Vos King Fist-er-rick. We helped, right, yes?" she asked.

Turning to the woman, still on her hands and knees, I blinked and nodded slowly. "Yes. You did."

She smiled wide enough I didn't need light to see it.

"Finish the fight!" Jomar ordered, turning my attention back to the camp before I could ask her any questions. "Archers! Let fly!"

Arrows dropped several soldiers before men snapped out of their awe and returned to the deadly dance.

Kneeling next to the Bane woman, I put my hand on her shoulder. "Can you do it again?"

She flinched away from my touch before answering. "No, Vos. Must rest first."

"What happened?" Bior asked, red-faced and breathing hard.

"The Bane put out the fire," I said, standing

"Aren't they stonesyths, m'lord?" he asked, face scrunched.

I nodded and explained what they did.

"Oh." He turned and pointed at two, Bane men, breathing harder than him. "So, we don't need them?"

"Not now," I said, "but we might as well keep them here in case there's another fire."

"Right. You two, stay with them." He pointed to the Bane stonesyths crouched on the ground.

"Yes, Friend Bior. Right," one of them said.

"I'm never going to get used to that," Bior muttered, shaking his head. "Did I miss anything else, Sire?"

"The fight seems to be going our way so far. We caught them off guard and used the surprise to our advantage."

An arrow struck the ground between my feet.

"Take cover!" I said, diving behind a tree.

One of the Bane stonesyths didn't move fast enough and caught an arrow in his shoulder.

As he cried out, another arrow hit the tree I knelt behind.

"Find that archer!" Jomar bellowed. "Put him down!"

Pushing my talent into the ground, I raised a chest-high dirt wall for some protection. "Bior, see to his injury."

Dirt flew after an arrow struck near the top of our cover.

"Aye, Sire. I'll do what I can."

The stonesyth screamed again as Bior went to work.

One of our archers was hit and stumbled behind the wall. Holding his right arm to his chest, blood flowed from between his fingers where his left hand pressed against the wound.

"There!" someone barked, before bowstrings thrummed.

I crawled to the injured bowman. "Let me see if I can help."

His breath came in short, ragged bursts. "Th — Thank you, Sire." He moved his hand, uncovering the hole in his forearm. His face lost color as blood poured out of his arm.

"Missed!" an archer ahead of us hissed.

"Where'd he go?" another asked.

"Bior, I need a bandage!" I yelled, pressing the archer's bloody hand back over his wound.

"You and me both, Sire. I've got this arrow out, but nothing to stop the bleeding."

Cloth ripped behind me. "Vos King Fist-er-rick, Friend Bior ... use this."

I turned as one of the Bane firesyths approached, holding rags.

I nodded and grabbed some strips. "Take the rest to Bior."

"Right, yes."

I rubbed the rough cloth between my hands, trying to brush as much grit off it as I could. *Best I've got for now.* "This is going to hurt," I warned.

More ragged breaths. "Already does," the archer said, a distant look in his glassy eyes.

Keeping the rag tight as I wrapped it around his wound, he groaned when I tied it to keep pressure on his arm.

The tan cloth quickly turned darker as it soaked with blood. The archer's face continued to lose color.

All of our herbalists are back at camp. "Bior, how are you doing over there?"

"Better than I should be, Sire. Why?"

"This man needs a herbalist...now! Can you get him to Asfrid?"

Another arrow struck the wall.

"I see him!" someone shouted.

Bows strummed.

"Missed again!"

"He went behind that tent."

"We can help, yes, Vos?" the Bane woman asked.

"We could use another wall, I suppose," I said.

"No, Vos. Get your man to Friend Asfrid."

"Of course. I'm sure Friend Bior would take all the help he can get."

"Help me carry him," Bior said. "We'll move faster."

"Right, yes, Friend Bior," she said. "Everyone lift."

The Bane stonesyths carried the archer. The two firesyths trailed behind, walking slower, supporting their wounded countryman.

Dirt stuck to my hands when I tried to wipe them clean on the ground.

A bowstring thrummed. "Got him!"

To the fire with that Satran archer.

"Keep a sharp eye for more archers," Jomar ordered.

"Yes, general."

"How long can the fight continue?" I asked.

He looked over the wall. "Hard to say, my king. Right now, it looks like they've lost more men than us, but I can't tell for sure."

As we spoke, two soldiers cut down one of my warriors. "Archers. Avenge him," I ordered, pointing toward their fallen comrade.

The closest bowman shook his head. "Sire, it's too far to take a shot with any confidence."

Closing my eyes, I nodded. "General, have you seen Fastulf or any of his men? It would be a serious blow to our efforts if we lose them."

"I haven't, but they're smart and sneaky. I'd bet several gold doubles they're still alive and fighting, m'lord."

Nodding again, I swept my gaze across the battlefield, watching my warriors hacking, stabbing, and chopping their way through the Legion camp. *I should be down there helping win this battle. My presence would help end the fight sooner.*

I crumbled a section of the wall in front of me and stepped through.

Jomar grabbed my shoulder. "No, m'lord. That's a bad idea. We do more good directing the archers from here. Not to mention, I promised Bior I'd keep you safe, and I don't care to face your queen's wrath should you get hurt."

"We have the numbers, the advantage ... you said so yourself," I said, twisting away from his grip.

He grabbed me again, pulling me back this time. "Trust me, this isn't the last fight before the war is won. Better to be alive for the final victory than fall during this one."

"My warriors need to see I'm not afraid," I argued.

"Your warriors want to see you're alive ... they already know you're not afraid, my king. From here, we can see everything as it happens, maybe learn something about Satra's tactics."

"What's going on, Sire?" Bior asked, from behind.

Jomar let go of my arm. "I stopped him from making a bad decision. How's the archer?"

"Asfrid didn't look hopeful. He lost a lot of blood."

"Where are your Bane friends?" I asked, glancing back.

"Sifet found out they'd returned and sent Branko after them. Something about wanting a report."

"Hope we don't need them again soon," I said, shaking my head.

Bior sighed. "If we do, I'll go get them, m'lord."

"Sire. Look," Jomar said, pointing.

I tried to find what he wanted me to see. "Where?"

"A few, Satran soldiers are glancing behind them instead of focusing on the fight. I suspect they're about to run."

"Maybe those are the cowards," Bior said.

"Possible," Jomar said, "but it won't take many runners to spread fear and doubt. If I'm right, we'll take the camp well before midday."

"And if you aren't?" I asked.

"Both sides will lose men to fatigue and mistakes," he said.

"So, the last men standing will be stonesyths," I quipped.

"Most likely," Jomar replied. "Archers forward, ten paces. Let's see if we can get them to run."

"General, we'll be on the slope. We'll be off balance, and our aim won't be as sure," a nearby archer said.

"I'm aware, but I'm not ready to send you into the camp."

"As you say, sir."

Stepping back behind cover, I watched our warriors moving through the enemy camp, hurrying around tents or slicing through them.

As more soldiers fell, our victory seemed certain. A group of five or six Satran dropped their weapons and ran for the river. Other Legion soldiers yelled at them as they fled but stood defiant as my men pressed the attack.

"Archers, forward twenty paces!" Jomar ordered. "And be ready."

Holding their bows low, they hurried ahead and readied themselves to let arrows fly when needed.

Before the archers steadied themselves, the Legion's will broke. Obviously outnumbered, the Satran soldiers turned and ran for the river.

"Archers, loose one volley to the river!" Jomar shouted.

Though I agreed with the general's order, and the arrows flew faster than men could run, I feared seeing our warriors shot in the back as they chased the fleeing Satran. "Warriors! Halt!" I screamed, hoping they'd hear me. I didn't have time to push my voice through the ground.

Fortunately, the archers aimed for the far side of the river, leaving our men safe while wounding a few soldiers sloshing onto the bank. Those hit continued their retreat with shafts lodged in their bodies.

Croian warriors stopped the chase at the river's edge and cheered.

"The camp is ours!" Bior bellowed.

I looked at Jomar.

He nodded. "Sire, let's see what they left us."

Lots of bodies to bury, if nothing else. Despite my dark thoughts, witnessing the victory made me smile. "Bior, let the exiles know it's safe to advance, tell Asfrid to expect more wounded, and meet me in the camp."

"Aye, Sire, as quickly as I can."

Chapter 70

Jomar and I walked down the slope, following the archers to the edge of the campground. As we got closer, the smell of blood grew stronger, along with the moans of the injured. A layer of dust from the Bane's efforts to put out the fire covered everything in sight. Dark, brown pools near fallen fighters marked where the fine dirt soaked up their blood.

"Archers, help our wounded. Kill any Satran still breathing," Jomar ordered.

"Gladly," the nearest archer said. "Get to work, men!"

They slung their bows over their shoulders, drew knives, and went about their task.

"Sire, head to the center of camp. I'll order the search to begin," Jomar said.

"Have the woodsyths and firesyths search. Anyone with stonesyth talent should work on burying the dead," I said.

"Even the Satran, Sire?"

"*All* of the dead, and bury them well. We don't need Bonetakers using this battlefield for supplies, making Stoneskins to use against us."

"Understood, m'lord. Stay safe. I'll meet with you soon," he said, saluting before jogging ahead.

Alone, I felt vulnerable and exposed. *What if the retreat was a trap?* The cut on my hand made it uncomfortable to grab my hammer, but being prepared was worth the minor pain.

Keeping my talent pushed through the ground around me, I walked through the Satran camp, passing dead bodies, Satran and Croian alike. Even though I didn't feel anything moving, I stayed alert, watching for unexpected threats.

At the splintered fence where the corral had been, I let myself relax a little. *If only they'd have used a wall, we'd have horses now.* More than anything, I did my best to ignore the soldier's body lying not far from me. Seeing arrows jutting out from him made my shoulder ache.

My talent told me someone approached from the east. My arms moved my hammer into a defensive position without me thinking about it.

General Jomar smiled and bobbed his head. "Relax, Sire. It's only me."

I returned his smile and clicked my hammer onto my back. "Anything to report, general?"

"Men are breaking into groups to search, m'lord."

"Have you seen Fastulf?"

He nodded. "Yes. I left him and his guides, with three other companies, guarding the river in case the Legion regroups to attack."

"Glad to hear they survived. Do you think they would counter-attack this soon?"

He scratched his chin. "Considering we took them by surprise, I doubt it, but I want to be ready in case they want some revenge." He pointed to the largest tent near us. "In the meantime, I'd like to search in there, m'lord. It looked like one of their leaders was in this tent. Who knows what we might find inside."

"As good a place to start as any. After you, general."

The tent's interior was clean but held the musty smell of old, weathered cloth, along with a hint of smoke from the earlier fire. Though not exactly pleasant, I preferred it to the odor of death lingering outside.

Looking around, it reminded me of my own tent, except the small table was knocked over, and the chairs were scattered. A backpack lay on the ground near the back wall, but the place was otherwise empty.

"No bed, no chest. General, either he wasn't a leader, or they packed light."

"I'm guessing they packed light, Sire," he said, grabbing the backpack and dumping it out. "Not much there either, a sack and a change of clothes."

"What's in the sack?"

"Food. A couple of apples, a few hard rolls, and some dried meat strips." He sniffed at the strips. "These don't smell right."

"It's not like those go bad," I said, holding out my hand.

He handed me a piece, and I smelled it. The earthy scent reminded me of the air in Tudal's kitchen back in Varia. "I'd guess it was prepared with the herbs used in Satran cooking. Likely the rolls were too."

"How do you know about Satran cooking?" Jomar asked, brow furrowed.

"There's an eatery in the Varian capital run by a man with Satran roots. It's not bad once you get used to it. Enjoy your meal." I smiled, handing the strip back to him.

"I'd rather not," he said, curling his lip while putting everything back in the sack. "You sure you don't want the food, Sire?"

I shook my head. "Keep it or give it to one of our wounded. At least the apples might be a comfort."

"Good idea, m'lord. I'll pass it on. And the clothes?"

"Maybe one of the Bane would use them, better than the tattered rags most of them wear."

"True. I'll send someone after them later. Where to now?"

"Since I'm well rested, I'll help bury the dead until Bior returns. Are you going to continue searching the camp?"

He nodded. "I'm sure they'll appreciate the help, m'lord. I'll let you know if we find anything interesting."

I left to help our other stonesyths cover the bodies of our fallen and our enemies. Though it pained me to do it, I made sure to press the ground hard against the bodies so their bones snapped. *Can't leave anything for the Bonetakers to use against us.*

Bior, red-faced and huffing breath, found me. "Sire. Sorry it took so long."

"Sit. Catch your breath." I said, pulling seats for us.

He nodded and sat next to me. "Anything interesting yet, m'lord?"

"I haven't heard of anything yet. A supply of clean bandage cloth would be nice, but I'd be surprised if we find anything useful. The tent across from us was pretty bare. What kept you? Or do I not want to know?"

"Asfrid asked me to help her prepare some ointments and pastes before the wounded arrived."

I patted his knee. "It was for the best. Hopefully, our herbalists join us soon. They can take most of the burden off her. Any idea of how many wounded we have?"

He shrugged. "I passed a few on my way back. If I had to guess, I'd say twenty ... maybe thirty, Sire. No more than fifty men, at most. Do you know how many were killed?"

"Haven't heard yet. I know Fastulf and his company are whole. General Jomar left them with a few other companies to guard —"

"My king!" General Jomar yelled, interrupting me, from somewhere nearby. "Where are you?"

"Over here!" I yelled back. "Talking with Bior!"

"We're almost through searching! Stay there; I'll come to you!"

Jomar jogged into sight and saluted after stopping in front of me. "Aside from the tents themselves, we've found swords, axes, a few bows, many arrows, food, waterskins, clothes, and Satran armor, Sire. We haven't cleared the dirt used to bury the flaming tents yet, though."

I nodded. "Do you expect to find anything of use under there?"

"I find it odd we haven't found any herbalist supplies, not even bandages."

"Until recently, our army didn't travel with herbalists. Maybe Satra's Legion doesn't," I said.

"It's also possible the fire was set on purpose to keep us from capturing something." Jomar paused. "More than anything, I want to be thorough, my king."

"After the stonesyths finish covering the dead, have them clear the dirt," I said.

"My thoughts exactly, Sire," Jomar said.

"Dispose of the armor. We don't need it, and I'd rather the Legion doesn't get it back. Burn it, bury it, throw it in the river ... whatever's best."

"Again, I agree."

"We'll invite the exiles to take the clothes. Whatever they don't want —" I paused and looked at Bior. "What should we do with them?"

He shrugged. "I doubt any of our men would want Satran clothes, Sire. And I see no reason to ask our warriors to carry a load we have no use for."

I nodded. "Then, whatever the exiles don't take stays here."

Jomar pursed his lips before shaking his head.

"Which leaves the food," I said.

"Be midday soon. Eating their food for lunch seems like a good idea," Bior said.

"It's flavored with Satran herbs. Our warriors might not like the taste," I said. "Offer it to the exiles first but don't leave any for the Legion to find later."

"I'll have it delivered to them, Sire," Jomar said. "Given everything we've done today, our warriors need to rest. I'd advise we plan to stay the night here. Gives us time to plan our next move."

"Also gives our herbalists time to catch up, assuming they move today," Bior added.

I looked at Jomar for a moment before nodding. "General, get food and water to the guards first. Once the burials are finished, send half of the stonesyths to relieve the guards so they can get some sleep, especially Fastulf's company. I want them leading the night watch."

"The exiles are fresh. Will they help?" Jomar asked.

"Do you trust them to guard us?" Bior countered.

I sighed. "Bior, find Rorec. Ask him to meet with me. I'll be in the big tent."

"Aye, Sire," Bior said, getting to his feet.

"Jomar, join us as soon as you can."

"Of course, m'lord." Jomar saluted.

As they left, I returned to the leader's tent and took a moment to right the table and place the scattered chairs around it.

• • • • • • • • • •

Though I expected Bior to return first, Jomar entered the tent.

"Everything's going well?"

"Well-trained warriors follow orders, m'lord. The joy of a victory helps too."

"Let's hope the triumph continues."

"I feel the same, Sire, but there are too many unknowns for me to have much confidence. We were tested today, and we won, but not without cost."

"How many men did we lose?"

He hung his head. "One hundred twenty-three, m'lord, including Sergeants Trygg and Gunnkel as well as Commander Ketill."

I sucked a hissing breath.

He nodded. "But, we killed nearly four hundred Satran soldiers, m'lord."

"If we knew how big the Legion was, that might seem like a fair trade," I said.

"Thus my reservation, Sire. Don't expect our men to beat them three to one for the entire war. Also, they can gather more men while we fight only with the men we have."

"But those won't be well trained and, maybe, not even willing to fight."

"A scared man with a weapon is still dangerous, Sire."

"True enough," I said, nodding. "But he's far less of a threat —"

Bior stepped into the tent with Rorec close behind.

"Welcome, Rorec. Thank you for coming, and please pass my thanks to Asfrid for tending to our wounded."

"Of course," he said, sitting.

"The general and I were discussing the possibility of Satra's Legion gathering men to replace their losses," I said.

"They will," Rorec said.

"Untrained men are less of a threat to our warriors," I said, "at least, in my opinion."

"The danger's less obvious but still real. Expect the Legion to put new fighters in harm's way first. Green warriors fighting for their lives may lack discipline but fight hard. They will all die, but the fighting wears your warriors down. Their seasoned soldiers will attack once yours are exhausted," Rorec said.

"Sound plan when you think about it," Bior commented.

"Good to know. Thank you, Rorec. Make sure you discuss this with the commanders, general."

Jomar nodded.

"Now, for the real reason I asked you here, Rorec. We need more help from the Bane. I lost a good number of warriors. The men left standing are tired, and I need guards for night watch."

"Why not go to Sift with this request yourself?" Rorec asked.

"I'm not sure he's giving me his full support."

"What makes you doubt him?" Rorec asked.

"The Bane he sent to help Fastulf guide us were called back after they carried an injured archer to Asfrid. They haven't returned."

"He wanted them to report something," Bior added.

"And I see no reason that requires keeping all of them," I said. "They are all strong stonesyths, and we could have used their assistance."

"I'm sure he has a good reason," Rorec said.

"But it doesn't help me — us. You have his trust. I need you to use your influence to Croy's benefit."

"I'll do what I can. What, exactly, do you need?" Rorec asked.

"I need people who can stand watch, guard the camp, while my warriors rest," I said.

"Preferably men who will fight if the Legion comes back," Jomar said.

"Most Bane aren't fighters," Rorec said, shaking his head.

"They don't have to fight to raise an alarm," I said. "Although we have plenty of weapons now, and Jomar's point about a scared, armed man being dangerous is not lost on me."

"Nor on me, but —"

"But nothing," Bior interrupted him. "Either Sifet wants us to win, or he's been lying the entire time."

"Tell Sifet his people should share the camp with us tonight," I said. "Makes it easier to protect everyone."

"I'll do my best, Fitzeirick. Anything else?"

"Yes. Although we haven't found any supplies to help the wounded, Asfrid is welcome to a tent so she can work in a cleaner space. Perhaps some Bane can help her move men and supplies when they come to take their place as guards."

"I'm sure she'd welcome the tent and the help," Rorec said. "Anything else?"

I looked at the general. "Jomar?"

"I need to know we have guards we can trust."

Rorec nodded. "Sifet's followers are loyal to him. If he's in camp, they'll do what they can to keep him safe."

"So long as they make enough noise to wake our warriors," Jomar said, nodding.

"Shouldn't be a concern," Rorec said. "Do I have your permission to leave, Fitzeirick?"

"Anything to add, Bior?" I asked.

"No, Sire."

"You may go, Rorec. Do your best to make Sifet see this is in everyone's best interest," I said.

"As I can."

"I'd like to see if there's been any progress clearing the dirt, Sire," Jomar said. "I'll report as soon as I know anything."

"Let's hope it's not a waste of time and energy, general."

"At least we'd know we didn't miss anything important, m'lord." He stood, saluted, and left.

"Hungry, Sire?" Bior asked.

"Best to eat when we can," I said. "Let's see what Satra left for us."

Chapter 71

We left the tent searching for captured food. It didn't take long to find the pile of sacks next to a mound of clothes and various weapons.

"Well met, Sire," Commander Osvif said, saluting. "Good to see you."

"Well met, commander. Word is we lost some leaders today," I said. "Sorry to hear it."

"The risk we all take," he said. "No time to grieve now, m'lord. And no doubt there's lots of fighting yet to do. We'll remember their sacrifices later. What can I do for you, Sire?"

"Bior and I were wondering what there was to eat," I said.

"Not much different from what we brought, m'lord. Except they have apples or pears," Osvif said.

"We'll take a sack and be on our way."

He nodded. "Help yourselves, Sire."

I grabbed a rough, woven bag.

"We put the waterskins inside the tent over there to keep them in the shade, m'lord," the commander said, pointing.

"Thank you. Bior, grab a couple and meet me in the big tent."

"Will do, Sire."

Dalibor was inside when I got there.

I raised my eyebrows. "Why are you here?"

"Vos Sifet sent me, wise king. But, while we're alone, we'll discuss the real reason."

"You'd best speak quickly."

"Sifet is causing you trouble, no?"

I crossed my arms. "People around me have some concerns, but your offer is not a solution I'm willing to consider."

He cocked his head. "Yet, it would be effective and to your advantage."

Yes, but it's not an option … regardless. I closed my eyes. "Why did your vos send you?"

"I'm here to let you know the Bane will help your men watch tonight. Also, I am to ask which tents will be set aside for us."

"We aren't through searching the camp," I said, opening my eyes and staring at him. "After we're done, we'll set aside a place for the exiles."

"Understood, wise king. We stand ready to come in once you give the word."

I pressed my lips together for a moment and took a deep breath. "Tell Vos Sifet he can bring his people into the camp now. There's no reason to wait. Everyone is welcome to help with the search or clean up and prepare the camp. Any assistance would show my men our alliance is useful. Some of my leaders have noticed we are doing most of the work. I tell them Sifet's people, your people, are here to help, but my words only go so far."

"I will let him know, King of Croy."

I stepped aside to let him leave.

Bior nearly bumped into the Satran adviser as he exited the tent.

Dalibor snorted at him before continuing on his way.

"Sire, what was he doing here?" Bior asked.

I put my finger across my lips and pointed to a chair.

He nodded, and we took our seats.

Glancing over his shoulder, Bior turned to me and raised an eyebrow.

Reaching out with my talent told me Dalibor was still walking away, and no one else would be close enough to hear anything we said. "Delivering a message."

"Good news or bad, Sire?" Bior asked, handing me a skin.

"A little of both, most likely."

"Why the secrecy, m'lord?"

"I suspect he's spying for Sifet. Even if he isn't, the less he knows, the better."

"Aye, Sire, I agree. What's for lunch?"

I emptied the sack onto the table; six hard rolls, a dozen strips of meat, two apples, and two pears.

The rolls and meat were seasoned differently than what we carried. Their earthy flavor reminded me of Tundal's food back in the Varian capital.

Bior wrinkled his nose. "What did they do to this?"

I took a drink of sweet water from the skin. "Tastes like Satran food to me."

"I'll take your word for it, Sire. Can't say I care for it much."

I nodded. "Don't get me wrong, I've had better. What I'd like to know is why their water has a sweetness ours doesn't."

He shrugged. "Couldn't tell you, m'lord. What's the rest of the day hold?"

"Depends," I said. "If Jomar's efforts to clear the dirt uncover anything interesting, we'll likely be involved. On the other hand, Sifet's actions could demand my attention before the day's over."

"What do you mean, sire?"

"For a man who insisted on a binding pact between us, he doesn't seem eager to offer much aid."

"Perhaps he's worried about tensions between our warriors and his people, m'lord."

"I've made it clear the exiles aren't our enemy; there should be no tension. Fastulf accepted their help. If he'll have a Satran at his side, anyone should."

"Sire, I'll be the first to admit I'm not entirely comfortable having them around. Hard to trust people who could be ordered to stab you in the back."

"I know what you mean, but something tells me not everyone standing with Sifet blindly follows his orders. The Bane ..." I shrugged. "They'll do whatever it takes to avoid punishment. That's the life they live. I would never treat anyone like that."

He scratched his head for a moment. "The only others with Sifet are his advisers, Rorec, and Asfrid."

I nodded. "And Rorec swears he's loyal to Croy. Asfrid's had *his* back for almost her entire life. Her loyalty is rock solid."

"Leaving four advisers to watch out for." Bior rubbed his hands together. "Tell me, Sire, which do you suspect?"

I trust Bior with my life, but I can't risk him saying something to the wrong person. "I'll leave it to your own good judgment."

He frowned. "You mean I can't kill Dalibor simply because I don't like him."

I flashed him a smile before crossing my arms. "Sifet's rat is no friend of mine. Regardless, do not act on any decision you reach without my permission, or I risk breaking the blood pact."

He nodded. "What if I have credible evidence one or all of them intends to harm you, m'lord?"

"I expect you to bring said proof to me before taking action. Except for, possibly, Mecik, none of those men pose much of a physical threat unless they attack while I sleep. In which case, you *are* expected to protect me."

"Exactly what I wanted to know, Sire. Thank you."

"Glad we understand each other," I said. "This conversation's getting a bit too serious for my liking. Let's check on Jomar's progress. If he hasn't found anything notable from those burnt tents, I'm going to call the search off and focus on getting everyone settled for the evening."

"Sounds like a solid plan to me, Sire."

Jomar's orders were heard well before we found him standing near a dozen or so men. "I know you're tired ... we all are, but the king wants this done as soon as possible. Get that dirt cleared."

"General," I called. "Anything of interest?"

He turned, saw me, and bowed. "Nothing yet, Sire."

"General," I said, crossing my arms. "Let them rest. We need to get this camp ready for the evening. After they have rested, anyone who wants to search this dirt pile is welcome to do so, provided we have sufficient guards."

Jomar nodded. "As you say, my king."

I flashed a quick smile. "Whatever might be left of those burned tents isn't worth the effort."

He looked from me to the pile of dirt and back before nodding. "You heard the king, leave this and get some rest. We'll ready the camp before dinner."

Judging by the looks on several faces, they would have cheered if they weren't exhausted.

"One more thing, general."

"Of course, Sire. What can I do for you?"

"I've asked the exiles to camp with us tonight. Considering our losses, I wouldn't be surprised if their presence upsets some of our men."

"Agreed, m'lord," Jomar said, nodding.

"I'll leave the decision to you but posting a few trustworthy watchmen between us and them, assuming we have the men to spare, might be a good idea. No sense in spilling allies' blood over misplaced frustration."

"Understood, my king. I'll take it as sound advice," Jomar said. "Is there anything else I need to know?"

"Nothing I can think of at the moment. Bior, anything to add?"

"No, m'lord."

"General, you have a lot to do. Move quickly and let me know if you have any problems," I said.

He saluted. "Yes, Sire."

"What now, m'lord?" Bior asked, as Jomar jogged away.

"I'm going to see what Sifet's planning to do with his people."

"Not to question your judgment, Sire, but if Dalibor went straight to his leader from your tent, Sifet hasn't had much time to decide. I got the impression he's the kind of man who doesn't like to be pestered."

I looked at him and rubbed the stubble on my chin. "You're right. So, what are we going to do while we wait?"

"Well, m'lord, you've been concerned about Fastulf since the fighting started. Why not find him and see how he's doing?"

"Good idea. I should have thought of it myself," I said.

"Another reason to keep me around, my king," Bior said, smiling.

I chuckled. "Among many. Let's see what he has to say."

Bior nodded before taking his place beside me as we headed for the eastern side of the camp.

Chapter 72

We found Garda and asked where we could find his leader.

He pointed toward the river. "Cleaning blood off his armor, m'lord."

Someone else's, I hope. I thanked him, and we continued on.

Fastulf stood, wiping his hands down the leather on his forearms as the river came into our view, about thirty paces from the camp.

"Well met," I called.

He turned and nodded when he saw us. "Well met, Sire."

I waved him over, not wanting to get too far from camp.

After shaking like a dog, he hurried toward us. "Any fight you live to clean up after is a good one, m'lord."

Bior chuckled.

"I wanted to thank you for your part in the attack and make sure you were well," I said.

"Your concern is appreciated, Sire, as is your praise, but my men contributed as well. I don't deserve all the glory."

"Pass on my thanks. I lost track of you once the fighting started. What happened?"

"The Satran soldiers seem to like leaving themselves open for surprise attacks. We dropped three guards without making a sound before spreading out and going from tent to tent, slitting throats. I got six before anyone realized they were under attack."

"And your men?" Bior asked. "Were they as effective?"

"More or less." He shrugged. "They know what their job is, and they do it well. I do have a question, Sire. Where did the dust cloud come from?"

"Before I explain that, do you know anything about how the fire started?" I asked, grinning.

"I don't, m'lord...wasn't working in that part of the camp. None of my men mentioned seeing anything either."

He nodded as I told him about the Bane stonesyths raising the dirt wall and collapsing it onto the burning tents.

"Smart," he said, still nodding. "Jitka's got a good head on her shoulders, m'lord. Shame her people don't see her potential. I am surprised they could syth a wall that high from so far away, though."

"Never thought I'd see the day you would praise a Satran," Bior remarked.

Fastulf shrugged. "She's not like the Satran we've fought."

I explained how it hurt when my talent brushed against their energy as I tried to figure out how they raised the wall together.

He shook his head. "Never heard of such a thing, Sire. No idea what it could mean."

"I've never woven my talent with another stonesyth either. It could be the combined energy that protects itself ... or something. Or maybe it has something to do with their techniques?"

"Seems the Satran do many things different from us, m'lord," Bior commented.

"That's the truth," Fastulf said, yawning.

"Let's get you back to your men before you fall asleep out here, alone," I said. "You should have guards to relieve you soon so you can get the rest you deserve."

"I'm good to sunset, if needed, Sire," he said.

Bior shook his head. "A tired warrior is a sloppy warrior."

"And a sloppy warrior is a dead one," I finished.

Fastulf raised his hands. "I know, Sire ... believe me, I know."

"So, do as you're told and rest when you can," I said.

He nodded. "We'll rest once Jomar sends more men."

We bid them farewell and continued back to my tent.

As we got closer to the center of camp, the smell of woodsmoke grew stronger.

"Another fire, m'lord?" Bior asked, looking around.

"Doubtful," I said. "No one seems upset. I'm thinking someone made cooking fires."

"Possible," Bior said, "or, at least, as good a guess as I have."

Before the tent came into view, I noticed the top of a stone building standing where the corral was. Smoke curled out of a hole in the roof.

"That's new," Bior quipped.

"For a group who was supposed to be resting, some stonesyths have been busy," I said.

Bojan and Branko stood outside my tent.

"What are they doing here?" Bior asked.

"I'll find out. Go see why we have a new building," I said.

"Aye, Sire. Be careful."

I tapped my hammer's handle. "Shouldn't be a problem."

He smiled and jogged ahead.

I saw no reason to hurry and kept a steady pace to my tent. "Bojan. Branko. Well met. What can I do for you?"

"Vos Sifet waits for you inside, King Fitzeirick," Bojan said.

"I see. How long have you been here?" I asked.

Branko glanced at the sky. "Not long enough for Vos Sifet to get restless."

I nodded and stepped into the tent. Sifet was alone, sitting in my chair.

Where's Dalibor? I pushed my talent out, searching for the shady adviser but found no one but Sifet, Bojan, and Branko.

"Welcome, young king. Sit, so we can talk."

"Sorry I kept you waiting," I said, leaving my talent flowing while taking the seat across from him. "Had I known you were coming, I'd have returned sooner."

Lacing his fingers together, he rested his wrists on the edge of the table. "No worries. Most of my followers have not come yet. We still don't know where we're staying tonight."

"General Jomar is supposed to be preparing the camp for everyone. Did Dalibor not tell you everyone was welcome?"

He nodded. "I wasn't sure he understood your meaning. One of your commanders, Oz-fif, I believe, said as much when we arrived. He met us at the edge of the camp and told me where to find your tent."

"Osvif," I said, correcting him.

"Yes. I asked him if we could be of help. He said your cooks were unhappy with working in tents. I understand there was a fire during the attack. Seems they feared starting another. The Bane who helped you earlier offered to make a suitable place to cook."

"The stone building behind me?" I asked.

"Obviously, young king. There are no other stone workings here."

No sense in being rude. If not for our pact, I'd make you pay for it. "Please pass along my thanks for their effort."

"Words of praise mean little to their clan. They do their job and know they did right because they didn't get punished."

I closed my eyes and sighed. "That may be your way, but it isn't mine. Good work is recognized, bad work is corrected."

"Remember, young king, you are not yet in a position to change Satra's ways."

Crossing my arms, I leaned forward. "I'm aware — painfully aware. Doesn't mean I have to follow them. If you will not thank them, I will do it personally. Is there anything else?"

He rolled his eyes before nodding. "Where were you planning to go tomorrow?"

"I planned to discuss that with my leaders over dinner. You are welcome to join General Jomar and me for a meal, share any advice you may have."

"I need to eat with my followers, but I can tell you where to go next now if you'd like." I nodded. "I'm listening."

"Follow the river south but stay off the banks ... use the forest to your advantage. At a good pace, you'll reach a village before dark. Wajda's elder was friendly to me and mine before. It's likely we'd be welcomed there again."

"I won't trade more people for safety or lodging," I said.

"Shouldn't be a concern in Wajda, but a wise king would know an oiled wheel stays quiet, moves easier."

"People aren't coin," I said, standing.

"Not in Croy, young king, but this isn't Croy." He gave me a toothy smile as he rose to his feet. "I believe this meeting is done."

I nodded. "Thank you for the information."

He chuckled as he passed me. "I do what I can, young king. I do what I can."

And when necessary, you'd best be ready to do more.

The rough tent cloth scraped against his hand as he left.

"Oh, one more thing, Vos Sifet," I said, turning to watch him go.

"Yes, King of Croy." He didn't turn to look at me.

"Will Jitka and the others be guiding us again? My men appreciated the help."

He shrugged. "I see no reason why not."

"Thank you, once more, for your assistance."

He nodded and left.

Bior walked in as I moved to my seat.

"Thank you for waiting outside," I said. "Did you have a good conversation with them?"

He looked over his shoulder and growled before sitting. "I didn't want to wait, Sire. They stood in my way and wouldn't move."

"You should have said something," I said, frowning.

He raised his eyebrows. "I was afraid to cause a commotion and interrupt you getting Sifet to cooperate."

I snorted. "I've seen mules more willing to help. At least he let me know we're not far from a friendly village. As far as you being kept from joining me, I'll make sure it doesn't happen again. On to a happier subject, how's the kitchen? Are the cooks pleased with the work the Bane did for them?"

Bior's gawked for a moment. "I'm guessing Sifet told you."

"He did, but you didn't answer my question. Is the work satisfactory?"

"Did my best to stay out of the way, but everyone looked pleased. Did he tell you they sythed big stone pots to make stew for dinner?"

"No."

"Well, they did. And the cooks seemed to appreciate them. More importantly, the village Sifet mentioned it won't be like the last one, will it?"

I gave a quick summary of where he recommended we go next.

"Do you trust him, Sire? I'm not sure many of us are willing to allow that kind of trade again."

I shrugged. "I said as much to him. He assured me Wadja was friendly. I suppose something could have changed between now and the last time he was here. Still, it seems like a strange time to set us up for trouble when he could have let us wander into a hostile village without warning before."

"True enough. But does it warrant trust, though, Sire?"

"I want to discuss this with Jomar before making a final decision. Also, the Bane guides are coming back to help Fastulf's company ... surely they would warn us of any problems they know about."

"Right," Bior said, nodding.

I crossed my arms. "Given where we are, how little we know of these lands, passing through someplace friendly would be welcome. Who knows, maybe we could gain more allies there."

He sighed heavily and shook his head. "Just what we need, Sire, more people most of us don't trust."

"I didn't say it was a given conclusion, more like a possibility. There must be Satran citizens who are unhappy under Bonetaker rule."

"Other than the exiled ruler and his followers, you mean, m'lord," he said, smiling wide.

I glared at him for a moment. "Goes without saying."

"Hey! You there! Stop!" Someone yelled nearby.

Bior and I looked at each other before jumping to our feet.

"On the ground! On your knees! Now!" The voice came from behind my tent somewhere.

Chapter 73

We ran in the direction of the yelling but saw no one as we passed the large tent.

What is going on? Bior's limping gait couldn't keep up with my strides, and I left him behind as I passed another row of tents.

"Don't move!"

Beyond the next group of tents, I found a warrior, axe in hand, approaching a small group cowering on the ground.

"What is the meaning of this?" I demanded.

"My king." He saluted. "I caught them sneaking around, looking through these tents."

"They're our men," I said.

Bior arrived, sucking his breath loudly.

"They're Satran, dressed as us, Sire," the guard said, gesturing with his weapon.

"They are here at *my* invitation," I said, putting my hands on my hips.

"Best put your axe away," Bior warned.

"Jitka, are you unharmed?" I asked.

"Yes, right. Friend King Fist-er-rick."

"See," I said. "She knows me. I appreciate your concern but return to your post."

He saluted again. "Yes, m'lord."

"Jitka, what are you doing over here?" I asked, as she slowly stood.

"Looking for Friend Fast-elf."

"He's resting with his men. Why didn't you look for him after you made the kitchen?"

"Vos Sifet didn't tell us we could."

Bior grunted.

"I see. Let's see if we can find out where Fastulf is. How long are you going to stay with him?"

"At least to Wajda."

"Everyone, come with me. Bior, it might be best if you bring up the rear in case we run into another zealous guard."

"As you say, Sire."

We paraded through the camp, gathering fewer stares than I expected until I found Commander Galtis. He didn't know where Fastulf was but pointed us south to where General Jomar should be.

It didn't take long to reach the southern edge of the captured camp. Jomar was easy to find by following the sound of shouted orders.

"General," I called. "Well met. A moment or two."

He turned, saluted, and eyes grew wide when he looked past me and saw the Bane gathered behind me. "Of course, m'lord. What can I do for you?"

"First, do you know where Fastulf is resting?"

"No. Not exactly. But I'd check the group of tents near the eastern edge of camp first, Sire."

I nodded. "Second, I'd like for you to join me for dinner this evening so we can discuss plans for tomorrow. I have some information for you to consider."

He smiled. "Gladly. Can't wait to hear it, m'lord."

"Good. General, I leave you to your work."

"I take it they are willing to help again, Sire?" he asked, tilting his head toward the Bane.

"They are. That's why I'm looking for Fastulf."

"Understood, my king. Hope your search doesn't take long." He saluted before turning to shout more orders.

We made our way northeast and found Fastulf asleep, with three of his men, in the second tent we checked.

"Wait out here," I said, to the group of Bane before Bior and I stepped inside.

"Wake him carefully, m'lord," Bior warned. "Considering what he does, he could be jumpy."

I nodded and called Fastulf's name softly.

He didn't budge, not even a twitch.

I know I hate to be grabbed in my sleep, so ... Tapping his boot with mine made him move his leg a little.

Progress. "Fastulf," I said, a little louder.

"Lemme sleep. General said we could rest."

"Warrior, I need you on your feet," I said.

His eyes flew open. "S-S-Sire," he stammered, rising clumsily to his feet, disturbing the warrior lying nearby.

"Sorry, my king," Fastulf said. "Didn't know it was you. What can I do for you, m'lord?"

"No need to apologize," I said, before turning to hold the tent flap open. "Your Bane friends got in a little trouble looking for you."

He leaned to look past me and smiled. "Jitka, it's good to have you — your group — back with us. I'll be out in a moment."

"Right, yes, Friend Fast-elf. Happy to see you," she replied, nodding.

"Try to keep them out of trouble," I said, to him. "And, maybe, arm them ... teach them how to fight. If they're going to wear our armor, they need to be ready to face our enemy."

"Understood, Sire. I'll do my best," Fastulf said, saluting.

"One more thing. I'm having dinner with General Jomar to talk about our next move. Join us since you're going to lead the way."

He nodded. "Gladly, m'lord."

I smiled, hoping more good than harm would come from us helping the Bane, and stepped out of the tent. "Bior, let's see if we can get an idea of when dinner will be ready."

· · · · ● · ● · · ·

Entering the kitchen, smiles greeted us even though everyone dripped with sweat. Smells of boiling meat mixed with the smoke made me feel warm, almost comfortable.

"Well met, men," I said, returning their smiles with one of my own. "The food smells good. When will it be ready?"

"Well before sunset, my king," a nearby cook said.

"So long as everyone gets a hot meal. They deserve it," I said.

"No worry, Sire. The building holds heat well," he said, looking around.

"Next time I see the Bane who raised it, I'll give them your thanks," I said.

"Who knew a group of Satran could be so helpful," he said, nodding.

"The Bane live to serve," I replied. "Most try hard to do their best."

"Not a bad way to live life."

"Trust me," I said, frowning, "you don't want to live the life of their clan. You work hard for pride. They do so to avoid punishment."

"So, they're slaves?"

"Close enough," Bior commented.

I nodded. "He's right, but don't treat them as such. Show them Croians are better than their own people."

"Aye, Sire. We will."

"Thank you for your effort," I said.

"You're welcome, Sire. I'll make sure you are the first served," the cook said.

I shook my head. "Make sure the warriors are fed first. They deserve it after fighting this morning."

"If you insist, Sire."

"I do. Also, along with Bior, General Jomar and Fastulf will be in my tent for dinner. Make sure we have enough to eat."

"Aye, my king. I'll see you're well taken care of."

I nodded. "Not asking for special treatment, as long as no one goes to sleep hungry."

"Understood, m'lord."

I turned to Bior. "Now, we have nothing left to do but wait."

"I'm following you, Sire," Bior said.

"Interested in a few rounds of King's Table?" I asked, as we entered our tent.

"Is now the best time to play games, Sire?" Bior asked.

"I need something to take my mind off Sifet and his stubbornness. Plus, thinking over strategies will help me focus better in the coming battles," I said.

He shrugged. "Sound reasoning, I suppose."

I sythed a small board and the playing pieces from the ground and set the game on our table.

"Your attack," I said, nodding to Bior.

He smirked and made his first move.

• • • • • • • • • •

"Sire," someone said. "You might want to put that away."

"What?" I asked, rubbing my temples while trying to figure out how Bior was ahead three games to one.

"My king, General Jomar isn't far behind," Fastulf said.

"Oh," I said, turning the game to dust and brushing the pile off the table. "Guess we'll have to continue our competition some other time."

Bior frowned and looked over his shoulder as Fastulf took the seat to my left.

The general stepped into the tent before my assistant could say anything. "Good evening, Sire. Bior. Fastulf. Porters are heading this way."

"Best be seated," I said, gesturing to the seat across from me. "Before we eat, I want to thank you for your efforts in this war. Please pass my gratitude on to your men. At the same time, caution everyone against expecting an easy victory. Yes, we won today but not without losses. We caught the Legion by surprise, don't expect it to happen again."

Three porters entered the tent. "Dinner, Sire."

"I'll do the honors," Bior said, as they left. He ladled my bowl full of steaming liquid, then served Jomar and himself before giving Fastulf a portion.

From the smell rising out of my bowl, the cooks used the meat strips we'd captured to make this meal.

"Wise words, my king," Jomar said. "I agree."

"If they don't post more guards, we'll always catch them unprepared," Fastulf commented.

"Would be nice," I said, nodding, "but don't expect it. Surely they'll learn from their mistakes."

"One would think, Sire, but we've often noticed the Satran do things for reasons we don't understand," Bior said.

Fastulf, mouth full of stew, nodded enthusiastically.

"Sire, you mentioned you had information to share," Jomar said.

I swallowed the thin stew. "Met with Vos Sifet earlier. He advised me to travel south, through the woods, and we would find another village. One friendly to him as far as he knows."

"Any chance this is a trick?" Jomar asked.

"Same question I asked," Bior commented.

"Considering he didn't let us blindly wander into a hostile village before, why point us toward a trap now?" I asked.

"We killed a lot of Legion men today," Fastulf said.

Jomar nodded. "Perhaps the exiled ruler thinks we hurt them bad enough he can finish the job himself."

"With less than sixty unarmed, untrained people, most of whom have never stood up for themselves?" I asked, looking from one man to the next. "The Satran way of thinking may be strange, but no one's that foolish."

"The Bane aren't fighters," Fastulf said. "I couldn't get even one of them to swing a *stick* in anger, much less wield a real weapon."

"Regardless, Sifet doesn't have enough fighters to face the Bonetakers, much less the Legion," I said. "Rest assured, he doesn't have my complete trust. There were opportunities for him to reach out to me when Eirickson broke the deal between Croy and Satra. Sifet chose to attack my lands. Instead of talking, he killed our people. I haven't forgotten. Eirickson paid for his treachery, but the debt is not yet erased."

"Good," Bior said.

"Did he say anything about where to go after we reach the next village?" Jomar asked.

"We didn't discuss it. I invited him to join us this evening. He declined," I said.

"For someone who insists they are our ally, he isn't very forthcoming," Jomar said.

"Let me worry about that," I said.

The general dipped his head.

"I'll talk to Jitka and the others, see if they know," Fastulf offered.

I nodded. "But don't press too hard. Could be they won't talk without Sifet's permission."

Fastulf nodded for a moment. "She seems particularly friendly with me, Sire. Maybe she'll tell me things she might not say to anyone else."

"Knowing what we might find beyond this village would be helpful," Jomar added.

"I'll ask, nothing more," he said.

"This village, assuming it is still friendly like Sifet claims. Is it worth the extra time it takes tromping through the woods to get there?" Bior asked.

"The trees help hide us from the Legion," I said.

"We have no reason to hide," Fastulf said.

"The forest also makes it harder for them to attack us with a large force," Jomar said. "Hiding or not, the trees work to our advantage."

"Good point, general," Fastulf said, nodding.

"Another problem," Bior said, raising his hand. "We don't know when our herbalists will arrive. How do we keep them from getting lost, or worse, if we go south from here?"

"He has a point," Jomar commented.

"We won't move until after breakfast tomorrow. If the herbalists haven't arrived, we'll leave a message," I said.

Jomar pointed at me. "Leaving information for our enemy to find is a bad idea."

"Is it worse than letting our people wander around to potentially get captured?" I asked.

"We could leave a company or two behind to wait for them," Fastulf suggested.

"And risk them being overrun when the Legion returns to this camp," I argued, crossing my arms. "The Legion will be looking for us anyway. Is it so bad to tell them where we're going? By the time they find the message, we could be a day or more ahead of them."

"Would the Legion attack the village for aiding us?" Jomar asked.

"Be surprised if they didn't," Bior commented. "Or, at least, force the men to join the fight."

"I'm sure the villagers would get a choice; give up their men or die," I said. "Not ideal and not what we want. I'm open to suggestions."

"Rorec seems capable of moving about at will," Bior said. "When we reach the village, have him backtrack to the herbalists and lead them to us."

"Asfrid won't like the idea," I said.

"M'lord, does her opinion carry more weight than the lives of our herbalists or our warriors?" Jomar asked, frowning.

"No, it doesn't. I'll ask him to help once we know the village is a safe haven," I said.

"I know you don't like it, Sire, but it is the best pick from a heap of bad choices," Bior said.

"Listen to your adviser, my king," Jomar said, nodding.

"I know," I said, scowling. "Doesn't mean I have to be happy about it."

Fastulf sighed. "I have a full belly and need to let my men know we'll be heading through the woods tomorrow before seeing if Jitka will talk to me. May I leave, Sire?"

"General Jomar, do you need anything else from Fastulf?" I asked.

"Nothing I can think of, m'lord. If anything comes to mind, I can get with him later." I turned to my adviser. "Bior?"

"No, Sire."

"You are excused, Fastulf. Thank you for your time and observations."

"Anytime you need, my king," he said, standing. "General, I'm likewise available to help as needed."

"Like our king, I appreciate your service," Jomar said. "May your efforts with the Satran girl be to our benefit."

"Thank you, general. I'll do my best." Fastulf saluted before leaving.

"M'lord, why haven't you made him a sergeant?" Jomar asked. "He leads a company and does more work than most commanders."

"General, I prefer to not get involved in the organization of the army unless necessary. If you believe he should be a sergeant, promote him. However, his superiors are all in Croy ... correct?"

Jomar nodded. "True, though Fastulf has operated under what ... three different generals now. Does he truly belong to any leader, m'lord?"

"Command structure on the battlefield flows like water," Bior said. "It's not unheard of for promotions to come from generals other than the one a warrior is under, especially in these conditions."

"Handle it as you see fit," I said. "I won't pressure you either way. Fastulf seems happy doing his job. His men follow him, with or without a title."

The general rubbed his hands together. "True. Maybe I'd best leave well enough alone."

"Again, general, the decision is yours," I said. "What else do we need to discuss? Any problems I don't know about?"

"I'd still like to know what's buried under the dirt in those burned tents. Leaving a stone unturned doesn't sit well with me."

"While I admire your dedication, I don't share your unease. The chance there could be a few bandages or remedies doesn't warrant the effort to recover them."

Jomar nodded. "Understood, my king."

"If there's nothing else, I'd advise you to get some rest. Traveling through the forest will likely be slow, so the earlier we start, the better."

"I agree. A stomach full of warm food is weighing on my eyelids. Best I call it a night while I can still walk to my tent. Sleep well."

"And may you sleep well, too," I said.

The general stood, saluted, and left.

"Go ahead and rest, m'lord. I'll get these back to the kitchen," Bior said.

"Thank you, Bior. I'll help if you need it."

"No. It's not far, even if it takes a couple of trips."

I was asleep before he returned.

Chapter 74

It wasn't often I woke before Bior. Doing my best to move quietly and not disturb his quiet slumber, I crept out of the tent. The moon sat low on the horizon, casting its glow through thick clouds. The smell of smoke drew my attention to the kitchen. Shadows crossed through the glow shining from the entrance. *Didn't expect anyone but guards to be awake.*

Scents of boiling stew filled the air when I stepped inside. Cooks busied themselves stirring large, stone pots over low fires.

"Morning, men," I said, after watching the activity for a moment.

One of them flinched and turned toward me. "Good morning, Sire. Wasn't expecting you," he said, before bowing.

"Pay me no mind," I said, grinning.

"Breakfast is almost ready, m'lord."

"What are you making?"

"Boiling meat strips for a simple stew and thickening it with the extra hard rolls. Should be ready soon, Sire."

"Sounds good," I commented, leaning against the wall to stay out of the way.

"This is ready," someone said, from the far end of the building. "Take a bowl to the king."

A young man hurried toward me, thick stew sloshing side to side in the stone bowl he held. "For you, Sire."

I took it, thanked him, and ate a few spoonfuls. "I'm sure everyone's going to appreciate a warm meal to start the day."

"Good to hear it is to your taste, m'lord. We wanted to use food that may have been wasted or left behind."

"Good thinking, men. I'll finish this and be on my way."

"You're welcome to stay, my king."

"Thank you, but I need to wake Bior and prepare to leave. You'd best be ready to feed everyone before much longer."

"We'll be ready, Sire. Don't worry."

"Sounds good. Expect Bior to come sniffing for something to eat soon."

Several of the cooks laughed, and the noise followed me out of the building.

Streaks of the first sunlight ran through the clouds. I tried to be quiet entering the tent, but Bior stirred before I said anything. He sat up and blinked several times before rubbing his eyes. "Sire? Why are you up so early?"

"Haven't been awake long. Breakfast is ready in the kitchen."

He jumped to his feet and hurried outside.

Sitting, I tapped my fingers on my helmet for a moment before closing my eyes. Pushing my talent into the ground, I let out a long sigh and relaxed. *Should have taken time to do this yesterday.* Not searching for anything or anyone, my energy mixed with the ground, draining away my stress.

The smell of stew announced Bior's arrival.

"You look happy, Sire," he said, as I opened my eyes.

"Enjoying a moment of calm," I said. "Won't be happy until this war is over."

He sat across from me and ate.

General Jomar entered the tent and saluted. "Well met, Sire."

"Good morning, general." Standing, I returned his salute. "What can I do for you?"

"Wanted to let you know we would be ready to go south once everyone has eaten. Shouldn't be long now."

"Good to hear. Thank you. Any sign of our herbalists?"

"Nothing yet, Sire."

I nodded. "Have you talked to Fastulf this morning?"

"No. Should I send him your way?"

"Not necessary. I'm going to tell Rorec to look for our herbalists, then head to the front and get ready to leave. I'm sure we'll find out if Fastulf got any information from his Bane friends in due time."

"Hopefully not after it's too late," Bior commented.

"He wouldn't withhold information," I said. "General, if you hear anything, have someone let me know."

"Of course, Sire."

I nodded. "Perhaps this trip will be less eventful than yesterday's."

Jomar chuckled. "Would be nice, Sire, but I wouldn't expect it."

"He doesn't either," Bior quipped. "He likes to sound hopeful from time to time."

I shook my head and laughed. "No one asked you."

"No, but I am right."

"Yes, you are," I said.

Jomar laughed as he left us.

"M'lord, why don't you head to the southern edge of camp? I'll gather our lunch and meet you there?" Bior suggested.

"I'll meet you there after I talk with Rorec," I said, putting on my helmet and clicking my hammer onto my armor.

Bior hurried out of the tent.

I made my way to the Satran side of the camp and asked Bojan if he knew where Rorec was.

The adviser pointed me to a tent not far away and said Rorec was talking with some Bane.

Rorec stepped out as I approached.

"Well met," I called, waving.

"I understand we're leaving soon," Rorec said, waving back.

"We are," I said, "but I have a favor to ask."

"I'll do what I can," he said, smiling.

"We expected to have our herbalists join us by now. Considering the only herbalist we have now is your wife and we're preparing to march on the Satran capital, would you be willing to go back, find them, and lead them to us?"

He closed his eyes. "To be clear, you want me to look for men who may or may not arrive. If they do, I'm to lead them to you when you could be days ahead and actively fighting. All the while, my wife is alone and possibly overrun with dead and dying warriors. This is what you ask?"

"I know it is a lot, but I wouldn't ask if I didn't believe you were up to the task. If you do get them to us before the fighting starts, it will be a benefit to your wife. Consider this as service to her *and* Croy."

Opening his eyes, he stared at me for a moment before sighing. "You're not asking for more than I can do. I'll leave after gathering some supplies."

I nodded. "Leave when you're ready."

He offered me his hand. "Keep Asfrid safe while I'm gone."

I shook it. "No harm will come to her."

Rorec bowed and turned to leave.

I hurried to the far edge of camp, hoping Bior didn't decide to come looking for me. Two lines of archers and a company of footmen greeted me when I arrived at the southern edge. "Everyone well rested and fed?" I asked.

"Never, my lord," someone quipped.

Several laughed, and I joined them after a moment.

"Thus, the life of a warrior, it seems," I said, shaking my head.

"Aye, Sire," a nearby archer said.

"Anything moving this morning?" I asked.

"Nothing, m'lord. All's clear as far as we can see," the archer explained.

I nodded. "Sounds like good news. I'm not here for a report. Just waiting until we get moving. I'll do my best to stay out of the way. Pay me no mind."

"My king, if you don't mind me asking, any idea how far until we reach the village we're supposed to find?"

I shook my head. "Like so many other details, I don't know. Assuming it's still there. If those Satran stayed loyal to their exiled ruler, the Legion might have slaughtered them."

He frowned. "Didn't think about that, Sire."

I nodded and crossed my arms. "Believe me, I wish I didn't have to consider the possibility."

The archer looked away. "Aye, Sire."

"If we win, we can change this country ... keep those kinds of things from happening again. Not immediately, though. It will take time."

"Understood, m'lord. A solid, noble goal," he said. "Let's hope it happens."

"With our victory, it will."

He looked at me and saluted.

Bior called to me from behind, approaching with two waterskins across his chest.

"I have food, Sire," he said, patting the backpack Jomar found in the Satran commander's tent. "And we have plenty of water."

"And now we wait," I said.

"Shouldn't be too much longer, according to General Jomar, Sire. He wanted me to tell you to give the order to leave when Fastulf gets here."

"Assuming he arrives before the general, I will. For now, give me one of those skins. No sense in you carrying everything yourself."

"As you say, m'lord."

After hanging the waterskin across my chest, I pulled two seats from the ground. No sooner had we sat than General Jomar approached with Fastulf beside him.

"My king, Fastulf has good news," Jomar said, pointing to the short warrior.

"Sire, Jitka told me the capital is no more than a day's walk southeast of Wajda."

"And how far is Wajda?" I asked, looking southeast.

He shrugged. "She guessed about half a day using the road, but we're going through the forest, so it will be longer."

Jomar shook his head. "And even longer still if we get attacked. Fastulf, take your men to the front, and let's get going."

"Stay alert," I said. "We need to move quickly, but I don't want to be taken by surprise because we weren't careful."

"Understood, Sire." He saluted before turning to the group of people behind him and pointing south. "Spread out ahead. Eyes and ears open. No surprises. We're the best at what we do, so get to it."

"Aye," the group responded, before rushing through the archers and warriors to take positions in the lead. Jitka and the rest of the Bane stayed close to Fastulf.

"Move out!" Jomar yelled.

After climbing the sloping river bank, we entered the forest, and progress slowed to a crawl. The dim sunlight, passing through thick clouds and treetops, did little to light our way. Between weaving around trees and keeping a constant watch, everyone moved slowly.

As we walked deeper into the forest, every noise drew attention. Leaves rustling in a breeze, twigs snapping underfoot, swooping birds protecting their nests; everything was seen as a potential attack until the source was located and found harmless. My right hand spent more time reaching for my hammer than it did at my side.

I jumped when Bior asked if I was ready to eat something, offering a handful of meat strips.

Halfway through the snack, a quiet call to halt came from ahead.

"Think we're near the village, Sire?" Bior whispered.

"No one raised an alarm, so I hope that's why we're stopped."

"Good point, m'lord."

"Let's look for Jomar," I said.

The general found us first. "Sire, Fastulf stopped us when he spotted farmland. He thought a couple thousand armed Croians trampling their way into town might give the wrong impression. I tend to agree. How should we proceed?"

"Not stomping in like an invading horde is a good start. Have everyone wait here. I'll go talk to Sifet. If this place is friendly to him, he should be willing to make proper introductions."

"And if he isn't, m'lord?" Jomar asked.

"We'll burn that bridge after we cross it," I said, grinning. "Bior, wait here."

"Aye, Sire. Hope he cooperates."

Me too.

Sifet and his followers made no effort to mingle with the Croians, which made them both easy to find and more of a walk to reach. Already tired from walking non-stop most of the day, I was frustrated by the time I reached the exiles. Branko was the first non-Bane I found.

"King Fitzeirick, why have we stopped?" he asked.

"Where's Sifet?"

He nodded. "Come with me."

We wandered deeper into the group to Sifet, circled by his other advisers.

"Young king, what brings you?" Sifet asked.

"We're near your friendly village. Instead of storming in like a gang of boors, we want you to lead a few of us into the town and introduce us."

"Dalibor, escort the King of Croy—"

"No!" I barked.

Mecik shifted his weight and reached for his axe.

I cocked my head. "Don't. I'm not in the mood, and neither of us would like the outcome."

The big Satran hesitated, taking a step back when Bojan grabbed his arm.

I nodded. "Sifet, you will escort me and General Jomar, maybe a few others, into Wajda. You will make the introductions and explain we are friendly."

The vos stared at me for a moment before crossing his arms. "Are you done, young king?"

"Yes."

He nodded. "As I was saying, Dalibor will walk with you back to your general while I change to meet with the elder. I will join you soon. Acceptable, young king?"

I glared at him. "Is this necessary? My men are tired and ready to rest for the evening."

"As are mine, young king."

"Then I'll wait for you here," I said. "Make it quick."

"Patience in this matter will likely bring a better result. I will arrive when I am ready ... no sooner. Take Dalibor and introduce him to your council so we look friendly with each other to the elder."

Why do I put up with this? I sighed and looked at the skinny adviser. "Are you ready?"

"I am, King of Croy."

After several paces, Dalibor cleared his throat and leaned close to me. "Give me the word, and I can remove your frustration."

I didn't turn to look at him. "Does our blood pact mean nothing to you?"

"Has he not shown you he's no longer fit to lead?"

"How do I know you haven't made the same offer to Sifet?"

"My ancestors have been the power behind our throne for generations. We're raised to recognize worthy leaders and dispose of those no longer capable of ruling. Your actions speak beyond your borders. What you make of this fact is up to you, King of Croy."

"Regardless of your rearing, my commitment to this pact is binding. What you make of that fact is up to you, adviser."

He snorted but, otherwise, kept quiet.

Passing between groups of my men talking, we drew more attention than I expected. *Guess some still aren't used to the idea of working with these Satran.*

"General Jomar, this is Dalibor, adviser to Vos Sifet."

Jomar nodded. "Welcome."

"Dalibor. My field general."

The adviser bowed. "I've heard your name. An honor to meet you."

Jomar cocked his head for a moment. "Where is your leader?"

"Preparing for the meeting," Dalibor said.

Bior raised his eyebrows but didn't say anything.

"Anything I need to know?" I asked.

"A farmer and two young men were tending their crops a short while ago. From what we could tell, they didn't notice us, m'lord," Jomar said.

"Good," I said, nodding. "Surely they would have raised an alarm if they knew we were here."

"The villagers are familiar with the area," Dalibor said. "You might be surprised at how easily they notice changes. This many people hiding in the forest." He shook his head. "Likely they know you're here."

"Why aren't they preparing to defend their land?" Jomar asked.

"Though not as passive as Bane, Devoted are certainly not like the Legion. They do not fight unless threatened ... most have to be cornered first."

Bior crossed his arms. "And we pose no threat?"

A smirk spread Dalibor's lips. "You let them leave without attacking. No doubt they have told the elder as much. If they are still friendly to Vos Sifet, you are in no danger. If they are not —" He paused and looked over his shoulder. "It's why you have an army, is it not?"

Jomar chuckled. "He's right, Sire. If the villagers attack —" His eyes focused on something behind me.

"Vos Sifet." Dalibor bowed low.

I turned to see Sifet approach with Bojan and Branko on either side. The exiled leader wore dark red robes with a wide, gold collar. Red ribbons were woven into a skull cap. The loose ends fell below his shoulders as if they were meant to look like long hair.

I bowed. "Welcome, honorable Vos. I'd like you to meet General Jomar."

Jomar stepped next to me and bowed. "Your Majesty."

"You flatter me, general. I am no longer majestic ... though I will be again with a Croian victory."

"So, I understand," Jomar said.

"General, this is Bojan and Branko." I nodded to the men flanking Sifet.

"Well met," Jomar said, dipping his head to each.

"Vos Sifet, the Wajda elder likely knows the Croians are here," Dalibor said.

Sifet smiled. "As I would expect. Young king, are your escorts ready?"

I nodded. "Bior, General Jomar, and Fastulf ... with me."

"Aye, Sire," Bior said, saluting.

"I see no reason to carry our supplies with us," I said, placing my waterskin on the ground.

Bior took off his pack and leaned it against a tree.

"After you, Vos Sifet," I said, bowing again.

Sifet swept his arm toward the village. "Branko, lead the way."

Bior moved to walk ahead of me as the Satran lined up.

Seeing Dalibor close behind Sifet made me shiver as I pictured his knife plunging into Sifet's back.

Chapter 75

Branko set a slow pace, carefully moving through the farmer's field to avoid disturbing the crop. We passed a simple, wooden house. I couldn't tell if anyone was watching us from inside.

The next few structures were gray stone with thatched roofs. I guessed they were storehouses. Wooden homes and workshops became more common as we continued into the village.

Branko led us to a two-story, wooden building near a modest market square. The structure looked to be about twice the size of the homes we'd seen so far.

By now, we had attracted a crowd. Sweat rolled down my back as I fought the urge to grab my hammer. Bior's fingers tapped a steady rhythm on his sword's pummel.

"Hand at your side," I whispered.

He nodded and moved his hand away from the weapon.

Sifet cleared his throat.

Branko knocked hard.

The door creaked as it swung inward.

Branko straightened his back and squared his shoulders. "Is the elder in? We require an audience."

"Who makes such demands?" someone demanded.

"Vos Sifet and his allies."

"Bah. Sifet hasn't been this far south in many moons. Most say he's dead. Elder Draza—"

"Radi," Sifet said, voice raised. "I assure you I am not dead."

A Satran man, maybe a few years older than me, stepped out. He wore a tan shirt and brown pants. "Sifet? Is it really you?" he asked.

"Yes, Radi, it's me. Let us in before there's an incident."

The man smiled and waved us in. "Of course, Vos. Come in. Wait in the meeting room. Draza's resting upstairs. I'll send him right away."

Radi climbed a staircase to the right of the doorway.

Branko led us through the wide entry and turned left. He opened a door in the right-hand wall and looked inside. "After you, Vos Sifet."

The exiled ruler nodded before stepping through the door.

We paraded behind him into a large room holding a long, wooden table with enough chairs to seat at least twenty.

Branko stayed in the hall.

What is he waiting for?

Sifet took a chair on the far side of the table, across from the door. "Advisers on my left. King Fitzeirick, on my right. Your men should sit next to you."

Bior growled.

"Be calm," I said, patting him on the shoulder. "Traditions must be honored."

Sifet spoke quietly with Dalibor while we waited.

Closing my eyes, I tried to listen to their conversation but couldn't hear what they said.

Bior's chair squeaked as he fidgeted next to me.

Clunking footsteps echoed in the hall before a barrel-chested, silver-haired Satran stepped into the room. His long beard matched the short-cropped hair on his head. He wore a similar tan shirt and brown pants, similar to Radi's, with the addition of a weathered, leather vest.

"Elder Draza," Branko announced.

Vos Sifet stood, and I rose to my feet as Draza looked from me to the rest of my men.

"Sifet, seems reports of your death are mistaken," the elder said, a crooked grin on his face.

"Thank you for your time, Elder Draza. I am alive and, mostly, well."

"So, I see. Tell me, is Rorec still with you?" Draza asked.

"He and Asfrid are among my followers," Sifet said.

"Good to hear. I always liked him. Am I to assume he's responsible for the interesting company you're keeping these days?"

Sifet dipped his head. "He contributed ... in his own way. This is King Fitzeirick of Croy, son of the late Jarl Eirick, and his men."

"A Croian king?" Draza tilted his head. "This is a new development."

"Not so new as you'd think," Sifet said.

"Your home is impressive," I said.

"One must make the proper impression," Draza said, smiling at me. "I take it those are your advisers, King of Croy."

"Of a sort." I looked to my right. "Bior is my steward, next is General Jomar, and to his right is the leader of our guides, Fastulf."

He nodded then returned his focus to the exiled vos. "Sifet, why have you returned? If Vos Stesha gets word you are this close to the capital, he will find you and kill you."

"Stesha wears the koron now?" Sifet asked, steepling his fingers. "Interesting. I wasn't sure which of the serpents would rise to claim it. As for why I'm here, no doubt you know there's an army outside Wajda."

The elder stepped forward and squared his shoulders. "Are you threatening me?"

"I don't make threats, especially not to old friends," Sifet said, smiling.

"I don't want to get involved," Draza said, lowering his gaze.

"Draza, your loyalty to me has deep roots," Sifet said. "Give us a little of your day. Sit. Let's talk."

The elder looked at Sifet for a few heartbeats and sat across from us.

Sifet nodded and returned to his seat.

I followed his example.

"I'm sitting," Draza said. "Speak."

This is what Sifet calls friendly?

"I have a blood pact with Fitzeirick. We—my followers and the Croian army—are on the way to the capital. Together we seek to eliminate the Bonetakers and restore my rightful position."

Draza raised his eyebrows and gave a long, low whistle. "Your claim is hard to believe, Sifet. Why would the nation of Croy want to help you regain the koron?"

"Though he doesn't care to admit it, King Fitzeirick has many of the qualities of his father. At the least, he cares more for people than his saz-tongued half-brother did," Sifet said.

Draza tilted his head and looked at me. "The jarl I remember didn't let others talk for him."

I never knew Eirick was so involved with Satra.

"Croy has no jarl, and I am not my father," I said, fighting the urge to glare at our host.

"I meant no offense, your Majesty," Draza said. "Still, I would like to hear your words."

"You're not the first to compare me to a jarl, no offense taken," I said, forcing myself to relax. "I believe it takes a strong man to admit when he was wrong. Misunderstandings, caused by hidden truths, brought me to a dangerous conclusion. Vos Sifet saved my life — showed me some of my beliefs were not based on facts. He offered me a chance to benefit my people and yours. I chose to save innocent lives instead of waste them."

"Your words carry conviction. You speak with conviction. Reminds me of your father." He held up his hands. "I say so with respect. There is a sameness to your tone. Your words carry a familiar weight. You have his certainty when you speak."

"If you insist," I said.

He nodded again. "Much has been said, yet I haven't heard *why* you came *here*. What do you want, Sifet?"

"Is it not enough to want to see a friendly face?" Sifet asked.

Draza let loose a loud, cackling belly laugh. "You are surrounded by friendly faces. Save your sugary words for those who don't know better. Speak the truth. Why are you here?"

I tapped my finger on the table. "A safe and secure place to sleep tonight would be welcome. A night's rest for my men would go a long way toward helping our cause."

Sifet glared at me.

The elder's smile disappeared. "This army of yours, how many?"

I looked at Jomar.

"Better than twenty-two hundred people, all told," the general said.

Draza sighed, looked at me for a moment, then shook his head. "Even if I ordered everyone in Wajda to sleep outside, we still don't have the room. Food you want? Supplies? We're lucky to hide enough from the Legion to stay fed until the next harvest. Ignoring the punishment we would face if anyone found out we met with you, I simply can't help you."

"Perhaps you could spare a soft bed and a warm meal for an old friend and a few of his allies?" Sifet asked.

What is he doing? My turn to glare at the vos.

"Your own comfort over that of your followers, Sifet?" Draza asked, frowning.

"He speaks for himself," I said. "I stay with my men. If they are cold, uncomfortable, and hungry, so am I."

The elder scowled. "Don't roll your eyes, Sifet. His men follow him because he's willing to sacrifice. There's wisdom in those words. You'd do well to learn it."

"The King of Croy does not understand Satran ways, Draza."

"The same traditions which cost you your family and your power. Maybe it's best he doesn't take those to heart. It doesn't matter. Wajda cannot offer what you seek."

"Wise elder, will you allow us to stay in the forest and not alert the Legion to our presence?" I asked.

"Your men keep to themselves and take nothing of our crops, animals, or people?" he asked, arms crossed.

"So, I swear," I said. "My companions will see your village remains untouched while we are here."

"Aye," Bior said.

Draza closed his eyes and lowered his head. "You are welcome to stay outside my village, King Fitzeirick. If only we had more to offer."

"Perhaps you do," I said. "How many soldiers are stationed in the capital?"

He looked at me and shook his head. "Since the Bonetakers seized power, I do my best to avoid travel south of here. I can tell you this, Legion soldiers are not the only force guarding Vos Stesha and securing the city. You will face Stoneskins."

"I expected as much," I said.

"Also, from what I'm told, there is a wall protecting the voret where once none stood."

"Voret?" I asked.

"The Vos's home and seat of power," Sifet explained, before turning to Draza. "Why did they raise a wall?"

"Pride, fear, or ..." He shrugged. "Who knows."

"Does this wall protect the city or just the one home?" I asked.

"I have not seen it myself. All the traders tell me is there's a wall where there wasn't one before," he said, resting his hands on the table. "I've told you all I know. It will be dark soon. Best you all be going."

I suspect he's hiding something. I stood. "Again, Elder Draza, thank you for your time. Your information is helpful and appreciated."

Sifet slowly rose to his feet. "Yes, old friend. It was good to see you. Perhaps we'll meet again soon and celebrate victory."

"That sounds nice," Draza said, before looking away from Sifet.

"Branko, lead us back to camp," Sifet said.

Chapter 76

We left the building to find the crowd in the marketplace had grown during our visit.

I don't know how many people live here, but this must be about all of them.

"Stay alert," I said softly. "I suspect this place isn't as friendly as Sifet believes."

"Aye, Sire," Bior said.

"I agree, my king," Jomar added.

Fastulf stayed quiet.

My talent brushed against his as we turned north.

Exactly what I expected of him.

Branko's pace was slower than I would have liked, considering the number of eyes turned our way.

Once we cleared the farmland, I walked faster to get next to Sifet. "When we reach my warriors, I want to talk with you."

"My advisers and I have things to discuss, young king. You may see me afterward."

"No," I said. "You are here, now. There's no reason to wait. After we talk, you have the rest of the evening to spend speaking with whoever you like."

"You would do well to consider how you speak to me, young king."

"It's time you did more than hide among the Bane trailing behind my army."

"How dare you?" He glared at me. "You would have walked into a hostile village in complete ignorance had I not warned you. I traded people for your safe passage, saving untold numbers of your warriors. Even now, my presence afforded you a valuable connection."

"Yet, you did not come to me and freely offer your knowledge. I had to seek you out and ask for your advice. If you do not stop and talk with me now, I will not come to you again."

"Now you sound more like your half-brother. He grew fond of making similar threats. Spilled a lot of blood before he paid the price."

By itself, my hand wrapped around my weapon's handle. "Eirickson's blood once coated this hammer. Accuse me of being like him again, and I'll add yours to it. The time for playing games is over. We have a blood pact, and you need to honor your end of the agreement."

"I've long forgotten the passion and sensitivity which burdens young rulers. You don't yet have the wisdom to temper your anger." He nodded. "We will talk, King of Croy, once we've entered the forest."

"Good," I said.

Dalibor cleared his throat.

When I turned to look at him, his hand rested near his knife's handle.

He raised his eyebrows and tilted his head toward Sifet.

I shook my head. *If I kill Sifet, the rat dies soon after. He's too much trouble to keep around.*

The warriors waiting for us in the forest gave me plenty of room to pass through their lines. *Guess I look as angry as I feel.*

Sifet stopped a few paces past a group of archers. "Dalibor, Bojan, Branko ... go ahead. I'll speak with you soon."

I looked south. "We are two days, maybe less, from the Satran capital."

"I know," Sifet said, crossing his arms. "Anything else?"

I glared at him. "You will enter the city with me, freely giving information to help our victory, or you may find yourself outside ... wondering how to get in."

He raised his wrapped hand. "This says otherwise."

"Our pact binds us both. My aid in exchange for yours. It's time for you to show your value against what I bring to this table. So far, your effort has felt weak and wanting ... and not just *my* men have noticed."

Sifet glanced over his shoulder. "Now is not the time for such bickering."

"I am not bickering. Listen closely. I now know where we are, where my goal lies, and some of the challenges ahead of us. You are bound by blood to aid me in this war. You cannot provide fighting men, and I already have most of the information I need. All you can do is guide me to the easiest, most certain path to victory. Do so, and the pact stands. Choose to continue walking in the shadow of my army, and you show yourself unwilling or unable to honor your oath. Only you can make the decision, but I'm sure you'll want to discuss it with your trusted advisers first."

His face turned dark red as I spoke. "Are you dismissing me, young king?"

"He is," Bior said.

I tilted my head. "I expect an answer before we reach the capital."

"Good evening," Sifet growled, before turning and stomping away.

I called for Fastulf.

"Here, Sire," he said, closer than I expected.

"I hate to ask because you deserve a decent night's sleep, but take half your men and watch the village tonight. We need to know if anyone leaves."

"Don't trust them to keep us secret, m'lord?" Bior asked.

"Do you?"

"No, Sire."

"Me either, my king," Jomar added.

"What about Jitka and the others?" Fastulf asked.

"Leave them with your men here unless you trust them to stay quiet," I said, before clapping my hands together. "Your life could depend on their silence. Do you trust them that much?"

"They're Bane, Sire. How many times have you said they live by going unnoticed?"

"You *have* mentioned it several times," Bior commented.

He's right ... they both are. I sighed. "Do as you see fit, Fastulf."

"Thank you, m'lord. I'll ask my men before deciding. When should we return?"

"First light, unless something happens before. We won't leave until you're back."

"We won't be late," Fastulf said. "Sleep well, Sire."

"Stay alert and be careful," I said.

"Always, m'lord."

Chapter 77

"I'm parched. Anyone have a waterskin?" I asked.

"Here, Sire," Bior said.

I took the offered container and enjoyed a long drink.

"Sire," Jomar said. "Will Sifet march with us?"

I swallowed, took another drink, and nodded. "If he took me at my word, he will."

"He seems attached to the blood pact," Bior said.

"Yet does as little as possible to honor his word. I overlooked his lack of cooperation while everyone got comfortable with the idea of our agreement. Now, it's time he pulled his own weight," I said. "As far as I'm concerned, if he's not at my side when the Bonetakers fall, he did not uphold his part of the pact. While I was with the exiles, it became clear where my vengeance should be focused. I decided the innocent would be spared my wrath. Without the blood pact, Sifet and his advisers are not among the innocent."

"Sire, if we come to blows with them, I'm killing Dalibor first," Bior said.

I smiled. "If we fight, I expect you to be at my side."

"Understood, m'lord," Bior said, nodding.

Jomar chuckled. "Never knew you had such blood lust, Bior."

"Open disrespect of my king tends to make me angry. Can you blame me for holding a grudge?"

"No, good guardsman, you'll get no blame from me," Jomar said, still smiling.

I walked closer to the forest's edge and glanced at the sky. The clouds, earlier blocking the sunlight, grew darker. *A betting man would put a few coins on getting wet tonight.*

"Bior, find your pack. I'd like to eat before I raise a shelter and get some sleep."

"Aye, Sire. Give me a moment."

I nodded. "Jomar, I'd advise you to ask our stonesyths to raise some protection for the men. The sky looks angry; we're likely to get soaked tonight."

"Agreed, m'lord. Commanders, pass the word. We need cover."

Several men saluted and hurried away.

I found a sturdy-looking tree and knelt beside it to see what I had to work with. Pressing my fingers into the dirt, I forced my talent past the roots near the surface to search for stones. No matter how deep I pushed my energy, I couldn't find any sizable rocks to bring to the surface. *Dirt won't keep us dry for long.* Looking at warriors searching the ground nearby, I saw nothing but frowns. "Seems like we don't have much to work with," I said, to no one in particular.

Dirt rose around me as I poured energy into the ground. When the highest point reached about shoulder high, a cool wind carrying the familiar smell of rain blew through the trees. I forced the walls another arm's length higher and bent them inward until they formed a roof.

Sweat burned my eyes, forcing me to take off my helmet to wipe my brow. I stepped out into the cool breeze, and Bior called out to me.

"There you are," he said. "Got room enough for me?"

"Of course, but I'm not done. Water?"

He nodded and handed me a waterskin. "Plenty, Sire."

I took a long draw to quench my thirst and handed it back. "Give me a moment to harden this against the rain, and we'll eat."

"Take your time, m'lord. It's not raining yet."

"No, but I'd rather be tired and ready than rested and wet," I said, going back to work.

Resting my hands against the crude shelter, I pushed my talent into it, forcing the dirt together. The structure shook as it hardened. *It won't stand up to an endless downpour, but it should keep us dry.*

Thunder rumbled in the distance.

"Sire, you're looking a bit pale. Perhaps this is good enough?"

No fire and barely enough room for us to lie down. Far from ideal, but better than getting soaked. "As good as I can do, for now," I said, nodding. "Time for food and rest."

"Thank you, Sire, for taking care of us," Bior said, offering me a roll and a few strips of meat.

"It's not much," I said, nodding. "Would've been better if there was real stone to be found around here."

"Better than the other choice," he said, tilting his head toward the forest.

"My thoughts exactly. Hope you don't mind if I eat fast and go to sleep."

"Do what you need, Sire. No doubt you're exhausted."

"Wake me if something happens."

"Of course, Sire."

· · · · · ● · ● · · ·

Commotion outside disturbed my sleep.

"Where's King Fitzcirick? There's Legion in the village!"

The word 'Legion' got my attention. After shoving my helmet over my head, I shook Bior and pointed outside before grabbing my hammer and leaving the shelter.

The ground squished under my feet as I stepped out to the morning twilight. "What's wrong?"

Gavid turned to face me. "Sorry to wake you, Sire. Fastulf sent me. A Legion force entered the village, m'lord. We stayed unnoticed, hidden. I was sent to tell you they dragged someone—Draza, according to Fastulf—out of a big house."

I was afraid someone in the crowd would give us away. I closed my eyes as my blood ran cold. "How many?"

"From what I saw before I left, fifty, m'lord, maybe more."

"Did it look like they were taking Draza away?" I asked.

"Not from what I saw," Gavid said, glancing back toward the village.

"Did Fastulf say what he planned to do?"

"No, Sire."

"Hope he stays put," I said, shaking my head. "Bior, find General Jomar. Tell him I want everyone ready to fight as quickly as possible but try to keep the warriors quiet. Surprise attacks have worked well so far. Maybe they'll help us drive the Legion out of Wajda."

"Aye, Sire. Where will you be?"

I pointed to where the trees met the clearing. "There. Gavid, if you can find a safe path back to Fastulf, let him know we're coming."

"I will, my king. Hope to see you soon."

"I hope you do, too. Stay out of trouble."

He nodded and jogged south.

I followed him until the trees gave way to open ground.

The guards saluted me when I stopped. A misty fog hung above our heads, concealing the tops of the buildings to our south.

"Any movement?" I asked.

"Other than Gavid, nothing to report, Sire."

Boots splatted the soaked ground behind me while I strained to see anything happening in the village.

Bior and Jomar stopped on either side of me.

"Archers will be here soon, Sire," Jomar said. "Footmen aren't far behind."

A bellow of pain filled the air.

"That didn't sound good," Bior commented.

"How much longer, general?" I asked. "If they find out where we are, we lose the element of surprise."

"My king, we need a bit more of a plan than charging blindly into a fight," Jomar said.

Another scream raised the hair on my arms.

"And while we plan, Draza is most likely being tortured," I said.

"I hear the same cries you do, m'lord, but thirty or so archers is not enough to put those soldiers on the run," Jomar said.

I looked over my shoulder at a group of men heading our way. "How about thirty archers and two companies of warriors?"

"Against an unknown number of soldiers in a place we don't know well?" The general shook his head. "Not enough, my king. We need to overwhelm them quickly and keep ourselves from getting flanked."

Bior tugged at my arm, gripping it tighter. "Listen to him, Sire. I know you don't want anyone to die, believe me. I don't like it any more than you, but I like the idea of you getting hurt much, much less."

I know he's right, but everything about this is wrong.

Another bellow assaulted my ears.

I grunted and yanked my arm away.

"Sire, I was told three more companies are close behind. When they arrive, we'll attack," Jomar said.

"If we can't beat fifty Legion soldiers with nearly two hundred of our men, we should turn around and go home now, general."

"Gavid *guessed* at fifty, m'lord, and we don't know how many more may have arrived since," Bior argued.

Clenching my jaw when the victim cried out again, I nodded. "General, give the word. We've waited long enough." My hands gripped the hammer tighter with each scream. *If that's Draza, he's tougher than he looked.*

Jomar ordered our advance with the archers leading the way.

Chapter 78

Mud squished from under our boots as we advanced cautiously. With each step, the damp ground squelched. I wasn't sure which would give us away first, our rattling weapons or the soaked soil.

Somehow, we reached the edge of the village without being noticed.

A living corral of Satran soldiers herded the villagers into the square. Horrified expressions were evident on most of the innocents forced to watch the torture.

Draza stood in front of everyone, shirtless, facing away from us. Two soldiers held him by the arms. Another towered over the elder, bloody knife in hand.

Our first volley of arrows hit the men holding Draza; three arrows hit the back of the soldier on the left, and two more hit the man on the right.

The injured elder toppled to the ground with them.

Confusion froze our enemies for a moment before the Legion roared and ran toward us.

Villagers screamed and ran as their captors sprinted into battle.

My heart racing, I gathered strength from the ground before running after my men. Bior loped along next to me, keeping up as best as he could.

Two warriors cut the torturer down before I reached him. I smashed the heads of soldiers holding Draza and knelt to see if the elder still lived.

He groaned when Bior and I rolled him over. The gray blotches on his face seemed darker against pale skin. Both made a stark contrast to the blood flowing freely from several long slices across his chest. Fat and muscle pushed up through most of them. His rib bones were uncovered by two wide cuts on his right side.

Bior sucked in a hissing breath.

He's not going to make it without help.

Frightened screams from the villagers caught between us and them added to the chaotic sounds of steel against steel as the two forces clashed. Considering they were outnumbered, the Legion held their ground until Fastulf and his men pierced their right flank.

I guessed we killed over half their force before the soldiers fled. My footmen gave chase like hounds after a wounded deer.

"Bior, take the archers and find a herbalist ... find help. Beat on every door in town if you have to. Draza doesn't die today if I have anything to say about it."

"Aye, Sire. Archers, with me!"

Alone, I watched for threats in the now-empty square.

"Radi died," Draza rasped, "trying to stop them."

"Save your breath, good elder. We're looking for help."

"They wanted Sifet."

Someone talked. "Tell me about it after you're cared for."

"I didn't say anything."

I grabbed his hand. "Rest now. Talk later." *Where's the herbalist?*

I looked across the empty marketplace again, searching for anyone coming our way.

"I'm cold," Draza muttered.

"Yeah. The fog," I said, eyes still looking for help. "It's a bit chilly this morning."

The elder's hand went limp.

"Hold on," I pleaded. "Stay with me."

His eyelids fluttered before closing.

"Where's the herbalist?" I yelled.

"Coming, Sire!" someone yelled back.

I didn't recognize the voice and wasn't sure where it came from.

"Did you hear, Draza? There's a herbalist on the way."

His chin twitched.

An archer appeared on the far side of the marketplace, practically carrying an old woman. Another archer followed close behind, hefting a trunk.

I nodded and squeezed Draza's hand. "Not long. You're going to be fine."

His hand felt cold in mine, skin paler than when I first reached him. "Hurry!"

"Moving as fast as we can, Sire!"

"Hold on," I whispered. "She's nearly here."

The herbalist's knees popped like dried sticks as she squatted next to Draza. "Poor, poor man. Should've given them what they wanted."

"Even more blood might have been shed if he had. Can you save him?" I asked.

"Not sure. I'd guess there's more blood out of him than in," she said. Her voice reminded me of dry leaves rattling in the wind.

I nodded before getting to my feet. "I'm going to check on Draza's assistant. Have either of you seen Bior?"

"Not since we split up to find help, m'lord."

"Where'd you see him last?"

The archer pointed southeast. "He ran off toward some buildings over there, Sire."

"You two stay here. Help the herbalist if she needs it. Otherwise, stay out of her way. Above all, keep her safe."

"Of course, Sire. Stay safe yourself."

I saluted and jogged toward the marketplace to start my search.

Several of the shops had broken doors; a few were torn off their hinges and lying on the ground. *Our fault, or was it the Legion?* Pushing my talent through the ground told me no one was near. When I heard footsteps behind a row of houses, my heart sped up again.

I found two archers opening doors and asking for herbalists. According to them, Bior was searching the next cluster of homes to the south. I explained a herbalist was treating Elder Draza and sent them to let everyone know they could stop searching and return to the market square.

I located Bior and two more archers. A young boy scurried away from them as I approached.

"We found a herbalist," I said, "Call off the search."

Bior turned. "King Fitzeirick, I wasn't expecting to see you. Will the elder live?"

"She's doing her best," I said. "Who was that?"

Bior smiled. "A new friend, trying to be helpful, Sire. Telling us where the soldiers ran when they fled."

"I'm sure our warriors know where they went," I said, returning Bior's smile. "Men, rejoin the archers. Bior, come with me."

The archers saluted and hurried away.

"Aye, m'lord," Bior said.

I guessed word had spread to return to the square because most of the archers were there when we arrived. I glanced at the herbalist. An archer held her hand and patted her on the back.

A dark blanket covered the elder.

My heart sank.

"Sire," Bior said softly.

"I know. This is not good."

"What are we going to do, m'lord?" he asked.

"Exactly what we came to this country to do," I said. "I need four volunteers."

The group of archers looked at each other before anyone stepped forward.

I pointed to one. "Find General Jomar and tell him I said to secure the southern edge of this village. Let him know I'm sending the rest of the army to join him there."

"At once, m'lord."

"You, go back to our camp, to the first commander you can find. Tell him to march around Wajda, avoiding all people and farmlands, and meet with the general in the south."

"Of course, my king."

"Next man, go to the exiles and find Vos Sifet. Let him know the elder's dead, and I want his people here as quickly as possible. I'll wait for him and his advisers in the elder's meeting room."

"What if the Satran won't listen to me, Sire?"

"Make them," I said, scowling.

"Understood, m'lord."

I pointed to the last archer and frowned. "Come with me and Bior to the elder's house."

"Of course, my king."

"I want two of you to see the herbalist back home, safe and sound. The rest, guard the body."

I opened the door without knocking.

"All things considered, Sire, is invading the elder's home a good idea?" Bior asked.

"I suspect there are other concerns on their minds right now," I said, looking at the grizzly scene in front of us.

Radi's body lay near the door. His head was nearly removed, and there were two obvious stab wounds in his chest. A dark, sticky pool of blood covered the entryway.

I nodded to the archer. "Stay with me. Bior, find ink, a quill, and something to write on. Bring it to the meeting room."

"Aye, Sire," Bior said, boots making a slurping sound as they left bloody footprints marking his trail.

The archer followed me to the elder's long table.

"You've been on your feet a while, sit," I said, pointing to a chair near the door. "Who knows how long we might have to wait."

Bior hurried into the room. "Here's what I could find, Sire."

He handed me a short, thick quill before placing an inkpot and several sheets of dark, rough parchment in front of me.

"Thank you. I hate to ask but go wait for Sifet and his men."

He cocked his head and stared for a moment. "They know we're waiting for them here."

"I want you to make sure Sifet finds his way here in a timely manner," I said, raising my eyebrows.

Bior nodded. "Understood, Sire."

I quickly wrote a message to Rorec.

Folding the letter, I realized something was missing. "What I wouldn't give for some wax." I shrugged. "Oh well, Desperate times. I can trust you to keep this secret, yes?"

"I swear on my life, Sire."

I tapped my finger on the parchment, folded it once more, and slid it across the table. "Retrace our path until you find a Croian man named Rorec. This message is for him and him alone. He should be waiting for our herbalists and escorting them back to us. Once you deliver this, guide him back to us."

"I'm honored you trust me with this task, my king. Thank you."

I nodded. "Travel safe and swift."

The archer saluted and left the room.

Don't know if I'm fixing things or making them worse ... maybe both. Won't know for sure until everything's done.

Echoes of footsteps let me know someone was coming. I kept a hand on my hammer, in case.

Bior looked into the room. "The exiles are in the village, Sire. Sifet insisted on paying his respects before coming to see you. I told him not to keep you waiting."

"Thank you."

"Anytime, m'lord."

I gestured to the seat on my right. "Sit. This shouldn't take long after the Satrans arrive."

Chapter 79

Sifet entered the room ahead of his advisers. He sat across from me, and his men took seats on either side of their leader.

"I'm sorry we couldn't save him," I said.

He frowned. "I'm sure you did everything you could though I did not expect you to move in so soon."

"I'm borrowing an available resource," I said, brow furrowed. "I doubt Elder Draza would object to us meeting here to discuss what must be done before we can continue toward our goal of overthrowing the Bonetakers. Truth be told, I'd wager he'd advise us to work together to destroy those who tortured and killed him. It's time for you to do your part."

"What do you expect from me?" Sifet asked, head cocked.

"I know nothing of Satran burials, but Elder Draza died protecting you — us. He should be buried with honor."

"It will take time. Do we have much to spare, young king?"

"Considering I expect you to enter the capital at my side ... no, we don't. Still, he didn't deserve this. Something can be done, yes?"

Dalibor leaned over and whispered something to the exiled leader.

Sifet steepled his fingers and nodded. "Unfortunately, you have my best Bane stonesyths leading your army through the wilderness."

"If the villagers support you, as you claim, they should be more than willing to help. How long do you need?" I asked.

"Longer than you're going to give, I'd guess, King of Croy," Sifet said, not answering my question.

"Can it be done by midday?"

"Hardly. For an honorable burial, we wouldn't be done preparing the body by midday. Then the words of remembrance, the list of honors, carving the headstone, followed by the burial itself. Done properly, he'll reach final rest by first light tomorrow."

He can't be serious. I closed my eyes. "We don't know how many soldiers escaped, but word will reach the capital. I have to believe the Legion will do everything they can to attack us before we reach the capital. My army will protect Wajda, but we aren't staying here overnight. You have until midday."

Muscles in Sifet's face flexed. He fixed me with a hard stare, eyes closed to nearly slits. "Do not push me, young king."

Once more, Dalibor leaned toward him and whispered.

The exiled leader relaxed before nodding. "Mecik, watch over Elder Draza. Bojan, Branko, organize the villagers and find herbalists to prepare the body and stonesyths to prepare the ground. Dalibor and I will bestow his honors."

"And you will join me south of the village by midday," I said.

"Will you not attend the burial, King of Croy?" Dalibor asked.

"I doubt the villagers want to see the outsider who endangered their elder at his funeral. Unless Vos Sifet thinks otherwise, my time is best spent making plans with my leaders." I stood and pointed at Sifet. "The only way you regain the power you so deeply desire returned, is by entering the Satran capital at my side. Otherwise, the koron will go to someone of my choosing, and you will never touch it again."

Sifet stood, still glaring. "We have a pact."

"We do," I said. "But my oath did not include me carrying all the risk and giving you an easy reward."

His shoulders drooped. "Men of the League, you have your assignments. See to them quickly."

I cleared my throat as they turned. "Dalibor, I'd like some of your time. Once you are free, of course."

Bior kicked my foot.

Sifet's face turned red when he turned to look at me. "Why do you need him, young king?"

"He's a man of much knowledge, including many secrets forgotten by others. Perhaps he knows ways to move about the capital unseen. Such information could turn the fight in our favor."

Dalibor turned and bowed. "Anything I can do to help, King of Croy. I will find you when I am available."

I nodded. "I look forward to speaking with you."

Bior stood as they left the room. "Fitzeirick, what are you thinking?"

"After we tell the archers to leave the body to Sifet's followers, let's find Jomar."

"I'm not taking a step until you tell me what you're planning."

"You can't know everything, Bior. Sometimes it's for your own safety, and sometimes it's to keep others from getting hurt."

"I don't like it when you keep secrets, Sire. Especially from me."

"Some plans are best held in confidence until the right time."

Villagers packed the square, wailing and chanting. Mecik stood at Draza's head, staring down anyone who got too close.

I nodded to him before ordering the Croian archers to come with me.

Bior grumbled as we worked our way through the crowd. Passing several rows of houses, we came across more farmland near the southern edge of Wajda. Their crops stomped, fruits and vegetables crushed. *Hope that was the Legion's callousness and not my men.*

A company of warriors stood watch across the path heading south. One of them pointed into the trees on the western side of the way when I asked about General Jomar. I ordered the archers to take cover in the trees on either side before continuing my search.

Bior and I found him sitting with several commanders behind a large tree.

"All is well, General?" I asked, approaching him from behind.

"Everyone's present and accounted for, Sire. I heard the elder didn't live."

"I was with him when he died. He's in Sifet's hands now. They'll see to his burial. Sifet and his followers should join us before midday. Then we head for the capital."

"With your permission, I'll find something to eat, Sire," Bior said.

"Good idea, we'll eat while we have time," I said.

Commander Osvif pointed west. "Cooks are deeper in the woods."

Bior walked away as I stood my hammer on the ground and sat with my back against the tree. "I don't know what we may face between here and the Satran capital, but we best be ready for a fight. Any idea how many soldiers escaped the village earlier?"

He shrugged. "Can't say for certain, m'lord. I would guess somewhere between five and ten."

I nodded. "Our losses?"

"No deaths. A few minor injuries, from what I was told, Sire. Didn't hear anyone asking for a herbalist."

Several commanders nodded their agreement.

"Speaking of which, I asked Rorec to find our herbalists and guide them to us. Hate to enter the battle without healers."

"Their aid would be appreciated," Commander Ottar commented.

"But what about midday, my king?" Osfiv asked.

"If the Legion marches this way, I'd like to meet them away from innocents, like the villagers they terrorized here."

"I tend to agree, Sire, but I'm concerned about the unknown land ahead of us," Jomar said.

I nodded. "Only one way to learn about the unknown: we go there."

"Or we send scouts ahead," Commander Galtis suggested.

"I'd rather keep the army together. We're getting close to the Satran capital. No doubt they've gathered the bulk of their forces to defend it. Scouts could get separated, captured, and tortured. They could give away valuable information. I don't doubt any warrior's loyalty, but everyone has a breaking point."

Bior stopped next to me with a small sack. "You want rolls or meat first, Sire?"

"Give me a roll and lots of water," I said.

Bior dropped a waterskin next to me and sat.

"Send Fastulf's Satran friends ahead," Jomar said. "They don't know much about us."

I swallowed the dry bread and took a drink. "They aren't mine to command. Even if they were, how much progress would they make before we move again?"

"Good point, Sire" Galtis said.

"I don't like having people with us who answer to someone else, m'lord," Jomar said.

I nodded. "Yet they are a useful resource in the right situations."

"As you say, Sire," Ottar said, frowning.

"General, assuming we make it to the capital with most of our force intact and healthy, what's the plan?" I asked.

Jomar shrugged. "Won't know until we see the wall and its gates, Sire."

Pursing my lips for a moment, I shrugged. "So, another unknown."

"Unfortunately, Sire," he said, frowning.

"At least we know there's a wall," Bior said. "Sifet didn't."

I glanced toward the sky, but the tree blocked my view. "Speaking of Sifet, where's the sun?"

"It's not midday, Sire," Commander Alrik said.

I nodded. As the general and his commanders discussed plans for what we might face, I glanced toward the village and prepared myself for the coming chaos.

Chapter 80

"Sire, Dalibor's coming this way," Bior said, tapping me on the hand.

I stood, clicked my hammer onto my back, and looked at my assistant. "Wait here."

"I'd rather be with you when the rat is around," Bior said.

"He does seem suspect, my king," Jomar added.

"I'm surrounded by warriors, not to mention I can take care of myself against one man."

"But if you two are discussing the best ways to move through the capital, wouldn't a second set of ears be useful, m'lord?" Bior asked.

"Bior," I said, forcing myself to keep my voice calm, "your concern is appreciated, but this conversation will likely include things you're better off not hearing. Anything I learn about the capital, I'll pass along before we get there. Sit, enjoy the day while you can."

He frowned. "Aye, Sire."

I strode to Dalibor and extended my hand. "Nice to see you. Where's Vos Sifet and the others?"

He looked at my hand and turned up his nose. "He is assisting the villagers in picking a new elder. My fellows stayed with him to keep order, a task I'm not well suited for. How may I help you, King of Croy?"

Flashing him a smile, I swept my arm toward a dense stand of trees not far away. "Let's walk together and discuss opportunities that may present themselves over the coming days."

He nodded. "Gladly, wise king."

"What do you know about secret passages in and around the capital?" I asked.

"We were exiled from Mazhur many moons ago. Considering the Bonetakers are powerful workers of stone *and* wood, it's likely none of the passages I knew of still exist. Truth be told, any left could be traps."

I pushed some underbrush aside to let him pass. "But there were such ways before, correct?"

"There were."

I looked around and pushed my talent out to make sure there was no one close enough to listen to us. "Does your offer to remove one of my problems still stand?"

He laced his fingers together, holding his hands about chest high. "Which offer?"

"King of Croy, I must be certain. You want me to kill Vos Sifet ... correct?"

"When the time is right."

He tilted his head. "I take it the time is not right now?"

"Sifet lives until the Bonetakers are defeated, but he will not touch the koron."

"He complied with your demands, yet you plan to eliminate him? Interesting indeed."

Crossing my arms, I squared my shoulders and stared at him. "So, you'll do as you offered?"

He nodded. "Are you prepared to honor your part in this agreement?"

"Rest assured, you will be there when Satra's new leader is selected." I paused and smiled. "If all goes well, I expect you to contribute greatly to the decision."

"As is my birthright," he replied, nodding.

"For many generations, so you claim. I see no reason to ignore time-tested methods."

"I'll admit, your choice comes as a surprise. Young, inexperienced rulers rarely have the wisdom to understand why such actions are necessary."

"Never doubt my wisdom, Dalibor."

He smirked. "Know this, young king, I don't make offers I cannot deliver on. I will make my family proud."

"Make sure you are in position to cut down Sifet when the moment presents itself. You'll open the way to a better Satra for everyone."

He nodded.

"I should return to Bior before he starts looking for me," I said, glancing toward the large tree I came from.

"He won't be a problem, will he?"

I shook my head. "He's loyal and more than capable of doing everything I ask, but he's not aware of our deal because he doesn't need to be."

"Understood, wise king. No doubt Sifet will head this way soon, also." He bowed. "To your success, King of Croy."

"To success, adviser Dalibor."

He chuckled as he turned to leave.

Hope the reward is worth the risk.

Bior was pacing when I returned.

"See," I said. "Nothing to worry about."

"What did he tell you?" Bior asked.

"Nothing I didn't already suspect. His knowledge is old, and any remaining passages are likely traps."

"More unknowns," Jomar muttered.

I nodded. "As has been the case since we set foot on Satran soil, general. I expect Vos Sifet and his men soon. Are we ready to march south when he arrives?"

"Most of our warriors are well rested now, m'lord. We'll move on your command."

I nodded. "Anyone know where Fastulf is?"

"Near the river holding a wet cloth against a bump on his head, last I saw him, Sire," Commander Ottar said.

"What? Why didn't anyone tell me he was hurt?"

"I said we had a few injuries, m'lord," Jomar said.

I stepped toward the general. "But you didn't mention him."

"You didn't ask for specifics, Sire," he said, standing to face me.

"You're right." I raised my hands. "Sorry, I —"

"You care about him," Bior said. "No one can fault you for caring, m'lord. I'll go find him if you want."

"No. I expect Sifet soon, and Fastulf likely needs the rest anyway. Are there any other injuries I should know about?"

"Nothing worth worrying about, Sire," Jomar said.

Branko approached, halting our conversation. "King Fitzeirick, Vos Sifet is on his way. Selecting a new elder for Wajda took longer than expected."

I frowned. "While I'm not pleased by the delay, it is understandable. What can you tell us about Satra's capital while we wait?"

"Mazhur is a large, magnificent city. No doubt much like your own capital, good king. Cobbled roads. Sweet wells. Homes and markets made of the finest wood and stone." His shoulders sagged. "At least that's how I last saw it. With the Bonetakers in power, who knows what they've done."

"Do you believe in my cause?" I asked.

"Vos Sifet does."

"I didn't ask about him. How do *you* feel?"

Branko closed his eyes. "Honestly? I'm afraid, your Majesty."

"Why?" I asked. "What do you fear?"

"Not knowing what may come, should you win and take over my country. While I hate the Bonetakers for what they did to my clan, they are still Satran. You are not."

"Why come with us?" Bior asked.

"I am loyal to Vos Sifet. He believes siding with King Fitzeirick is the right thing for Satra. You seem an honorable man and a respected leader from what I've seen."

"Can you judge me by my actions, not by your fears?"

"I'll try."

Someone called for me.

We turned to see what was wrong.

A tall, thin warrior ran to me, stopped, and saluted. "Sorry to interrupt, King Fitzeirick, but our herbalists are here."

"Good," I said, smiling. "Was Rorec with them?"

The warrior nodded. "Led them here, my king."

"Branko, return to your Vos. Tell him to get moving, or we'll leave him behind."

"I'll deliver your message, King Fitzeirick."

"General Jomar, I'm going to see if Rorec has anything to report. Have everyone ready to leave when I get back."

"Consider it done, m'lord."

"What of me, Sire?" Bior asked.

"Assist as you can. I shouldn't be long."

"Aye, Sire."

"Good warrior, take me to Rorec."

He bowed. "Follow me, m'lord."

Dodging around trees, we moved quickly, and I knew we were close when I heard Hakon complaining about having to leave most of his supplies behind.

"Perhaps you should swallow your pride and ask Asfrid to help you find what you need," I said.

He nearly tripped himself turning to face me. "Oh, yes, my king. You give sound advice, as usual. I'll consider it."

"It is good to see you, Fitzeirick," Rorec said.

"Happy you all made it safe. I hate to bring bad news, but there is more walking before the day is done. We move south soon."

Hakon threw his hands in the air. "I should have known. None of us have eaten. Where can we find food, Sire?"

Looking back, I pointed toward where I left Bior. "Warrior, take them to the cooks."

Hakon bowed. "Thank you, m'lord."

"Also, we fought a small Legion force earlier. No major injuries, but some warriors may benefit from your attention."

"We'll do our best, given our lack of supplies and tools, Sire."

"I have no doubt you will, Hakon. I need to speak with Rorec a moment. You're free to go."

The herbalists bowed and followed the warrior back the way we came.

"You seem well, Fitzeirick. Has Dalibor —"

"Done nothing to cause suspicion. I take it you got my message."

Rorec nodded. "You're certain Dalibor made the threat?"

"Do you doubt his ability to kill?" I asked.

"No, not at all. In his own way, he's more deadly than me. Still, it doesn't make any sense. Dalibor has to know what would happen to him if he assassinated his vos."

I sighed. "Much of what goes on in Satra makes no sense to me. Still, you will act if necessary."

"Of course, but why not kill him now?"

I shook my head. "My relationship with Sifet has grown tense, almost like he's working against me and hoping I don't notice. Accusing Dalibor without absolute proof would only make the situation worse."

Rorec frowned. "Unfortunate but understandable."

"I have to ask...you still work for Croy, right?"

He bowed. "Until I draw my last breath."

"Stand ready to do as I asked, and don't say anything to anyone else."

"I've spent much of my life doing this kind of work. I haven't forgotten how."

"And you will be rewarded for it," I said, nodding. "No doubt Asfrid misses you. Go to her."

He smiled. "Gladly, King of Croy."

I laughed and waved him away before returning to see if Hakon was causing trouble. Instead, I found Vos Sifet and his advisers waiting for me. "When do we leave, and how long will we be walking?"

"As soon as General Jomar gives the word, we'll be on the move. How long? Until we can no longer enjoy the cover of trees or we see the capital, whichever comes first."

Sifet smiled. "Unless things have changed, you should be in sight of my city when this forest ends."

I nodded. "Good to know."

"What's good to know?" Jomar asked, from behind me.

"Vos Sifet said this forest ends within sight of the Satran capital."

"How far?" Jomar asked.

Sifet shrugged. "We may reach it before dark but likely a short time after sunset."

"Good." I nodded again. "Are we ready to move?"

"I believe we are, m'lord," Jomar said.

"Give the order."

Chapter 81

Bior tapped my arm. "Let me know if you get hungry or thirsty, Sire."

"As late as I ate breakfast, it will be a while."

He nodded. "Making sure you're taken care of, m'lord."

"Thank you."

Sifet and his men dropped back as we continued south. They stayed close enough for me to see them when I glanced back but kept enough distance that I couldn't hear their conversations. *Annoying, but I can live with it.*

Watching for patrols and hidden threats slowed our pace. On one hand, it kept us from getting exhausted. On the other, we didn't cover ground as quickly as I'd have liked. *Caution over speed will keep us out of trouble.*

We reached the edge of the forest as the moon peeked over the horizon. As Sifet said, we could see the nearest buildings in the capital along with the top of the wall separating his old home from the rest of Mazhur.

"A shame," Sifet said. "I lived there without need for such an ugly thing. The Bonetakers must live in fear to feel they need to close themselves off."

"We'll help bring it down," I said.

"Thank you for the offer, young king. Once the koron is on my head, my people will destroy it as part of the celebration," Sifet said.

"Regardless, my offer stands."

He nodded.

"Jomar, have the commanders set a watch schedule. We attack at the first sight of dawn unless a Satran force is spotted before then."

"As we planned, m'lord."

"Bior, find Rorec. Ask him to come see me."

"Aye, Sire."

"Sifet, you and Dalibor stay with me when we enter. Of your remaining advisers, who knows the city best?" I asked.

The vos scratched his chin while looking at his advisers. "Branko, most likely."

He stepped forward. "Myself or Bojan, yes."

I nodded. "I'll ask you two to stay close to General Jomar as guides."

They looked to their leader.

He nodded. "They will do as you ask. What of Mecik?"

I shrugged. "I assume he's a formidable fighter but — how would you best use him?"

"Though he's not as strong a stone worker as the Bonetakers, he should prove useful when we face Stoneskins," Sifet said.

"What can you tell us about these constructs?" I asked, looking at Mecik.

"Hit them hard and break them apart or find the man making them move and kill him."

"Would you lead the charge if we face any Stoneskins?" I asked him.

He laughed. "It's not if, King of Croy. It's when. And yes, I will take the fight to them. Gladly."

Sifet smiled and nodded.

Bior returned with Rorec close behind.

"Thank you for coming," I said, offering Rorec my hand.

He shook it. "I go where I'm needed. What's the plan?"

"A moment," I said. "Bior, take Mecik to Fastulf. He's going to help when we face Stoneskins."

Bior looked from the big man to me. "Are you sure, Sire?"

"I am," I said, crossing my arms. "No doubt Fastulf will appreciate the assistance."

"As you say, m'lord." He pointed to Mecik. "Come with me, please."

"Your assistant is interesting," Sifet said, as they left. "He never hesitates to disagree with you. Why do you keep him, young king?"

"For the exact reason you find him interesting. My word may be law, but my decisions aren't always correct."

"Again, your wisdom surprises me," Sifet commented.

"He was raised by a good man," Rorec said.

I nodded. "Who lived by his father's example."

"I wouldn't know for sure, but I'd hoped so," Rorec said.

It's my hope you get to see for yourself soon. I smiled at him. "You asked about our plan. We'll rest here and attack before sunrise. I hope we, those of us here, along with Bior, can avoid getting caught in the fighting and charge the castle directly. Once we're through the wall, we strike swift and take the koron, overthrowing the Bonetakers."

"And after?" Rorec asked. "How do you rid this nation of their kind?"

"It will take time." I nodded to Sifet. "And cooperation."

"With my country under my control, I can provide the resources needed to eliminate our enemies, young king."

"I hope you're right," I said. "For now, find a place to get comfortable and try to rest. We're going to all be busy soon enough."

· · · · ● · ● · · ·

Blurry faces and words I couldn't make out haunted my troubled sleep.

A voice I barely recognized called my name, asking me to wake.

Sitting up, I yawned and rubbed my eyes before looking at Sergeant Anund. "What's wrong?" I asked.

"The moon is halfway gone, Sire. General Jomar sent us to wake everyone and spread the word to get ready for battle."

Better to be early than lose our advantage. I nodded. "Anything happen while we slept?"

"As far as I know, nothing, m'lord."

"Thank you. I'm sure someone would have woken me if there had been contact. Work quickly, sergeant, and when the fighting starts, strike fast and true."

He saluted. "Thank you, m'lord. Stay safe, and may our victory come quick."

"If only," I said, before yawning again. I woke the men around me as Anund hurried away.

Bior groaned, getting to his feet. "Feels like I closed my eyes only moments ago."

"Same for me," I said.

"I suspect no one feels like they got enough sleep," Rorec said, glancing at Dalibor. "We all have our worries about this day."

"No worry on my part," Sifet said. "Win or lose, I will no longer suffer this exile."

"If we lose, I leave Croy with a grieving queen, no heir, and an emboldened enemy," I said. "Not the best way to ensure lasting peace at home."

"Yet you still chose to invade Satra, King of Croy," Dalibor said. "Is the reward worth the risk?"

"If we win, yes. If we lose, or I fall, others will judge the wisdom of my decisions."

"Surely you left someone behind to aid your queen," Rorec said.

"He did," Bior answered, before I could say anything. "Your son is next in line."

"Oh," Rorec said, and looked away.

Sifet smiled. "Are you surprised, Rorec? No doubt you prepared your boy for greatness."

"I thought so," he said. "But his life hasn't been what we expected."

I smiled and put my hand on Rorec's shoulder. "Roi's been my mentor and adviser as long as I've been alive. He earned his place at my side."

Dalibor mumbled something.

"Best we get something in our stomach before the fighting begins. We might not have much of an opportunity to eat again before the battle is over," I said.

· · · ● · ● · · ·

The rolls felt like stones in my stomach as we approached the edge of the forest. General Jomar stood in the shadows, sending men left and right.

"General," I said quietly. "How is everything?"

"As well as can be expected, m'lord. Everyone's watching the sky. Won't be long before we enter the city."

"Have you seen any guards or patrols?" I asked.

"No one has shown their face," Jomar said.

"But they have to know we're here," Rorec said.

"Watching from windows, no doubt," Dalibor suggested.

He's right. My eyes searched for signs of anyone in the openings facing us. Unlit rooms and shadowy alleys between dark buildings made it impossible to tell if there were any soldiers lurking about, waiting for our first move.

I was tempted to push my talent out to see if I could detect hidden threats but decided against it. *No sense chancing an enemy stonesyth discovering it and tracking the flow back to its source.*

"So, why not test us?" I asked.

"Perhaps the Legion are scared," Sifet said. "Your army has won many victories now."

"Any chance they'll surrender without a fight?" Bior asked.

"No," Sifet said. "They are cornered in their place of strength. Beyond Mazhur lies cliffs with the ocean below. With no place to run, they must fight here."

"Field Masters will drive their men hard. We do not face an easy battle," Dalibor said.

"If my warriors fight as I expect, we will win ... easy or not," I said.

"You are not inside the voret yet, young king," Sifet said.

I crossed my arms and turned to look at the vos.

"Time to stop talking and find out what the day holds, Sire," Jomar said.

Glancing toward the sky, I flinched when Jomar said, "Go! Go! Go!" in a loud whisper, ordering our first wave forward and gesturing toward the stone buildings in front of us on the other side of the clearing.

Chapter 82

Fastulf hurried past him, scurrying across the open field with Mecik and the Bane stonesyths close behind. He paused near the closest building and pointed to the right. Roughly half of his company veered away as he directed. He guided the rest to the left before scampering around the corner and out of sight.

Hundreds of warriors rushed out of the woods. Twice I heard clangs of metal clashing before someone cried out.

Torchlight flickered to life. A horn sounded. My heart raced, beating loudly in my ears.

The battle was on.

"When do we advance?" Sifet asked.

"Not yet," I said. "I want most of my force in the city before we enter."

"Understood, wise king."

Jomar ordered more warriors forward, sweeping his arm toward Mazhur.

Another swarm of men exploded from the trees. This time they roared battle cries, rushing into the fight.

Bior paced in front of me.

"Stay calm," I said. "I need you focused when our time comes."

"Aye, Sire," he replied, without looking at me, continuing to pace.

Again, Jomar directed a wave of men to advance.

"Young king, is it not time?" Sifet asked.

"How many soldiers are defending Mazhur?" I asked.

He looked at me for a moment before shrugging. "I have no way of knowing for certain."

"Neither do I, so I want most of my warriors engaging them, drawing them away, so we can skirt the main battle and reach the wall unchallenged."

Rorec moved to stand next to me. "He's right, Vos Sifet. We can't win if we fall on the way to the voret."

As the sky brightened, I saw Satran soldiers for the first time since we arrived at Mazhur. They left the edge of town and circled back to flank our warriors.

Jomar called out. Another mass of warriors stepped forward. This time, a flight of arrows covered the advance. The combination dropped several of the attackers and drove the others back, trapping them between our advancing warriors and those already in the city.

"Now, we go," I said. "Bior, lead the way and keep an eye out for Fastulf. I'd like to have him with us if you see him."

My steward drew his sword. "Aye, Sire."

We took a path to where Fastulf had stopped at before entering Mazhur.

I stayed close to Bior, holding my hammer in a defensive position.

Weaving through bodies, blood, and worse, we passed stone buildings. I guessed there were more Satran on the ground than there were Croians but had no doubt both sides suffered losses.

We flinched when the next wave of Croians yelled after Jomar sent them forward.

"Hope it scares the Legion, too," I commented.

Rorec chuckled and shook his head.

A lone soldier came around the corner ahead of us, nearly bumping into Bior.

My companion dropped him with two sword strokes, spraying blood on the side of the building next to us.

Rorec, axe in hand, strode forward to stand shoulder-to-shoulder with Bior. "Next one might not be alone."

Resigning myself to the fact that we likely wouldn't reach the wall without fighting, I drew strength from the rounded stones under our feet, adding small amounts as we walked.

Going by the sounds of fighting, we were well away from the main battle when we surprised a small group of soldiers heading west.

Rorec struck first, hacking the nearest soldier's arm off as the fighter raised his sword.

The harsh scream urged us into action. Bior fought a man back, sword against axe, as I positioned myself to attack.

Shifting my grip, I struck the one-armed soldier in the side, collapsing his chest.

He fell in a heap as Rorec swung his axe again, taking the next soldier's head.

Bior yelped when his attacker's axe sliced the back of his hand. As he stepped back, Dalibor's hand snaked forward, sliding this blade into the gap between the soldier's leather shirt and pants. With a flick of the wrist, the soldier's belly opened, spilling his guts.

Bior ended the man's suffering before bringing his bleeding hand to his chest.

A spear thrust into the space between Rorec and me.

Rorec caught it with his axe, twisting the pole out of the attacker's hands.

I stepped forward and knocked the man to the ground with a thrust of my hammer to his chest.

Three more soldiers stepped forward while the empty-handed spearman got back to his feet.

Bior feigned several quick attacks, drawing attention away from me.

Rorec bellowed a challenge and swung his axe again, barely missing his target.

Two soldiers shifted their focus, aiming to take advantage of the opening Rorec left them.

I smashed the soldier nearest me in the shoulder, full force.

He dropped his axe and fell into his partner.

Between Bior and Rorec, the two men were soon dead.

Now, it was five of us facing two Legion. One held a sword and shield; the other was unarmed.

When the empty-handed soldier moved, Rorec and Bior charged the swordsman.

Rorec bashed the shield down with the flat of his axe, and Bior's blade slid over the rim as the soldier tried to recover.

The unarmed man shifted away from the attack and tripped himself. He hit the ground at nearly the same time my hammer smashed his head.

Neither fighter got up again.

I glanced back to make sure Sifet and Dalibor were still with us. "Bior, wrap your hand," I said, "then we'll press on."

"With what?" Bior asked.

Dalibor knelt and sliced a strip of cloth from a dead Satran's undershirt. "This will do for now, yes?"

"Aye, it will. Thank you." He quickly covered the bleeding slit. After flexing his hand a couple of times, he nodded. "On to the wall, Sire."

The sounds of fighting followed as we moved forward. We took our time, checking each corner for threats before scurrying to the next building until we reached the barrier between us and the voret.

I pressed my hand against the wall to see how it was built. *Stone and wood woven together.* "I can't get us through with my talent," I said, shaking my head. "Bashing a hole would take too long and draw unwanted attention."

Rorec rested his hand against the barrier and shook his head. "No doubt this is Bonetaker work. We have to get through the gate."

"Do you happen to know where the gate is?" Bior asked, looking at Sifet.

"No," Dalibor said. "But I would guess it's on the main street. East of here."

"And well guarded, no doubt," Sifet added.

"A safe assumption," I said. "I'm open to suggestions."

Dalibor cleared his throat. "Find a building where we can hide, watch the gate, and wait until your army arrives, King of Croy."

"Sounds like a good idea, Sire," Bior said.

"Best option we have," Rorec added.

"Let's get away from the wall and move east behind the first row of buildings. Hopefully, the fighting stays away long enough for us to find a good hiding spot. Bior, lead the way."

Our search stopped at a small home, away from the main street, with a clear view of the gate and the Legion soldiers defending it. From our perspective, it was hard for me to judge exactly how wide the gate was, but I guessed three wagons could pass through at once with room to spare.

Bior posted himself at the door, sword at the ready. Rorec and I stood where we could watch the gate. Sifet sat at a small table in the far corner of the room. Dalibor searched the dwelling while we waited and announced, "I found a roll of clean bandage cloth. Bior, do you want it?"

"Toss it to me."

"Better be quick," Rorec said. "Looks like the guards are getting ready for something."

"Spears!" someone shouted.

"Spearmen on top of the wall," I said. "My army must be close." *Surely Jomar will order the archers forward ... if any are alive.* "We should know how this is going to go soon. If my men don't breach the gate, the battle is lost. Dalibor, Vos Sifet, stand ready. One way or another, the time draws near."

"I tend to agree, young king," Sifet said.

"Spears!" The call came again.

"Archers ready!" Jomar's voice rose above the clatter of spears impacting the cobblestone.

"The guards look jumpy," Rorec said.

"Bior, how's your hand?" I asked.

"Well enough, Sire."

"Spears!"

"Archers! Let fly!" Jomar roared.

Some of the bowstrings sounded like they were nearly in the room with us.

Men cried out in pain, but I couldn't tell from where.

"Again!" Jomar yelled.

More screams. Closer this time.

"He's using archers to attack the guards," Rorec said.

"A few are down, but he can't charge the gate with those spearmen covering it," I said.

"I'd guess the throwers aren't as effective with archers ready to poke holes in them. Once the guards fall, there are no threats keeping the archers from covering our warriors' advance to the gate," Bior said, flexing his hand.

"Again!" Jomar ordered.

"Spears!"

"The guards look nervous," Rorec said.

Can you blame them? "If they run and try to come in here, they die," I said. "Otherwise, let them pass. It would do us no good to give away our position."

Rorec nodded but didn't look away from the window.

"Anyone believe the gate is only wood?" Bior asked, shifting his weight back and forth.

"Archers, let fly!"

"If it isn't, there's a builder or a Bonetaker on the other side. Someone just opened a hole and let the guards in," Rorec said.

"Do we charge the gate now?" Dalibor asked.

"Into a rain of spears? No. We wait for my army to go through first," I said.

"Young king, we don't know if word of your attack has spread. Messengers could have snuck out. Reinforcements could be on their way. If they arrive, your men will be smashed against the wall," Sifet said.

"If I know Jomar, we won't wait long."

"Something's happening," Rorec said. "The gate's wide open now."

Stone impacted stone.

Chapter 83

"What's that?" Bior asked.

Twice more, the sound came through the walls around us.

"Stoneskins," Rorec said, "two of them coming through the gate."

"Mecik better be ready," I said.

"If he's alive, he's ready," Sifet said.

I moved to the window to see what my men faced.

The gate closed behind two large, stone statues with massive hammers where hands should be. They stood at least an arm's length taller than any man I'd ever seen. They lacked eyes and most other features one would expect on sythed stone monuments or decorations.

"Why aren't they attacking?"

"I suspect the Bonetaker controlling them is climbing the wall now so he can see your men," Dalibor said.

"So why aren't *we* attacking them?" I asked.

"General Jomar won't send warriors against something we've never seen before *and* expose them to a wall topped with spearmen," Bior responded. "He knows that's a fool's errand and a waste of men."

"Young king," Sifet said, "your warriors will be forced to take action or flee soon."

I jumped when the statues stepped forward.

"Archers!" Jomar roared. "Make them pay!"

Several Satran fell to the ground when arrows found their targets.

Good thinking, general.

"Gives your men a chance to hit the Stoneskins," Rorec commented.

"But we're no closer to getting through the gate," I said.

The Stoneskins smashed the structures on either side of the road.

"Why knock down the buildings?" I asked.

"Removing cover," Rorec said.

"Good strategy," Bior said. "Our men will have to move, exposing themselves or risk being crushed."

"If those Stoneskins reach our men, the battle is lost," I said.

"Perhaps Mecik is dead," Sifet muttered.

"An army stopped by two stone fighters," Bior commented. "Hard to believe."

Another building collapsed as the Stoneskins advanced again, moving out of our sight.

Cold sweat wet my back and chest. *Think of something, Jomar, or we're all as good as dead.*

Someone bellowed a challenge, and stone cracked against stone.

Something hit the ground hard enough to shake the home around us.

Cheers roared from nearby.

Cries of surprise, maybe disbelief, came from the top of the wall.

"Don't let it get up!" Jomar yelled.

I turned to Bior, wide-eyed. "Did we fell one of them?"

"Sounds like it, Sire."

The ground trembled as the second statue took another step.

"Rorec, watch the gate." I hurried to the back wall and sythed a small opening, hoping no one would notice. One Stoneskin was visible, swinging at men swarming it. Axes and hammers slammed into its legs with little effect.

A warrior stumbled, and the statue smashed him to the ground.

Spears flew again, scattering my warriors.

Arrows took flight in response. Going by the sound, another spearman caught one.

Mecik ran from somewhere, swung a huge stone hammer, and shattered the Stoneskin's leg.

Large chunks of rock and wood splinters flew as the giant statue fell over. Again, the walls shook when it hit the ground.

Someone screamed from atop the wall.

"Archers! Cover them!" Jomar roared.

"The legs," I whispered.

"That's their weakness," Bior said, finishing my thought.

When did he move over here?

"What happened?" Sifet asked.

"Mecik," I said, turning to him with a feral grin. "He shattered a leg. Those big piles of rock and wood can't do much with only one leg."

"Smart," Dalibor commented. "And good to know."

"I told you he would deal with them," Sifet said, looking and sounding too smug for our situation.

"Charge!" Jomar bellowed. "Bring down the gate!"

His order shot a shiver through my body, and I hurried to watch the attack from the window.

"Do we join the charge?" Sifet asked.

"No," Rorec and I replied together.

"We wait for my warriors to fight through whatever waits beyond the wall and clear a path to the voret," I said.

Rorec nodded.

Fewer spears rained down, striking a handful of warriors.

Arrows flew in answer, dropping two or three soldiers.

"But stand ready," I said. "It won't be long, I expect."

Woodsyths removed the lower half of the gate in the blink of an eye.

Arrows streamed out of the opening, and the charge stalled as warriors fell like harvested wheat.

The line surged forward again as the Satran archers readied their next flight. Screams of pain mixed with battle cries as more warriors were struck inside, but no arrows flew beyond the gate this time.

Croian archers let fly again when spearmen stood to lob their deadly missiles at my men.

Many Satran fell; few of my warriors were struck.

The sounds of battle changed, dull thuds of bodies being struck and clangs of metal clashing.

Must have taken the archers out of the fight.

"Now?" Bior asked.

"Not yet," I said.

It seemed like the fighting raged forever. Warriors attacked the few spearmen still atop the wall before Jomar ordered the archers to enter the gate.

"Time to go," I said. "Let me lead. Maybe we won't be attacked."

"Are you sure, Sire?" Bior asked.

I nodded. "The archers are ready to loose an arrow into anything moving. No one else wears armor like this. Maybe I can convince them to hold their strings before I find out how well this protects me."

"Fitzeirick makes a good point," Rorec said. "Let him go first."

Bior raised his eyebrows and motioned toward the door.

"Bior, I'll call for you once it's safe. Lead Sifet and Dalibor out. Rorec, watch their backs."

"Aye, Sire," Bior said.

"Agreed," Rorec said, eyeing Dalibor.

I took a deep breath, opened the door, and stepped out. Holding my hammer across my chest, I scurried past the buildings and stopped before exposing myself.

A line of archers, bows held ready, jogged into view.

I stepped to the edge of the road. "We're not the enemy."

Bows raised as they turned to face me.

"Hold!" Jomar yelled.

I saluted him, called for Bior, then pointed my hammer toward the gate.

The general nodded. "Archers, forward!"

Bior joined me as the second line of archers passed.

Jogging, we caught Jomar before he reached the wall.

"My king, good to see you. I was starting to get worried," the general said.

I tilted my head toward the bloody end of my hammer. "Got into a bit of a tangle on the way. Bior's cut. He'll survive."

He nodded. "We've lost men; they've lost more. And those statues ... "

"Stoneskins are horrible things," Sifet said.

"Good thing that big Satran knew how to stop them," Jomar said. "If we win, it's because of him."

"I'll give Mecik your praise when I see him next, general," I said. "For now, I'm more worried about getting to the voret."

"It won't be easy," Jomar said. "But we'll do our best to make a path."

"We'll make our own way if we must," Rorec said.

"Bior, lead on," I ordered.

He raised his sword. "Aye, Sire."

"Strike hard and swift, my king," Jomar said, as we jogged toward the gate between the rows of archers.

Bodies, Croian and Satran alike lay scattered. Blood tinted the cobblestones and grass red. Clangs of steel clashing against steel and the slaps of flesh striking flesh mixed with angry shouts and anguished cries echoed off the tall, stone wall surrounding the courtyard. The horrific, metallic smell of blood combined with the stench of opened guts hung in the air, hitting my nose like a fist.

I froze in my tracks.

Twanging bow strings broke me out of my shock. Out of instinct, I ducked before looking beyond the gore.

A wide staircase leading to a tall, columned porch and a pair of polished, wooden doors sat almost directly ahead of us. All we had to do was wade through the battle still raging between us and our goal.

I turned and waved Rorec to me.

"You and Bior get us to the stairs," I said. "Dalibor, keep Sifet safe."

Rorec looked at Bior before fixing his eyes on our goal. "On your word, Fitzeirick."

"Go."

Dodging dead bodies and haphazard attacks, my talent pushed against the wills of an untold number of stonesyths trying to pull strength from the ground. Even though we skirted around the chaotic fighting, Legion soldiers turned to attack us. Ignoring the warriors they were already engaged with cost them their lives.

Fewer bodies littered the stairs. The blood there was splattered or sprayed, not pooled. Compared to the scene behind us, it was calm. *The calm before a bad storm.*

"Sifet, what's behind the doors?" I asked.

"When I lived here, a long hall of artwork. Now," he shrugged, "who knows, young king."

"And they are what ... barred, bolted?"

"When this was mine, nothing secured them. I had no reason to lock myself away."

I raised my eyebrows. *Impressive or arrogant ... not sure which.* "I doubt the Bonetakers feel the same way."

Sifet nodded.

"Bior, get ready to check the doors. Syth them open if you can."

"Aye, Sire. Gladly."

Climbing the steps, the stench of blood and sweat seemed thicker as we rose above the fighting below.

I glanced back to see several Legion soldiers running toward us. Arrows and blades stopped every man before they came close enough to threaten our advance.

"Sire!" Bior yelled over the din. "The doors are wood *and* stone. I can't do anything with them."

"Walls are the same," Rorec added.

I turned to Sifet. "Why didn't you tell me?"

"I didn't know," he said, looking away. "The Bonetakers must have changed them."

And I should have guessed. Turning back again, I looked over the battlefield. *No one down there can help me — us.* Gripping my hammer, I pushed a spike out of the head and spun to face the door. With a roar, I swung with all the might I'd drawn as we crossed the courtyard.

Splinters flew. A fist-sized piece of the wood-skin shattered. The spike made a hole the size of my finger in the woven material underneath. "To the fire with these doors." I struck again, shaking from the effort. "To the fire with this whole place!" More material flew. The doors trembled. I'd removed more of the skin, made two more finger holes, but felt no closer to being through the barriers than when we'd arrived.

As I reared back for another swing, Bior grabbed my hammer. "Sire, wait."

I glared at him before turning. Fastulf and three Bane rushed up the stairs.

"M'lord, Jitka wants to help," Fastulf said.

"Where's Mecik?" Sifet asked.

Fastulf glanced over his shoulder. "Dead."

I looked from him to her.

She cast her eyes down.

"You can get through this?" I asked.

"She's nothing more than a Bane stone worker," Dalibor said.

I shook my head. "Jitka, can you get us through these doors?"

"Yes, right, Friend King Fist-er-rick. Think so."

"Let them try, Sire," Fastulf pleaded. "What do you have to lose?"

I looked at my progress, or lack thereof, and nodded. "Do your best."

Fastulf patted her on the back, and Jitka stepped forward. She placed her hands on the stone in the door and looked at her fellow Bane stonesyths before nodding.

They joined her, standing shoulder to shoulder. The ground quivered. As one, they grunted. The door creaked and cracked. Small faults crept through the exposed stone. "More, yes!" Jitka ordered.

The Bane men shifted their feet as if they were bracing against something.

I stepped back, the energy flowing from the three stonesyths made me nervous.

The door groaned. Loud cracking sounds, like tree trunks snapping, echoed off the walls.

Jitka screamed words I couldn't understand. The door burst inward, and the three Bane collapsed.

Fastulf knelt next to them. "They're breathing."

I nodded. "Keep them safe while they recover, and do your best to guard this door."

Fastulf stroked her hair and nodded. "Gladly, Sire."

"Why worry over Bane?" Dalibor asked.

"They've more than proven their worth to me," I said. "Earned my respect and protection. If you want to argue with me, you can stay out here. I have a vos to kill."

Chapter 84

I didn't wait for his answer before stepping through the rubble into a long hall. Daylight shining through the hole where the door once stood showed bare stone walls. Two rows of statues, armed men standing watch, lined the walls. Several near the door were toppled and broken.

"Sifet, is this your artwork?" I asked.

"No, young king. I had tapestries and murals on the walls. These figures are not to my taste."

"Anyone care to risk some gold doubles these are Stoneskins?" Bior asked.

I took a quick count. A dozen on each side, including five broken statues. "I wouldn't put a copper single against your gold. How many Stoneskins can one Bonetaker control?"

"We do not know, King of Croy. More than one, for certain, but —" Dalibor shrugged. "Can one man control all of these? I cannot say."

"Sifet, where does this hall go?"

"Assuming nothing has changed, young king, straight ahead is the court room."

I nodded. "Where should we look for Vos Stesha?"

Sifet peered ahead and shivered. "I have no idea."

"Dalibor, what about hidden doors, rooms?"

"None from here, so far as I know, King of Croy."

I nodded again and looked at the closest statue. Pushing my talent toward it, the stone crumbled with little effort. "Wasn't a Stoneskin," I quipped. "Bior, Rorec, take the lead...just in case.

"Aye," they responded together.

I glanced back at Fastulf before following the fighters into the unknown ahead.

We reached the double, stone doors into the courtroom without incident. I pushed on them and wasn't surprised when they didn't budge.

I looked at Sifet and shook my head. *Not going to waste my breath.* Soon after I sent my talent into the doors to see if I can find how they were secured, stone ground against stone behind us.

"Sire," Bior said, fear in his voice.

I turned to see six statues move to block the hall and take a step toward us.

"Remember. The legs." My hammer struck the first hard enough to drive through both knees, toppling the stone man.

The next pair moved to join the five we already faced.

Rorec grunted when he blocked the nearest Stoneskin's attack.

Catching an axe blow with my hammer drove me back.

Bior cried out in pain next to me. A stone hammer knocked him to the ground. He dropped his sword, clutched his arms to his chest, and curled into a ball.

I swept the statue's legs out from under it and smashed the head when it hit the floor. Farther down the hall, two more came to life.

An unwelcome chill formed between my shoulders. *They'll wear us down.*

Sifet cowered behind Dalibor. The rat's expression told me the adviser knew he could do nothing to protect his leader.

"Bior. Get back," I spat. "Go to Dalibor."

"Sorry, Sire," Bior said.

Two Stoneskins kept Rorec on the defense.

My arms ached from blocking heavy blows from the two nearest me.

Shoving against a stone sword, I turned and shattered the other's axe and almost tripped, dodging the fist aimed at my face.

Something Dalibor said earlier came to mind. *These are controlled by Bonetakers who need to see to attack. Where are they?*

One of the statues to my right crashed to the ground. *Rorec, I assume.*

More statues came to life farther down the hall.

I landed a glancing blow, opening a small crack in one's thigh, but the stone man stayed on its feet.

My heart raced. *We came all this way to die.*

I parried three more attacks before a stone sword sliced across my stomach. The leather split, but the metal sheet kept it from opening my gut. Still, the blow knocked me off balance, and I stumbled back. *The controller—where is he?*

Rorec bellowed. From pain or anger or frustration, I couldn't tell, but I didn't dare look his way.

My heart screamed attack, but all I could do was parry and dodge while I shoved my talent into the floor, searching for the controller's energy. Wood woven through the stone resisted my will. Two more attacks stung my arms, threatening my focus. Continuing to defend myself didn't make the effort any easier. Flashes of light floated in my vision as I pushed more energy into the floor, hoping to find something to follow.

Another statue fell, but it wasn't one I faced. Rorec's breath came in huffs loud enough for me to hear over the statue's grinding movements.

Another heavy blow knocked me back before I figured out energy flowed through the entire floor. They weren't pushing streams to each Stoneskin but flooding the area, making it harder to track.

"Rorec," I said. "Come closer, cover me."

"I can't ... fight ... all of them ... alone."

"Just take some pressure off me," I pleaded.

He groaned. "Stay put."

I dodged a punch and parried a sword. When his foot touched mine, I stepped back to use his body as a shield and searched for the energy source.

An attack knocked him into me, smearing sweat on my leather sleeve. I stepped out, smashed the attacker's knee, and moved back. When the statue fell, I noticed a ripple in the energy. Following the wave, it led to the doors behind us.

"Dalibor, come here," I commanded.

"I'm no good against those things," he said.

"Come. Here," I growled.

He shuffled to me.

I leaned close to his ear. "The controller is behind the door. Find a hole where they can see us and stab your blade into it. Rorec and I are almost spent."

"As you say, King of Croy."

I moved to stand shoulder-to-shoulder with Rorec. *If this doesn't work, we're done for.*

The next strike drove Rorec to a knee.

I smashed the attacker's arm, shattering it but not dropping the Stoneskin.

A stone sword scraped against the metal in my armor. It didn't cut me, but the force of the blow knocked me into Rorec.

A scream filled the air, and the Stoneskins froze.

I turned to see Dalibor pull the knife from a slot in the door. Its long blade was covered in blood. "Success, King of Croy."

"We survived. Not the same thing," I said. "How do we get through these doors?"

Though no one touched it, the right-hand door swung inward.

Chapter 85

My chest tightened.

Dalibor moved away, nearly tripping over Sifet.

"Enter," a raspy voice beckoned. "You've earned an audience before you die."

"Trap?" Rorec asked, blood running down his cheek.

Resting my hammer on my shoulder, I looked at him. "Almost certainly, but it's not like we have a better option. Perhaps we can convince him to surrender."

Bior's laugh turned into a groan.

Pointing toward the other end of the hall, I smiled at him. "Go to Fastulf, friend. You're in no shape to fight."

"But Sire, I promised —"

"I know. And you've done your best. If we win, Queen Tindra won't care. If we don't." I shrugged. "None of us will suffer her wrath."

He nodded. "Aye, m'lord."

"When you reach Fastulf, make sure he doesn't do anything stone-headed."

"Not sure I could stop him, m'lord." He grimaced as he saluted. "Until I see you again, strike swift and hard." He turned to shuffle toward the shattered doors.

"Sifet, I trust you're ready to be persuasive," I said.

"I will support you as best I can, young king," he said.

"Dalibor, I trust you are prepared to do your duty," I said, turning to the rat.

He wiped the blood from his blade. "Expect nothing less, King of Croy."

"Rorec, are you with me?"

He took a deep breath and nodded. "I'm ready to do what must be done."

Hiding my exhaustion, I strode confidently through the door.

Though the body of the Bonetaker Dalibor had killed was nowhere in sight, we walked through a puddle of blood near the door.

A large brazier, fire burning bright, hung in the center of a large, round room. Giving enough light to see stair-stepped benches rise up the walls, it took a moment for my eyes to adjust before I could make out six chairs facing a substantial, stone podium. Behind it, a tall, broad-shouldered man stood. A skull-shaped mask covered his face matching his weathered-bone-colored armor.

"Vos Stesha?" I asked.

He nodded. "Murderous King Fitzeirick."

Maybe he'll see reason. Squaring my shoulders, I readied my hammer. "You are outnumbered. Your army dwindles with each passing moment, and your Stoneskins are of no use. Your reign is all but ended. Surrender, and your death will be painless. Fight, and you will suffer."

He laughed.

Still expecting a trap to spring, Rorec and I advanced together, with Dalibor and Sifet a couple of paces behind. The floor beneath us went soft, letting our feet sink calf-deep. Faster than I could react, the material hardened, fixing us in place.

Glancing at Rorec, the concern on his face mirrored my own. Gooseflesh prickled my skin. I pressed my talent into the stone and found wood woven through it. Before I could swing my hammer to smash the bindings, we were yanked toward the chairs. I fought to keep my balance, nearly dropping my hammer.

Something sounding like a bone snapping came from my left.

Sifet screamed.

I turned to see him grab his left knee.

"It's a shame we have to meet like this, self-proclaimed king," Stesha rasped. "You do have my gratitude for sending Porsey. Without his deceptions, the Bonetakers would have never convinced the Legion to help us seize power from the outdated and ineffective League. With even the slightest amount of understanding on your part, You and I could have sat together and discussed the future prosperity of our nations. You chose to attack instead."

"Lies," I spat. "Satra invaded Croy. Slaughtered thousands of innocents. Such an act of war must be answered in kind."

"Do not mistake Sifet's Satra for the nation you now stand in," Stesha said.

"You and I can still decide our nation's futures. Let me go, and we'll settle this now," I said. "You can end the bloodshed going on outside."

We stopped at the chairs, which grabbed us and forced us to sit.

"Unlike your greedy, shortsighted half-brother, I will not fall to you."

The brand on my face throbbed as I fought panicked memories of the moment Eirickson bound me in a stone chair and marked me a traitor with a blazing iron on my cheek. Now, as before, my talent couldn't overcome the will of my captor. My heart drummed against my ribs. Blood pumped in my ears, roaring like a river. My vision narrowed until all I could see was Stesha.

"Face me," I demanded. "Man to man. Let muscle and metal decide who lives and who dies. The last one standing will declare victory and end the war."

Stesha shook his head. "Whose loss would bring tears from you first, child king? I'm guessing it's the Croian lap dog. Unless you've formed a bond with Dalibor." Crossing his arms, his gaze swept across us. "I find it unlikely you'd care if a single Satran died for you. Rorec, stand for your sentence."

My mentor's father bellowed his frustration, struggling against stone and wood as the chair shifted and flowed, forcing him upright.

Stesha stepped from behind the podium and drew a sword. Its long, broad blade gleamed in the flickering firelight from overhead.

Stopping in front of Rorec, the Satran stared at me. "I will cover you in his life's blood, would-be-conqueror."

"I won't beg for my life, usurper," Rorec said, before spitting at the Bonetaker.

Stesha laughed and raised the sword, resting the blade on Rorec's shoulder.

Again, the fire flashed brightly off the steel as Stesha drew it back to swing.

Muscles in his arms clenched. The sword's tip quivered before he swung the blade.

Stopping mid-stroke, Steshsa cried out in pain, arching his back and stumbling forward before turning.

A sword, Bior's sword, lodged near Stesha's spine in a gap between his armored shirt and pants.

Should've known he wouldn't listen. Fire surged through my body. I pressed my will against the Bonetaker's, wanting nothing more than to free myself and help my friend.

"Who dares?" he roared, raising his sword to attack my steward.

Again, the big Satran screamed in pain and stepped back.

Someone in Croian armor ran past me.

That wasn't Bior.

Stesha turned, Fastulf's sword buried in his gut.

Oh. He's sneaky enough.

The grip of stone and wood loosened as Stesha searched for Fastulf.

"Show yourself!" he yelled.

If I can get free, Fastulf and I can end this.

The Bonetaker grabbed the blade lodged in his stomach, grunted as he pulled it free, and tossed it away.

Faint footsteps raced behind me.

Stesha turned again, trying to follow the same sounds I had heard.

I caught a glimpse of Croian armor entering the shadow behind the podium.

Fastulf isn't one to hit and run, and he certainly isn't going to hide. Who's in here?

Pushing my will against Stesha's, I nearly had an arm free.

The Bonetaker made it to the podium before I could move.

"There you are," he said, raising his sword again.

A faint flash from the shadow caught my eyes.

Stesha dropped his sword and reached for his throat. Turning toward us, blood ran through his fingers, down the front of his armor.

Free from the chair, I rushed toward the podium. "Fastulf, you saved us!"

"Not Friend Fast-elf, no." Jitka appeared from behind the podium. Blood covered her knife and sprayed across her chest and face. Glassy-eyed, she didn't look steady on her feet.

"A Bane?" Sifet barked, leaning against Dalibor. "How fitting for Stesha to be felled by the lowest of the low."

Dalibor struck, slicing Sifet's throat. "Satra will be in better hands now. A proper ruler will be chosen."

Blood sprayed from the open wound.

Jitka stumbled back, swaying as Sifet crumbled to the floor.

Rorec yelled and pushed me out of the way.

Before Dalibor could raise his hands, Rorec's axe separated the rat's head from his body.

Jitka fainted.

Poor girl.

"You told me he made the threat, but I didn't believe it," Rorec said, breathing hard. "It seems unthinkable. Sifet's closest adviser, a lifelong confidant, actually killed him. What do we do now?"

"By the pact, I had with Sifet, I choose the next leader of this nation," I said, clicking my hammer onto my back before checking on Jitka.

"Your Majesty, I would be honored to help you find the right man."

Once I knew she was breathing, I nodded and pulled the mask off Stesha. Wide bands of silver, gold, and fiery opal woven in a circle sat on his head. "Is this the koron?" I asked, holding it toward Rorec.

"Yes."

"Must admit, it has a certain beauty. Might fit me. Should I try it on?"

"I won't stop you," Rorec said, head cocked.

"Perhaps there's a better option," I said, smiling. "Come here."

"Why?" he asked, not moving.

Moving behind him, I slipped the crown on his head. "Because it fits you."

He chuckled. "Seems it does. Now take it and find someone worthy."

Grabbing his shoulders, I turned him to face me. "No. My chosen leader should wear it for his introduction."

"What? No. I can't."

"Why not? Do you not serve Croy until your dying breath?"

"Fitzeirick ... are you serious?" His fingers brushed the bands.

"Croy needs someone trustworthy to help me fix everything wrong with this land. Who better than you to be my skald here?"

"Are you sure?" he asked, bowing his head.

"Yes. You know these people, and you know Croy. I believe you will speak your wisdom, pronounce fair judgment, and act as my mouthpiece when needed as these people learn to live under Croian laws."

"I... Asfrid's going to be—"

"Busy," I said. "She's going to be busy. Now, let's make the announcement and see if we can put a stop to the battle in the courtyard."

"I'd like nothing more," Rorec said, smiling ear to ear.

I carried the unconscious Jitka to find Fastulf crouched where we had left him.

"Is she?" he asked, rising to stand with concern on his face as we approached.

"Overwhelmed, I think," I said, nodding to her. "She fainted. Let her wake on her own. Where's Bior? He needs to know I'm safe, and we won."

Fastulf's smile faded, and his face lost color. "Sire...he —" The leader of my guides pointed to a pile of stones. "He arrived, pale and breathing heavy. I helped him lie down. When he coughed up blood, I sent the Bane to find help. I haven't seen them since. Bior didn't make it, my king."

Rorec put his hand on my shoulder.

I froze. A burning knot formed in my stomach.

"Sire, he asked me to tell Sibbi what happened so the family would be proud," Fastulf continued.

"I will speak to his brother," I said, wiping my eyes again.

"Jitka," Fastulf said, then paused. "You should know, she held Bior's hand when he breathed his last. Once we covered him, she took our swords and ran to help you."

"She saved our lives." I lay the brave girl on the ground near Fastulf's feet. "We would have died if not for her. She won this war." I stood and looked him in the eyes. "I may not get the chance to thank her. Make sure she knows she's a hero."

He looked away from me for a moment before meeting my gaze. "Of course, m'lord."

Chapter 86

Bodies littered the courtyard. Blood flowed like water across the ground. It was hard to tell which side had more fighting men on their feet. Still, the fight continued.

Red haze crept in from the edges of my sight. Prickling warmth flooded my muscles as an ache gripped my chest. Approaching the edge of the platform, tears blurred my vision.

Emotions gave my talent extra strength as I shoved it into the ground and spoke with as much force as I could muster. "I order all men, Croian and Satran alike, stay your hands and listen."

Fighting slowed as my voice rumbled from below the ongoing battle.

"Vos Stesha is dead. The age of vos rule is over. The nation of Satra bows to the will of Croy now. Skald Rorec, wearer of the Koron of Satra, will see my orders are carried out across this land. Men of the Satran Legion, surrender. Lay down your arms and live. Let us work together for everyone's benefit. Let all countries coexist in peace starting now. So I declare."

Rorec went to one knee beside me.

Silence blanketed the expanse before us. My heartbeat pounded in my ears.

Dull clangs split the quiet as many Satran soldiers dropped their weapons and fell to their knees, hands raised over their heads.

A few Legion soldiers foolishly tried to take advantage of the lull and attacked. When the last one fell, cries of victory filled the air.

"What now?" Rorec shouted, over the commotion after standing.

"First, you should find your wife and tell her the good news."

He chuckled. "Should go well, especially since I have a couple of cuts for her to treat."

I nodded.

He sighed. "Dalibor ... can you believe?"

Believe it? I knew it. Regardless, it was the best thing for everyone.

"I wasn't sure he would make good on the threat." I shrugged and looked back. "Now it's too late."

"What happened in there?" Fastulf asked.

"I'll explain later," I said. "Rorec, when you find Asfrid, tell her I want her to prepare Bior's body for his journey home."

Frowning, he nodded and strode down the stairs.

I turned to Fastulf. "How's Jitka?"

"Waking, Sire."

"Good. Find a herbalist and get her looked at."

"I will, my king," Fastulf said, smiling.

"Whatever she needs, she gets. I'll never forget her bravery."

Chapter 87

It took the better part of two days before something resembling peace settled across the Satran capital. More than a few of the Legion soldiers swore allegiance to Croy and agreed to help spread our message. Even with their help, I had no doubt it would take far longer before the former nation adapted to Croian rule.

Some of my stronger stonesyth warriors worked with Satran Devoted to make a passable road from the capital, down the cliffs, to the sea. Using horses from the capital stables, I'd sent a messenger to our barges, ordering them south to take me back home once the planning meetings were through. It seemed like a faster route than going north to Croy and continuing west to get home. It was time to carry Bior back to Croy, to his final rest, and I was more than ready to go.

Rorec and Asfrid settled into the voret once she understood we weren't playing a cruel joke. Sunlight streamed through the windows in the skald's study. *This meeting won't be over soon enough.* Jomar took a long drink from his cup. "I can't be the only general here, Sire. I need another to help coordinate our forces while we hunt the rest of the Bonetakers and quell uprisings."

I nodded. "Choose the commander best suited for the job and promote him. While you're at it, make all necessary promotions to give you the leaders you need."

"I still don't understand why I'm in charge, Fitzeirick," Rorec said. "General Jomar can handle everything without me."

"These people need an arbitrator, a judge, not a general. You are my voice to the Satran people. Your wisdom will change this country. Something my army, *our* army, cannot do. The old clan system does more harm than good. The League no longer exists, and the Legion is dismantled. There's no reason everyone can't live and work together as equals. That's your primary task."

He sighed. "Change is never easy."

"Believe me, I know," I said. "We've already spilled more than enough blood. Guidance is what's needed most now. You are more than capable."

After draining his cup, Rorec nodded. "Thank you for your confidence."

"I want to speak with Fastulf before I leave." I glanced outside, taking note of the position of shadows. "I must leave you two to work out the details, but I expect regular updates."

Rorec and Jomar stood and bowed. "Until we see you again, Sire."

The hall felt much larger without the statues standing watch. The shattered door hadn't been replaced, but repairs to the city as a whole were underway.

Fastulf was on the porch, pacing, when I stepped past the workers. He saluted when he saw me.

I smiled. "How is Jitka?"

"Doing well, m'lord. Though she hasn't slept through the night since."

I raised my eyebrows. "How would you know?"

He blushed and looked away.

"Are you sleeping with her?"

"What? No." He raised his hands and stepped back. "Well ... yes, but ... but only sleeping. Together. I mean all of us. While we were traveling, Sire."

I chuckled. "Fastulf, look at me. Are you falling in love with Jitka?"

He stepped back again, bumping into a column. "Would it be so wrong? I mean — She saved your life. If not for her, we might have lost the war, m'lord."

"So, you took interest in her because she saved my life? Curious."

"No, Sire. She caught my eye long before."

I nodded. "Why are you so defensive?"

"You ... and me. We hated the Satran, Sire. You had good reason, considering ..." He shrugged. "And I let hate take root because of what they did to our people. I hunted them for sport, m'lord."

"But one person is not the same as an entire nation," I said. "Hard lesson for me to learn, but an important one, in the end. If she has your heart, so be it. Don't let your past get in the way but don't hide what you did from her either. Tell her the truth and let her decide if she wants to stay with you."

"Do you think—"

"It's not what *I* think," I said, stopping him. "It's what *she* deserves."

He nodded. "Right, m'lord."

"You have my support if you both decide to live in Croy ... by her own will."

"Yes, Sire. By her own will ... of course. But —"

"But what?"

"I think it will be easier if we stay here. You don't know how long it will take our people to accept your decision to let Satra live. Jitka's life has been hard enough; I don't want to make it worse."

I nodded and tapped a finger on my chin. "Bringing us to why I wanted to meet with you. General Jomar needs sergeants, and he needs commanders. If I were to recommend you for a promotion, it would give you another reason to stay. If you'll take it."

"If you believe I am worthy of the authority, Sire."

"You already do most of the same work as a sergeant. One thing to remember: a title isn't just authority; there's also responsibility. It will be more work and keep you on the move for some time."

"Of course, Sire. I understand. Thank you for everything you've done for me."

I offered him my hand. "You've earned everything I've done for you."

"As you say, m'lord," he said, shaking my hand.

"I will give your name to the general when I see him next. One more thing before I go."

Fastulf raised his eyebrows and nodded.

"I never got a chance to ask; do you know why she attacked Stesha? It seems out of character. She'd always been so timid. Why her and not you?"

"You treated her with respect, m'lord, thanked her for helping us," he said. "Most of the Bane didn't understand why. I'd told them you wanted to make things better for all Satran people. I think Jitka was the only one who listened. When Bior died, she said you must need help ... you know the rest."

"Except how she reached Stesha without him seeing her."

Fastulf smiled. "She did what Bane do best and stuck to the shadows to avoid being noticed."

I nodded and patted his shoulder. "Thank you for your time. Go share the good news with Jitka. I have to get ready to go home."

He saluted. "I will, my king. Thank you again. May your travel be swift and safe."

"And may your life be happy."

Chapter 88

I stepped onto the deck after Bior's wrapped body was loaded. Several, wounded warriors traveled back with me, along with three herbalists. Another barge, loaded with goods, left with us. The rest would wait for more wounded.

While faster than traveling by horse, traveling by water was unpleasant. Waves rocked the barge to and fro, making me sick. I spent most of the trip with my head hung over the side. *No doubt Bior would find this amusing. I wouldn't even be angry at him for laughing at my misery. I just want to hear him laugh again.* By the time we reached Croy's southern shore, I swore I'd never ride on a barge again.

Legs shaky and stomach empty, I rolled out of the wooden craft as soon as it stopped and fell into the salty water. Sputtering and wobbly, I staggered onto dry land and sat, not caring my armor's pants were caked with sand.

The herbalists approached, carrying Bior. "Sire, we have a spot in a wagon returning to the capital. Bior's body will be loaded soon."

I nodded, pushed myself to my feet, and escorted my fallen companion to the wagon, saluting his body as the herbalists placed him onboard. *Not much farther, my friend.*

"An honor to have ya in ma wagon, King Fitzeirick," the driver said, as I climbed into the back. "Lotsa folks gonna be glad yur home safe 'n sound."

"Slow and steady," I said. "You're carrying precious cargo."

$$\cdot \ \cdot \ \cdot \ \bullet \ \cdot \ \bullet \ \cdot \ \bullet \ \cdot \ \cdot$$

The sun was low in the sky by the time we entered the capital. I did my best to return every greeting and salute I received along the route to the compound where I lived. Part of me wanted to cheer at the sight of the dark, stone wall surrounding the courtyard around my home, the home of my guard captain, and the barracks where the guard lived. My joy was dampened knowing Bior's friends lived there, and I carried terrible news. The wagon stopped outside the gate.

"Here we are, ma king," the driver said. "Again, it's been ma honor."

I thanked the driver while the herbalists unloaded Bior's body.

"Wait here," I said, to the healers.

Cheers rose from the courtyard when I walked through the gate.

I waved and asked the men to stop. "Where's Captain Agrim?"

As if he knew I was looking for him, he stepped out of his quarters. "What's all the noise about?"

"They're happy to see their king," I said, not quite smiling. "Are you not, captain?"

Turning to face me, he saluted. "Sire, I didn't know you'd returned. How long have you been here?"

"Not long. Came straight from the southern beach. Where's Sibbi?"

He glanced toward the sky. "I'd expect him to be leading the new recruits to the mess hall about now, m'lord. Why?"

"We need to talk. Send someone to get him." I glanced over my shoulder. "And I want four men to carry a heavy burden."

"Of course, Sire. Sigric, get Sergeant Sibbi," he ordered. "Ivar, Hedin, Erland, Orn, help your king with his load. Is it still on the wagon, m'lord?"

I shook my head and waved for the herbalists to carry Bior through the gate.

Agrim's jaw dropped as he looked from the body to me. "Is that the dead Satran king, Sire?"

I shook my head. "If it were, I'd be smiling. Bior fell. In battle. At my side. It's only right I see him home, to his brother."

Agrim gasped before hurrying to my side. Sigric stopped mid-stride and fell to one knee. The rest of the men followed soon after.

"That's Bior?" the captain asked.

"It is," I said, nodding. "Get Sibbi. Take the body to my meeting room so we can honor him together. First, give me a moment to tell Tindra before you enter."

"She's not here, Sire," Agrim said. "Likely, she's still at the castle site."

"I'll find her after I've spoken with Sibbi."

"Aye, m'lord," Agrim said, turning to jog to my door.

We followed him inside. The men placed Bior's wrapped body on the table and stood at attention. I placed my helmet next to Bior's head and stood with my hammer across my chest, waiting for his brother.

The door crashed open. Sibbi rushed into the room, ashen-faced and cheeks shiny. "Is it true?" he demanded.

"Yes," I said, putting my hammer away and stepping back from the table, struggling to hold back my own tears. "We stood shoulder to shoulder, fighting for our lives."

"He died a warrior's death?" Sibbi asked, placing his hand on Bior's head.

I nodded. "He did. You should be proud. I'll tell you what happened if you want."

"Aye, Sire,"

Sibbi shuddered as the story poured out of me. By the time I finished, the guards stood at his side, supporting their sergeant.

Once I'd finished, Sibbi embraced me tightly. "Thank you for seeing him back to me, Sire. It's more than he would have asked for."

"But no less than he deserved," I said, squeezing him back.

"May I take him to our family, Sire?" Sibbi asked. "There's much to prepare."

"Agrim, see Bior makes it home," I said, releasing Sibbi.

"Aye," Agrim said. "It would be an honor."

"Sibbi, whatever your family needs, it's theirs for the asking," I said.

"Thank you, Sire. Your generosity is appreciated."

"Now, I need to find my wife," I said.

Sibbi nodded. "She's burned all her worry ordering builders around on the castle grounds, m'lord. I'm sure they'll welcome the relief."

Agrim chuckled. "He speaks the truth, Sire. The sooner you get to the build site, the happier everyone will be."

I grabbed Sibbi's shoulder. "Anything, and I do mean anything, you need. Let me know."

"Aye, my king. Thank you."

I saluted again as the guard took Bior out of the room, then waited a moment longer before leaving my home. I got to the under-construction castle as quickly as well-wishers would let me. Bior's absence weighed on me the entire way.

Entering the grounds through an opening in the low wall around the property, several workers recognized me and bowed. One told me Tindra and Roi were discussing something in the main hall. Following the directions, I found them in the middle of a loud but civil debate.

"The fireplace *must* be on the right wall. Otherwise, it blocks passage to the small meeting room," Roi insisted, waving his hand toward the wall.

"But the Einns laid out his kitchen with cooking fires on the *opposite* wall," Tindra countered. "Nothing will line up if we do it your way."

"Maybe you two should worry about security first," I said. "Anyone can walk in like they belong here."

My wife and my mentor turned together to face me.

Tindra looked confused for a moment before shocked recognition changed her expression, and she ran toward me.

I reacted in time to catch her when she launched herself at me.

Wrapping her legs around my waist, she hugged me tightly before planting a long, hard kiss on my lips.

Roi laughed. "Welcome home, King Fitzeirick. I'm surprised all of Satra was eliminated so quickly?"

"When did you get back?" Tindra asked, pulling back to take a breath.

"Long enough to see you two being almost civil toward each other," I said. "It's good to be home."

Tindra released me, stepped back, and looked me up and down. "Good to see your armor did its job."

"It served me well, even against a danger we'd never heard of. Thorgault will need to fix the damage, but it protected me. I'm healthy and whole. We won. Croy is safe," I said. "Bior did his job ... did everything asked of him. In the end, he paid the ultimate price."

"He —"

"Oh, no," Roi gasped, interrupting her. "What happened?"

I gave them a much shorter summary of the fight than what I told Sibbi.

Tindra hugged me tight again. "I'll miss him. At least that barbaric nation has been removed from our life."

"Not exactly," I said, shaking my head and stroking Tindra's hair. "A Croian leads the good people of Satra."

"The good people — You let some of them live?" Tindra asked.

I rubbed her back. "There's much to explain." Looking at Roi, I cocked my head. "Perhaps over dinner."

He smiled. "I'm sure it can be arranged."

I returned his smile. "One more thing before you leave. After we've mourned Bior's death and celebrated our victory, I want you to travel to the Satran capital."

He squinted. "Why?"

"Rorec contributed a great deal to our victory," I said.

A scowl twisted Roi's face. "After killing our people during Satra's invasion?"

"Was he the stranger you mentioned in that message?" Tundra asked.

"Yes," I said. "I learned he was trying to save as many Croian lives as he could. Rorec had no choice in riding with the Legion. It kept your mother safe. When we met again, he supported me while I met and negotiated with Vos Sifet, the disgraced Satran leader.

Rorec fought at my side. We would have lost the war without his help. He earned the title of skald but faces many challenges changing Satran minds. In my opinion, he could benefit from your presence. Take Grima and Einns with you. I'm certain Asfrid would like to meet your family. And you can't tell me Grima wouldn't want to spend time with the woman who raised you. Consider it a working vacation for a job well done while I was away."

Roi crossed his arms. "I would like to see my mother again, but I'm not sure I have much to say to my father."

"Rorec is a better man than you realize. He's given his life to Croy, much the same as you. Do this to tighten the bonds between us and our new land." I kissed the top of Tindra's head and shrugged. "Who knows, reconnecting with your father might be good for both of you."

Roi nodded and relaxed. "I'll discuss it with Grima."

"Don't get me wrong, there is much work left to do...both here and in our new territory. All I'm asking is for you to help me guide everyone toward a prosperous and peaceful future for your children and mine."

Tindra hugged me tight as Roi offered me his hand.

"I've always been proud to serve my country," he said. "You have my word that I will always be there for you."

I shook his hand and hugged my wife as Roi turned to leave.

"A peaceful future," I said. "After so much pain, so much loss, I'd do it all again as long as I knew my people could look forward to a peaceful future."

To the reader:

Thank you for reading this novel. I encourage you to leave a review at your preferred book retailer. If you enjoyed my story, please recommend it to your friends.

You are welcome to follow me on social media at:
www.facebook.com/JAGuynnAuthor
www.twitter.com/JAGuynnAuthor

Also follow my publisher at:
www.facebook.com/3220Group

Other titles by J.A. Guynn

Branded Book 1: Skald
Branded Book 2: King
Water Princess: Through the Storm